D0914346

N, NJ
8

BLIND WAVES

Tor Books by Steven Gould

Jumper

Wildside

Helm

Blind Waves

BLIND WAVES

STEVEN GOULD

A Tom Doherty Associates Book  New York

This is a work of fiction. All the characters and events portrayed in this novel are either fictitious or are used fictitiously.

BLIND WAVES

This book is printed on acid-free paper.

Designed by Jane Adele Regina

A Tor Book
Published by Tom Doherty Associates, LLC
175 Fifth Avenue
New York, NY 10010

ISBN 0-312-86445-0

www.tor.com

First Edition: February 2000

Printed in the United States of America

0 9 8 7 6 5 4 3 2 1

This book is for Gilo.

I had a sister,

Whom the blind waves and surges have devour d.

—William Shakespeare, *Twelfth Night*

BLIND WAVES

1

Beenan: *Vomitar debajo del agua*

Once upon a time in America, Patricia's father told her, you could say what you wanted in public, buy cheap land in the mountains, and the Immigration and Naturalization Service wasn't the second largest division of the armed forces.

That was before the Antarctic Volcano field. That was before the Ronne-Filchner ice shelf slid.

That was a hundred feet of water ago.

This is now.

Terminal Lorraine was fifty miles from the Houston dikes, inbound, seventy feet of water under her keels, passing over Fort Jacinto Military Reservation, the old northeastern tip of Galveston Island. The sky was mostly clear, blue diamond with white puffy cumulus clouds scudding northward, and the sun beat down hot enough to make the deck uncomfortable. A trio of oceangoing shrimp boats were passing to the north on their way out to the deep water. A giant container ship had passed them earlier, headed for Houston, and was slowly shrinking in the east.

Patricia could've saved time by passing more to the south, but their escort and client, the hundred-foot-long workboat *Amoco Mechanic*, drew a lot more water than *Terminal Lorraine* did and they didn't want to risk running into the top of one of the old Baylor Medical School buildings.

Terminal Lorraine handled rough water pretty well, for a

trimaran, but when the wind and seas aligned on her rear she developed a corkscrewing motion that got Patricia every time.

Toni, Patricia's new crew, was telling her a joke, and Patricia was listening carefully, trying to distract herself from simulcasting lunch.

"So, during the Deluge, the mayor of San Francisco sees the water rise and he says, 'Oh, my god!' The mayor of New York sees the streets filled with water and he says, 'Oh, my god!' The mayor of Miami sees water everywhere and he says, 'Oh, my god!' Then the mayor of New Orleans watches the fish swim through his office and says, 'I do declare. Humid, today, eh?' "

Patricia had heard it before, but she laughed anyway. Toni did a great Cajun accent and Patricia was still trying to get her to relax.

The fathometer dropped back to 140 feet, meaning they were past the old shoreline and over Bolivar Roads, the historic mouth of Galveston Bay. The Amoco boat turned again, following the old Texas City ship channel, and Patricia adjusted the sails, letting the thick Dacron rope run through her fingers, while Toni brought the boat around to the new heading, then recleated the sheets. Toni had been aboard only for the last two days, and Patricia was mostly happy with her, but she wished her regular crew could've come.

Terminal Lorraine's two outer hulls were elegant forty-foot-long fiberglass blades, each sporting a single unstayed mast forty feet high. She carried fully battened "junk" sails, Kevlar-reinforced Mylar with composite ribs that stretched the width of the sail. They were easy to handle single-handed since they were self-reefing; in high winds the crew just lowered them a span or two and the bottom battens stacked neatly.

The pitch was a little better on the new heading, Patricia faced into the wind and breathed deeply, trying to settle her stomach. She smelled salt water, sunscreen, the barest hint of diesel exhaust, and her own sweat.

Toni looked sideways at her new boss. "You okay, Patricia? You look a little green."

Thanks so *much for the reminder.* Patricia shook her head, irritated. "Not *your* problem. Mind the helm."

Toni shrugged and her face closed up a little.

Patricia was pleased Toni didn't get seasick—the topside hand needed to ride out rough weather sometimes—but she could keep it to herself. Toni'd learn, hopefully.

Toni was sixteen years younger than Patricia, a sun-browned blonde with big breasts and a small nose, unlined face, and a long and lean body that was a head taller than Patricia—hell, Toni was everything Patricia wasn't. She seemed to live in Speedo suits and T-shirts. Her parents were from peninsular Florida, but she'd been born during the Deluge and, as a cash-poor Displaced American, she really didn't have a chance of getting land outside the wet-foot ghettos or a homestead in the Nevada "Displaced Citizen" projects.

Toni's sailing experience was extensive, since she'd lived all her life on a forty-five-foot ketch, and, though she didn't have any experience with multi-hulls, she was doing all right.

"We gonna hit them in the ass," Toni said.

Patricia looked forward again. They'd picked up a knot of speed on the new heading, and the distance between them and the workboat was dropping. "Pass them to port."

"Passing to port, aye, Moth—Captain."

Patricia laughed. "Do I really remind you of your mother?" Toni's mother was in her early fifties, twenty years older than Patricia. Patricia had met the woman briefly the week before and thought she looked a lot like Toni—the same build, and the same face if you accounted for the difference in mileage. Certainly she looked nothing like Patricia. "You'll make me feel my age, child."

Toni shook her head. "No. It's habit. Mom would skipper. Dad did maintenance. I was crew. Our boat was already forty years old before the Deluge, so it's over sixty, now. Everything was jury-rigged." She shrugged. "Keeping it afloat was a full-time job for Dad. Parts."

She didn't need to say anything more. Most yacht and marine supply warehouses and manufacturers went underwater that year.

"That's pretty cool about your mom," Patricia said. "My mother gets seasick driving across bridges."

"She does? How does she handle the storm surge on the Strand?"

"She doesn't. She lives in Austin. Won't go near water." The old familiar guilt rose up inside Patricia. "We used to call her the 'Ruler of the Queen's Navy.' "

"I don't get it," Toni said.

"*HMS Pinafore.*" Toni still looked blank, so Patricia explained further. "The song is about the Lord High Admiral who is appointed to the post after an extremely successful legal and political career landside. He sings, 'Stick close to your desks and never go to sea, And you all may be rulers of the Queen's Navee.'"

"Oh, they said you spouted Shakespeare."

Patricia froze and counted to ten before saying calmly, "Well, yes, but that wasn't William Shakespeare—that was William Gilbert. Anyway, when my parents divorced, my mother stayed in Austin, and I came out here with my dad."

"How old were you?" She looked wistful.

"Fourteen."

"Wow. And she let you go?"

"*Let* me go? It wasn't that simple." Patricia shook her head. "She was very busy. She was a full partner in a firm and in her first race for Congress. She didn't want a messy and public custody fight."

"I wish I could get my mother out of *my* hair."

"Would you have your parents divorce?"

"No, they're happy. Did your dad remarry?"

"No." *He just slept around a lot.* "Uh, he dated. He could recite Shakespearean verse for hours. It was his shtick. He was very popular." Patricia could recall a host of "aunts" who came and went like candles.

The VHF crackled. "Hey, Beenan?"

Patricia picked up the mike. "I hear you, Mateo." Mateo was the tool pusher on the Amoco boat.

"We'll be on station in ten minutes."

"Right—we'll power up."

Patricia went forward, bare feet quickstepping over sun-heated white textured fiberglass, following the deck above the middle hull of the *Lorraine*. The middle hull was slightly less than thirty-five feet long, a big titanium pipe four feet in diameter, with stubby wings in the middle, a big ducted fan with vertical and horizontal stabilizers at the rear, and a transparent acrylic nose. It was a stupid design for a sail-boat hull, but a darn good submarine.

"You ready for this, Toni?" Patricia called back.

Toni shrugged. "No prob, boss."

"Okay. Just remember she's a lot more lively without the sub attached," Patricia said. "And if that INS Fastship drops back by, just show them your papers and cooperate. Mateo will back you up."

There was an Immigration and Naturalization Service patrol boat, a 110-foot ex–Coast Guard Fastship, about six miles northwest of them. The INS Fastship had already queried Mateo's people by VHF, but they were used to *Amoco Mechanic* working this area, and Amoco still had a lot of clout, even if its largest refinery was underwater.

It was the INS that made Patricia leave her regular crew back home. They were floaters—displaced aliens—and the INS had a mandate to keep them out of the U.S. Exclusive Economic Zone. They were fair game anywhere within two hundred miles of the coast. Toni, as a mere wetfoot, was legal here.

"You told me a hundred times already," Toni said, but smiled. "Besides, why would they mess with Assembly-woman Beenan?"

Patricia felt her face twist like she'd bitten into something intensely sour. "First, I'm just an alternate on the assembly, and second, why should the INS care? New Galveston is only vaguely associated with the U.S. What the INS *should* care about is that we have the legal right to be here."

Toni looked skeptical. "Yeah, they *should*."

"The youth today." Patricia shook her head and lifted the fiberglass hatch on the personnel tube. "Christ, I remember when my dad used to say that to me!"

"When do I meet your dad?" Toni asked.

Patricia froze in the mouth of the personnel tube, silent for a moment. Then she said, "You don't, Toni. *Full fathom five my father lies; of his bones are coral made*. He went down four years ago, in the *Cobia*, our second submarine."

"Uh, I didn't mean—" Toni's mouth was open, searching for words.

"Of course you didn't. How could you know?" Patricia flashed her a grin she didn't feel and pulled the hatch shut, muttering to herself, "*Those are pearls that were his eyes: Nothing of him that doth fade, but suffer a sea-change into something rich and strange. Sea nymphs hourly ring his knell,* the son-of-a-bitch."

Patricia was still pissed at Dad.

He was into act four of *Comedy of Errors*, calling back and forth on the underwater telephone. She took the part of Angelo and left him with Antipholus of Ephesus arguing over just who had the golden chain. That's the trouble with identical twins (and there are a lot of them in Shakespeare and *two* sets in *Comedy of Errors*). It's never clear whom you're dealing with.

Dad had just said, *As all the metal in your shop will*— And she hung there, waiting, waiting, waiting. *It's "answer." As all the metal in your shop will answer.* But he never completed the sentence. He did not "answer."

The personnel tube was a short fiberglass shaft that protected the pilot hatch of the submarine from flooding while it was on the surface. It ended with a pneumatic gasket snuggled tight to the titanium hull of the sub. With her feet still on the bottom rung, Patricia contorted in the narrow tube, reached down, and snaked the transparent acrylic hatch open. The thing was two inches thick, and getting it open in the narrow space was always awkward, even with years of practice.

Patricia's dad had never seemed to have trouble with it. Longer reach.

She dropped through the hatch and latched it shut above her. She was in the back of the pilot's station, a space reminiscent of a sewer culvert, stuffy, barely three and a half feet across on the inside diameter, and lots of that was taken up with boxes, plastic conduit, canisters, and oxygen tanks, all mounted to the walls. Carefully, she eased forward and sat in the backward-facing chair, tucked her knees up, and spun it until it faced forward. It locked with a loud click that reverberated in the confined space.

The front half of the chair stuck out into the acrylic nose of *SubLorraine*. Patricia's feet were bare, so she pulled on a pair of socks before lowering them to the plastic surface to avoid smudges. Surface water foamed greenish white along the top of the nose and green below. She could make out the outer hulls through the water.

It was on the warm side of comfortable, and Patricia could smell her own armpits, a whiff of ozone, the vinyl chair cover, and something like blue cheese. Her stomach gave one minor heave, then settled. It was time to pull the charcoal filters and bake the volatiles out of them again.

She pulled her sunglasses off and put them in the baseball cap, then stared at her distorted reflection in the acrylic dome: spiky red hair matted from the hat, oversized blue eyes, pronounced cheekbones, small breasts under a worn green tank top, bicycle shorts, and a long nose with perpetual sunburn. She straightened in the seat and tried the confident look—the grown-up woman of business. *Christ—you're starting to get crow's-feet, and you still look like a kid!*

It was hard for her to climb into *SubLorraine* without thinking about Dad. They never found *Cobia*, so she didn't know what had gone wrong. It made her very careful.

First things first: life support. Carbon dioxide scrubber fan on. Oxygen tank at full, valve on auto. Emergency tank full. Now if she'd just changed out the charcoal filters. Ah, well. At least it was only her own farts—not somebody else's.

She didn't notice that her motion sickness had vanished, dropped like last night's pajamas the instant she stopped waiting and began to work.

She took the computer off standby and called up the diagnostics on the electrical system. Green lights all around. She'd spun the flywheels up two days before, when they'd powered out of the Strand, and they were still spinning at eighty percent capacity, about forty-eight thousand revolutions per minute. The reserve kinetic energy was probably enough for everything they'd be doing today, but still she wanted them at full capacity, just in case.

Dad always did.

She flipped the snorkel switch, opening the intake and exhaust doors for the turbogenerator, and then hit the start button. There was a slight shudder after the turbine sped up, when it ignited. It was a forty-five-kilowatt natural gas–burning jet turbine generator, spinning on compressed air bearings and self-cooling from intake air. It could run only on the surface since it pulled in several hundred cubic feet of air every minute, and the exhaust temperature was over 550 degrees Fahrenheit, but it could spin up all three storage flywheels from a dead stop to full speed ahead in less than five minutes.

While the flywheels were spinning up, Patricia flipped on the rest of the subsystems. GPS, sonar, pressure depth gauges, CO_2 monitor, VHF, acoustic telephone, external strobe lights.

"You there, Toni?" she asked over the VHF, speaking loudly over the roaring hum of the generator.

"Yes, Patricia."

"Try the Gertrude."

The speaker from the acoustic telephone said, "How's this?"

"Radical," Patricia said, over the same system. "Receiving?"

"Loud and clear, assemblywoman."

"Wiseass," Patricia said aloud in the chamber, but didn't transmit. "Try *this*." She switched the acoustic phone back on. "Hang on for a minute."

"You mean wait?"

"No, silly woman—I mean *hang on* to something."

Patricia kicked in the big ducted thruster at ninety percent, and *Terminal Lorraine* jumped forward. She tested the control surfaces, first shaking the boat side to side, then porpoising it up and down.

"My, how *refreshing!*" Toni's voice sounded like she was talking from between clenched teeth. In a more relaxed tone she said, "We passed *Amoco Mechanic,* and you put enough water into the cockpit to soak me."

Patricia grinned and shut the thruster down. "You're dressed for it. Drive check complete. Flywheels fully charged. Shutting down generator. Securing snorkel doors."

Five minutes later the VHF crackled, and Mateo's voice said, "This looks like it, Beenan. We were about here when we picked up the diesel plume, but we haven't been able to trace it any further topside—between surface contaminants and wind dispersion, it hasn't worked."

"Gotcha, Mateo. I'm switching on the HCD now." One didn't so much turn on the hydrocarbon detector as access it through the instrumentation bus. Patricia tapped through a menu on the touch screen, and a small readout window appeared. "It's running from zero to two point three parts per million, Mateo. You have any sense of the normal contamination here? I mean, we are talking about Texas City."

"That's pretty much background for here, sweetie."

"Gross. Any higher and you guys wouldn't have to drill for oil. You could just filter this stuff." She dragged the HCD display window to the corner of the display, where it wouldn't obscure the flywheel readouts. "Okay. What's the current doing?"

There was a pause; then he came back. "Tide is on its way in, maybe one and a half knots, but other than that, who knows? There's so many structures down there that the currents are all over the place."

"Okay. I'll start hunting. Out."

"Mateo out."

Patricia switched back to the Gertrude. "Toni, bring her into the wind."

Toni didn't answer, but *Terminal Lorraine* slewed around until she was facing due south. Patricia buckled her seat belt and shoulder harness.

"Into the wind, Patricia." Toni's voice said.

Before *Lorraine* lost headway and her bows were pushed back around by the water and wind, Patricia hit the button on the sling control.

The water completely covered the acrylic nose and Patricia counted to five slowly, then gave a gentle push backward, reverse thruster. The hulls above slid forward and the sling passed by. She waited until the twin rudders were well ahead, then killed thrust.

In her usual configuration, *SubLorraine* was slightly buoyant, though Patricia could change that in either direction. As she sat there, she was wallowing on the surface, the waves trying to push her around. She was also slowly rolling over to starboard.

Patricia could see the sails on *Terminal Lorraine* cutting hard to port, back across the wind. "How's it going, Toni?"

The Gertrude came back. "Whoa, baby! I'm doing thirteen knots."

"Told ya. Hang with *Amoco Mechanic*, right?"

"Aye, aye."

"Starting my run."

She put the thruster on twenty-five percent, and *Sub-Lorraine* submerged, her inverted wings giving her negative lift. Patricia put the stick on its side and did a quick barrel roll to test the trim, hanging upside down for a moment by her seat harness. *SubLorraine* was slightly bottom-heavy but not so much that she needed adjusting.

The GPS beeped as it lost signal, the water cutting out both the satellite signals and the VHF. Upright again, Patricia cut northwest and descended to ninety feet, moving four knots. At this depth the visibility dropped markedly, but the forward sonar was giving her a pretty good picture of the old ship channel: Five minutes later she acquired the old breakwater, off to starboard, its top just level with the sub. Patricia eased over until it loomed out of the murk, big car-sized hunks of rock and concrete less than fifteen feet away; then she ascended ten feet and edged over it, a nice visual road into Texas City.

The hydrocarbon count kept flickering up and down, though the peaks began edging up to three and a half parts per million. Patricia had a pre-Deluge digital video disc U.S. road atlas in the drive, and she called up the street map of Texas City. She was too deep for the global positioning system to work, but with the breakwater as a reference, she hit the old shoreline near the junction of Bay Street and Ninth Avenue.

She'd worked Texas City before, both legally and ill-. The Flood Salvage Bill, passed seven months after the Deluge, retained property rights to the original owners for thirty years, which could be extended by ongoing salvage operations or permanent moored or seabed occupation. That was back when they still thought the waters might recede.

In its previous life, the titanium hull of *SubLorraine* was a high-pressure heat exchanger pulled from the effluent side of a catalytic cracker unit at Marathon Refinery. That was twelve years ago, at night, and Patricia's dad towed it home submerged. The serial numbers were gone now, and the hull's papers of provenance pointed to a company well under the Sea of Japan.

The flywheels came out of several Galveston City buses, legally salvaged under contract. They'd pulled up fifteen, but the containment chambers were flooded in twelve of them and the interiors were corroded; but the three they still used were intact. The turbine generator was the auxiliary power unit from a computer firm in south Houston, but it went astray when the company evacuated its equipment during the Deluge. It ended up in the gray market out on New Galveston.

Patricia cruised up Ninth Avenue, ten feet off the silty road. This put her above most of the abandoned vehicles and junk scattered by the first flooding, but under the existing utility wires. Visibility improved slightly, though current eddies around the buildings kept her constantly correcting her path to avoid drifting into a storefront or light pole. The sonar screen made the street look almost normal, like people should be on the sidewalks and the cars should be moving, but through the port she could see mullet eating algae off brick walls, and once, after Ninth Street turned into Palmer Highway, a shark cruised across the intersection at Center Street, low and smooth on the crosswalk.

The HC gauge spiked up to fifteen parts per million, and when it dropped back down again it didn't get below five.

B–I–N–G–O, *B–I–N–G–O, and Bingo was his name-oh.*

She eased up to fifty feet of surface water, looking out for power lines, and banked hard to starboard, heading north. The meter dropped back to background levels almost immediately, surprising her. The Amoco plant, once the country's largest refinery, was in this direction, as were a few others, and they were the expected source.

Perhaps the plume was hugging the bottom, a heavy crude fraction, heavier than water. She descended again, coming down to the bottom at the Bayou Municipal Golf Course. The readout dropped further, undetectable quantities below the limits of this field meter.

She turned around, passing a golf cart up to its hubcaps in silt, past three skeletal cottonwood trees, and over a fiberglass pole with a flag that moved slowly in the current. Hole number seven—dogleg to the right, the water trap is a real mother.

Dad missed golf when they'd moved to the Strand.

The count slowly picked up as Patricia crossed Palmer Highway again, and she started an east-west grid fifty feet below the surface bounded by state road 146 on the east and route 3 on the west. It took her another fifteen minutes to zero in on it, somewhere near where Texas Avenue merged into Preston Street.

Oh, well, she thought. *It's probably another gas station tank that's failed from corrosion.* This should make Mateo feel better. Amoco wouldn't be liable for this leak and could claim recompense for pumping out the remaining fuel. As she descended, she reduced her speed to less than a knot. There were a lot of power lines in the area and she had no intention of spitting *SubLorraine* on one of the poles.

She was easing up a side street a couple of yards above the silty asphalt and watching the meter go berserk, when the forward sonar reflected an image across the street about two hundred feet away. It was odd because the map showed clear road there, and the obstruction was rounded, rising thirty feet or so above the road. Still, it wouldn't be the first time storm currents had rearranged the landscape.

She crept up to it with just enough headway to keep *SubLorraine* neutral. Several sandbar sharks scattered, surprised as she loomed out of the murk, and then the hulk loomed out of the murk at *her*. It was covered with weed, but surprisingly, surface weed, like you'd get where the sunlight is stronger. Then she saw the keel.

It was a ship. Well, a shipwreck, lying on its side, keel toward her, pushed right up against the bulk of a warehouse.

She killed her forward motion with reverse thrust and deprived of negative "lift," *SubLorraine* started drifting upward, slowly rolling to starboard as she rose. Patricia waited until she was clear of the wreck, and then eased the sub forward. There was no weed above the ship's waterline—not even a tinge. This boat had sunk recently—very recently.

The ship was about 130 feet long, an old coastal freighter with a lot of rust on her even before she sank. Her cargo holds were still closed, locked in fact, with stainless chain and brass padlocks that gleamed faintly through the murk.

She turned on the video camera and the external floodlights and began narrating into the mike. Her voice was shaky, and she hardly recognized it.

"The wreck is located in Texas City near the intersections of Texas Avenue and Preston Street. She's on her side in seventy feet of water with about forty feet of clear water above her starboard rail. As you can see, the vessel came down between these two warehouses, then rolled over, with the bridge crushing this section of the second structure."

She took a deep breath before continuing. "There are several shell holes along her waterline, probably twenty-five-millimeter cannon fire. The bullet holes scattered across the bridge bulkheads and windscreens are probably fifty-caliber. Most of the bridge windows have simply starred, but one has given way completely, and that's where the sharks are gathering.

"The presence of sharks makes me think that the crew went down with her."

She moved the submarine back to the bow where she read the faded paint. "*Open Lotus*, Shanghai." The leak—diesel fuel oil—was there, in one of the forward tanks, visible, a two-inch hole—possibly another twenty-five-millimeter cannon shell—poked inward, dark fluid oozing out and up.

She turned off the camera for a moment and switched on the Gertrude. "Toni, do you read me?"

"I do."

"Tell Mateo that I'm working an area of higher readings, but it looks like I'll be awhile."

"Will do."

She moved *SubLorraine* back to the street on the deck side of *Open Lotus*, then flooded the forward and aft ballast chambers. The sub settled slowly, this time bottom-heavy for sure, onto the silty roadbed. She bumped, first on the two safety skegs that protect the ducted fan at the stern, then on the thin ventral fin just forward of the lockout hatch.

Patricia shut down everything but the Gertrude, the CO_2 scrubber, and the floodlights and camera, now zoomed in on *Open Lotus*'s number two hold cover; then she unlocked the seat and swiveled it around.

She squeezed past the black boxes and canisters and conduit, and passed under the pilot compartment hatch, coming to another hatch, also acrylic, that divided the rear of the pilot's compartment from the lockout chamber. She pushed it open easily—both compartments were still at surface pressure—and squeezed through.

The lockout chamber was four feet long and no wider than the rest of the sub. It had separate life support—scrubber, oxygen, plus tanks of helium for mixed gas decompression. Patricia latched the hatch behind her and duckwalked down to the gauges.

They were about seventy feet deep, no biggie, but Patricia had to add a couple of atmospheres to equalize pressure. She unlatched the hatch in the floor and rested one foot on it. It held firm, supported from without by 452 pounds of pressure difference spread across the two-foot hatch. She twisted the valve to the air bank, a heavily pressurized section of the hull directly behind the lockout chamber. Air shrieked in, attacking her ears with both noise and pressure. She swallowed, encouraging her ears to pop, doing the descent in thirty seconds. The hatch dropped open and her foot dipped momentarily into the cold water, soaking her sock.

She felt foolishly surprised that it was wet, and she couldn't remember if she had a spare pair of socks in the pilot's compartment. *I could go back to the boat for more.* She laughed, a short explosive "ha" totally without humor. *Stop stalling.*

Her gear was clipped to the back of the chamber: rebreather, emergency pony bottle, dry suit, polyfleece undersuit, weights, fins, gloves, mask. Below it, in a closed plastic bin mounted on the wall, were tools. She put her hand in the water, held even with the hatchway by the pressurized pocket of air. The water was cool, 69 degrees per the readout, but not *that* cold and she didn't want to take the time to worm into the dry suit.

She took off the socks and went with the mask, fins, and the backup pony bottle, a little ten-cubic-foot tank pressurized to four K psi. She strapped the tank to her waist, spit in the mask, and donned it, put on the fins, and dropped her legs out the hatch. She took the big bolt cutters from the plastic bin, put the regulator in her mouth, and dropped through the hatch.

Dad wouldn't have liked this. He wanted divers to be tendered or partnered. Solo diving is dangerous.

Tough. If you were here, I'd do it your way.

Her first thought was that she should've gone with the dry suit, but that quickly passed as she adjusted to the chill. *SubLorraine* sat two and a half feet off the bottom on her "tripod," and Patricia had to scrunch down to clear the hull, wiggling clear and kicking up some silt, which was rising around her in a dark brown cloud. She rose well off the bottom to clear the silt, kicking strongly up to offset the weight of the bolt cutters. Except for some padding on her butt, she was pretty scrawny, negatively buoyant if she didn't take deep breaths, but she didn't want to kick up any more silt between the camera and the ship. She wasn't thrilled to be swimming into the camera's view, but, if necessary, she hoped to edit that part out.

She settled to the ship's deck and braced one foot on a

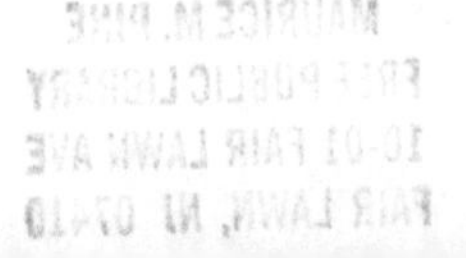

ventilator, the other on the railing, and tried the bolt cutters on the padlock hasp. The chromed surface was barely dented, but the chain was softer, and though she had to make two cuts to get completely through a link, it dropped clear and she was able to snake the free end through the latch. She looked around, nervous, checking for sharks and other less nameable things, then released the two starboard latches on the hold cover.

It wasn't very heavy, but it had a lot of surface area, so it lifted slowly as the water flowed around it. For a second, as she strained to lift it high enough for the floodlights and camera, she didn't notice what she was uncovering.

Vomiting underwater is dangerous—you can clog your regulator—but fortunately, she spat the mouthpiece out in time. It was two violent spasms, clouding the water with tan unidentifiable chunks.

The crabs and smaller fish must've entered through the ventilators or the cannon holes, but the bodies hadn't been down long enough to look "nice." There were too many to count but it was all too clear that their number included women and children. Some of them were still bloated and bobbed at the top of the compartment—what used to be the starboard side. The rest either hadn't reached that stage or were beyond it. They floated along the bottom of the compartment, mostly upright, their shoes holding them down, like guests milling around at a party.

She half-expected to see Dad among them. To see him drift forward, a drink in his hand, eyebrows raised, quoting devastatingly from *Coriolanus* or saying something snide about solo diving.

She got the regulator back into her mouth and cleared it while backing away. The metal hold cover slowly dropped back down, and Patricia saw the worst thing of all—there were fresh scratch marks on the inside of the hatch, near the latches. Someone had been alive when the boat went down.

It took all her courage to move close enough to secure the latches again.

They're dead, Patricia, they can't hurt you.

Oh, yeah? The dead have hurt me every day for the last four years!

She broke a record swimming back to the lockout hatch. She stood on the bottom, her upper torso inside the sub, and threw the bolt cutters back into the toolbox. There was nothing more she wanted than to climb back in, seal up, and get the hell out of there, but she grabbed the big tank of salvage foam, then ducked back in.

It took her two minutes to swim to the oil leak, insert the nozzle and block the leak with expanding plastic foam, and swim back. The pony bottle expired as she squirmed under the sub, but she didn't care anymore. She was shaking with cold and breathing oddly, in short ragged gasps. There really wasn't any difference in the air, but her imagination was supplying the scent of rotting meat. She pulled the hatch up as quickly as she could and turned on the compressor, pumping the lockout chamber's atmosphere back into the air bank.

It took ten minutes to bring the pressure down, long enough to strip off her equipment and wet clothing. There was a scrap of *Hamlet* droning in her head. *The graves stood tenantless, and the sheeted dead did squeak and gibber in the Roman streets.*

As she put the polyfleece undersuit on to try and warm up, she recognized the pattern of her breath.

Big girls don't cry.

She curled into a ball by the forward hatch and rocked back and forth.

The hell they don't.

2

Beenan: *Jugar al escondite*

Patricia found a railroad tank car near the intersection of Twenty-fifth Street and the SP railroad line bearing a diamond-shaped flammable sign with the DOT code "UN 1202"—light diesel oil.

It wasn't full of air, or it would've floated away during the Deluge, but it wasn't full of water, either, since it'd drifted about three hundred feet from the tracks. The worst case was that it had a pocket of air and the rest was water, but nosing up to the valve manifold, Patricia got a slight jump on the hydrocarbon meter.

Most important of all, it was a good four miles from the wreck of the *Open Lotus*.

She flooded her tanks and settled to the bottom beside it; then she popped the radio buoy—two short antennae, one for the VHF and one for the GPS, connected to a reel of coaxial wire. It only worked in two hundred feet of water, or less, but here was no problem.

"Mateo, I think I've found your leak." Her voice was hoarse from throwing up, strange to her, despite her best efforts to act normally.

He came back immediately. "Well, it's about time, girl. What have you been doing down there?"

"My nails. Shut up and home on my signal. The GPS says twenty-nine thirteen point three north, ninety-four fifty-four point seven west. Get close enough and you can't miss my little orange antennae buoy."

"We're moving. What's the leak? That's not near the refinery."

"It's a railroad tank car. I don't know how much is left, but the DOT code is for diesel. It's not linked up—you could probably winch it to the surface and deal with it there."

"No, darling. If it has a gas pocket, it could expand as it rose and force the oil out. We'll drain it in situ."

"Your call, Mateo."

It took them ten minutes to get overhead. She tracked them on passive sonar, but by the time they were close, she could hear their big diesel engines right through the hull.

Their divers must've suited up as they traveled because they touched down on the sub hull just five minutes after the engines revved back to station keeping RPMs. Patricia waved through the bubble, and one of the divers took his mouthpiece out and blew a kiss. She stuck her finger in her mouth like she was gagging and both of them shook their heads; then they kicked off to the tank car, trailing an orange tender line that rose up through the murk.

Once they were by the valve manifold, they pulled it tight and tugged. The line immediately slackened and they began pulling it in, keeping it tight. After a minute the end of the rope appeared, tied to a four-inch flexible hose with a quick-connect valve. The divers took a minute to clean the algae and scum off the output valve; then one of them swam halfway back to Patricia and made a circling motion with one of his hands.

"Mateo, looks like they're ready for you to pump. You got enough capacity for this thing?"

He laughed into the mike. "You kidding? We only call a tanker when we find something big. I can drain this thing, separate out the water, and still handle twenty more."

The hose shifted downward and the diver opened one of the other manifold valves, to let water replace the outgoing material. The pumps on the workboat sucked the tank empty in fifteen minutes, a definite no-decompression dive for the boys out there.

"You gonna pull the car up?" Patricia asked Mateo. In a remediation job like this they were entitled to recover associated equipment.

"Nah. It's probably ninety percent rust. Doesn't seem worth it."

The divers finished disconnecting the hose, pantomimed blowing kisses with their hands, and followed the hose up into the green murk.

"So, any more chores while we're in the area?" Patricia asked this lightly, dreading the answer.

"Sorry. We've got some salvage work over at the refinery, but we've got all that stuff located. Can't justify the expense."

Thank god. "What? You drag us two hundred miles from home for this piddling little job?" It took all she had to sound pissed.

Mateo came back. "You know the drill, darling. If I can do it without outside contractors, I have to do it with my boys alone. I thought you'd like it—after all you get travel time, both ways, plus you milked this job for over twice the bottom time I estimated. You'll make out. Considering how small the recovery was, we're going to lose money."

"Milked? That does it, Mateo. You're definitely off my Christmas card list. You there, Toni?"

"I'm here, boss."

"Good, cause we're leaving these raggedy-ass bozos behind. Give me a minute to wind in my antennae; then start home—bearing one thirty-five. Keep it under three knots and I'll be there shortly."

"You got it, boss."

Mateo came back on the VHF. "Now, darling, don't go away mad . . . just go away."

"You'll never drown, Mateo."

"Huh?"

"I have great comfort from this fellow: methinks he hath no drowning marke upon him; his complexion is perfect gallows."

"Say what?"

"You'll never drown because you were born to be hanged. Go do your salvage job, bozo. I'll see you next time."

"Right-oh."

"Beenan out."

She blew the ballast tanks with high-pressure air rather than pump them out. She didn't like to do it, since it took a long time to replenish the air bank, but she was in a hurry. The radio buoy clicked into its slot about the time the sub started drifting off the bottom and she kicked the thruster in at one hundred percent, zero to thirteen knots in twenty seconds. The flywheels, already down to forty percent, dropped farther as she pulled over four hundred kilowatts from them.

She didn't care. She switched back to the Gertrude and said, "Start singing, Toni."

"What?"

"Start singing. I want a homing signal for the passive sonar."

"O-kay."

There's a little switch on the *Lorraine*'s Gertrude that runs an automatic pinger, but Patricia didn't want that. She needed something warmer, human—something alive. Later, she couldn't remember what Toni sang, something bluesy, perhaps, and she could remember thinking Toni had a nice voice, but mostly she wanted something she could run to.

She nearly overran *Lorraine*, dropping the thrust to nothing when the hulls came out of the murk, and she had to use a little reverse thruster to match speed. The sling was still trailing in the water, pulled down by streamlined weights. She nosed *SubLorraine* into it without thought and hit the switch to tighten the winches, concentrating on matching headings until the wings met the frame guides and eased the submarine up to its mating collar.

She pushed the seat back around and opened the top hatch.

Toni, at the helm, waved as Patricia popped out of the personnel tube. "Did it get that cold down there?"

Patricia frowned, then realized she was still wearing the polyfleece undersuit. "Umm. Cold . . . yes." She looked around. To reduce speed, Toni had let out the sheets on both sails. "Let's get some speed on."

Toni switched on the autohelm, and trimmed the sheet on the port side. Patricia took the starboard sail. The boat crept up to eight knots, taking the wind two points off the starboard bow. Patricia picked up the binoculars and began sweeping the horizon, finding what she was looking for all too soon. The INS Fastship had moved farther south from its previous position. Not toward them, but not away, either.

Patricia wanted to go back below, fire up the turbogenerator, and run the thrusters at one hundred percent, but even then they could hope, at best, to achieve twenty knots. The INS Fastship with its jet turbines and water jets had a top endurance speed of thirty-five knots and a short-duration pursuit speed of forty. It had a semiplaning monohull with a slight concave bottom that generated lift at the stern, reducing drag.

Toni watched Patricia, perched on the edge of the cockpit. Patricia put the binoculars back in their cabinet and said, "There's five lithium hydroxide cartridges in the starboard storeroom, the one forward of the galley."

Toni nodded.

"Put them in the sub, in the lockout chamber. Then get together some grub—stuff we can eat uncooked, put it in the lockout chamber, too." Patricia could still taste the vomit in the back of her throat despite several drinks of water on the way back. Food didn't sound appealing at all. "Oh, and get your stuff."

Toni stared at her. "My stuff? What's going on, Patricia?"

"I'm sorry, Toni. This isn't fair and it isn't right, but I found something when I was down there and it could get us both killed."

Toni frowned, her head askance, her lips pursed. "Take off your sunglasses."

Patricia pulled them off, blinking in the bright sun, and looked at Toni.

Toni's tan paled two shades. "You're not kidding."

Patricia shook her head.

"What did you find?"

"Survival first. Information later."

Toni swallowed and turned away.

Patricia checked the GPS and adjusted the autohelm, then went down into her cubby in the port hull. Her sat-phone and portable workstation were stowed in the locker above her bunk. She hooked them together, then took the video data cartridge from the polyfleece jacket and slid it into the workstation.

She was sweating like crazy and while part of it was the polyfleece, part of it wasn't. Still, you work on the factors you can control. While the workstation booted, she stripped, then put on some fresh underwear, light shorts, and a long-sleeved T-shirt.

The entire video file was twenty minutes long but it contained stretches of stillness while she was cycling out and into the lockout chamber. She trimmed it to the original narration and the footage showing the shell and bullet holes, plus the entire sequence from the opening of the hold hatch to the closing. This gave her a file of just over three minutes running time, including a lovely shot of herself vomiting. She couldn't edit it out—she was in the frame the entire time the hold was open.

The file was twenty megabytes of full-frame, six-hundred-line video. She started it compressing and climbed back up to the cockpit.

Toni was carrying her duffel, her portable stereo, and a

plastic bag to the personnel tube. "How's it going?" Patricia called.

She shrugged. "Okay, so far. I've got the lithium cartridges down there, and this is food." She held up the plastic bag. "What about water?"

Patricia nodded. "Good point. There's a bunch of water jugs under the sink. They should be full."

She looked to the southwest. "Better hurry."

The INS Fastship was easily seen naked-eye now, and it'd changed aspect: much narrower, indicating it was heading toward them. While Patricia watched, a tiny dark shape separated from the main mass and rose into the air. She felt nauseated and it had nothing to do with the boat's motion.

Toni was watching, too. "What is *that*?"

"An RPV."

Toni looked blank.

"A surveillance drone—a remotely piloted vehicle. They're coming to check us out." Patricia turned back to the port hatch. "Hurry!"

Besides enhanced video the damn things were wired for radio capture. If it got overhead before she finished her phone call, they'd know she was broadcasting. Her satphone provider was based in Houston and subject to the surveillance provisions of the Emergency Immigration Act. The INS might have the escrow keys to decipher the phone call.

The file wasn't finished compressing, but it was close. She connected to her net provider and started cee-ceeing everybody she could think of: the *Houston Post,* the Texas Department of Public Safety, the UN Refugee Monitoring office in New Galveston, the New Galveston Assembly, the *Chicago Sun Times,* and even the INS themselves: national headquarters on D.C. Island. After a moment's hesitation, she added the Honorable Katherine Beenan, U.S. Representative from the state of Texas, then started to delete it.

No. Mom can just deal with it.

The compression finished, and she attached the file and hit "send."

The connection was good, one fifteen kilobaud, and the file had compressed to a quarter of its original size so it took just a little less than a minute. As soon as she had the upload confirmation, she killed the connection and took the phone and workstation on deck.

Toni was just coming back on deck from the starboard hull, carrying four gallon-jugs of water. Patricia looked for the drone and couldn't see it until she craned her neck back.

Well, there wasn't any doubt that they were its target. It was making a slow circle overhead, about a thousand feet up, and Patricia knew it could stay there for about twenty-four hours on its fuel load.

Patricia followed Toni over to the personnel tube and lowered the jugs to her, then the workstation and satphone. Toni stowed them, then started to climb back out again and Patricia said, "Stay there, okay?"

"Why?"

"If we have to bug out, it's going to be very soon."

Toni swallowed. "It's a little tight down there. How about I just stay here in the hatch?"

Oh great! She's claustrophobic! "Sure. Just so we can get going quickly."

Patricia went back to the cockpit and slung the binoculars around her neck. She didn't really need them to see the growing bulk of the INS Fastship.

The VHF crackled and a voice said, "Boat on my bow. This is the INS vessel *Sycorax*. Lower your sails and prepare to be boarded."

She used the binoculars. They had a boat swung over the rail on the port davits, men already aboard.

Make your decision, girl. Tough it out or run.

The guilty flee where no man pursueth. They could be doing a standard screen for illegals or boat safety or smuggling or a noncompliant toilet.

Or they could be coming to find out if she'd seen what she'd seen and to keep them from ever telling anybody else.

She turned the VHF off. If it ever came to court, she

could always claim she'd never received their hail.

The autohelm was slaved to the GPS and as long as the winds remained favorable and the batteries held, *Terminal Lorraine* would head for the Strand. Patricia turned on the underwater telephone and set it to ping every minute. As long as they didn't sink her, or turn off the Gertrude, or any of a number of more likely and less sinister things, they'd be able to track the boat from the sub.

If Patricia messed around any more, the cruiser would be within audible hailing range and she wouldn't be able to pretend not to have noticed it.

"Out of my way, girl," she said to Toni and dropped through the tube into the sub and slammed the hatch. Toni had gone forward to get out of Patricia's way as she climbed down, so, of course, she was now in Patricia's way. Patricia jerked her thumb back toward the lockout chamber and said, "Move!" Her voice wasn't kind and it wasn't soft, but she was more interested in keeping Toni alive than being diplomatic.

Toni moved awkwardly past in the tight cylinder, unable to avoid rubbing against Patricia; then Patricia wiggled clear and scrambled for the chair, spinning it forward and hitting the sling control and then reverse thrust, dragging *SubLorraine* back even before the sling was fully distended.

As she'd hoped, *SubLorraine* was negative now, with the extra crew and gear. Patricia pushed the stick forward, but left it in reverse thruster. This sharply tilted the front of the sub up and the ducted fan pulled them down. Behind her, she heard Toni swear sharply as the girl slid backward and banged against something in a cascade of bags, water bottles, and other equipment.

The hulls of *Terminal Lorraine* passed out of sight and the surface receded in front of Patricia. She killed the thrusters and switched off the active sonar and kicked in the directional hydrophone of the passive sonar. The high whine of the Fastship's turbines was loud in the speaker and bearing thirty degrees off the sub's stern.

Without the reverse thruster, all the extra weight in *SubLorraine*'s forward section caused them to tip forward, causing yet another slide of equipment.

"Quick. Shift everything to the back of the lockout chamber."

"Why are you whispering?" Toni asked.

"Because they might have passive sonar . . . so don't bang around. Okay?"

They were back over Bolivar Roads in waters 140 feet deep. The bottom was also nice and silty, something Patricia wouldn't mind hitting at the rate they were sinking, but she didn't want to hit it nose first. They could get stuck.

Toni shifted back, practically climbing up the sub, dragging water bottles and Patricia's workstation with her, but the nose stayed down. Patricia watched the pressure-depth gauge. They'd been dropping slowly, at first, but now that the nose was pointing farther down, the depth was increasing by ten feet a second and had just passed seventy-five feet.

Patricia could've changed things several ways. She could've blown ballast. She could've used reverse thrusters. Instead she flew the sub down, using the forward speed to glide, so to speak. A few seconds later, they passed a hundred feet and Patricia pulled the stick back. The nose came sharply up and she leveled the sub. As her speed dropped, *SubLorraine* began sinking again, this time more slowly, on an even keel. They'd lost most of their headway when the sub skidded into the bottom, kicking up a cloud of silt which removed what little vision they'd had through the water and blocked the dim green light from above. The interior of the sub dropped to deep darkness relieved only by the glow of display panels.

"Are we okay?" Toni hissed from the back of the lockout chamber.

Patricia turned the speaker down on the sonar and said, "Yes. Now let me concentrate a minute, okay?"

They could hear the INS Fastship's turbines and water jets through the hull now, growing steadily louder.

"How could they possibly hear us over that racket?" Toni said.

"Signal processors. They can subtract their own noise profile. So hold it down." Patricia turned her seat halfway around, so she could reach the sonar controls, and waited, her legs propped against the bulkhead.

The Fastship passed a hundred yards to the south of them. The bearing from the pinger on *Terminal Lorraine* was merging slowly with the bearing of the INS Fastship's turbines. Then the turbines revved back, dropping substantially in volume, and the sound of outboards came through the speaker.

"They put an auxiliary in the water. They're going to board her."

"Isn't it about time you told me what's going on?"

Patricia tried to think of a way to tell her—something simple, something that wasn't as horrible as the truth. In the end, she chickened out. "Turn on my workstation—in the tan case. There's a file on the desktop called 'wreck video.' Play it."

She plugged a headset into the sonar and listened with one earpiece pressed to her head. Her other ear could hear the muted sound of her own narration from the workstation.

"—presence of sharks makes me think the crew went down with her."

The rest of it was silent, thank goodness, but her memory readily filled in the images and she shivered again. She half expected them to emerge from the murk outside and press their mangled hands and bodies against the port.

Toni's face was clearly lit from the glow of the screen and Patricia watched her frown increase in intensity; then she saw her entire body flinch back from the screen. "Jesus!"

Toni was silent long after the video stopped playing. Finally she asked, "We're not going back there, are we?"

"No!" Patricia was surprised at the intensity in her voice. She was the one who talked about keeping quiet after all. She whispered, "No. Definitely not."

"It was horrible, but why is it dangerous to us?"

Patricia pressed the headset back to her ears again. The outboard motors were still revving, possibly keeping station with *Terminal Lorraine* after dropping men aboard to search the boat. She pictured faceless men rummaging through every compartment aboard *SubLorraine* and felt like some sleazebucket was groping her in a crowd.

She answered Toni's question. "Did you hear me talk about the shell holes in the wreck? The machine-gun holes? The standard armament on a Witch Class Fastship—that thing that was coming after us—is fifty-caliber machine guns and twenty-five-millimeter cannon."

In the earphones, the *Sycorax* revved up its turbines and Patricia picked up the sound of its wake deepening.

"You're saying the *INS* sank her?"

She pronounced it "ins" as in "ins and outs." She'd been an "out" all her life, so it made sense.

"It's possible. I don't know. I'm not taking the chance. I'll apologize all they want once we're safe on the Strand, but I don't want to deal with them out here. Not without witnesses."

"Why would they do that?"

"Kill us? Or sink that ship?"

Toni waved her hand irritably. "Sink the ship."

"I don't know. Maybe they didn't know they were in the hold. Maybe the crew fired on them. But she was deliberately sunk. There was no other reason for cannon fire at the waterline. And the only reason to sink her would be to keep it quiet."

Toni muttered something.

"What?"

"I said I wouldn't put it past them. I've heard stories," Toni said.

The bearing on the Fastship shifted and Patricia tweaked

the settings on the hydrophone, refining the angle. As it moved, the frequency changed, first dropping, then raising again. "Doppler shift. She's coming back."

Toni's eyes widened. "The Fastship?"

"Well, it's not Santa Claus."

The bearing stopped changing and Patricia knew they were retracing the boat's path, the old ship channel. Then she heard a ping, strong and loud, about twenty-five kilohertz.

"Dammit! They're actively sounding the bottom and we're right in their path." The titanium hull would return a strong, distinctive signal.

Patricia swung the seat forward and kicked the engine in—only ten percent power at first, since *SubLorraine* was chewing through as much silt as she was water. The nose came up and the sense of dragging stopped. Patricia pushed the thruster to ninety percent and cut starboard, to the southeast, and they came out of the silt cloud into the murky green. If the *Sycorax* had passive sonar, they'd hear *SubLorraine* for sure. At ninety percent thrust, the engine hummed like a loud dishwasher and the blade tips cavitated enough to be audible.

Patricia risked one active sonar pulse, forward, and got a strong return at five hundred yards. It was the old stone breakwater lining the ship channel on the north end of Pelican Island. She pulled the nose up until the gauge showed 105 feet of surface water.

"What's happening?" Toni asked, a hint of panic in her voice.

"I'm running for Galveston."

"Huh? You can go submerged all the way to the Strand?"

"Not New Galveston." New Galveston was the official name of the Strand. "Old Galveston. Drowned Galveston."

The bearing on the Fastship had been changing as they continued up the channel, but now it stopped shifting. "Shit! They've turned toward us. They *must* have passive sonar."

She dropped the thrusters back to ten percent and banked hard to port, changing course forty-five degrees. At ten percent thrust the sub's noise signature would vanish into the background wash of surface waves and shrimp clicks. Unfortunately, their speed would also drop to less than two knots. Patricia didn't want to use any more active sonar. That'd be like ringing a bell and shouting "come and get it!"

The bearing on the Fastship began shifting slightly and Patricia hoped they were headed for that last contact. She was looking for the old ship channel between Pelican Island and Galveston proper, a deep, narrow channel.

The water clarity was not great, but at their current speed Patricia saw the breakwater in time to avoid running into it. She cut further port, following the breakwater west. Bearing separation on the INS Fastship increased and she felt slightly better.

A weed-shrouded tower with navigation markings loomed out of the gloom and she cut hard to starboard, cutting up over the corner, then dropping down into the old ship channel, pushing down to 130 feet.

The noise signature from the Fastship disappeared, cut off by high sides, and Patricia pushed the thrusters up to fifty percent, figuring that if she couldn't hear them, then they couldn't hear the sub.

She was tempted to shut down, pull out the sleeping bags, and stick there, on the bottom, until they went away. With the lithium hydroxide cartridges that they'd added, they had enough life support for five and a half days. They were more limited by power since they'd have to surface to recharge the flywheels, but still, even at their current reserves, they could stay on the bottom for a day and a half before they had to start hand-cranking the circulation fan to pump air through the CO_2 absorbent.

But at the end of the five days she and Toni would still

be here, deep inside the EEZ and two hundred miles from home.

After ten more minutes Patricia shut the thrusters off and pulled back on the stick, rising thirty feet from momentum alone. When she swept the hydrophone around, the *Sycorax*'s turbines showed up immediately, fifteen degrees starboard of the stern, which meant they'd given up on the other bearing and were heading out.

"What's happening?"

"The Fastship is moving out to sea." Patricia put the hydrophone on speaker. The whine of the turbines filled the sub with loosely organized white noise. Patricia shifted the phone slightly and the noise diminished.

"And now?"

It came after a moment, a clear high-frequency ping. "That's the *Lorraine*. Heading for home." Patricia checked back on the other bearing. "Shit. Less separation. They might be shadowing her—waiting for us to come back."

She dropped back into the channel. Two more minutes at fifty percent brought them to the end of the channel where the bridge crossed over to Pelican Island. Without slowing she raised the sub out of the channel and cut port, up above the docks, past the container gantries, and into the rail yard.

She kept the sub ten feet above the tracks, weaving between old boxcars and switch towers. She kept checking the passive sonar, but what bits of noise she got were scattered and reflected by the many flat surfaces around them.

"Look out!"

Patricia had already pulled the nose up. A nasty tangle of telephone poles and high-tension wires blocked the edge of the yard at Avenue E and they barely cleared it, rising above the sheltering buildings before she cut power.

"Backseat driver." Patricia kept the power down and coasted fifty feet above the bottom. On the sonar, the *Sycorax*'s turbines were revving up again and her bearing shifted, then became constant.

"Dammit! They heard us. I bet they have a navy sonar operator."

She dropped down into Avenue E on the other side of the telephone-pole tangle and kept it low, barely ten feet off the street, trying to maximize the acoustic barrier of the drowned buildings. She ran at twenty-five percent, fast enough to keep moving, but slow enough that she could avoid any obstacles that twenty years of currents had put across the street.

After a bit she cut across to Avenue J and continued southwest past rows of skeleton trees and caved-in Victorian houses, then into the downtown area where some buildings reached as high as the surface.

As soon as the sub was among them, she rose forty feet, drifting along dark windows. She heard Toni shift forward behind her to get a better view. *SubLorraine* tilted slightly and Patricia corrected with the stick.

"I don't care where you sit, Toni, but pick a place and stick with it. The trim gets out of whack when you move forward or back." She kept her voice soft.

There was a sharp tang to Toni's sweat, overwhelming her deodorant, and when Patricia looked back at her, Toni's eyes were wide open and her mouth a thin line.

"Is this okay?" Toni asked, her voice tentative.

"It's fine," Patricia said. "There's a sleeping bag tucked under my seat base. It makes a fair butt pad." Patricia pumped some water out of the forward trim tank. The tendency of *SubLorraine* to nose down ceased.

She used the headphones to check her bearing on the *Sycorax*. The turbine/water jet noise was breaking up as they put more and more submerged buildings between them and it.

She pushed the thrust up to ninety percent and ran at eleven knots.

"Won't they hear us?" Toni asked, an edge of panic in her voice.

"The ambient noise in this area is particularly high—surf

against the old buildings. With luck our noise profile will be blocked and distorted by the buildings and lost in the background roar."

"Hopefully?"

Patricia looked back at Toni and grinned a grin she didn't feel. "Hopefully."

She had other worries. They were dropping below twenty percent on the flywheels, and the sub was going to have to surface at some point to run the turbogenerator. The noise profile running full out was bad enough, but the noise from the turbogenerator could be heard through water a good thirty miles if you had the right equipment—and it was clear the *Sycorax* did. Worse, the exhaust plume was two times hotter than boiling water, and it would stick up into the air like a giant arrow pointed right down on them—a glowing finger on any IR scanner.

SubLorraine covered another seven nautical miles before Patricia got a positive ID on *Sycorax*. The cruiser had moved outside of Galveston, deeper into the gulf, and was paralleling the island, moving roughly in the same direction as the sub and about fifteen nautical miles away. Patricia had been stopping every five minutes to listen and now that she had them, there was the possibility that they had *SubLorraine*, but their bearing didn't change.

She tried to locate the Gertrude ping from *Terminal Lorraine* and finally found it, but not where she'd hoped. After five minutes of listening, she confirmed the worst. It wasn't headed toward the Strand—it was headed back toward the coast. *Shit, they've impounded her.*

Considering the range, Patricia thought twenty percent thrust—four knots—would be safe. She put the compass on south-southeast and slowly descended to a hundred feet of surface water once they were past the old shoreline and out into the historic gulf. They still had ten percent of usable PE in the flywheels, and that meant a half hour at their current consumption.

Patricia engaged the autopilot and turned the seat ninety

degrees. This put her shoulder right next to Toni's knee. She slumped in the seat and put her feet up on the bulkhead. "So, what's to eat?"

Toni's mouth dropped open and her eyes went wide. "Eat?"

Patricia wasn't really hungry but she was worried about Toni. "Yeah. Eat. Food, preferably. I'm wasting away here." She wanted to give Toni something to do, to take her mind off the tiny quarters.

"How can you think of food now?" Toni's voice rose in pitch, but her shoulders dropped, relaxing some.

Good, good. "Well, I pay attention to my stomach and there it is—hunger."

Toni rolled her eyes and turned away. "If I get you something to eat, will you tell me what the hell is happening?"

Ignorance isn't bliss. "Sure."

Toni put together cheese and crackers. "I figured the cheese would spoil first. We can switch to peanut butter later." She sliced the cheese using the cardboard cracker box as a cutting board—neat quick strokes with a stainless steel rigging knife. As she worked, the crease between Toni's eyes slowly eased.

Better. Patricia called up a chart of the northwest gulf. "Okay, here we are, just off old Galveston, about sixty miles from the Houston dikes. We've got enough fuel to get to New Galveston." She pointed at the dot representing the Strand, about 160 nautical miles from their current position, just outside the EEZ. "But, we've got to avoid the INS until we're in international waters and, frankly, I'm not sure if it's safe even then."

Toni nodded, chewing mechanically.

"The *Sycorax* has pretty good sonar equipment and that airborne drone. If they keep after us, they'll find us every time we surface to spin up the flywheels. On the other hand, by the time they get to us, we can be submerged again and, hopefully, safe." *Unless they have torpedoes or depth charges.*

"How long can we stay submerged? And breathe, that is."

"Well, that's the crux of it. We've got about five days of life support. We can make it on that, but not if we have to creep along to avoid making too much noise. If we could run full out on the surface, we'd make it in by tomorrow, but we'd be sitting ducks." Patricia put air between her cheeks and gums and squeezed it out, making a quacking sound.

Toni blinked, surprised. "Are you sure they're really after us?"

Patricia reviewed the data in her head. "I'm *sure* they're after us. I'm *not* sure whether they just want to talk to us and check our papers, or whether they want to kill us and keep us from telling anybody else what we've seen." *What I saw. Maybe I should've left her aboard and run for it. Maybe they would've left her alone.* Patricia looked at Toni's face, smooth, untouched by the hand of time. *And would you like to be the one to tell her parents if they didn't?* "I don't want to risk it."

Toni shrugged. "Well, if they just wanted to question us, we look guilty as hell, running like this."

Patricia shook her head. "*I* look guilty. It's *my* name on the registry. Unless you left your ID aboard, they have no idea who *you* are." *Unless they dust the boat for prints.*

"Oh."

An alarm sounded—a light tone. Patricia sighed and shut down the thrusters.

"What was that?" Toni asked.

"We're below five percent on the flywheels. We're going to have to surface and run the turbogenerator to get anywhere."

SubLorraine drifted slowly to a stop and listed slightly to port as she lost dynamic stability. Patricia shifted her weight to starboard and closed her eyes. With the engine off and the gain turned down on the sonar speaker, the only sounds were the faint whirring of the circulation fan and, because Patricia was close to her, the sound of Toni's breathing.

"Aren't we going to surface?"

Patricia opened her eyes again. "Eventually. The longer we wait, the farther away they'll get. That's my hope. That's my plan."

"Why do you even do this?"

"What are you talking about?"

Toni shrugged. "You're richer than Midas and you take on these stupid jobs for Amoco when you've got all that stuff back on the Strand."

Patricia sighed. "I am *not* richer than Midas. And I got a good rate for this job."

"You've got the Elephant Arms Apartments and that school and the garden thing and this sub and that boat. Don't tell me you're not rich."

It must look like riches to you. "Yeah, I've got that stuff, but I also don't make that much from them. I've got over thirty people working for me, and they all have salaries, health plans, and retirement packages. And if I don't keep bringing in money with jobs like this, the whole mess breaks down." *And I don't even want to think what happens to them if I die out here.*

"Oh." Toni tried to stretch and her long arms hit the bulkhead before she'd even started. "D-dammit! This thing is so tiny!"

Patricia reached out and put a hand on her shoulder. "Shhhh. Here, trade places with me." She swung the seat toward Toni and squeezed past her, hoping she wouldn't freak as Patricia crowded her even more. Toni moved into the seat quickly. Patricia lifted Toni's feet up onto the edge of the cushion and turned the chair a full one-eighty, so she faced, and actually stuck out into, the acrylic nose of the sub.

This far off the coast the water was relatively clear, free of silt in the top hundred feet of the water column. When you sat in the front of *SubLorraine,* you didn't feel like you were contained in a narrow steel culvert—you felt suspended in an enormous green-blue vault.

The water was changing color, gathering more blue as the amount of suspended silt dropped and the visibility increased. It was far less confining than the backseat, like sitting in an enormous cathedral, the moving waves above defracting shafts of light down into the vast space like the glow of stained glass touched by the sun.

"Try deep breaths, now. Deep breaths." Toni shuddered and then visibly relaxed, taking Patricia's advice and breathing deeply. There was a med kit aboard, but short of major pain medication, Patricia didn't think there was anything she could use to tranquilize Toni. *Make a note: add Valium to the first aid kit. Also, screen for claustrophobia in future employees.*

"I've no intention of dying out here. I'm way behind on the routine inspections of the Strand submerged structures and I've got to get back by Wednesday, for a shift of playground duty."

"What? Don't you have people to work there?"

Patricia grinned to herself. *That's it. Get her out of her own head.* "We're always shorthanded. Sing me that song," Patricia said. "The one I homed on."

"Huh?" Patricia could see Toni's reflection, surprised, distorted. " 'DNA Blues'?" Toni asked.

"Is that what it was?"

Toni nodded.

"Sing it now."

The dome acted as an acoustic reflector, focusing sound back at Toni's body and adding an almost tactile resonance to anything she said while in the seat. Toni started out weak and tentative but strengthened as she felt the reflected vibrations.

Patricia had wanted to distract Toni, to keep her calm, but it ended up helping Patricia, too. She hadn't realized how tense *she* was.

Big surprise, that.

When Toni finished, Patricia could see a smile flash in Toni's distorted reflection.

"Nice. Very nice," Patricia said, earning another brief glimpse of teeth. "I'm going to need to use the sonar set now."

"Do you want me to move?" There was some anxiety in Toni's voice.

"No. Just hand me the headset. You can work the controls for me." It would be awkward, but it had the double advantage of keeping Toni in the less claustrophobic nose *and* giving her something to do.

"What are we doing?"

"Looking for a . . ." *Miracle?* ". . . a decoy. Well, not exactly a decoy—some nice noisy traffic heading our way that can hide our sonar signature. Sort of a moving screen." Patricia took the headphones from her and told her how to kick the nose around until they were pointed back toward the coast. The hydrophone for the passive sonar sat in an acoustically transparent dome on the keel of the hull directly beneath the pilot's seat. The lockout hatch and the fan duct distorted sonar reception from the aft quarter and Patricia wanted as much range as possible.

"Okay. That handle right under the edge of the seat is the hydrophone direction control. I want you to twist it around until it's pointed about plus thirty."

"Plus thirty. How can I tell?"

"Look. There's a dial and a pointer."

Toni tilted forward. "I didn't see you do this."

"You do it long enough, you don't have to look. It clicks every five degrees." Patricia checked the headset. "Turn the volume up a little." She reached past Toni and took the clipboard wedged between the O_2 tank and the bulkhead, then put the headphones fully on.

"Now . . . we listen."

There were seventeen candidates in the first ten minutes. By the end of the half hour, there were only two. Of the other fifteen, six were going into port, five were fishing boats rattling their nets across the bottom, and four were fast transports, moving at over forty knots. They were noisy enough, with their turbines and water jets, and they were going in the right direction, but even if the sub could intercept one, they couldn't keep pace long enough for it to hide them.

The remaining two were diesel-powered with big screws whose bearings changed more slowly than the rejects. One of them had an odd hull sound, far in excess of the other, and Patricia had a notion about it. "There's our boy," she said. "But we're going to have to haul ass to catch them."

"What is it?"

"I think it's an oceangoing tug pushing a string of barges to the Strand. Maybe raw materials for the Industrial Park. Maybe beach sand for Playa del Mar. We need to change places, Toni."

Toni kept her voice brisk. "Right, then. Let's do it." Her shoulders were hunched up again, though, as she squeezed past Patricia.

Patricia strapped in, then powered up and eased *Sub-Lorraine* back to the surface. *Sycorax* was south of them, perhaps seventeen nautical miles, but moving very slowly, playing a waiting game.

"Here we go."

After their time of quiet, the turbogenerator sounded like God's own coffee grinder, filling the interior with noise. For the five minutes necessary to spin the flywheels up, Patricia couldn't check on the whereabouts of the *Sycorax* either; the noise overwhelmed her one hydrophone. What she could do, however, since she was on the surface, was get a good GPS fix and take a listen on the VHF radio.

"—below me. Stand to and prepare to be boarded. I repeat, submarine below, open your hatches and prepare to be boarded."

"Jesus, Joseph, and Mary!" Patricia leaned forward and craned her head. Distorted by the thin wash of water overhead, a large orange-and-white shape hung above. As she watched, a dark blob detached itself from the larger shape and dropped, splashing into the water about twenty feet ahead of them. When the bubbles cleared Patricia saw a wet-suited figure kicking his way toward the sub.

"What is it?" Toni asked, reacting to Patricia's voice.

Patricia kicked the thruster in, pushing the lever all the way up to the stop while she gave the sub full port rudder. They surged forward, and she felt Toni grab the back of her seat to keep from falling.

"INS helicopter."

The diver jerked to a stop and kicked back for a moment before he realized the sub was turning away from him. Then he was gone, well behind them.

"HEAVE TO IMMEDIATELY OR WE WILL OPEN FIRE," the voice on the VHF said.

The flywheels were only up to forty percent and Patricia was wondering how long she could push it when a sheet of bubbles cut through the water in front of her like a bead curtain.

She didn't bother to shut off the turbogenerator. She just pushed the stick all the way forward and prayed the safety interlocks would work.

There was a heavy *thud* that shook the entire hull as the float-operated flap valve on the snorkel intake flipped shut onto a jet engine sucking several hundred cubic feet of air a minute. The sudden vacuum sucked exhaust gas back up into the combustion chamber, stopping the turbine dead. Red lights came on and alarms sounded, but the fan kept thrusting. When the nose of *SubLorraine* was fifteen feet under and the stern barely awash, there was a loud bang, as if someone had struck the hull with a ballpeen hammer, and then another.

Then the sub was deeper and the only things that comforted Patricia were that the gauges weren't showing any water in the engine compartment and those bastards didn't dare drop explosives while their diver was in the water.

The sub pointed straight down now. Toni perched on the back of Patricia's chair and moaned, while Patricia hung in her seat, the seat belt pressing into her bladder with painful intensity. She shut down the thrusters and let *SubLorraine* coast deeper, gaining speed.

"It's going to be all right, Toni. Deep breaths."

"That's easy for you to say!" Toni's voice was shrill with more than a hint of panic.

They'd probably found the sub visually, Patricia thought. This far out, the water was clear enough that, looking down from altitude, the helicopter spotted *SubLorraine*'s shape even a hundred feet underwater. She was going to fix that. The bottom here was just under three hundred feet and she was going to get right down on it.

"Patricia—could we level out anytime soon?"

"It's all relative. Become a fish. Surrender the chains of planar thinking. Jeez—surface dwellers!" They passed one hundred feet, and Patricia picked up the sound of turbines and water jets to the south on the passive sonar. *Sycorax* was headed their way.

Toni was muttering, "I'm not a fish. I'll never be a fish. I eat fish. And I like gravity under my butt, too."

Patricia called up the instrumentation menu and enabled a water-temperature readout in the corner of her panel—67 degrees Fahrenheit and dropping very slowly, perhaps a tenth of a degree for every ten feet down. The gulf is a soupy mass of water, hot-to-warm, but you get deep enough and you can find cold water underneath. Sometimes there's a gradual transition between the cold and the hot, and sometimes it's sharp as a knife. Patricia was hoping for the knife.

The sub passed two hundred feet and she rolled it ninety degrees without changing the nose-down attitude. The hull was creaking, sharp popping sounds that were probably audible all the way to Houston, as the pressure increased. Patricia wasn't worried about the hull—it was designed for half a mile of water column—but the noise worried her.

Apparently it bothered Toni, too, because every time the hull popped, she whimpered.

"Don't worry, girl. The noise is a normal adjustment to pressure changes."

Toni muttered, "Normal for *you* maybe.

Patricia adjusted the hydrophone on the passive sonar. The *Sycorax* was still coming on strong.

Then it stopped, the sound cut off sharply to nothing.

Patricia looked at the temperature readout—48 degrees Fahrenheit. "Yes!"

Toni cursed again as Patricia pulled the nose up sharply, headed due east, and kicked the thrusters back up to forty-five percent.

"'Yes,' what? What is it with the 'yes,' already?"

"We've got a thermocline and we're under it. A thermocline reflects sound. Our sound, underneath, doesn't make it to the surface. I can't hear the *Sycorax* either, but we can rise above the thermocline to check them. They can't drop below to check us. We can make progress without them tracking us."

"What about that helicopter?"

"We're too deep now for them to track us visually."

The hull popped again and Toni whimpered. "Too deep."

"I've had this sub over two thousand feet down, Toni. The hull sounds are normal adjustments to changes in pressure."

Toni didn't speak for a moment, and when she did she said haltingly, "If you say so."

Just don't spaz on me, girl.

Patricia didn't want to tell her their real problem. Patricia's original plan had been to close with some noisy and heavy surface traffic that was slow enough for the sub to match speed—then keep it between them and the *Sycorax*, a sonic barrier. Now, though, since they hadn't been able to fully charge the flywheels, they didn't have the reserves needed to reach the barges she'd identified earlier.

She called up the charts again and plugged in the GPS data she'd acquired on their brief stay topside, looking for anything, something that might give them an edge.

"What's that?" Toni asked after Patricia had centered the chart on their current location. She stretched her arm over Patricia's shoulder to indicate a small square south of them that read "DP52: submerged structure: surface clearance 50 feet."

Patricia didn't answer her for a moment. *From the mouths of babes*. Finally Patricia said, "It's an oil rig."

Patricia closed on the rig slowly. She didn't want to come this far only to crack open the nose on a massive steel column. The rig towered above them, ranging from fifty feet of surface water at the truncated end of its mostly salvaged derrick to its legs, buried in silt and sand at 295 feet. The sub, approaching at a depth of 230 feet, was well below the majority of its mass.

"As it is above, so it shall be below."

Toni, looking over Patricia's shoulder, said, "What are you talking about?"

"Refugees." She gestured.

There were fish everywhere. Schooling horsehead jacks, ling, solitary grouper, three swordfish cutting through shimmering clouds of pinfish, and a hammerhead shark cruising the outer edge of the schools. Patricia felt Toni's breath on her ear as the girl craned forward to get a better look.

The rig, sea life, water, everything, was painted in shades of blue, the other colors of sunlight filtered out by the water column like a painting from Picasso's blue period. As they cleared a massive triangular brace and entered into the deep shadow between two of the rig's legs, Patricia switched on the two floodlights that tipped *SubLorraine*'s wings. Fish, suddenly painted vivid hues of yellow, orange, and red, scattered, fled to monotone anonymity beyond the beams' scope.

"Ohhhhhhhh," sighed Toni. "Do it again."

"Later," Patricia said. "Hang on tight, we're going up." She pulled the stick back and heard items sliding down the floor of the chamber as the sub climbed to the vertical. The thermocline held here beneath the rig, but she was moving the sub slowly, stealthily, and merely noted the temperature rise as she passed two hundred feet.

Toni swore for a moment beneath her breath, and Patricia spared a glance behind—now below—her.

"Give a girl some warning, why don't you!" To keep from first sliding, then falling to the back of the sub, Toni had braced her feet and was pushing her back against what had been the ceiling, chimney-style, one hand on the back of Patricia's seat, the other holding on to one corner of the sleeping bag she'd been sitting on, which dangled down the length of the sub toward the lockout chamber.

Patricia turned back around, quickly, worried that she'd run into something, but the space beneath the platform was vast. Even though the riser assembly led down through the middle of the space, they were nowhere near it. She let her head drop back against the headrest, easing the strain from her neck. The sub was pointed straight up now and the rest of the loose gear had slid or dropped to the lockout chamber hatch.

"There. Do you see it?"

"That shiny thing?"

The bubble was a flat mirror, reflecting the floodlights back down at them, increasing steadily in brightness as they rose. There was a crosscurrent, but the bubble was sheltered from it by the massive beams that formed its walls, and the silver surface seemed flat as glass. Without changing their orientation, Patricia killed the thrusters and let the sub coast upward, slowing. When they were ten feet short, she stopped them dead with reverse thrust.

"Wave in the pretty mirror," she told Toni.

Their reflections, distorted by the curved acrylic nose, stared back at them, doppelgängers suspended above in an outlandish electric light fixture. Patricia pumped a small amount of water from the forward ballast tank and the sub crept upward. Their reflection grew as well, dropping slowly to meet them until, at the last, even Patricia began to worry what would happen when the two subs collided, but, of course, they didn't. Instead, the acrylic nose of its reflected twin and the mirrored surface rippled out in circle after circle of distortion around a widening hole.

"Why so slow?" Toni asked.

"Didn't know how much clearance there was. Didn't want to break anything."

The chamber above had at least six feet of clearance between the surface of the water/air interface and the lowest of the steel beams above. Patricia could've risen normally, in a horizontal configuration, but at least now she knew there were no nasty surprises waiting to smash them from above. She pumped water from the rear trim tank and the stern began to rise.

"Well, what now?"

"We're going to run the turbogenerator to recharge the flywheels," Patricia said.

"Oh! Cool. You're going to use the bubble for air so we don't have to surface."

"Right. There is a problem, though."

"A problem—"

"Well, several."

Yeah, several problems.

Patricia put on the full outfit this time—dry suit, rebreather, and the fully enclosed helmet with its built-in Gertrude so she could talk to Toni while she was outside.

She'd gone over the procedures with Toni several times before closing herself in the lockout chamber. She dropped out of the chamber clutching her two-pound sledge and a waterproof bag holding Toni's portable stereo.

"You read me?"

Toni's voice came back clearly in the headset. "Oh, yeah. You're really going to replace my stereo, right?"

"Cross my fingers—" *hope not to die.*

The stereo floated, buoyed by air trapped in the bag, and

as Patricia pushed it clear of the hatch, it slithered up the side of the sub to bob at the water/air interface. Patricia followed, venting a bit of nitrogen into her dry suit to counteract the tendency of the hand sledge to pull her toward the bottom.

"I'm moving to the back of the sub now." She let her helmet push the stereo along in front of her, bobbing along, while she slid her free hand along the side of *SubLorraine* and kicked her fins.

"Confirm fan locked out, please."

There was a pause and then Toni's voice came back. "Confirmed. The thruster display says 'disabled.' "

Patricia wedged the floating bag with the stereo into the shroud surrounding the thruster fan, then slipped off her fins and clipped them to a ring on her rebreather harness. She used the horizontal stabilizer as a step and hauled herself awkwardly up onto the sub, the weight of her rebreather, ballast belt, and suit becoming suddenly onerous as she lifted them above the supporting embrace of the water. The rear of *SubLorraine* settled noticeably lower in the water, eliciting a startled query over the Gertrude.

"It's okay, Toni. I've climbed on top, and it's just my weight. The snorkel is still above water."

Toni had not wanted to be left alone in the sub, but there was no way that the snorkel was going to open by itself. Not with the engine compartment being at surface pressure and the air bubble at two atmospheres gauge.

Patricia turned her attention to the snorkel, an integral part of the vertical stabilizer. Just behind the titanium pipe of the snorkel there was an ugly hole in the composite skin of the stabilizer. Patricia shuddered. If the bullet had hit the snorkel instead . . . She decided not to tell Toni about it.

The intake was covered by a solenoid-driven titanium flapper valve with a Teflon seal. A float and water-pressure-actuated arm would close it—had closed it—in the event of unexpected submersion. At depth, the solenoid was insufficient to open the valve against water pressure.

Unless it gets a little help. "Toni, on my mark, activate the intake valve." Patricia adjusted her grip on the sledge. "Three, two, one, *mark*!" She brought the sledge up to the overhanging lip of the flapper valve. It didn't budge. "Again, three, two, one, *mark*!" This time she felt it move slightly, but the pressure differential was still too great, sucking the titanium piece firmly down onto its seat. Patricia began to worry about cracking the valve. If she flooded the engine compartment on submersion, they wouldn't be going anywhere but down.

"One more time." Again, she counted to the mark, and this time she used both hands on the sledge, throwing her body back to increase the impact.

The cover flipped back, and Patricia could hear a shrieking whistle inside her helmet as the compartment equalized with the bubble, followed by a *ka-chunnnng* as the hull of the sub rang like a bell.

"Whoa. I heard that," Toni said on the Gertrude. "Hell, I *felt* that."

Patricia inspected the flapper valve, frowning. There was a hairline crack on the edge, but it didn't seem to extend as far as the seat seal. *Fingers crossed.* "It looks like we've got step one taken care of. Give me a minute to prepare for step two."

"Okay."

Patricia didn't want the stereo too close to the sub. The noise levels would be bad enough, but there was the possibility that the exhaust gases would raise temperatures in the bubble enough that the waterproof bag would melt. She retrieved it from the fan shroud and opened the bag while she was still perched on the sub. They'd disabled the write protect on one of Toni's Grand Mal minidiscs while the stereo was still inside, but Patricia still had to turn on the record button.

"It's my favorite disc, you know," Toni said over the Gertrude.

"I'll download you another copy when we get home. Are you ready?"

"Snorkel and exhaust are green. Why shouldn't I be ready?"

Patricia bit her lip, then decided to tell her. "I'm not exactly sure what's going to happen, Toni. The partial pressure of oxygen at this pressure is three times what the engine is used to. It may burn hot, or the extra air mass may cool it more efficiently, or it . . . it might overheat really quick." Patricia pushed the record button on the stereo and sealed the bag before sliding off the sub into the water. "So watch your readouts. Hell, better yet, turn the display screen sideways and we'll both watch the readouts."

She shoved the floating bag toward the front of the sub, then put her fins back on and kicked after them. At the front of the sub, she shoved the bag farther away, then bled nitrogen from her dry suit until she was neutral, hovering just outside the seam between the acrylic nose and the titanium hull.

"Can you see it okay?"

Inside, Toni had rotated the plasma display ninety degrees, and though slightly distorted, Patricia could read it fine.

"Drop your knee and it's perfect. Okay, do it."

The jet engine whined up to speed, then coughed suddenly before catching. Patricia held on to a recessed mounting bolt with one hand and crossed her fingers on the other. The temperature readouts climbed steadily, reaching normal operating temperatures more quickly than usual. The noise level was tremendous, even through the rubber helmet and headphones.

Here kitty, kitty, kitty. You hear that, Syco Witch?

"No explosions," said Toni. "That's good."

Not yet. "Always a plus," Patricia said loudly, to be heard over the sound of the turbine.

The exhaust temperature readout passed 550 degrees Fahrenheit. Patricia lifted her hand and cautiously poked her bare fingers above the water's surface. The air temperature was rising rapidly as exhaust gases swirled into the enclosed chamber.

On the readout screen, the temperature readout on the recuperator housing was in the yellow and heading for orange. The storage flywheels were up to sixty-five percent, but Patricia expected the turbine to fail catastrophically at any time.

She looked at her watch. *It's not worth the risk.* "Okay, shut her down. We'll see if that will do it." The relief from the noise was palpable. "God, that's better. Time to see what we got on the recorder."

She swam over to the recorder under the surface. When she reached her hand up to take it, the plastic surface of the upper bag was hot and slightly sticky.

She rolled it over to cool it. She'd been planning on taking it back up into the air pocket to check the recording, but the air was so warm that she decided against it, returning instead to the lockout chamber and muscling the buoyant bag back under the surface, to pop up through the hatch.

Perched inside, legs down in the water, she pulled off her helmet and wiped down the bag closure before opening it.

She put it in play mode and specified track one. Even at low volume, the sound of the turbogenerator was perfect. When she boosted the bass and increased the volume, it was scary.

"Okay. Let's see what we can do."

Timing is everything.

"Are you sure this is going to work?" Toni asked.

Patricia laughed. "Hell, no."

"It's *not* going to work?"

Patricia laughed again. "No. I'm just not *sure* it's going to work."

The sub was perched on the truncated gantry, a mere fifty feet below the surface. The water around them was dimming as the sun neared the horizon and Patricia was no longer worried about being picked up visually by aircraft, especially profiled by the dark mass of the rig.

Patricia was back outside again, perched on the top of *SubLorraine* right behind the acrylic nose, feeling like a bull rider right down to gripping a cinch strap. She'd tied a heavy mooring rope to the forward lifting eye, and had the coiled excess tucked under her butt as she gripped the rope close to the hull. They had the settings on the Gertrude turned all the way down, but even so, they intended to stop using it when the *Sycorax* closed on the rig. The acoustic telephone translated voice frequencies up into the kilohertz range to broadcast through the water and passive sonar could certainly detect it. An operator could even drop the frequency back to hear what was being said.

"She's still coming strong and her bearing hasn't changed a bit."

Patricia closed her eyes. "Yeah. I can hear her now. Get ready. Remember—no more than five percent thrust and watch my hand signals."

"Aye, aye."

Patricia checked her chronograph. They were pushing it. They had less than two minutes until their diversion happened and if *Sycorax* wasn't in place, the diversion would be useless.

Come on, you overpriced heap of scrap.

The stereo, still down in the air pocket below the rig platform, started up precisely on time, full volume. Patricia could hear it clearly through the water, unaided.

Hopefully the very expensive sonar equipment on the *Sycorax* could, too.

She'd programmed it to repeat the first track on the disk five times, which, with a slight stutter every time it repeated, should give them ten minutes of turbogenerator noise.

"No more Gertrude, Toni."

Toni answered by holding her thumb up where Patricia could see it.

The noise from *Sycorax* was growing, threatening to overwhelm the sound from the stereo. *Their signal processors probably filter it out.* She kept twisting around, her eyes to the southeast, looking for the dark shadow of the *Sycorax*'s hull.

The sound of the *Sycorax* grew and grew, to the point where she was feeling the pressure waves on her skin, an oppressive, ominous force. *Where are you, dammit?* Five minutes into the diversion, she saw it, more southerly than she'd expected, long and narrow and big. Even as she acquired the visual, the *Sycorax* throttled back completely, surprising her by how tiny and tinny the stereo reproduction of her own turbogenerator sounded by comparison.

The *Sycorax* still made noise even with her jets shut off. She'd been doing over forty knots and she didn't exactly stop on a dime. The hull wash sounded like distant surf and she coasted past faster than *SubLorraine*'s top speed.

Stop already or come back.

Almost as if her captain had heard her, *Sycorax* dropped her deflector plates over her jet nozzles, and kicked her jets back in. The reversed thrust dropped the forward motion quickly, bringing *Sycorax* to a stop at the far edge of visual range.

Patricia stuck her hand forward where Toni could see it and pointed her finger forward. *Come on, girl. Let's see what you can do.*

In less than three minutes, they'd run out of diversion.

It took most of that three minutes to close on *Sycorax*. Patricia clung to the rope and streamlined her body with *SubLorraine*, trying to minimize drag. The closer they got to the INS Fastship, the less sure she was about the plan.

Can they hear us? Are they still listening to the decoy? They must've heard us when we were really running the generator. Can they tell the difference?

Toni headed *SubLorraine* straight for the stern of *Sycorax*, keeping at fifty feet. When they passed into its shadow, Patricia waved her hand and pointed up. Toni didn't waste time acknowledging but pulled the stick back.

Too fast, too fast.

Toni must've felt the same because she kicked the thrusters into reverse. *SubLorraine* drifted to a stop ten feet below the intake grates of *Sycorax*'s massive water jets.

Down below, the tinny sound of the recorded turbojets stopped, and after a few seconds of silence she heard the bass and drum intro of Grand Mal's "I Don't Like the Clothes You Wear."

Too soon! Patricia kicked hard off *SubLorraine*, uncoiling the rope as she went. She approached the water intakes with dread. The grating was stainless steel with six-inch spacing and the constant flow of water and small debris had polished the leading edges to knife thinness. If the *Sycorax* were to start up its jets right now, she suspected she'd be pulled through the grid like cheese though a grater.

She threaded the rope through the aft edge of the grate, tied a bowline then tucked, rolled, and kicked off the *Sycorax*'s hull.

Almost immediately she heard the turbines above whining as they increased in rpm's.

They must've figured out it's a decoy and they think we ran for the Strand. Oh god, oh god, oh god!

She got as far as the nose of *SubLorraine* when the rope suddenly went rigid tight and *SubLorraine* jerked forward, knocking into her shoulder. As she slid underneath the sub's nose, she saw Toni looking down through the acrylic with a horrified expression on her face.

The ventral fin struck Patricia in the knee, and she nearly passed out from the pain, but flailed around to grab it. The water was moving by very fast now, tugging at her helmet, her equipment. The lockout chamber hatch was right behind her, but it was closed, and unless they stopped, there was no way she'd be able to open it against the rush of the water. Hell, even if she could open the hatch, to do so she would have to let go of the ventral fin.

This was such a stupid idea!

She wouldn't be able to hold on much longer. She felt one of her fins flutter as the streaming water caught the edge of the foot pocket, and then it was gone, torn off like tissue in the wind.

She shifted her grip on the fin and freed one hand to flip the Gertrude power switch as high as it could go. *Hope Toni doesn't answer.* She used her thickest Central American accent, half Nicaraguan guttural, half Belize singsong. "Yo, Beenan. Look at them run! They bought it!" Then, cranking the control down to the halfway mark, she answered, using her own voice, "Can it, you idiot! They can still hear us!"

With a little bit of luck, the sonar operator on *Sycorax* might think the second signal came from a different source, because of the difference in amplitude. In any case, Patricia hoped they would think they were cruising *away* from their quarry.

The drag was increasing and even with both hands on the ventral fin, the water pulled at Patricia's helmet, rebreather, and limbs like some relentless giant. Her other swim fin tore away and she wondered, abstractly, if she would be swept clear or break her back on *SubLorraine*'s fan shroud.

She could feel the space between the finger joints increasing and her fingers slowly unbending. *Sorry, Dad.*

Then the noise slowed—the massive overwhelming drone of the water jets and turbines wound down to a mild droning—and the pressure eased, slowly at first, then more. She risked one hand to reach back to the hatch, and pulled the purge lever, venting the excess pressure in the lockout chamber into the water. It sounded like someone farting loudly in a bathtub and Patricia wondered what the sonar operator would make of it.

She freed the hatch and it dropped slightly open, but as she suspected, the water was still holding it mostly closed. She pulled on it, but the best she could do was pull it down forty-five degrees. *Come on!* The *Sycorax* was still slowing, but her captain could speed up again at any moment, either to turn back to look for the source of the Gertrude transmission, or to return to their original course.

The *Sycorax* slowed even more and the hatch came down further. *Now or never, girl.* She let go of the ventral fin and clung to the hatch latch, streaming downcurrent before she transferred her grip to the trailing edge of the hatch opening. Here she found she could wedge her body between the hatch and the hatchway, forcing it open by worming through, twisting to get the rebreather through. She'd gotten her helmet and torso up into the chamber when that sound started again, turbines and water jets revving up. The pressure on the hatch increased sharply, pinching her thighs between the hatch and the hatchway. She used her weight to push down on the hatch and pulled one leg through, then the other. The act of pulling her right foot through before the water forced the hatch shut tore her dry-suit boot open, abrading the skin raw on her instep. Blood mixed with salt water splattered drops on the acrylic.

Shit! Just what she needed. Her suit was patched in a dozen places already.

It took longer for Patricia to squirm out of her equipment than it took the pumps to bring the lockout chamber back down to surface pressure.

Toni was incoherent. "But—you—. How—?"

"Shhhhhh," Patricia whispered when the hatch was opened. "They're listening. Mind the helm."

They had to keep a slight downward pressure on the horizontal dive controls to keep *SubLorraine* from swinging up and bumping into the bottom of the *Sycorax*.

"What's our speed?"

Toni turned back around to look at the readout. "Uh. Thirty-three knots."

Patricia whistled silently. "She's never gone so fast." She unclipped the first aid kit from the bulkhead, working as quietly as she could.

"What do we do now?"

"We wait. The *Sycorax* makes a stop at the Abattoir every Wednesday, when the INS transport brings the latest deportees in from Texas and Arkansas." The Abattoir was the nickname for the Abbott Base Refugee and Detention Center, the INS processing and detention camp at New Galveston.

Toni's expression darkened. "Yeah. I've seen 'em. Why the *Sycorax*?"

"Three years ago there was a bad riot. They want the extra firepower. You weren't here then, were you?"

Toni shook her head.

"A lot of people died, guards and inmates. That's when they started calling it the Abattoir." Patricia found some gauze and began wrapping her foot. "This is Monday. We just have to imitate a hole in the water for thirty-six hours and the bastards will tow us home."

3

Becket: *Centro de interés*

Thomas hitched a ride to the site on an INS helicopter from Houston Intercontinental, skirting east of the Houston dikes. The brown gulf waters were spotted with the shadows of clouds and occasionally interrupted by local boat traffic or the projecting tangles of taller pre-Deluge structures not yet pulled down by storm surge and the persistent wear of waves. Closer to shore the ever-present fingers of telephone poles and power-line towers climbed from the water, getting shorter and shorter until all but the tallest utility towers rose above the waves.

The gray naval tender and a smaller oceangoing shrimp trawler were anchored in an otherwise unremarkable stretch of that same brown water.

But their very presence is the indicator. Their very presence defines the focus, the locus of this investigation. It made Thomas stir inside, come back to life, just to think about it. He tried to put the scene in context with the video, but it wasn't the same. The video had been taken eighty-five feet below the surface of the water.

There was a landing pad on the fantail of the naval dive tender, but the pilot didn't land—just hovered a few feet above while Thomas hopped down, then turned to catch his bag, dropped by the copter's crew chief.

It was hot and humid and the sun shining off the water hurt his eyes. He'd been traveling all night in uncomfortable dress whites, now wrinkled and sweaty, and he felt like hammered shit.

His XO, Lieutenant Graham, met him at the edge of the platform, but remained silent while the noise and wind of the helicopter followed that vehicle away to the east. Graham was a slight black man, and he looked cool and comfortable in khakis.

"Sorry I'm late, Jazz," Thomas said, speaking first. "They kept me on the stand all afternoon."

"Yes sir, I know. I called Admiral Rylant yesterday, uh, five P.M. D.C. time. He also said the sitting court threatened the honorable counsel for the defense with contempt if he didn't show some substantive reason for continuing the cross-exam. Did the prosecution rest?"

"Yeah. I may get recalled during the defense, though. Hope not—I was just giving context to the video."

"Hmph. Why didn't they plea bargain? We got the bastard cold, with the cocaine, with the weapons, with the cash."

Thomas shrugged. "He wasn't offered a plea bargain. The decision came down from the attorney general. They want him made an example. He's a senior officer of the INS and they want to send a message."

"That you better not wear the uniform and be a bad guy?"

Thomas laughed. "Maybe. But certainly that you better not wear the uniform and get caught." He pointed at the large oceangoing shrimp boat moored next to the dive tender. "What's that for?"

Graham started moving again, walking forward toward the bridge of the tender. "Got it from Houston impound. We're using its freezer as a morgue."

The remnants of Thomas's smile dropped from his face. "Oh, yeah. How many so far?"

"The divers are still bringing them up, but the rough count is forty-seven from the hold. The freighter's crew is iffier—the sharks have been pulling them around, so I'm not sure we'll get a good count on them. Certainly we've got at least three different crew members. It remains to be seen if the other parts match up."

"You got facilities lined up?"

"Yeah. Harris County will lend us their morgue and lab. Most important, they've got a freezer semitrailer for overflow and we're going to need it."

"Who'd you get for examiner?"

"It's still up in the air. You asked for Lawson, but the FBI says he's too busy with something in California. The old man says they'll push them for someone of similar quality."

They reached the steep stair, almost a ladder, that led up to the bridge. "Might as well leave your bag here. We've been hot bunking it with the crew, so I don't know where we'll end up putting you."

The bridge was dark, tinted shades pulled down over the front windows, and the two khaki-clad officers inside were facing a pair of video monitors mounted at the back of the room. They turned around as Thomas and Graham entered.

Graham did the introductions. "This is Captain Nathan Elmsford," he said, referring to a man with the brass oak leaf of a lieutenant commander. Captain, in this case, was his job, not his rank. "And this is his exec, Lieutenant Martin Callard. My boss, Commander Thomas Becket of INS CID."

Captain Elmsford and Commander Becket shook hands. "Welcome aboard, commander." His eyes lingered on the right side of Thomas's face. "That's quite a scar you got there."

Thomas smiled, causing them to stare even more. His smile was a lopsided affair, the scar tissue that covered most of the right side of his face was stiff and unresponsive at the corner of his mouth and right eye. "What can I say—I thought it was an electric razor." He said it deadpan, used to this reaction.

The two naval officers smiled uncertainly.

Thomas continued. "It's good of you to extend facilities to the investigation."

"As if we had a choice. I go where I'm told." Elmsford

gestured at an active screen, which showed an irregular dark shape framed by squares. Looking closer, Thomas saw it was the freighter *Open Lotus* and the sunken warehouses that he'd seen once, already, on the footage from the Beenan woman. The angle was very different, though, and he realized that the camera must be on the hull of the dive tender staring down through the water.

Two divers in Mark VII rebreathers were rising toward the camera, each pulling a long dark bag behind him.

Elmsford said, "And frankly, I'd have been glad not to. I've got some pretty tough personnel but this—" He shook his head. "My lead diver woke up screaming this morning. Nightmares."

Thomas closed his eyes briefly. "Does he have kids?"

"You got that right. Anyway, we're professionals. We'll do our job."

"I never had any doubts. Have you found any ordnance?"

"Weapons?"

"Projectiles. Jacketed slugs. Anything we can use for ballistic matching."

"Ah. We haven't been looking but we can. In fact, I had to pull some of my men off the hold detail—the bodies were too much for them. This'll give them something to do while the rest of my divers build up some surface interval after we finish recovering the bodies."

"It can't have been easy on anybody." Thomas took another look at the screen. A different pair of divers had left the hold below, another pair of body bags in tow. Thomas exhaled air between clenched teeth. "I'll let you guys get on with it, then. Uh, I know you guys are crowded, but do you have someplace I can bunk?"

Elmsford and his XO exchanged looks; then Elmsford said, "Certainly. You can hot bunk with one of us, if you'd like, but the owner's cabin on the shrimper is downright luxurious. It's just that nobody wanted to sleep near the . . . you know."

Thomas looked at his own XO, Graham, who suddenly

found his own shoes extremely interesting. "I see," Thomas said. "Well, I'm not particular." He offered his hand again to the two men and turned to leave.

"It's not the dead who worry me."

The owner's cabin boasted a double-wide bunk, air-conditioning, and a stereo, as well several oil-painted female nudes more photorealistic than impressionistic. Thomas left his bag and followed Graham to the aft deck, where his people were using the shrimper's gantry to transfer the body bags from the water to the refrigerated hold.

"Who are they, Jazz? Where are they from?"

Jazz shook his head. "I have no idea. The crabs have really done a job. I know this, though. They weren't poor. Their clothes are Chinese knockoffs of American and European fashions. Good dental work. Some crowns. But whoever put them in the hold took their ID. There's not a purse or wallet to be found. No jewelry, no luggage. A few toys but they're generic."

"Fingerprints? Tattoos?"

"Crabs and fish, but I think we'll be able to get some plantar prints from those who wore lace-up shoes. We'll have to go after birth records, then."

Thomas nodded. "Okay. Have the medical examiner try for stomach contents. Give me an idea of their diet and we'll know where to send the footprints."

They walked to the edge of the open hold. The humidity of the hot gulf air was mixing with the cold below, making fog. A ladder leaned against one corner of the hatchway and they climbed down into the fog.

"That feels good," Thomas said, as the cold air enveloped him.

A voice from below said, "The first five minutes is nice. Can't recommend it for much longer, though."

At one end of the hold a plywood table had been rigged, three feet wide by seven long. The speaker was one of two figures standing at the head of the table. He was holding a camera against the mouth of a corpse in a zipped-open body bag, taking shots for dental matching. It was easy to do since the crabs had eaten away the cheeks and tongue. As he worked, the acquired images began appearing on the screen of a portable workstation set on two crates against the wall.

"How are you doing, Leo?" Thomas asked.

Master Chief Investigator Leo Bernstein, a slightly heavy man with male pattern baldness eating up patches of his hair, was the unit's forensic supervisor. He wore a field jacket and a decidedly civilian sweater over his undress denims. "I've been better. I'm going to get pneumonia going in and out of this hold."

The other person at the table, First Class Investigator Barbara Mendez, said, "Maybe you shouldn't go back and forth. Why don't you just stay down here so that nasty hot air doesn't throw your metabolism into unbalance?" Mendez was using a measuring tape to record the length of the corpse, then recording the information on the workstation with the dental and facial shots.

"I'll give you unbalance," Bernstein told Mendez.

Thomas said, "You trying for the plantar prints?"

"Not here. Don't want to mess them up. We could just as easily rip the skin off by removing the shoes and socks. If it were one or two, I'd go ahead and do it, but I won't really have enough supplies until we get them in the lab."

Thomas nodded. "Okay. As soon as the navy brings up the last body, we'll get this bucket moving over to Houston. You can finish the cataloging under way."

"Aye, aye, sir."

"Carry on."

Thomas and Jazz climbed out of the hold and walked back to the owner's cabin. "You got any word on the submersible that found this mess?"

"Our Fastship *Sycorax* has been trying to intercept it, but it gave them the slip yesterday and they haven't been able to reacquire it. You think they had anything to do with this?"

"Do they carry twenty-five-millimeter cannon? How

about fifty-caliber machine guns? What became of their surface tender, anyway?"

"*Sycorax* put two ratings aboard. They sailed it back to Buffalo Bayou."

"I don't suppose they found a cannon aboard?"

"No, sir. No weapons of any kind."

"Well, then, I don't think they had anything to do with it."

"Then why did they run? Doesn't that sound suspicious to you?"

Thomas shrugged. "If I had to guess, I'd say it sounds like they're scared, Jazz. But it doesn't mean they did it. But I don't like to guess. I'd rather ask them." He stretched and a jaw-popping yawn reminded him how tired he was. "I'm going to get some sleep. Wake me up in four hours, okay?"

Floating morgue or no, he was unconscious in five minutes.

Jazz's voice, vibrating the walls of the cabin greatly amplified, woke Thomas. He stared blearily at his watch. It was less than two hours since he'd closed his eyes.

"—is Lieutenant Hamilton Graham of the INS. You are intruding upon a crime investigation and are subject to arrest for obstruction of justice if you do not leave the area immediately. I repeat, if you do not leave this area immediately, you will be arrested, detained, and your vessels confiscated."

Thomas stumbled to the head and splashed tepid water across his face, then opened his bag and took out a clean set of khakis and dressed quickly.

He stepped into the shrimper's pilothouse and found Jazz talking into a handheld radio. "I don't care if they're from NBC. I don't care if they're from CN-fucking-N. If they don't pull that boat back, I'm going to throw their asses in the Abattoir faster than you can say 'citizenship check.' "

"I hope you're on a secure channel, Jazz."

Jazz turned and blushed. "Yes, sir. Scrambled and spread spectrum. Sorry to wake you up." He pointed at a thirty-foot cabin cruiser sitting two hundred yards away. "They started to put divers down. They're from NBC News out of Houston."

Thomas looked closer and saw a Zodiac inflatable pulled up by the boat's stern. "Who'd you send?"

"Ensign Terkel and Seaman Guterson. Captain Elmsford lent us the boat and a rating to crew."

"Good of him. You send for help?"

"Yes, sir. Buffalo Bayou Station is sending a patrol hydrofoil, but it won't be out here for another thirty minutes."

Terkel's voice came from the radio in Jazz's hand. "They're going, sir."

Jazz answered. "Escort them until they're at least a half-mile out before you come back."

"Aye, aye."

Jazz put the radio back in his belt holster.

"Is this the first appearance of our friends from the fourth estate?"

Jazz looked confused, then said, "Oh, the press? No, we've been buzzed by news helicopters out of Houston. The crew from CNN tried to land on the pad of the dive tender, but Elmsford put three men out there with M-22's and they sheered off."

"How many people got the damn video? Damn that woman, Beenan."

"Yes, sir."

"Any word on that sub?"

"None. They haven't heard her since yesterday. *Sycorax* forwarded her audio signature to the navy, and they've been listening on the SONUS net, but there's been no trace."

Thomas frowned. *Did they sink her?* "See if you can get someone from the New Galveston unit to keep an eye on her residence in the Strand. Does she have an apartment?"

"An entire apartment building. Uh, I asked them for a profile, which they'll be sending, but she owns an entire hex. Her father was one of the original investors, even before the Deluge."

Thomas whistled. "A hex? What's on it?" A hex was the

basic flotation unit of New Galveston, an inverted hexagonal cup two hundred feet across the flats. They were the floating city's equivalent of a block, over thirty-four thousand square feet of area.

"He said she has a twenty-unit apartment, a day-care center with a K-6 school, and a garden co-op. Patricia Beenan is also an alternate for the city assembly."

Thomas whistled. "Rich woman. Beenan. Beenan. I know that name from someplace else."

Jazz nodded. "Katherine Beenan, U.S. congresswoman from Texas. She's on the Joint Immigration Oversight Committee."

"Right! Any relation?"

"Her mother."

Thomas sat down heavily on the padded bench at the back of the pilothouse. "Perfect. It's *perfect*. You couldn't ask for a more perfect situation. Well, maybe if the president had a stake in it, or maybe the pope. Or perhaps if you caught the president and the pope in bed having sex with a sheep—and they *both* had a stake in it. And the sheep were on the committee."

Jazz waited patiently for Thomas to run down.

Thomas finally stopped. "I don't suppose there's any chance of getting a cup of coffee, is there?"

Jazz lifted the radio. "Coming right up, sir."

"Well, send it to me on the tender's bridge. I've got to go talk Elmsford into raising the *Open Lotus*."

Convincing Elmsford to raise the *Open Lotus* took about five minutes. Getting him authorization from his chain of command took the rest of the afternoon with many calls back and forth to Washington. By the time Thomas had finished, his satphone was on its second battery and his voice was a croaking husk.

He was sitting in the tender's wardroom when Jazz came in. "We've got what seems to be the last body, Commander."

"Okay. Get that shrimper headed for Houston. You take it and the unit. Leave me Guterson and have him secure our gear on the tender. When we get *Open Lotus* afloat, we'll take it to Buffalo Bayou." He paused, thinking furiously. "I'm hoping we'll need someone to work with waterlogged documents, but I guess we shouldn't ask until we find same. Tell you what. Get on your phone when you're under way, and get me some travel history on *Open Lotus*. Find out who owns it and where it's been. Give me twice-daily reports unless you've got something hot. Then call at any hour."

"When shall we expect you, sir?"

Thomas shook his head. "I don't know. I might go out to the Strand. I'd like to find out more about the Beenan woman."

Jazz blinked, suddenly very still. "You don't have to go out there. I could go for you."

Thomas grimaced. "Stop it. Just stop it. You have your orders."

Jazz was about to say something else when Captain Elmsford stuck his head in the doorway, then came the rest of the way in. "Got a present." He set a Styrofoam cup on the table and slid it across to Thomas. Partway, it tipped over and four pieces of metal tumbled out.

"Fifty-caliber, like the lady said."

Thomas picked up one jacketed slug, nearly perfect in its shape. "This can't have hit anything hard."

"It was on the floor of the bridge. If I were to guess, I'd say it was fired as the boat was sinking and it hit water first, then settled."

Thomas shook his head. "Okay. I guess the next thing is a ballistic check on every INS fifty-caliber machine gun in this region. I want our people to do it, Jazz. Don't let the local personnel retrieve the rounds, you understand?"

"Aye, sir. I'll put Ensign Terkel on it. Shall I get a helicopter out of Buffalo Bayou?"

"See if you can get that hydrofoil assigned. That model

came on line after the Coast Guard was brought into the service so they have the M-30 instead, right? So they're a clean base of operations."

Jazz shrugged. "Unless they brought one on board special."

"That scenario works for anybody in or out of the service. We know we use the M-61A1 twenty-millimeter cannon and M-2 fifty-caliber machine guns. If we don't hit pay dirt then we can cast the net wider."

"Uh, dig wider? Mixed metaphor and all that," Jazz said.

Thomas grinned. "Do you really want to start doing body-cavity searches on all those victims, Jazz?"

Jazz straightened. "No, sir."

Behind him, Elmsford looked slightly green.

"Any other ideas, questions?" Thomas asked.

Jazz shook his head.

Elmsford said, "This is a pretty busy area. A lot of traffic moves through here. Commercial fishing, freighters, tankers, you name it. Someone may have seen something, even at night."

"Gotcha," said Jazz.

Thomas added, "We look for witnesses."

With Jazz safely away in the shrimper and Ensign Terkel safely away on the hydrofoil, Thomas put Seaman Guterson to work with Thomas's workstation, organizing a summary of results to forward to the old man, Admiral Rylant, director of the INS Criminal Investigation unit charged with internal affairs.

Thomas slept, using the exec's cabin. Lieutenant Callard offered it freely, saying he'd be on duty until midnight. When Thomas's wrist alarm woke him at eleven-forty-five, he found Guterson waiting with a fresh pot of coffee in the officer's wardroom.

"Lieutenant Graham called thirty minutes ago. They're at the Houston dikes, and they'll be transferring the bodies immediately, using the refrigerated semitrailer the county provided."

"Good. Have you secured a bunk yet?"

"Yes, sir, they've set me up in the decompression chamber aft. It's not being used right now." Guterson, a young blond, kept his voice deadpan, but his eyes were a little wide.

"How . . . cozy," commented Thomas.

"Yes, sir. I've got the draft memo to Admiral Rylant done. It's on your desktop." He was referring to the virtual desktop on Thomas's workstation.

"Fine. Get some rest, then—if you can. I'll see you in the morning."

"Yes, sir."

Reading the summary was chilling. Besides the three crewmen, the preliminary age and gender ID's were eighteen men, twelve women, and seventeen children dead in the hold. Alone, in the wardroom, Thomas felt the weight of their deaths. *Fifty in all. What a horridly even number.*

He took his coffee cup out onto the deck. The clouds had dissipated during the evening and stars dotted the sky from horizon to horizon, fading slightly to the northwest, where the night lights of Houston painted a false dawn in the sky. A faintly visible line of yellowish lights on the horizon defined the near edge of the dikes. It was still hot, but far more bearable with the sun down and a light breeze from the south.

He'd been raised on this coast in a series of small towns with names like Ingleside, Port Aransas, Port Isabel, and Orange. His father had been a Coast Guard officer. *My childhood is well and truly drowned,* he often thought, but he never said so, since it wasn't exactly an uncommon experience. Ninety percent of the planet's population had lived in the first hundred feet above sea level before the Deluge. With the exception of a few dearly bought square miles like those at Washington Island or the lands inside the Houston dikes, the former homes of billions now rolled below the waves.

The images from the videotape pulled at him in a way he didn't understand. The drowned warehouses juxtaposed with the ship and its cargo of death. *Not death. Just the dead. The death had been carried on another craft—a craft with weapons and men who operated them.*

Something inside of Thomas was making a connection between his drowned childhood and these drowned men, women, and children. Something intangible and elusive.

He took his empty coffee cup back inside and spent the rest of the night reviewing the data, downloading the catalog of victim data compiled by his team, and finalizing the daily summary for Admiral Rylant.

> *. . . and while it is true that many service vehicles (air force and navy) use the twenty-millimeter cannon, the INS uses it in combination with the M-2 fifty-caliber machine gun still in service on our older vessels—inherited from the Coast Guard.*
>
> *So, preliminary investigations have to treat INS involvement as a possibility.*

He encrypted it and sent it off without any sense of accomplishment. He didn't feel he'd lost any of the burden. Sharing the nasty details hadn't released him. It was a burden that didn't lessen on distribution.

N divided by 2 should be one-half N. But it's not working that way. It's bad math and it's even bad therapy. Talking about it should lessen the load.

He shook his head.

Talking about it and talking about how it affects me are two different things, aren't they? It'll have to wait.

This time he laughed out loud.

I've heard that before.

4

Beenan: *Llegando a casa*

While *Sycorax* thundered overhead, sleep was possible, barely, if Patricia took cotton from the first aid kit and wadded it into her ears. But even then it was difficult. She could feel the noise from the *Sycorax*'s engines through the hull, even when lying on top of the sleeping bag, and her dozing was haunted by images of the *Open Lotus*'s hold.

She and Toni took turns resting in four-hour shifts. They stretched out in the lockout chamber, feet sticking through the open hatch into the pilot's compartment, head pillowed on Toni's clothes bag.

Fortunately, the *Sycorax* stopped to listen, sitting still for a blessed hour of silence at a time, then running at top speed for another hour to another listening spot.

They were twenty-five feet underwater and normally beyond the depth where Patricia could receive radio transmissions, but the giant steel hull just above them was acting as a radio guide, enabling Patricia to use the GPS to track their course.

Initially, the *Sycorax* hunted inshore, returning almost to old Galveston before heading southwest, some hundred miles off the coast, zigzagging along. Then, a full thirty-six hours after they'd attached themselves to her, the Fastship turned southeast and headed out to sea, toward the Strand.

By this time, Toni's claustrophobia had worsened to the point that Patricia was considering giving her a life jacket and shoving her out the lockout hatch. The last ten hours she kept Toni in the pilot's chair staring out into the clear blue, but unfortunately, it had been night and the darkness pressed in as readily as the titanium hull, relieved only by phosphorescent tinafores.

It was late afternoon and the light streaming past their constant overhead companion took on a red tinge when the *Sycorax* finished rounding the southern seawall and entered the INS shipping channel.

Toni shuddered at the thought of entering the INS lagoon at all. "You know what the refugees call this channel, don't you?"

Patricia did, but shook her head anyway. *Talk, girl, all you want. Distract yourself.*

"They call it *la Boca del Infierno*, the mouth of hell. They have a saying about it."

Es un viaje sin regreso hacia la boca del infierno, thought Patricia. "What do they say?"

"It's a one-way trip down the mouth of hell."

"Ah. Perhaps we shouldn't take that journey?"

Toni twisted in the seat, looking at Patricia's face. "I thought we couldn't get away until they stopped again. You have to go outside to cut the rope, don't you?"

Patricia shrugged. "Perhaps. Perhaps not. Our rope has been rubbing on that steel grate for forty-eight hours with a great deal of strain. Frankly, I'm surprised it's lasted this long."

"I'm not sure that helps us. Unless you're just hoping it parts at this exact moment?"

"Not exactly. Time to change places, again."

Toni's eyes widened for a moment. "Uh, do we have to?"

"Well, we can stay with the *Sycorax* and wait until she docks at *el Infierno*."

"The hell you say."

"Exactly."

They traded places carefully.

Toni sounded surprised when she said, "I have definitely

been in this piece-of-crap submarine for too long."

"What makes you think that, my dear?"

"We just traded places without me banging the shit out of some part of my body."

Patricia laughed. "Here goes."

Sycorax was headed up the channel at a sedate five knots, keeping her bow wake down in the enclosed waterway. Patricia brought the thruster on-line and pushed *SubLorraine* forward, first matching *Sycorax*'s speed, then pulling ahead, putting slack in the towrope. When she was even with *Sycorax*'s water-intake grate above, Patricia threw the thruster into full reverse.

Overhead it seemed like the hull of the *Sycorax* suddenly accelerated and they watched the rope come back overhead, then go wire taut. The submarine jerked forward, and behind her Patricia heard Toni fall backward, cursing. Through the port, Patricia saw the rope part from the grate. She shut the thrusters off immediately and pushed the control stick forward.

She'd trimmed *SubLorraine* to negative to help keep her from rising into *Sycorax*'s hull and now she coasted gently downward.

Toni scrambled back up, saying, "Did it work? Oh, it did. I figured it must have. Everything else we've done that's worked has caused me to bang myself painfully somewhere."

Patricia waited, watching the fathometer drop: thirty feet, forty, fifty; then she engaged the thrusters at ten percent and banked to the west. They passed under one of the great floating walls, moving from an ethereal blue light-filled space to dark green shadow. Above them, the great open hexes loomed, like giant honeycombs two hundred feet across. The seawall was made up of two rows stretching off in either direction. Large pipes, over fifty feet in diameter, dropped into the depths, OTEC intakes pulling cold water from over three thousand feet below.

The water was clear and the pipes in the distance looked

like some surreal forest with a canopy of linked hexes above.

Beyond the wall a different canopy stretched, a barely translucent tight mesh that defined the floor of one of the mariculture lagoons. Here Patricia brought *SubLorraine* back up, to right beneath the canopy, and pushed the thrusters up to ninety percent.

"Won't they hear us?" Toni asked.

"Doubt it. Don't care. We're out of their jurisdiction and the barrier should block our signature. I doubt they're listening anymore, but even if they were, they'd have to plow through four hundred feet of seawall to come after us. They certainly can't track us by drone or helicopter with *this* overhead. And I want a bath so bad I would . . . well, really bad."

It took them another forty-five minutes to traverse the Strand, moving under lagoons and floating walls, twisting around OTEC pipes and hexes that dropped deep into the water, their increased submerged volume indicating how high above the water they rose. Occasionally they'd hit one of the directed outputs from the OTEC plants, jets of mixed warm and cold water used to keep the Strand in its present location—outside the EEZ and in water deep enough for OTEC operation—and the current would slew them around.

Finally, they were in the clear water of the municipal lagoon, boat traffic of all kinds crossing the surface above them, from little water taxis to hovercraft ferries to a giant cruise ship whose keel stuck down so far they had to drop another thirty feet to clear it.

Patricia had Toni pack up her belongings while she steered a course to the marina where Toni's parents' boat was berthed. Toni peered over Patricia's shoulders and then pointed up at one of the hull silhouettes lining one of the foam-buoyed fingers of dock. "There. That's the one, on the end of the T-slip where we get all the wake from outside the marina. That's why it's the cheap berth."

Patricia brought *SubLorraine* to the surface parallel to the forty-five-foot ketch and gave it a last nudge over. "Go, girl. I'm not hanging out here a minute longer than I have to."

She almost wavered when the hatch opened and the fresh, salt-laden air hit her nose and she could suddenly tell how smelly the interior of the submarine had become.

Toni boosted herself up through the hatch, then reached back for her backpack. She looked liberated, the captive released. Patricia knew the look. She'd seen it a thousand times on refugees leaving the Abattoir with a work permit, free. *No mires atrás*—don't look back.

"I'll call you," Patricia said. "By the way, if anybody asks, you were shacking up with a hot date. You weren't on the *Terminal Lorraine.*"

"Right. Be careful." Toni flung her backpack over the lifelines on her parents' boat and jumped, rocking *SubLorraine* slightly. Patricia took one more deep breath of clean air, then dogged the hatch.

Come on. It's only for a little bit more.

She put *SubLorraine* back under by force of thrusters and diving planes, letting the buoyancy pumps catch up slowly. If she were returning from a normal trip, she would've been on the surface, strapped to *Terminal Lorraine,* and sailing or motoring across the lagoon to her own hex, a waterside module in the outer ring of the Matagorda subdivision.

She turned on the Gertrude and hoped that Perito was listening.

"Perito," she transmitted, using the lowest power setting.

There was a long silence and she thought he wasn't there, was at supper or out drinking *cerveza con sal* with his friends.

But then the voice came back, hesitant, surprised, "Patricia?" His accent rendered it *Pah-treesia,* which Patricia had always liked.

"Well, it's not the Easter bunny."

"*¡Gracias a dios!* It's been three days!"

Every hour of that time settled on Patricia like a leaden shroud. "It's been longer than that. I want you to shut the door on the pen and drop the harness. *¿Entiendes?*"

"*Sí. ¿Cuando?*"

"*En seguida*. I'm right under your *extremo*." She brought the sub beneath a silvery rectangle framed by silhouetted dock modules and waited for the harness to appear. It took a moment. The lighting changed on the rectangle above and then a moment later, the harness frame splashed down through the surface, trailing bubbles as it sank.

Patricia eased *SubLorraine* into it, then flooded the tanks, settling the wings onto the harness arms and tightening the cable. "Okay, Perito. *Hazlo*."

As the cable lifted the sub, she shut everything down, locking the console with a password. It broke the surface, then lifted into a rectangular space lit with flickering strokes of light coming under the door, muted and twisted by the water. Perito waved at her, one hand on the crane controls. She smiled, very glad to see his wide mestizo face.

She ached to move, to be out of the sub, but waited until Perito moved another sling under the rear portion of *SubLorraine*, stabilizing it. He walked forward again and gave her an "okay" sign.

The air in the pen smelled sweet and clear when she opened the lockout hatch. For good measure, she opened the top hatch to let air circulate through the sub. Perito brought a reinforced floor panel from the stack at the head of the pen and put it across the water gap, resting it on both side docks. She lowered herself through the lockout hatch and onto the panel before Perito brought the plastic step stool.

She ducked out and crouched there, taking deep, deep breaths of wonderful, clean air.

"Are you all right, Patreecia?"

"I'm fine. I'm better than fine—I'm alive."

"Where is *la rubia*? Her parents have been here every day."

The anxiety on Perito's face told Patricia a bigger story. Perito had recommended Toni for the job, and Patricia was surprised that he hadn't asked about *Terminal Lorraine* first. "I dropped Toni at her parents' boat. She's okay, but I don't think she's ever going to get back in a submarine."

Perito's shoulders, raised and tense, dropped back down. "The Engineering Office has been calling about the inspections." He looked around and suddenly jumped. "*¡Madre de dios!* What did you do to the tail?"

She turned. The hole in the vertical stabilizer was vivid, fracture cracks radiating through the plastic.

"Well, we were shot at."

"And? . . ."

She reached back in the sub and took out her satphone and workstation. "And I've been three days in the sub, and it stinks and I stink and I really don't want to talk about it right now. However, I would like you to put the rest of the floor plates down and bolt them. And if you have to leave the pen for any reason, I want you to find someone else to watch it."

Perito looked around, staring at the door as if something hostile was about to come through it. "Okay. And *Terminal Lorraine*?" he asked.

"The INS has it. Hopefully, I'll get it back." With a groan, Patricia began walking, dreading the four flights of stairs up to her apartment. "Anybody asks, I'm not back, okay?"

"*Mis labios están sellados.*"

She nodded tiredly and started up the stairs from the pier to the hex proper.

"How long will we need to leave *el submarino oculto*?"

"*Hablaremos mañana.*"

"H'okay, boss."

She called Moses using Celeste's phone, a cheap voice-only model with the most basic of encryption sets. Unlike mainland phones, though, this model didn't have its encryption keys held by the FBI.

"Bill Moses," the voice said.

"You really shouldn't stay at the office so late."

"Patti! Where are you?"

"A neighbor's. Did you get the video?"

Moses let out a breath, sharp, almost a bark. "Who *didn't* get the video is more like it. It's been all over the Web and print news, and Channel Seven ran the whole clip on the eleven P.M. show, Technicolor yawn and all."

Patricia closed her eyes and groaned. "What was the reaction in the assembly?"

"To the bodies or the vomiting?" Moses was on the New Galveston Assembly, the twenty-nine-member council that ran the city. Patricia was his alternate for the Matagorda District.

"Very funny."

"We were discussing the new industrial regs when Sylvia got the download and she interrupted the session. You weren't the only one to throw up, you know. Paul Nagoya messed up his trash can.

"That idiot Landers wanted to know why you'd sent something so gross and actually proposed a motion to censure you. Before *that* fight started, though, Major Paine pointed out the significance of the weapons used and things really got nasty." Major Paine was the New Galveston police commander. "You know what a tightrope we walk out here, especially with the federal government in general but with the INS in particular."

"Yeah. Why was Major Paine there?"

"The new industrial regs. He's got to enforce whatever changes we come up with. He was asked to consult. Where have you been?"

"You don't want to know. Okay, maybe you do, but I'm still trying to put it behind me. I'm going to have to talk to the INS. The bastards took my boat, but I got back here with my crew and *SubLorraine*."

"Did you break any laws?"

"I ignored a call to be boarded, but it can be argued my radio was off and I didn't receive it. They shot at me once, too, but I can also argue that I didn't know who was doing it and ran to save my life. We were in the sub at the time."

"Actually shot *at* you?"

"Warning shots first, then direct shots when I dove. I can show you the hole in the vertical stabilizer."

Bill whistled softly. "I'm glad you're all right. We can work with those circumstances, I guess. Why *did* you ignore their call to be boarded? Did you think they were the ones who sank the *Open Lotus*?"

"I didn't *know* and I wasn't going to take the chance."

"Hell, there's lots of precedents for running from the law because of reasonable fear of harm. Even if we admit you heard the call to be boarded."

"Well, I believe you, but the Emergency Immigration Act's search-and-seizure provisions make it really hard to get something back from the INS once they've grabbed it."

"So you want to talk to them and ask them nicely?"

"Yeah. But on our turf, not theirs. I won't go mainland for it and I sure as hell won't go out to the Abattoir."

She could hear Moses nod, his cheek rubbing the receiver. "Right. I'll suggest a conference room here at the assembly, and if necessary, we'll fall back on Major Paine's offices. In either case, I'll be there as your attorney and we'll record."

"Not before tomorrow, though, okay? I've got to sleep."

"You got it."

Patricia woke up rested, clean, and in her own bed but, alas, not alone. Sharp hard things poked her in the back, and she rolled away from them with a groan and sat up.

A small black girl, dressed like Patricia, in panties and an oversized T-shirt, whimpered in her sleep and shifted, questing blindly for the missing warmth with her knees and elbows.

Why me? Patricia looked blearily at the clock on the bookshelf above her bed. Six-thirty. She'd been asleep for six hours and, despite bad dreams, would gladly have slept for four more, but she knew she wouldn't. Once awakened she'd never been able to manage the trick of going straight back to sleep.

I'm being punished.

Her bedroom was a loft over the bathroom with waist-high bookshelf walls running around the three open sides, separating it from the rest of her apartment, a large open space with twenty-foot ceilings. There were skylights showing dim light above the main floor and one long expanse of window on the far wall opening onto a riot of greenery.

Patricia pulled the covers up over the sleeping girl. Then she stumbled down the stairs, one hand on the wall, and turned back to enter the bathroom, closing the door to keep from waking the child. After using the toilet, she eyed the bath, but she'd spent over an hour in it the night before, washing off the accumulated stink of nearly three days in the sub, leaving it only when her water-soaked hands, puckered and soft, began to remind her of the bodies in the *Open Lotus*.

She contented herself with brushing her teeth for five minutes before pulling a pair of neatly folded shorts from one of the many drawers built under the stairway. The dirty clothes hamper was empty, so Celeste had been through already.

She stared at her videophone. The message light blinked reproachfully. She turned on the menu and the screen lit up. Fifty-two calls. She sorted them by origin. The ID's on twelve of them were news organizations, both local and mainland. Ten of them were business calls, mostly dating from before she sent the footage off. Twelve of them were from concerned friends who'd seen the footage. Six of them were from her mother's office and another three from her mother's apartment. The other seven were from New Galveston Assembly members.

Five of them were from Geoffrey.

It was too early to call most of them, though her mother, in D.C., would probably be up. She skimmed the business calls, noting the Engineering Office's reminders about the inspections. She deleted the calls from Geoffrey, as well as the ones from reporters.

The many that remained were still too intimidating, but she called her mother's apartment, hoping she'd already gone into the office. Thankfully she got the voice mail and left a brief message saying she was all right.

Coward.

Her last three phone calls to her mother, like her last meeting in Austin, had been disastrous. *There's nothing more infuriating than someone who wants to help.* She shook her head. That wasn't quite it. *There's nothing more infuriating than someone whose offers of help imply you're incapable of managing your own affairs.*

She pulled the shorts on and, barefoot, walked out the door between the picture window and her dad's bronze bust of Shakespeare.

Will, I need coffee.

She came out into a large courtyard formed by three stretches of building and a chest-high wall overlooking a stretch of dark blue water with more buildings on the far side. Her immediate foreground was a patio defined by knee-high planters filled with bushes, flowers, and small trees.

Beyond the planters, a large open space in the middle of the courtyard was inset with dark red rubber tiles surrounding an enormous play structure made of colored tubes, steel platforms, bubbles of plastic, and nets of rope. It stretched almost three stories into the air, higher even than the tops of the surrounding buildings, and was connected by walkways to the building on her right at the next floor and roof levels.

The building on her left was distinguished by more planter-lined patios. She walked through a gap between planters, cut across the corner of the rubber tile, and entered another patio, one with white plastic tables and chairs. She settled slowly into one of the chairs and rubbed her eyes.

Almost immediately, a slight black woman appeared in the door opening onto the building. "*Bonjour, mademoiselle.* You are up with the birds."

"*Bonjour,* Celeste. Is there coffee?"

"*Mais oui.* A moment. I must send Philippe out to look for Marie."

"Don't bother. She's in my bed."

"Again! *Merde!* No wonder you are *réveillé. Je regrette.* I will beat her. I swear it."

Patricia suppressed a smile. Celeste's idea of a beating consisted of a barely perceptible swat on the bottom followed immediately by hugs and tears, mostly Celeste's. "It's not important. She likes me, that's all. If you'd sleep later, she'd stay in bed with you, but you get up very early."

"If you would just lock your door . . ."

She thought about the INS and shuddered. "Believe me, I did."

"*Merde*! When I picked up your laundry, I could have sworn I locked it after."

"I would forgive you," said Patricia. "But without coffee, my heart is hard and cold."

This time Patricia could see Celeste bite her lip to keep from smiling. "*Directement, ma chère!*" She vanished within.

Across the courtyard, Consuela Madrid, the principal of The Art of Learning School and Day Care, was propping open the doors. She looked up and waved at Patricia, calling softly, "I saw you on the news."

Patricia's original smile turned to a frown and a shrug.

Assembly Alternate Patricia Beenan, vomiter-at-large.

It had been the late news, so hopefully not too many kids would be having nightmares. *Now if I could do something about* mine.

She tried to think of something to say—something witty or trenchant or even relevant—but it eluded her. In the end she just shrugged again and said, "You still need me this afternoon?"

"Yes. Just from four to six. Belinda has a sonogram at the clinic and you know how long the wait is."

"I'll be there. We'll talk."

Consuela nodded vigorously. "You can depend on it."

Patricia groaned and hid her face in her hands until Celeste returned with a large double latte and half a baguette with butter and strawberry preserves.

"All right. I forgive you for not locking the door."

"*Merci*. I breathe easier now. I must collect Marie before I go to the factory."

"*Bien*. If those clothes I was wearing don't come clean—just throw them away."

"What a waste! Don't be absurd. Throw away good clothing?"

Celeste walked across the courtyard to Patricia's patio, muttering to herself. In a moment she returned, followed by Marie, who was yawning and rubbing her eyes.

As they passed, Patricia ran her fingers over the little girl's hair.

"Stop it, *Tante*," the little girl complained, stepping out of reach. She stuck out her tongue.

Patricia stuck her own out in return and Marie giggled as she was herded inside by her mother.

Other children, escorted by adults, began arriving for school, coming up from the public level by way of the stairway at the end of the courtyard, or from the inside stairs that led up from the rest of the Elephant Arms. The adults trooped inside the day-care center and then left, sans children. She knew many of them, and they waved, but only a few said, "Saw you on the news last night."

She couldn't help but think that the presence of children protected her from more explicit inquiries. *Thank god for small favors*.

Marie reappeared, dressed in a T-shirt, shorts, and sandals, carrying a cup of juice and buttered bread. She sat at the table with Patricia, silent and grave, eating steadily.

Occasionally her eyes would dart sideways toward Patricia, but she remained silent.

More small favors.

Celeste appeared again, this time carrying a child's lunch box and her purse. She put the lunch box on the table and kissed Marie on the head. To Patricia she said, "I forgot to mention but *votre vieux amour* came by yesterday, after the television."

Perfect. Patricia groaned. "And did Geoffrey leave, too?"

"Mais oui."

"C'est bon."

Celeste laughed. "When you are done eating, would you escort Marie across?" She tilted her head toward the school.

"*Mais oui,*" replied Patricia; trying for Celeste's Haitian accent and failing.

"*Au revoir.*" Celeste left at a brisk walk, anxious not to miss the next ferry. She worked for Sony America, putting together video player chassis on the assembly line, and it was a twenty-minute boat ride to the industrial park. After work, she would come home and do laundry and clean apartments. She was a woman of incredible industry and it made Patricia tired just to look at her.

As her mother disappeared down the public stair, Marie sat up straight and said, "Did you really find a whole bunch of dead people?"

Patricia rolled her eyes and sighed. "Why didn't you ask me when your mother was here?"

"She said not to."

"Oh, really? And what did you just do?"

"She's not here," Marie said reasonably, as if that caused all previous instructions to evaporate.

"I believe I'm going to tell your mother about this little conversation."

"*Tante!* You wouldn't!"

Patricia leaned back in her chair and cradled the hot coffee in her cupped hands. "And why not?"

" 'Cause you're not that sort!" the little girl said forcefully.

She's got your number.

"You know, you're right. I'm not that sort. However, I'm also not the sort to answer your question. Your mother had a very good reason to tell you not to bother me about it. You really should listen to her. She's really very wise for an adult."

"But I want to know!"

"It's none of your business. Are you done eating?"

Marie narrowed her eyes and looked stubborn, but there was nothing left on her plate but crumbs. "Yes," she said reluctantly.

"Very well, it's time to go to school." Patricia stuffed the last piece of her own bread into her mouth and, carrying her coffee, shepherded the girl across the courtyard, into the school, and to her classroom door.

Patricia crouched, putting her eyes level with Marie's enormous dark brown ones. "Someday we'll talk about it."

"When I'm older? That'll take forever!"

Patricia smothered a smile. "No, when *I* can talk about it. It's not easy, sometimes, to talk about certain things. Give me some time, okay?"

The little girl nodded.

"Okay. Give me a hug. I need it."

She drank the contact like wine, savoring it, storing every trace of it. Reluctantly she let go and let Marie run off into the classroom.

Thank you, child.

It was the first item in her new collection.

That's one memory to turn to. One memory to displace the floating dead.

She left, sipping her coffee.

What else *can I collect?*

5

Becket: *De vuelta al fuego*

At breakfast Thomas's memory swam with faces chewed by crabs and fish, and the closest he'd advanced in his investigation was to wonder if the people who'd sunk *Open Lotus* actually knew what was in her hold.

He was about to go to sleep in Lieutenant Callard's bunk when he received a call that caused him to shout for Seaman Guterson. "Get our things together. I'm getting us transport to New Galveston."

"Yes, sir. May I ask what's happened, sir?"

"That Beenan woman has resurfaced. Literally." He laughed to himself. "And I want to talk to her."

Thomas was tempted to recall Ensign Terkel's transport, the small patrol hydrofoil, from Buffalo Bayou, but ended up hitching a ride on a patrol helicopter to the sheltered water airport at Houston Galeria, to catch the noon SEA to New Galveston.

The SEA—surface effect airplane—was a giant two-engine turboprop with downward-drooping wings half a football field long. The wingtips ended in pontoons and the plane's tail section drooped down to another float. It flew fifteen feet above the waves, taking advantage of the decreased drag and thrust necessary when an aircraft gets down to one-tenth the length of its wingspan. Unlike those aircraft, the SEA didn't operate above this surface-skimming height with the exception of emergency "jumps" to clear unexpected obstacles. At 220 miles an hour, it could climb briefly up to three hundred feet if it had to clear a ship, but it couldn't sustain that altitude.

Radar and FLIR made this ability a last resort. Obstacles were usually navigated around rather than jumped. The surface effect increased fuel efficiency tremendously.

Thomas watched the water skimming beneath the SEA wings for five minutes before his head dropped back in the seat and his eyes closed. The attendant's voice announcing their impending arrival woke him. He checked the time: twelve-fifty-seven.

The edges of New Galveston, aka the Strand, were visible out his window. The extreme eastern border was reminiscent of the Houston dikes, an area of raised walls against invading sea, but as the SEA skirted the low border, beyond it Thomas saw what looked like a series of vegetation-cloaked hills, emeralds on a string, a Strand if you will. White towers projected from the summits, rising even higher. The SEA banked again, heading west about a mile away from the southern edge, passing between a large tanker and a cruise liner headed for the southwest channel, one of five channels that opened into the Strand's low sea barrier.

He saw a large passenger jet coming in from the west, flying parallel with them toward the conventional runway atop the barrier wall. As it touched down, the SEA banked sharply north again, headed directly for the barrier. The barrier was a mere ten feet in the air and the pilot lifted the SEA slightly; then they were skimming across it and the runway and dropping down into an interior lagoon, a truncated triangle over two miles across at its widest point.

They settled on the surface with a hiss and planed on the smooth water until their speed dropped. When the floats finally dug in, there was a sudden slowing and the nose of the SEA dropped briefly before rising again. They taxied slowly to their dock, one of many thin piers projecting out from the airport terminal. Other SEA craft, as well as smaller pontoon-geared aircraft, were moored alongside. The terminal, a sprawling structure made, like nearly all buildings on the Strand, of huge hexagonal prisms, stretched beside another conventional runway, this one running southwest to northeast atop an interior sea barrier—one separating the interior lagoon of the airport with the municipal lagoon of New Galveston.

He could've come on a conventional flight, but the overall travel time—helicopter to Houston Intercontinental on the coast north of the Houston dikes, then wait for the next flight—was actually greater. That flight wouldn't arrive here for another forty-five minutes.

The SEA pulled right over the end of the narrow pier, its wingtip floats straddling it, the tail section coming to rest against bumpers on its very end. The engines cut and the sudden silence, as always, surprised Thomas as the oppressive din lifted to be replaced by the chatter of passengers unstrapping, taking luggage from the overheads and beneath seats, and standing, just to be standing, since they couldn't get out until the front of the plane cleared.

Thomas, still tired, sat back and watched his fellow passengers. There were executives from the *maquiladora* offshore factories, tourists coming for the duty-free shopping and pristine though artificial beaches, sportsmen coming for the deep-sea fishing downstream in the nutrient-rich effluent of the Strand's OTEC plants or its floating lagoons, and expatriate Americans, either displaced wetfeet who couldn't find decent living in the shrunken States or fully landed citizens who preferred the freedom of offshore living.

The INS also had a strong presence aboard. There were several, in uniform and out, returning to duty at the Abbott Base Refugee and Detention Center. When they'd boarded, Thomas had spotted a plainclothes INS agent seated near first class handcuffed to a Latino, almost certainly destined for the Abattoir. He must've been more than just an illegal alien to be flown to the Strand. Most of the deportees were sent on the INS transport, a relatively slow, hot, and uncomfortable converted car transport that made a regular circuit, collecting illegals from all the gulf ports.

Thomas let Guterson retrieve their bags from overhead, while he stayed in his seat. They were way back in row forty-five, and he was still tired from traveling and messed-up sleep schedules. *I don't care what happens today; I'm going to stay in bed tonight.* He'd made reservations for two cubes at the airport Hilton while they waited for the helicopter back at the site and he intended to stop there first to get into civvies.

Going into certain parts of the Strand in INS uniform could be dangerous.

The passengers standing in the aisle began moving, and Thomas stood, partially crouched to avoid the overhead. Guterson stepped out into the aisle with their bags, abruptly blocking a large man in a corporate suit who was trying to slip past. Thomas grabbed the workstation off the seat and followed the moving horde.

Behind him, he heard the executive mutter something under his breath and Guterson replied with exaggerated innocence, "Oh, were you trying to get by? I'm sorry. I thought it was *our* turn."

It was hot on the pier; heat radiated up from the cement surface. As they walked in the long line of passengers toward the terminal, Guterson pointed at the water beside the pier and then across the runway to the lagoon that held municipal New Galveston. "How come this water is lighter than that water?"

"First time on one of the floating cities?"

"We have 'em all up and down the East Coast, but this is the first one I've been on that wasn't connected to land."

"Ah. Well, *that* water, over there," Thomas said, pointing across the runway to the deep blue water of the municipal lagoon, "is about a mile deep." He jerked his thumb back at the water beside them. "This stuff goes down to about thirty feet. There's a huge reinforced membrane that stretches across to that other side."

"Why on earth do they do that? To stop airplanes from sinking all the way to the real bottom?"

"Well, that *is* the reason they put the airport over on this side, but it's a fishery. They dump nutrient-rich deep water from the OTEC plants in there. It feeds phytoplankton and then shrimp eat the plankton and fish eat the shrimp and bigger fish and so on and so forth."

Guterson craned his neck, looking for fish, Thomas supposed. "Wow."

Thomas could remember before the Deluge when there were less than a thousand people on the Strand, ten hexes, a small surrounding breakwater, and one OTEC plant, a far-fetched utopian project funded by visionaries considered more crackpot than practical. That changed rapidly when the Deluge came. Then, for almost a decade it was a morass of construction surrounded by thousands of boats, rafted together like sargasso weed. The INS funded the Abattoir and flooded industries seeking new homes funded industrial development, beefing up the seacrete facilities and OTEC parts production. Now new hexes were floated every day.

The line slowly moved off the pier and into the welcoming cool of the terminal, but inside there were several delays in immigration control, including a tourist protesting at the top of his lungs.

"What's with the loudmouth, sir?" asked Guterson.

"He didn't cross his tees. You can't get onto the Strand proper unless they know you've got a place to stay and a way off when you run out of money. Or a job. Or city membership. He'll probably be given access to a phone to arrange his lodging and made to buy a return ticket before they let him through. Or he can put up a guarantee deposit, but that's even more money."

"Oh." Guterson looked worried. "Do *we* have a return ticket?"

Thomas laughed. "Don't worry. We're active-duty INS.

We're exempt." The laughter died in his throat when he saw a squad of Abattoir guards waiting on the other side of the barrier. They were wearing riot gear—flak vests, visored helmets, holstered sidearms—and carrying shock sticks. They stood in a tight bunch off to one side, watched closely by a pair of airport security. "Exempt. But not popular." They reached the head of their queue and the immigration officer briefly examined their ID's before waving them through with a too-neutral expression on his face.

The plainclothes agent and the Latino prisoner that Thomas had seen on the plane were standing with the armored squad, but none of them were moving yet, almost as if they were waiting for—

A khaki-clad chief petty officer stepped forward and saluted, a crisp regulation salute. "Commander Becket?"

Thomas sighed and returned the salute. "Aye, Chief—" He eyed the man's chest. "—Dallas. What can I do for you?"

"Admiral Pachefski's compliments, sir. He'd like a few minutes of your time."

Thomas winced inwardly. Rear Admiral William Pachefski was the commandant of the Abbott Refugee and Detention Center—the Abattoir. Thomas looked around. "And where might the admiral be?"

"In his office, sir."

His office was several miles away at the other end of New Galveston. At the Abattoir.

"Surely the admiral has a phone?" Thomas pulled his satphone from an outer pocket of his workstation carrying case.

The CPO looked uncomfortable. "Yes, sir. But he wanted me to bring you. Sir." The armored squad spread out slightly, half-surrounding them.

The admiral would like a few minutes of your time, not including time in transit. Well, Thomas was used to this from Pachefski. They had history. He sighed and shook his head. "Well, then, we shouldn't keep the admiral waiting, should we?" Without pausing, he turned to Guterson and handed him the workstation, keeping the phone. "Mr. Guterson, please call Lieutenant Graham and tell him why I'll be late for our conference call; then go ahead and check us into the hideways toward Patricia, but 479 she remained silent. otel." There wasn't any conference call, but Guterson didn't know that.

"Aye, aye, sir. When shall I expect you back at the . . . hotel?" Guterson's eyes were just a shade larger than usual and he looked only at Thomas's face. He had also avoided naming the hotel, as Thomas had.

Good man. Thomas turned to Chief Dallas and raised his eyebrows.

"Um. It's fifteen minutes over to the Abat—the base. If the admiral's business doesn't take long, we can have you back within the hour. But there's plenty of billets at our BOQ, sir. Ditto the EQ. No need to send tax money offshore."

And come and go under your watchful eyes. "That's a good thought, Chief, but our current investigation requires immediate access to the Strand proper." He stared the CPO full in the face. "Now if we were investigating improprieties out at the detention center, you can be sure I'd be staying at the BOQ." *A tidbit to relax your master.* "Shall we go?"

"Aye, sir. This way."

As Thomas walked away with Chief Dallas, he glanced back over his shoulder. Guterson, looking somewhat overloaded with all of their gear, was walking directly to a rank of pay phones. *Seaman Guterson, you are going to make investigator first class very soon.*

As they walked along, Thomas introduced himself to the plainclothes agent. "I saw you on the flight. I'm Becket, CID."

The other man, still watching his prisoner, nodded. "Yes, sir. Knew it. I'm Chief Warrant Patterson, Houston Field Office."

"Knew how?" Thomas asked.

"Well, not to be insulting, Commander, but there's only

one face like yours in the service. Even Armando here recognized you."

Thomas looked at the prisoner again. His hands were cuffed behind him now. The name or the face didn't ring any bells. "Have we met?"

"*No hablo inglés, Señor Cicatrizado.*" His Spanish was South American—Colombian or Ecuadoran.

Patterson looked appalled, but Thomas laughed.

"*¿Cómo me conoces?*" Thomas asked.

"Todo el mundo lo conoce."

Thomas sighed. "So much for invisibility."

Patterson shrugged. "It's true in the service. Everybody *does* know you."

It was a curse. He'd gotten the reputation before the face, but now, with the face, Señor Scar just had to show up at an INS operations area and everyone knew that CID was there. It wasn't always bad—sometimes it caused unsuspected perpetrators to do the most amazing things, exposing them.

The guilty flee where no man . . .

"What is Armando here for?"

"He was peddling fake ID's to illegals. Green cards, driver's licenses, social security numbers. They looked good on computer, too, if the check was cursory. But Armando's standing mute on his associates, his source, so the judge gave him ten years' detention, then deportation."

Which meant life, really, since to be deported you had to have a country willing to take you. So, Armando would spend his time in detention, then end up moving over to the refugee camp. At least it was coed in the refugee center. Unless Armando could find work on the Strand or sneak back into the U.S., he'd grow old and die out here.

They left the terminal outside the immigration control zone and made their way past the civilian ferries and water taxis to a gated dock guarded by INS shore patrol. A sixty-foot INS hovercraft was tied there, floating on its inflated skirt, and other INS passengers were boarding.

The armed detail went aboard in a clump, waiting their turn, stepping high to the deck. Armando stumbled, unable to catch the railing because of his handcuffs, and Thomas grabbed his arm to keep him from going down on his face.

Armando looked surprised. "*Gracias, señor.*"

Thomas shrugged. "*Cualquiera lo haría.*"

Armando shook his head. "*Muchos hombres no lo harían.*" *Many men wouldn't*. Unfortunately it sounded like the voice of experience.

Thomas sighed. "*Quizás.*"

There were rows of benches under a rigid awning behind the control cabin and the armored squad took over an unoccupied corner, waiting for Thomas, the two noncoms, and the prisoner to sit before distributing themselves across the remaining seats.

The CPO took off his hat and tucked it under his leg. "You might want to do the same, sir." He jerked his thumb at the two large ducted fans just now starting to turn at the back of the hovercraft. Thomas followed his advice just in time, taking his hat just as the fans generated a maelstrom of wind. The craft moved off, accelerating smoothly, until it was moving over forty knots, swinging north.

Conversation was impossible and Thomas was grateful. The last time he'd been here, he'd been investigating drug traffic passing into the refugee center with the complicity of a ring of INS personnel. His case had gone well professionally and very badly personally, and he wasn't at all happy to be going out to Abbott Base again.

He laughed to himself as he remembered the look on Jazz's face when Thomas had said he might come out here. Jazz knew.

All right, I could've stayed at the Bachelor Officer's Quarters, but it was more than the inconvenience of the commute, wasn't it?

Well, there were nice things about the Strand. The air was clean and the food was wonderful. If you stayed away from the Abattoir and weren't out here during a hurricane, it was practically paradise.

They cut into Main Street, the open channel running east to west down the center of the Strand, moving between the large enclosed area that bordered the airport and another large algae farm to the north. Then they passed into the industrial park, a diamond-shaped lagoon over four miles north to south lined with factories, wharves, and commercial shipping.

The channel passed between North and South Portland, two "islands" floating out in the middle of the commercial lagoon, green-draped structures over a mile per side. This close, one could tell that the hills were really steps, hexes within hexes, each circle rising higher as they marched inward to cumulate in center towers rising several floors higher than the closest ring. They were factory suburbs, a substantial step up from the Abattoir, but still more crowded residences than New Galveston proper.

The factory towns dropped behind them, and Thomas shifted, turning, reluctantly, to look ahead, past the control cabin. On both sides of them the factories and wharves were closing in, toward a gap that was much narrower than the passage from the municipal lagoon. Here the gap between the walls was less than a hundred yards and towers lined both sides, while crewed boats stood by below.

The official name was Abbott Security Passage, but the name used by the refugees and prisoners was *el Ano del Infierno*—the asshole of hell. Since they hoped to pass through and out of it, it didn't say much for their self-esteem.

Despite his best efforts, Thomas felt his shoulders hunching forward and the scar tissue on his face and neck began to ache. He forced himself to expand his chest and took deep breaths.

The ferry docked at Isabel Island, a half-mile-across complex similar to any New Galveston module, green-draped terraces marching up to a central tower. This was the base housing for dependents and personnel.

After offloading, the hover ferry ran across to another module, the same size as base housing but with very little greenery, and here the exterior of the island was made up of hex towers rising higher than the interior: Abbott Detention Center.

Some of the guards, Warrant Patterson, and his prisoner got off here.

Then they made the run to the camp's main landing, between the two islands, the north/south center point, which neatly divided the three-mile-long stretch of humanity in half.

It was always the smell that got to Thomas first. He'd smelled far worse, of course, on refugee ships so crowded that the sanitary facilities had been quickly overwhelmed. At least you knew, at the Abattoir, that the sewage was being treated and the OTEC plants provided plenty of fresh water. If the algae farm provided a much higher percentage of the Abattoir's diet than his own, it was a healthier one. But it was bland.

But you can't put four hundred thousand people in that small a space without some odor.

The hex they were in contained the long narrow maze of egress control, the booths where day workers showed their passes and left, to be ferried to the *maquiladoras* in the industrial park, or returning, processed through, back into the camp, to sleep and maybe to dream of bumping up to the next stage—slightly less crowded and more sumptuous housing in one of the factory suburbs.

They passed through the personnel gate and the guards took up position, forming a triangle around them to get through the crowd. This was Recruitment Square and thankfully, it wasn't an example of how crowded the rest of the Abattoir was, for people stood shoulder to shoulder, cruising the job-opening announcements, elbowing in and out in a constant Brownian motion.

The guards blew whistles and the crowd parted quickly,

anxious to avoid shock sticks that could cause a person to fall and be trampled by the crowd.

Becket inhaled sharply. *Ah, humanity.*

There was only one level of security to get into the administrative offices. Pachefski's suite of offices was on the top floor facing due west but built into the vertex of a hex so the view out across a short expanse of water took in both the green terraces of Isabel Island and the grim walls of the detention center.

Admiral Pachefski was thin and tall with the incipient stooping of old age. His posture, and his mostly bald head, had always reminded Thomas of a vulture. His nickname in the service, though, was "Mother Teresa." He'd had this post for over nine years, at his own request.

"Thanks for coming, Thomas. Have a seat. You can go, Chief." Both men waited for Chief Dallas to close the door behind him before talking.

Thomas, is it? Whatever happened to "you back-stabbing glory hog"? That's what Pachefski had called Thomas the last time they'd met.

"What's this about, sir?" asked Thomas. *Why are you messing with my investigation?*

Pachefski gestured at a television monitor mounted in the wall. "I saw the video. They ran it on Channel Seven—that's the local independent. This Beenan woman seems to imply there's INS involvement."

Not exactly. She just talked about ammunition. That conclusion could be drawn. You *certainly did.* "It's a possibility." Thomas considered keeping quiet about the ammo found on the *Open Lotus* but decided that as soon as his men started taking ballistics specimens, the word would be out. "We did find both kinds of ordnance were used."

"Hmmm. And your next step?"

"Sir, you know I can't discuss an ongoing investigation." Thomas paused a moment. "If I understood your concerns, perhaps I could help you without compromising my duty."

Pachefski stood abruptly and walked over to the window. "I have almost four hundred thousand refugees over there, not to mention almost sixty thousand in detention. We're barely surviving here. I've got UN refugee monitors *living* in the camp. I've got Amnesty International observers. I've got dozens of news organizations watching our every move. And now this. Christ, man, we're drowning as it is."

Interesting choice of words. Thomas kept his face perfectly still. "I don't see the connection." *But you seem to. Is there something you know that you aren't telling?*

"We can't do our job out here when everything we do is constantly being questioned and challenged. If the INS is implicated in particular, the INS will be implicated in general. And that will increase the pressure."

That was your argument against my last investigation here.

"It's not like the first years, when we'd get three thousand a day, but between births and new arrivals, the numbers are still increasing. We're between a rock and a hard place. The conservatives want to cut our funding to make the refugee center a less desirable destination. When we do get more resources, the international watchdogs want it allocated differently, pushing for things we can't afford. It's hard enough to provide bare subsistence, much less the schools and clinics they're clamoring for."

Pachefski shook his hands as if ridding himself of his tormentors. "If they'd spend just half the time they spend pestering me and my staff lobbying for international aid, their problems *and* mine would be solved."

This last was a bit unfair. The international aid communities poured millions into the world refugee centers, partly, Thomas suspected, to keep those refugees as far away from their borders as possible.

So you want me to suppress this investigation for the good of humanity? Or at least to keep your job from getting harder? Thomas steepled his fingers. *Or is it something more than that?* "I see your concern, sir. I would much prefer that this affair prove to have *nothing* to do with the service. It's my most heartfelt hope."

Admiral Pachefski nodded, but his eyes held doubt. "As it is mine."

Thomas shrugged and raised opened hands. "We'll just have to hope the villains of this event are not ours."

Pachefski sat back down at his desk and leaned forward. "Hope? That's a powerful force, but the Lord helps those who help themselves. Certain avenues of investigation may prove more . . . productive than others."

Thomas groaned inwardly. *Don't go there, Admiral.* "That goes without saying."

"And if one were to find insufficient evidence that the INS were involved, then, of course, one could even conclude that criminals were involved, absolving the service completely."

This is embarrassing. "I'm sure that whatever conclusions reached by this investigation will be supported by the evidence."

"The selection of *relevant* evidence must be quite an art."

Thomas was angry now, but his face was perfectly still. "Negative evidence would not undo the damage done by the release of the Beenan video. Positive evidence of non-INS involvement is the only thing that will counter public suspicions of an INS atrocity."

Pachefski furrowed his brow. "I hadn't thought of that, but you're right, of course. Positive evidence. We must see what can be found."

Found? Or manufactured? Thomas licked his lips, which were suddenly dry. "I'm sure our investigation will consider all possibilities."

"My intelligence office gets all sorts of news through the refugee community. Why don't we walk down there and see what they've got?"

"I'd rather not, sir. I need to be getting back to the city."

"Ah, you've leads then? You should coordinate with my intelligence section."

I'm not opening my investigation up to you or your lackeys. It was going to get ugly; Becket could feel it. Pachefski was passionately loyal to his people and he demanded the same in return. Becket had never been *his*. He steeled himself for the coming fight.

The intercom chimed.

Annoyed, Pachefski thumbed the button. "I'm in a meeting here!"

A nervous voice returned, "It's Admiral Rylant, sir. He insisted."

Pachefski's face stilled. "All right, Ramirez. I'll take it." He picked up the handset. "Hello, Larry." He listened for a moment, then held up the phone. "He'd like to talk to you."

Thomas stood and took the handset. "Yes, sir."

Admiral Rylant's voice said, "Jazz called me. Just give the phone back to him and leave. That, by the way, is a clear and direct order."

Thomas suppressed a grin. *Rock breaks scissors.* "Yes, sir. I'm on my way, sir." He handed the phone back to Admiral Pachefski and left the room.

There was no escort back to the dock and Thomas was glad. His uniform was enough to gain him passage, though he shifted his watch and wallet to the inside of his uniform shirt. He walked slowly, keeping aware, offering a polite "*Perdón*" and "*Excusa*" as they moved out of his way. At least once he heard whispered, "*¡El Cicatrizado!*"

Later, through security and waiting on the hovercraft dock, Thomas barely saw his surroundings, his head whirling with dangerous possibilities. *I really thought he'd called me in to see if my investigation ranged into his territory, but it seems he has a much more active role in mind. But is he just trying to keep the service image clean—or is it something more? Is he involved in this? Does he know who is?*

Regardless, the scope of the investigation had just increased.

6

Beenan: *Encuentros*

Patricia's satphone, hooked to her belt, went off while she was hurtling down a tube slide, three little girls clutched between her legs. They all tumbled out onto the rubber tile at the bottom of the play structure and after she made sure the girls moved clear of the slide, she answered the phone.

It was Bill Moses. "The INS officer in charge of the investigation is out here on the Strand. He'd like to meet with you. He didn't kick at all about our conditions."

"Not a bit?"

"Not a bit. I came on a little hard at first, saying you wouldn't go mainland or out to the Abattoir and he said, "Why should she? I'm here. She's here. Let's meet."

Patricia shook her head doubtfully. "Are you sure he's INS?"

"Positive. He's the CO of a CID unit. A full commander."

"What's a CID unit?"

"Criminal Investigations Division."

Patricia skipped sideways to avoid a shrieking knot of children running from one boy. The chase moved past her and up into the structure. She decided the shrieks were more in joy than fear and the boy's growls more feigned than real.

"Why isn't the FBI involved? Or even the Texas Department of Public Safety? It sounds like the INS is involved because they want to protect themselves."

"Maybe, but it's their jurisdiction. Crimes in coastal waters, especially involving shipping, are their meat."

"I reserve judgment."

Moses snorted. "Well, duh!"

"When and where?"

"I've booked conference room C here at the chambers. I told Commander Becket six o'clock."

"I'm stuck here until six. It'll take me at least a half hour to change and make it across the bay."

"Patti, you *own* that facility. Can't you get someone to replace you?"

"We're shorthanded here. We're always shorthanded." *And if you didn't maintain so many scholarship students, you could hire more help.* "If you like, I'll call the commander and explain why it has to be six-thirty."

"I don't know about that. I thought the idea was for me to buffer you from the INS."

"But I also want to talk them into giving me back *Terminal Lorraine.* Since I have to postpone, I'd rather take the sting out."

Moses paused, then sighed. "If you want. I guess that would work." He gave her the number. "Unless I hear otherwise, I'll meet you at the chamber at six-thirty."

"Thanks, Bill."

She dialed the number, a satphone area code she noted, but before she hit "send," she told one of the other attendants that she was taking a bathroom break. She wasn't sure she could make this call and keep her cool if, at some critical juncture, she was swarmed by children.

Inside she sat down on a bench by the restrooms and completed the call.

The voice that answered was fogged by sleep. "Hello?"

Oh shit. And I wanted him to help *me.* "Commander Becket?"

He started to say yes, but was interrupted by a jaw-cracking yawn. "Excuse me. Yes, this is Becket."

"Um, this is Patricia Beenan. I'm sorry to wake you."

"Beenan?" The voice suddenly sharpened. "Ah, Ms. Beenan. Yes, ma'am, what can I do for you?"

"Our meeting tonight—I have to postpone."

There was a pause on the other end of the phone. "I wish you'd reconsider. I may have to fly back to the mainland tomorrow."

"Oh! No, I'm sorry. I don't have to postpone that long—just a half hour. I'm tied up until six, and it will take me a half hour to change and get across to Palacios." The assembly chambers were in the central tower of Palacios, another subdivision of New Galveston. Like all the subdivisions of New Galveston, it was named after a drowned city on the Texas coast.

"Ah. Certainly. Not a problem. Um, look, I'm coming from the airport Hilton so I have to cross the lagoon anyway. How about I pick you up on the way? If that's convenient?"

And take me where? She closed her eyes briefly. *Remember, girl, you want him to help you.* "If that's not too much trouble. I can meet you at the Matagorda Intercity ferry dock at six-ten. That's on the south side, the one facing Playa del Mar."

"The resort? Ah, so Matagorda is on the south end?"

"Yes, it's the southernmost subdivision—pretty much straight across from the airport."

"That's handy. Um, I'll be in a Hertz boat, but I guess there's a million of them around so it would be hard to tell which one we were."

"Won't you be in uniform?"

"No," Becket said shortly. "I'll try and be on time, though. And . . ."

"Yes, Commander?"

"Well, I've got a bit of scar tissue on my face. It's kind of hard to miss."

"It's not a trench coat or a flower in a lapel," she said

brightly, "but I should be able to recognize you."

She heard him breathe out heavily. "Yeah. Can't miss me."

"See you then."

She dithered over clothes, torn between her most formal assemblywoman pants suit and a more informal sundress, festive and brightly patterned. In the end she went with the dress but threw on a dark jacket to tone it down. She pulled on flats and stuffed her wallet and satphone in a disused purse as she went out the door.

It was a three-minute walk to the ferry dock, a dash downstairs and then through the circular warren of public-access corridors opening, at the end, to a waterside elevated walkway dipping down to the dock proper. She avoided the Intercity ferry queue and walked over to the small-boat side of the dock where large Loading and Unloading Only signs were spaced every twenty feet.

There were several people waiting for boats that weren't there and several boats waiting for people who weren't there. Sailboats, motorboats, several solar/sail hybrids, a few sampans with junk sails or single sculling oars. There were even three gondoliers in striped shirts, their gondolas rafted together at a mooring buoy several yards away from the pier, probably waiting for tourists they'd brought over from Playa del Mar.

A vendor was selling fish tacos and black bean mango salsa from a pushcart, and the smells rising from his propane grill reminded Patricia that she'd only snacked at lunchtime.

A man stood on a box and ranted at the crowd. "The earth also was corrupt before God, and the earth was filled with violence. And God looked upon the earth, and, behold, it was corrupt; for all flesh had corrupted His way upon the earth. And God said unto Noah, The end of all flesh is come before me; for the earth is filled with violence through them; and, behold, I will destroy them with the earth."

Ah, Church of the New Genesis. They believed the Deluge was a renewal of God's original flood of Genesis. There were a lot of them on New Galveston—they thought of it as the new Ark.

She moved away from the speaker until his voice merged with the general roar, threading through the crowd on the edge of the pier and looking down into the boats. She spotted Becket, finally, farther down the dock, a medium-sized man dressed in a shirt and tie, with dark slacks. Even from a distance she could see how the scarring changed the skin tone on the right side of his face. He was leaning against one of the Loading Zone signposts, his arms crossed, watching the crowd, but he hadn't spotted her yet. She wondered where his boat was, for there wasn't one tied beside him.

"I saw you on the news," came a voice from behind her.

Oh, god. It was the last voice she wanted to hear. She turned slowly and glared at Geoffrey.

It still hurt to look at him. There he was, tall and lean and blond, a perfect match for Toni. He was wearing sandals, jeans, and a Hawaiian shirt with the top two buttons open, his curly brown chest hair showing. He'd been drinking. She could tell by the smile. There was a certain meanness that came out only when he'd been drinking. Near the end of their relationship, that had been often.

"Go away," she said.

He looked hurt. "Don't be that way, darling. It was just like old times seeing you on the news, especially the way that tank top clung." He let his eyes drop to her chest.

"Geoffrey, the court order is still in effect. If you don't leave this minute, I'm going to have you arrested."

Geoffrey laughed. "The pier cop left. Chinese man got in a fight with two Chicanos and he hauled them all off to the precinct."

"Go away, Geoffrey," she said, and turned.

He grabbed at her shoulder and she spun, inside his arms, raising her free arm level with her forehead. Her elbow smacked into Geoffrey's cheekbone and pain shot up her arm.

Geoffrey grunted and stumbled sideways, releasing her and clutching at his face. "Oh, shiii—" He reached the edge of the pier before regaining his balance and toppled over, falling the six feet down to the water's surface. She heard his breath leave his lungs on impact, then she stepped back, too late, to avoid getting splashed across the front of her dress.

Just great!

Geoffrey clawed his way back to the surface and gasped for air. Convinced he wasn't going to drown, Patricia turned back around, cradling her elbow.

Commander Becket was staring at her now, no longer leaning on the sign but walking slowly forward. Behind Patricia a string of obscenities floated up from the water.

Becket tipped his head toward her, almost more of a bow than a nod, and said, "Ms. Beenan, I presume."

She nodded, unwilling to trust her voice.

Becket glanced behind her and said lightly, "Ready to go?"

She nodded again.

"Very good." He looked out at the water, raised his hand over his head, and beckoned. A largish GE ElectraJet, free-floating beyond the gondoliers, started up and cut sharply around the mooring buoys before pulling neatly up to the pier. Becket looked back over Patricia's shoulder and stepped smoothly around her, until he stood between her and the place where Geoffrey had gone over. "Unless you want to talk with that young man some more, I suggest we leave."

He was larger than she'd thought, not so much tall or heavy as broad, as if he had the shoulders of a larger man. As she walked to the edge of the pier, he moved with her, slightly angled as if listening to her, his broad shoulders presenting the maximum screen.

A casually dressed young man holding the boat to the dock started to offer her a hand as she climbed down, but she was in the boat and seated before he could reach her.

I know how to get in a boat, thank you. She looked back up the pier and saw Geoffrey on the dock, his clothes dripping while he looked around wildly. He spotted her as Commander Becket dropped lightly down into the boat.

"Hey! Come back here!"

Becket murmured, "Mr. Guterson, a little speed please."

Up on the pier Geoffrey started running toward them, pushing through the crowd roughly, heedlessly, but the boat was under way before Geoffrey reached them, accelerating smoothly, planing almost immediately.

Becket dropped to the other end of the bench seat and looked back. "Oh, my."

Patricia twisted in time to see Geoffrey shaking his hands vigorously at a group. Angry voices drifted across the water, audible even above the sound of the electric jet and the boat's wake. Patricia looked away, pinched the bridge of her nose, and closed her eyes, but she couldn't help herself—she looked back just in time to see Geoffrey and two others topple into the water, entangled.

She winced and looked away again.

"I suppose I should explain," she said, turning toward Becket. *Oh, my, that* had *to hurt.* The scarring—it had been a horrible burn she realized—started below his shirt collar and rose up the right side of his face, warping the corner of the mouth and the corner of his right eye. It went back to the ear, which was withered and flatter to the skull than was his good ear. She presumed the scars went up under the hairline, but the hair, at least, had grown in normally. *Unless he wears a wig.*

Becket smiled slightly, a barely perceptible expression. "Depends." He jerked his thumb over his shoulder. "Did that have anything to do with your discovery of the *Open Lotus?*"

She found herself smiling slightly in response. "Not really."

Becket shrugged. "Well, then, explain what you would

like to explain, but there's no 'should' about it." He slumped in his seat and crossed his arms, yawning suddenly. "Excuse me."

"Certainly. Long hours?"

"Yeah."

She started to sit back, then leaned forward suddenly, speaking in a sudden rush, surprising herself. "Geoffrey's not really supposed to come near me. There's a court injunction to keep him away, but he saw me on the news—well, that tape—and it's stirred him up again. I don't know if it was coincidence on the pier or if he followed me from my hex."

Becket nodded, his face neutral. "How long ago were you involved with him?"

Involved. That's a nice unweighted term. "It's been three and a half years since I fired him, but the court order was just last year." She stared out across the water, seeing nothing. "I guess pride kept him away, initially, but then he started drinking more."

"So he was a disgruntled employee?"

She could've just agreed with him and dropped it. It was true, after all, but something compelled her to say. "I damn near married him."

Becket lifted his chin slightly and slowly dropped it. "Ah." Facing forward, as he was, she couldn't see the burned side of his face, and she wondered if he'd done it on purpose or if he was just as tired as he looked and couldn't be bothered to sit up, twist on the seat, and face her. She shifted to the backward-facing bench seat across from him and mirrored his pose, arms crossed, feet stretched out. He watched her, directly, both sides of his face visible.

"Geoffrey was the knight in shining armor. He was going to marry the princess and inherit the kingdom." She licked her lips. "Only when my dad died I discovered how much I'd tolerated from Geoffrey because Dad liked him. And the funny thing is, a friend of Dad's showed me one of my dad's old e-mail messages telling how much *Dad* had tolerated Geoffrey because *I* liked him."

"Ouch," Becket said.

This time Patricia shrugged. "It might still have happened—I really needed someone when Dad died—but Geoffrey wasn't the one. He was too busy trying to *manage* things. He was trying to manage the business, the properties, me. If he'd just waited or even *asked* before he started making decisions and commitments." She smiled a bright, artificial smile. "I gave him a good severance package." She scratched her head. "I don't know why I'm telling you this. I guess I'm just trying to explain that I don't knock people off docks every day."

He nodded. "I'll accept that." He grinned suddenly, a flash of white teeth oddly distorted on the right, but nonetheless pleasant. "Though I must admit it was very nicely done."

She shrugged. "Anything worth doing—"

Becket laughed, sitting more upright.

Are you sure you're INS? She stared down at the deck, suddenly uncomfortable. *You're a bigot, Patricia.* She peeked up at him. He was watching her, extraordinarily still, the smile still lingering.

"What happened?" she asked, suddenly, reaching out and almost touching the scarred side of his face. She drew back at the last second, turning it into a gesture.

His face closed up and she winced. "I'm sorry, it's none of my business."

Becket sighed. "But you'd like to know."

Patricia was flustered. "That doesn't make it my business. You didn't ask about Geoffrey."

Becket smiled softly. "No. You gave me that freely." He looked to the starboard side, west. They were out in the middle of the municipal lagoon, and when Patricia looked in that direction she could see up Main Street, the central channel. "It was out there, at the Abattoir." His voice was casual, but his shoulders hunched in slightly. His hands, previously flat on his thighs, bunched tightly.

"I was investigating a drug ring that targeted the refugee

camp. Fishing boats from Colombia, transfers at sea to an INS patrol vessel, patrol vessel to INS camp guards, camp guards to refugee dealers, dealers to users.

"My unit worked on it, mostly undercover, for six months, but near the end they got wind of our investigation. They didn't know how much we knew and thought they could still do something to stop us." He looked back at her, then down at his hands, flattening them consciously. "It was a gasoline bomb, spark plug in a gas can wired to the ignition in the small boat we'd been issued. I was lucky. I was still on the dock when Eugene—Ensign Parnasos—turned the key.

"That was four years ago last month."

Patricia frowned. "August nineteenth."

Becket frowned back. "Yes."

"My father died a few days before that—I hope." She shook her head suddenly. "That didn't come out right. My father went down in a new submersible that we were testing. It never came back up. When I said 'hope,' I meant that I hoped it was an implosion, not a failure of electrical and propulsion systems, because then he could've lasted for days, never knowing whether we'd find him or—" She shuddered.

"We never found the *Cobia*—the sub—but Geoffrey pointed out the news story—about the bomb—your bomb—to me. I think he was trying to show me something. That I wasn't the only one who'd lost someone that week, but he botched it, like anything he did involving feelings."

She smiled grimly. "That was the beginning of the end for us." She made a gesture with her hand, a closed fist releasing something into the air. "Anyway, I didn't remember the names, but I remember the picture of that boat, burnt to the waterline, barely afloat, with soot stains climbing up the wall and onto the dock."

Becket sat back, his hands lying loosely in his lap, still, his eyes distant. He cleared his throat. "Yes, that was the one." He looked even more tired than before.

He sat up, looking past her. "We've got a map, but perhaps you could help Mr. Guterson find the proper landing."

They'd cut across the mouth of Copano Bay and were approaching the multicluster of Palacios, a set of hex modules over a mile and a half across. The chambers were in the central tower, and though there was a covered waterway almost to the center of the cluster, it was still a hike to the elevator.

"Are you hungry?" she asked.

Moses met them at the landing deep under central Palacios and jumped in before the beat cop chased them away. His face was still as Patricia made the introductions. "Good to meet you in person." Moses had *not* been happy about the last-minute change in plans when she'd phoned from the boat.

Seaman Guterson kept the speed down, tooling gently along in the no-wake zone of the tunnel, then opening up when they passed out into the open air on the other side. It was a short dash across Chocolate Bayou to Cosas Muertas del Mar.

Guterson started to pull up to the restaurant landing, but Patricia directed him to a free mooring buoy in a thick cluster of parked boats. "They'll come get us. See?"

The restaurant greeter was already pulling out from the dock in the reception boat. The odors of burning charcoal, garlic, onion, broiling fish, and other unidentified but succulent things wafted across the water.

Guterson spoke quietly to Becket. "Should I stay with the boat, sir?"

Before Becket answered, Patricia said, "I told them we'd be four."

The reception boat pulled up beside them and the teenage girl driving smiled. "Hey, Patricia. Mr. Santos said you were coming."

Becket breathed deeply through his nose. "You have to eat, Mr. Guterson." He waved Guterson across to the other boat.

A heavy, smiling man was waiting at the landing. "*¡Bienvenidos, bienvenidos! Ha sido mucho tiempo.*" He pulled Patricia from the boat and hugged her before she'd properly set foot on the pavement.

"¡Tío Rodolfo! Yes, much too long." She hugged him back, then dropped free.

"I saw you on the news."

She winced. "Of course you did." Still holding on to Rodolfo's arm, she pointed toward the others. "My very good friend Rodolfo Santos. Do you remember Bill Moses? And this is Señor Becket and Señor Guterson."

"Of course I know the assemblyman. And I'm glad to meet your other friends."

Becket smiled and said, "*Mucho gusto. Tienes un restaurante bello.*"

"*Gracias, gracias.*" Rodolfo looked around proudly. The restaurant *was* beautiful, a series of multilevel, rough-tiled terraces spilling down from the side of a hex, looking as if it had grown there, an illusion furthered by thatched roofs on rough wooden posts and beams. Every table was occupied, and waiters threaded among them with a calm urgency.

"*Siganme, por favor.*"

Rodolfo led them up the terraces and into the kitchen, a more permanent building of seacrete. They went through it—past cooks, dishwashers, shouted orders, scurrying waiters, waves of heat, and mouthwatering odors—and then down a long narrow hall lined with storage rooms. At the end, they came out onto another patio, smaller in scale, tucked between the restaurant and the hex wall, perched a full story above the water.

A large table covered in rough linen stood out in the open, beyond the thatched roof, under the stars. There were low lights by the door and encased candles on the table.

"Are there any *alergias*—allergies—among you?" Rodolfo asked.

Becket and Guterson shook their heads.

"Then, if you do not mind, I will take the liberty of ordering for you."

Rodolfo vanished back into the restaurant. Almost before they finished sitting down, a waitress came through the door with two bottles of red wine and a pitcher of water. A second waiter brought glasses. Both of them greeted Patricia by name.

When they'd left, Becket said, "You're well known here."

Patricia, pouring wine into the glasses, nodded. "Yes."

"But you haven't come here recently?"

Patricia felt the blood rush to her ears.

Bill Moses interceded. "I don't think that question is pertinent to your investigation, Commander."

Patricia laid a hand on Moses's arm. "It's okay, Bill." She set a glass of wine in front of each of them. "Bill knows I've got painful associations with this place." She lifted her glass. "*A los que se han ido antes.*"

Becket, noting Moses's confusion, said, "To those who have gone before." He clicked his glass against Patricia's. "*A los muertos.*"

"To the dead." Patricia took a gulp of wine, sharp with tannin and rough on the throat. She noticed Becket only sipped his.

She pointed at one of the many rough posts rising out of the tiled floor to support the thatched roof. "My father and I salvaged all of these beams and posts. Most of them are telephone poles from the Port Aransas area; some of them came from drowned trees in public parks. It was one of the first jobs my father let me participate in fully. I was sixteen. Don Rodolfo finished the restaurant a terrace at a time, but there was always a crew out back scraping and sanding and shaping the posts and beams." She took another gulp of wine. "Don Rodolfo was from Tampico before the waters rose. Dad knew him from before the Deluge, when he'd eat in his restaurant there. Dad found him in one of the floating slums that lined the new coast and sponsored him for city membership."

The wine hit her empty stomach, and the sudden alcohol rush spread. She pushed the glass away from her on the table. "We practically lived here before Dad died."

Another waiter brought out a wooden platter of grilled prawns sprinkled with lime and red pepper, with a cloth-covered stack of fresh tortillas and a bowl of melted lemon-butter. Conversation stopped as the food was consumed.

"I'm surprised you could stay away from *this,* Ms. Beenan," Seaman Guterson said around a mouthful of shrimp and tortilla.

Patricia smiled. "It's not the food that kept me away." She glanced at Commander Becket out of the corner of her eye. He was chewing carefully, taking small bites. "You're not eating *con gusto, mi amigo.*"

Becket patted his mouth with a napkin before he answered quietly, "It's delicious, but I have to be careful." He touched the scarred side of his face. "There was some nerve damage. If I'm not careful, I dribble out that side."

"Oh. I didn't mean to—"

He held up his hand. "*No hay problema.* Tell me why you came back here tonight."

She looked down at the table. The glib answer was on the tip of her tongue—*for the food, of course*—but she couldn't say it. "Part of it has to do with being stuck inside a minisub for three days. Part of it has to do with almost dying." *And part of it has to do with you.*

He looked at her for a moment, as if he was searching for something. "This *does* have to do with your find."

She nodded. They'd avoided it so far. Was that yet another reason she'd detoured them here? To put off his questions?

He looked down at the table, at the shrimp and the glasses and the tortillas. "Later," he said.

Later eventually came, after black beans and *pico de gallo* and slabs of broiled shark and mole-covered enchiladas and mangoes sliced over ice cream. Later came with large mugs of cinnamon-flavored coffee mounded with steamed milk.

"I'm going to tell you what happened, but I'm going to hold back something." Patricia held her coffee in both hands, suddenly chilled by the open sky, the collection of her blood around her stomach, and the matter at hand.

Becket was on his second coffee already, and had just returned from the bathroom; his hair and face were wet, and the sleepy look was temporarily in abeyance. "You're telling me that you're not going to tell me something?"

She nodded. "I'm not holding anything back except the identity of my deckhand." *Or her gender.* "He wasn't there when I discovered the *Open Lotus* and though he was there when I was running from the INS, everything I did was my doing. He was just along for the ride, and he's barely an adult and I don't want him brought into this."

Becket was still for a moment. "Provisionally accepted," he said. "You had a run-in last March with the INS over working in the EEZ with a foreign national crew."

She rolled her eyes toward the ceiling. "I was blown into the EEZ by a storm. I was only three miles over the line and they wanted to arrest my crew and impound my boat for that. But that's not the case here. My crew this trip had wet feet, but his back was dry."

"All right. If I absolutely have to corroborate something you've said, I'll have to press you for access. It's possible I can leave his name off the record." He took an audio recorder from his pocket and placed it on the table; then rested his forefinger on the "record" tab. "Ready?"

She took a deep breath, then nodded. The recorder made a small tiny chiming sound. "My boat was about fifty miles from the Houston dikes. . . ."

7

Becket: *Testimonio*

. . . about fifty miles from the Houston dikes."
Thomas had no trouble concentrating on Patricia's story. He knew, in the back of his head, how near the end of his reserves he was, but for now he watched her face as she told him of her encounter with the death ship and he didn't feel tired at all.

He hadn't known what to expect after the videotape. The figure on the screen seemed almost unlikely to exist above water, the small pony tank she'd used was hardly visible, making her seem a water-breathing sprite completely surprised by the intrusion of corpses from the breathing world.

The creature on the pier, whom he'd spotted just before Geoffrey grabbed her arm, was equally different. He'd expected her to pull away or run, but instead, she'd whirled tightly, striking Geoffrey with her elbow and knocking him neatly into the drink. It was all Thomas could do to keep from dropping to his knees and roaring with laughter.

Then there was the woman who'd ridden in the boat with him, the one who'd pulled painful memories from him as easily as she shared her own. There was the woman who'd moved across to the other seat so she could see *both* sides of his face.

He settled back and watched her talk, letting the details flow past him. The recorder would catch those anyway and he wanted the nuances, the changes of expression that would lead him places that words would not.

Besides, her face, unlike his own, was not at all hard to look at.

She got to the part about finding the boat.

"Why didn't you tell the Amoco tool pusher what you'd found?" he asked.

She paused. "Two reasons. One, for the same reason I later ran. I was afraid of INS involvement. Two, if there was a salvageable cargo, I wasn't going to share it with them. Sunken boats aren't subject to the Flood Salvage Bill. Amoco hired me to find an oil leak, but they might not see it that way, and I didn't want to argue with them about it. When I found the bodies, though, I just wanted to keep it quiet while I ran back home."

Thomas nodded. "I see. How could you identify the types of ordnance, just from looking at the holes?"

"Two years ago, the INS contracted me to recover a small steel trawler in twelve hundred feet of water south of Louisiana. The INS intercepted her trying for the coast and the idiots fired two LAW rockets at the INS cutter. If they'd hit the cutter at the waterline, it would've been bad, but instead they punched a hole into the forward mess." She paused. "The second rocket killed the boarding crew as they were coming across in a Zodiac. The cutter responded with cannon and machine-gun fire, and that trawler went down like a stone—before they could see what she was carrying, though they pulled some of the trawler's survivors and corpses from the water."

Thomas raised his eyebrows. "I think I heard about that. What was the cargo?"

"Uncut cocaine. About two tons. It was in sealed plastic bags and except where some shrapnel tore some open, it was mostly recovered intact. Anyway, *that's* where I'd seen twenty-millimeter cannon and fifty-caliber machine-gun holes." She tilted her head and looked across the table at Thomas. "Was I right?"

"Yes. We recovered slugs." *Now why did I tell her that?*

Watch yourself, boy. "I know what you did from the time you opened the hold to when you closed the hold. Everybody who saw the tape knows. I'm also presuming from watching you cut the chains that it *was* the first time you saw the cargo. Well, from that and your, uh, reaction."

Patricia nodded.

"Was that the last time you saw it? Did you go back and look or remove anything from the hold?"

"No. I don't think I could've made myself go back in there even if I had a very good reason. Was it open when you got there?"

"No. Apparently it was as you left it." Thomas could understand her reluctance to reenter the hold. "What did you do next?"

"I went back to the sub, got some salvage foam, and plugged the oil leak. Ran out of air on my way back, too."

"What's salvage foam?"

She spread her arms apart. "It's an elastic plastic foam that you can spray into things to displace water and give them positive lift. It's really stretchy, for about an hour, so, even if you're bringing it up from depth, it can handle expansion without losing buoyancy. It makes a good temporary patch."

"Ah. Why'd you take the time to do that?"

"Are you kidding? Do you know how much oil ended up in the oceans during the Deluge? Not to mention other nasty chemicals. I work in the ocean. I live on the ocean. I don't want any more toxins dumped where I live."

Thomas nodded. *A better reason than, "I didn't want anybody else to be able to find it."* Well, her subsequent behavior had certainly proved she wasn't trying to *hide* the ship. "Tell me what happened after that."

He listened to her account of finding the railway car and returning to *Terminal Lorraine*. Then came the approach of *Sycorax* and her decision to run.

"It's not that I was sure about *Sycorax* or even the INS. For all I know, some third party loaded a twenty-millimeter cannon and fifty-cal aboard their rowboat and did the deed." She paused and licked her lips. "If it had happened officially—say, the crew opened fire on a boarding vessel—I would think I would've heard about it. But suppose an investigation was under way and the press hadn't gotten wind of it yet." She searched Thomas's face. "Did an INS vessel report sinking the *Open Lotus*?"

"No."

She exhaled. "Well, I feel justified in running, then. I don't know that it makes it any better. If it *had* been a case of the INS firing back, think how horrible it would be for the INS crew to find they'd accidentally killed all those people in the hold." She shuddered. "But then it's even more horrible if the people who *did* sink the *Open Lotus* knew what was in the hold." She took a swallow of her coffee and looked back down at the table. "How many people were in the hold, anyway?"

Thomas was surprised. "Do you really want to know?"

The corners of Patricia's mouth dropped down. "I can't stand people who ogle car wrecks and other disasters. It's the children, though. I can't stop thinking about the children."

Thomas sighed. "Eighteen men, twelve women, and seventeen children. There were three crew, as well. And no, we have no idea who they are yet. By the way, I didn't tell you that. I also shouldn't have told you about the ammo and I would be very grateful if neither of you talked to the press about it." He looked from Moses to Patricia.

"About the incident itself or just the details we've learned from you?" Moses asked.

"Just the details. If you weren't extraterritorial, I'd threaten you with obstruction-of-justice charges, but I wouldn't be able to make it stick out here. Instead, I'll just say 'please.' " He turned to Patricia specifically. "You'll probably be mobbed by the press when they know you're back here."

Patricia had been staring down at the table. When she

looked up her eyes were wet. "I'll be all right if I stay out of public places. My entire hex has only one section of public corridor where it joins two other hexes, but otherwise it's entirely private property. Unless a reporter had an apartment in my hex or a child in my school—which they don't—they can't enter. And my concierge is screening all visitors."

"No phone calls?"

She shrugged. "I can count the number of people who have my satphone number on one hand. I've been letting the voice mail get my regular line."

"I wish fewer people had *my* satphone number," Thomas said wistfully. "Tell me what happened after you started running from the *Sycorax*."

"Well, they took my boat."

"Navigational hazard. It's at BBINS." He pronounced it "bee-bins."

"I don't know what that is."

"Sorry. Buffalo Bayou INS Station."

"Oh. How do I get it back?"

"Um, I'm not sure. I'll be glad to check into it. If your only crime was justifiable flight, I don't see what the problem would be. What happened after they boarded your boat?"

She slumped back and her face fell into a shadow cast by her coffee cup. Thomas moved the candle minutely to the side, so he could see her face. He leaned his elbows on the table and supported his chin. The fatigue was catching up, but it left him in a rush when she described being shot at.

"They shot *at* you?"

"I can show you the holes. Not fifty-caliber, I believe. Why so surprised? We *did* flee."

"Yes, but you didn't fire at them. And since you weren't an immediate danger, the rules of engagement don't allow for anything past those first warning shots." He narrowed his eyes. "I'm going to be very interested in their log. Maybe they thought you were going to hit the diver."

"We were well past the diver when they fired."

Thomas shook his head.

"So you didn't fully recharge your flywheels. Did they break off the chase? Is that how you got back here?"

"As far as I could tell, they never stopped trying to find us. As to how we got back here, well, it really didn't have anything to do with finding the *Open Lotus*."

"I thought you weren't going to hold anything back but the identity of your crew." Thomas was so tired now that if Patricia balked on him, he wouldn't have the energy to pursue it. "Is it this?" He reached out and turned off the recorder.

Patricia looked at the recorder, almost as if she'd forgotten it was there. "I did something stupid," Patricia said. "It's rather embarrassing."

Thomas raised his eyebrows but otherwise just sat still. *Come on. You know you want to talk about it.*

She told them then about the portable stereo decoy and the bubble in the sunken rig and reluctantly, about almost being sucked into the intake jets of the *Sycorax*.

Thomas stared at her, openmouthed.

"I know it was stupid!" Patricia said.

He shook his head. "That's not what I was thinking. It's too bad you didn't have a suction collar like they use on the Deep Submergence Rescue Vehicles. Then you could've snuck up on the *Sycorax* and clamped on like a remora without having to leave the sub." He shook his head again. "I'm glad you *didn't* get 'grated like cheese.' I have enough witnesses to this crime who are unable to testify." He got momentarily grim, then laughed abruptly. "If the crew of the *Sycorax* had known! It's like spending all day trying to find your sunglasses when they're perched atop your head."

He dipped his hand into his water glass and slapped wet fingers across his cheeks. "Whew. So you rode back under the *Sycorax*?"

"Yes. That part's mostly boring. I broke us loose when it pulled into *la Boca del Infierno*—that is, into the INS shipping chan—"

He raised his hand. "No need. I'm familiar with *la Boca* and *el Ano*." He was silent for a moment. "Unless you can think of anything else, I think that concludes my business." He raised his eyebrows.

"Can't think of anything."

"How do we settle up the check?"

Patricia shook her head. "Feel free to come here sometime and pay, but Tío Rodolfo would be very unhappy if we were to try to pay. Especially after I stayed away for so long. The most I can get away with is the odd piece of salvaged restaurant equipment."

Thomas took a deep breath that turned into another jaw-cracking yawn. "Weren't you going to tell me why you decided to come back?"

She shrugged. "Yes. I was. But not yet." Her eyes darted sideways at Bill Moses and Seaman Guterson.

Don Rodolfo came with one last tray, five tiny shot glasses topped with blue flame. "*A los amigos ausentes.*" He handed the little glasses around.

Thomas eyed the fire doubtfully, thinking about other flames, other times.

"You blow out the flame, first," Patricia said. She demonstrated, knocking it back in one quick gulp.

"All right. To absent friends." The flame may have been out when Thomas swallowed the liquid, but it burned all the way down. He exhaled sharply, wheezing slightly. "What is it?"

Patricia shook her head. "Better not to ask."

Don Rodolfo leaned close to Patricia and whispered something in her ear. She closed her eyes for a moment and took a deep breath. "*Estoy de acuerdo,*" she said. She stood and turned to Thomas. "Commander Becket, would you come with me for a moment?"

Seaman Guterson and Bill Moses started to stand, but

Patricia waved them back into his seat. "We'll be right back. It's just for a moment."

Puzzled, Thomas followed Don Rodolfo and Patricia back through the kitchen, then out another hallway that led first to an office and then to a residence.

In the corner of a living room was a candlelit niche where a crucifix hung over painted saints on wooden *retablos*. In the foreground a rectangular grid of candleholders stood cemented to the niche by mounds of melted wax. A cluster of photographs stood just behind leaning against a *retablo*.

Patricia pointed to one of the photographs. "I'm going to light a candle for my father. I thought you might like to light one for your Ensign Parnasos—did I remember the name correctly?"

He didn't know if it was the fiery liquid or the food or the fatigue, but Thomas suddenly felt like he'd been punched in the stomach. "Yes. Eugene Parnasos. You remembered perfectly."

He took an unlit candle from the frame and touched it to one of the large votive candles burning at the side. He put it back in its place and took out his wallet. Tucked behind Thomas's driver's license was a dog-eared photo of a curly-headed young man with dark eyes and a wide smile. Thomas looked at Don Rodolfo and mimed putting the photo with the others. "*¿Se puede?*"

Don Rodolfo nodded. "*Sí*. It would be our great honor."

Thomas put the photo down in a gap between Patricia's father and an older woman smiling so large her face seemed all creases. He bowed his head for a moment. *You live, Eugene, in my thoughts and in my memories*. He stepped back and to the side, making room for Patricia.

Patricia picked up the photo of her father and stared at it for a moment.

Thomas could see the resemblance, though her father's hair was thin, his face was lined, and the long nose that anchored Patricia's features so nicely was rendered pleasantly ugly by masculine exaggeration. In the picture he was sitting at a table that Thomas recognized was at this restaurant and he was smiling as largely as Eugene.

Patricia put the photo back down next to Eugene, then lit her candle and replaced it. She was still for a moment, but when she turned away from the altar, she was smiling sadly. "Thank you, Tío." She hugged Don Rodolfo.

He patted her back, then held her out at arm's length. "*Todas las cosas tienen su tiempo.*" He smiled.

"*Cierto.*"

Thomas followed them back to the table, his hands deep in his pockets.

All the energy drained from Thomas when he stepped into the boat. He dropped back into the rear corner seat and barely managed not to fall over.

Patricia, stepping off the restaurant's boat behind him, said, "Are you all right?"

He shrugged. "Ask me in about ten hours."

She sat down beside him, in the middle of the seat. Moses sat in the other corner.

Seaman Guterson went forward and unclipped their line from the mooring buoy. Before he let go, he called out, "Where to, sir?"

Thomas flopped his head over, looking at Patricia, and raised his eyebrows.

"Where you picked me up will work for both of us, I think. You didn't take your boat in to work today, did you?" she asked Moses.

"No—the Intercity."

"Right then," said Patricia.

She smiled at Seaman Guterson and Thomas felt an unreasonable stab of jealousy. Thomas turned his hand over in lazy assent, and Guterson started the boat up and headed for the open middle of the bay, where he could run at planing speed.

The air was still warm and the lights reflected off the rippling water creating up-side down impressionistic towers. He was drowsily aware of her warmth, almost—but not quite—touching him. In a soft voice he said, "Was it almost dying? Is that why you decided it was time to come back to Cosas Muertas del Mar? Before you didn't have another chance?"

She looked at him and leaned closer, also talking softly. "Partly. Partly it was the encounter with Geoffrey. I'm almost grateful to Geoffrey, for showing up when he did. He's such an, uh, extreme. One of life's extremes. Like almost dying.

"I *am* grateful to you. If you hadn't been there—if I hadn't needed to explain it—I wouldn't have pulled the whole mess back to the surface. It dropped Dad's death into a greater perspective. Extremes do that, I guess." She slumped slightly, matching his posture, her shoulder touching his. "We carry these things around with us, unexamined, and only when we really look at them, take them out in the sunlight and dust off the cobwebs, do we realize we can finally put them down."

Again, Thomas felt like he'd been slugged in the stomach. He thought back to Eugene's photo. The guilt was still there, the grief. But something had changed. *Perspective?* He repeated what Don Rodolfo had said to Patricia. "*Todas las cosas tienen su tiempo.*"

He felt her nod. "Yes, all things have their time."

She stopped talking then, leaning her head back against the seat to look up at the stars. Thomas followed her example.

He woke up, startled, Seaman Guterson standing over him. He looked around. They were at the Hertz Rent-a-Boat facility by the airport Hilton. He sat up and felt something slide off him to his lap. He picked it up. It was a silk jacket, the one Patricia had been wearing.

He looked up at Guterson.

"When I dropped them at the pier, she said not to wake you, sir. I didn't realize she'd left her jacket."

Thomas carefully hung the jacket over his arm. "That's

all right, Mr. Guterson. I'll just have to make sure it gets back to her."

CONNECTED
ENTER USER ID CODE: XXXXXXX
PRESENT RIGHT EYE FOR RETINAL SCAN.
(IF YOU ARE WEARING GLASSES, PLEASE REMOVE THEM.)
WELCOME TO THE INSCID SECURE CONFERENCE SERVER COMDR. THOMAS BECKET. WOULD YOU LIKE TO INITIATE A CONFERENCE OR JOIN ONE IN PROGRESS?
CHECKING ATTENDEE LISTS FOR CURRENT SESSIONS. YOU ARE CONFIRMED FOR SESSION.
"JAZZ," ENCRYPTION LEVEL EPSILON. ATTENDING:
[BEEP] [VID WINDOW LT. HAMILTON GRAHAM]
Morning, sir.
[BEEP] [VID WINDOW ENS. BARTHOLOMEW TERKEL]
Morning, Commander.
[BEEP] [VID WINDOW MED. EXAM. RICHARD PRICE]
Good morning, Tom. It's been a long time.
[BEEP] [VID WINDOW COMDR. THOMAS BECKET]
Gentlemen. Thanks for connecting. I thought we'd review our progress to date. Why don't we start with the victims? Okay by you, Dick?
[VIDWIN PRICE]
Fine by me. You want to start with the crew or those unfortunates in the hold?
[VIDWIN BECKET]
Your choice.
[VIDWIN PRICE]
All right, the crew. They were pretty much stripped and scattered by sharks and lesser predators. We had to resort to gross DNA typing to sort the bones. Captain K. K. Mok was identified by the mandibular tori of his upper jaw. His lower jaw is still missing as are several other of the smaller bones as well as his left hip and femur. Several of the major bones were splintered consistent with ballistic impacts and

we found an embedded slug in his right hip. It's grossly deformed, but the ballistic wallas tell me it's jacketed fifty-caliber. Degree of trauma *almost certainly* indicates he died from gunfire and quickly.

[VIDWIN BECKET]

Where did the dental records come from?

[VIDWIN GRAHAM]

Abbott detention facility. Mok was skipper of another ship and did two years hard time for smuggling illegals. He was clearly a cog in a larger organization, but he always claimed he was an independent. The confiscated vessel was registered in Panama in his name, but his finances weren't up to that. When he was released, he spent a week in the refugee camp, then checked out via work sponsorship, signing on with a Panamanian freighter as second mate.

[VIDWIN BECKET]

And the registry of the *Open Lotus*?

[VIDWIN GRAHAM]

Panamanian.

[VIDWIN BECKET]

Well, we'll get back to the ship in a bit. Please go on, Dick.

[VIDWIN PRICE]

That's about it for Captain Mok's remains. Our next contestant is John Doe One. We're missing most of his head, so dental records were not an option. The fragment of the skull we did recover, a piece of the zygomatic arch, is splintered—consistent with gunfire, again. His head probably exploded, and the fish carried off the bits. I'd be willing to bet he died immediately.

[VIDWIN BECKET]

Sorry to interrupt again, but do we have an idea of when "immediately" was? That is, when did this attack take place? And was it sunk then or later?

[VIDWIN GRAHAM]

What we have are several complaints to the Federal Communications Commission on the thirteenth about oh-one-fifteen. The times reported vary by five minutes, but they all agree that there was a two-minute burst of white noise covering the entire VHF spectrum. Three of the plaintiffs got a bearing on the disturbance. The points of convergence are the current wreck site, plus or minus three hundred yards.

[VIDWIN BECKET]

Hmmm, five days ago. Three days before Ms. Beenan stumbled across it. So they jammed them, presumably during the attack. How does that correlate with the state of the bodies?

[VIDWIN PRICE]

The degree of faunal interaction can vary intensely in waters this warm, but the degree of bacterial gas buildup—in the tissues of those relatively protected in the hold—brackets that time.

[VIDWIN TERKEL]

Huh?

[VIDWIN PRICE]

That time of death and immersion works.

[VIDWIN TERKEL]

Oh.

[VIDWIN BECKET]

Okay. Please continue, Dick. I'll try and keep from interrupting again.

[VIDWIN PRICE]

John Doe two is pretty much the same story. Death by gunfire. Defleshing and scattering by the busy mouths of the sea. Parts are missing. No hits from CODIS-II or dental records.

[BEEP] [TEXTWIN] MSG FROM ENS. TERKEL:

what is codis two?

[VIDWIN PRICE]

Any questions before we move on to the hold?

[VIDWIN BECKET]

No.

[TEXTWIN] MSG TO ENS. TERKEL:

combined dna indexing system. fbi maintained. mostly convicted felons and unidentified crime scene data, but also any-

body booked for a crime or screened for military or police enlistment. you're in it.
[VIDWIN PRICE]
We have eighteen adult John Does, twelve adult Jane Does, nine minor John Does, and eight minor Jane Does. No hits through CODIS-II or dental. I've got one tattooed ankle that was covered by a lace-up boot—that's Jane Doe nine. It doesn't help much—it's a circlet of thorns motif that shows up all over the world.
[BEEP] [AUXWIN PRICE]
Jane Doe–9: Ankle tattoo
[Image]
[VIDWIN PRICE]
I've got lots of pierced ears and no earrings. I've got a few fingers with ring marks and no rings. I've got some watch-band marks and no watches. I do have one silver anklet chain, also hidden under a boot, and a labial piercing stud from Jane Doe eleven. The anklet chain is completely generic, but the piercing stud is handmade work.
[AUXWIN PRICE]
Jane Doe–11: Piercing stud
[Image]
[VIDWIN GRAHAM]
Wowwch!
[VIDWIN BECKET]
Uh, different. We got any clues?
[VIDWIN PRICE]
Yes. It's Incan handworked gold. Not a knockoff but a genuine pre-Columbian artifact. It was probably an ear piercing, originally. Nearly all the clothing is generic—mostly Chinese and Canadian knockoffs of American fashions. If I had to guess, I'd say they were dressing to fit in.
[VIDWIN BECKET]
You said nearly.
[VIDWIN PRICE]
Right. John Doe twenty-six was a minor between three and five years old. He was wearing this shirt.

[AUXWIN PRICE]
John Doe–26: Embroidered shirt.
[Image]
[VIDWIN BECKET]
Is that Guatemalan?
[VIDWIN PRICE]
No. It's Zuleteña embroidery—from Ecuador.
[VIDWIN BECKET]
You sent off the dental records and DNA?
[VIDWIN PRICE]
Dental records. They don't have a DNA database, though if we get some matches we can do interpolations from closely related living relatives.
[VIDWIN BECKET]
Better try Colombia and Peru, too. Next door.
[VIDWIN PRICE]
Right. Stomach contents were mostly inconclusive with the exception of fried green bananas. That's popular in most of Central and South America.
[VIDWIN BECKET]
Patacónes.
[VIDWIN PRICE]
Yeah, that's what my source called them. Cause of death in almost all cases was drowning. The one exception was an adult male with a chunk of shrapnel in his liver. It was probably a piece of ship hull taken ballistic by cannon fire. We'll compare it metallurgically after they raise the *Open Lotus*. He must've died quick for there wasn't any salt water in his lungs.
[VIDWIN BECKET]
Anything else?
[VIDWIN PRICE]
Yeah—these weren't poor people. Their dental work is good stuff—ceramic gold crowns, some implants, some expensive orthodontia on two of the kids. Jane Doe eleven has breast implants. Most of the adult women had their leg and armpit hair suppressed, which is nowhere near as common down

there as it is up here. We'll be doing computerized facial reconstruction on the men and women, but that's it for me for now.

[VIDWIN BECKET]

When we get the adult male images, we should run them past DEA, especially Agent Ortiz in the Colombian section. They might not be members of somebody's cartel, but since there seems to be a South American connection, we might get a lead. Did the *Open Lotus* put ashore in Colombia or Ecuador in the last month or two?

[VIDWIN GRAHAM]

We haven't been able to track the *Open Lotus*. As far as we can tell, the last time she put into an American port was three years ago when she was running a regular route in the Sea of Cortés up into the Imperial Valley. Nothing heard from since then. It's possible that she's been mothballed someplace, out of the country.

[VIDWIN BECKET]

Or running under a different name and registration. We better make sure *our* freighter and *that Open Lotus* are one and the same. Any word from the navy on raising the wreck?

[VIDWIN GRAHAM]

Yes, sir. Captain Elmsford believes he'll have it ready to float by tomorrow. He's got a two-hundred-foot mobile dry dock coming from Beeville Naval Base and weather permitting, they'll get it up and moved into BBINS.

[VIDWIN BECKET]

Okay. That's where I'll want the team excepting Ensign Terkel. Unless, that is, Ensign Terkel has found a ballistic match on our fifty-caliber machine gun?

[VIDWIN TERKEL]

Negative, sir, but I still have five vessels to check. Two Witch Class Fastships and three fifty-foot patrol boats.

[VIDWIN BECKET]

Have you checked the *Sycorax* yet?

[VIDWIN TERKEL]

Negative, sir. I caught them at BBINS yesterday, but they

are a gamma-level security installation, and I had to go through Admiral Rylant to get the authorization. By the time we were done futzing around, they'd pulled out for a scheduled patrol. The security issue is resolved, though. Just have to catch up with them.

[VIDWIN BECKET]

Oh, really? Do you have their schedule?

[VIDWIN TERKEL]

Yes, sir. They'll be on coastal interdiction patrol until next Wednesday, when they provide extra security when the INS detainee transport docks at the Abattoir.

[TEXTWIN] MSG TO ENS. TERKEL:

why the gamma level for sycorax?

[VIDWIN BECKET]

Jazz, get me their log data as reported to GulfComOps for the last two weeks. While you're at it, pull the same data for all Witch Class vessels in the region.

[VIDWIN GRAHAM]

Yes, sir. Do we actually want all that data?

[TEXTWIN] MSG FROM ENS. TERKEL:

the sycorax *is an advanced technology test platform. they didn't tell me what technologies.*

[VIDWIN BECKET]

No, we just want to avoid our *specific* interest getting back to them. Luckily we can pull their personnel files without going through anybody else. I want those.

[VIDWIN GRAHAM]

So we have a specific interest in the *Sycorax*?

[VIDWIN BECKET]

We do. According to Ms. Beenan, that ship pursued her submersible with an interest well beyond normal operations. A helicopter, working with Sycorax, also opened fire on the submersible outside the rules of engagement. It stinks, but it might just be overenthusiasm. Or they might be trying to cover up something.

[VIDWIN GRAHAM]

Might she be lying?

[VDIWIN BECKET]
She might, but why? What's her gain? So far, her testimony maps to all other evidence, and I can't see any motivation for her to lie.
[VIDWIN GRAHAM]
In that case, sir, I have a suggestion.
[VIDWIN BECKET]
Yes?
[VIDWIN GRAHAM]
We should pull the component-level weapons inventory on the *Sycorax*. Ensign Terkel has been checking fifty-cal weapons all over the region. The word has got to be out. When he does a ballistics check on the *Sycorax*'s fifty-caliber weapons, he should also make sure the weapons or their barrels haven't been switched out.
[VIDWIN BECKET]
Very good idea. Anything else?
[VIDWIN GRAHAM]
No, sir.
[VIDWIN BECKET]
Okay. I want the team over to BBINS. Ensign Terkel, you'll continue as planned, but I'd like you to avoid the *Sycorax* for now. When you're done checking the other boats, I'd like you to find out where the officers and men of the *Sycorax* hang when they're shoreside. Dick will be continuing to work on the ID problem, and Jazz will keep after the missing chapters out of the *Open Lotus*'s recent history. Last, I want to see about getting Ms. Beenan's surface tender released back to her custody. Find out why it was taken and under what pretext it's being held. Am I missing anything?
SESSION "JAZZ" ENDS.
WOULD YOU LIKE TO INITIATE A CONFERENCE OR JOIN ONE IN PROGRESS?
DISCONNECTED

8

Beenan: *Intimidades escasas y grandes*

Patricia was in landlord hell.

Mrs. Fong, the matriarch of apartment 3-C was talking a million miles a second, loudly, in Cantonese. Mrs. Fong's seven-year-old grandson, Lee, was trying to translate, but his English was much better than his Cantonese and Mrs. Fong never stopped talking, even when Lee was trying to tell Patricia what she was saying.

"Yes, I know the winds are high today and the Strand is shifting, but the city controller will have the orientation back to normal very soon now."

Lee tried to translate this, but his grandmother held out a magnetic compass and pointed at it, speaking rapidly.

"Good evening."

Patricia spun, surprised. Commander Becket was standing in the hall, Patricia's jacket hanging off a shoulder-slung workstation case. He was wearing the same or similar civilian clothes that he'd worn the night before.

She was wearing cutoffs, bare feet, and one of her father's old T-shirts. It was not the meeting she'd hoped for.

"Your concierge said I would find you here."

Mrs. Fong never stopped talking. Becket turned to her, smiled, and said, "*Nei hou ma?*"

Mrs. Fong closed her mouth with a snap.

"You speak Cantonese, Commander?"

Becket shrugged. "A bit. There are lots of Chinese refugees. I'm not fluent. What does she want a *feng shui* consultant for?"

"Well, her patio door normally points to the east, which is auspicious, but the Strand is rotated today because of the higher winds. They diverted OTEC output to keep us on station at the expense of keeping the orientation just so, and now Mrs. Fong says all the good energy is flowing into Ms. Carlisle's apartment instead of her own."

Becket nodded. "*Doi m'jui.*"

Mrs. Fong turned to Becket and began another long string of Cantonese. He held up his hands and said, "*M'hai. M'hai.* I'm not getting this. What's the conflict here? Do you object to her having a *feng shui* man in?"

"Not at all," said Patricia. "I object to paying for it, which is what happened last time she wanted one. The bill was three hundred dollars for a thirty-minute visit."

Becket shook his head. "Clearly I'm in the wrong business." He turned back to Mrs. Fong, spread his hands, and said, "*Hou gwai! Doi m'jui. M'hai.*"

"Aieeeee. *Tsi leng sin gwai!*"

Becket looked surprised; then he laughed out loud, wagging his finger at Mrs. Fong. "*Doi m'jui. Joi kin.*" Aside to Patricia he said, "Time to say bye-bye."

She followed his advice, smiled, and said, "Don't worry. The weather report says the front will be past by tomorrow, and your door will face the east again. Good-bye!"

She didn't wait for little Lee to translate this, but turned and followed Becket down the hall. When she was around the corner, she heard Mrs. Fong's door shut loudly. "Whew. What did you say to her?"

"I said, sorry, too expensive, no."

"And what did she say to you?"

He laughed again. "That I was a fucking crazy foreigner, which was rather rude but certainly gets into the Cantonese I *usually* hear. It also shows she accepted the answer since she wouldn't have been so rude if she still hoped to talk you into it."

"Thanks, I think. She isn't going to do anything crazy, is she?"

"Does she normally do crazy things?"

Patricia laughed. "Depends. She set off a huge string of firecrackers on Chinese New Year that tripped most of the smoke alarms in the building. But no, not usually."

Becket spread his hands apart, palms up. "Well, there you have it." He noticed Patricia's jacket still slung in the crook of his elbow. "Oh. Your jacket." He paused in the hallway and held it out. "That's why I came. Thanks. Uh, you left it in the boat."

I didn't leave it "in the boat." "Right." She took it from him and held it awkwardly. *Say something!* "Thanks." Then, suddenly "Do you have a moment?"

He tilted his head to one side and raised his eyebrows.

"I wanted to ask you about my boat, but I have a fifteen-minute meeting right now."

"I can wait."

She smiled and pointed to a stairwell. "It's up a few flights."

They came out into the school courtyard. Over the railing the stretch cf water was dotted with whitecaps, but the courtyard was mostly sheltered from the wind's direct effects. Patricia led Becket to her own patio and said, "Will you be all right here? I've got to talk with the teaching staff about schedule changes. Well, they're supposed to have worked them all out and I just have to approve them." *I hope.* "But I should be back shortly."

He pulled out one of the white plastic chairs. "This is fine."

She flashed him a smile and ran. When she got inside the school door, she made herself pause. Her heart was beating faster than the short dash warranted.

"Hi, boss." Toni was sitting in the waiting room just inside the door, wearing a dress and makeup.

Patricia stared at her blankly for a moment, her thoughts

still on Becket; then she shook herself vigorously. *Get a grip!* "Nice dress, Toni."

The girl was staring at Patricia's cutoffs. "Thanks. Too dressy?" The girl's anxiety was palpable.

Patricia took a deep breath and focused. "For work, perhaps. For the interview? No. You look fine. Come on. They should all be in the teachers' lounge." She punched the combination on the keypad door, and when the release buzzed, she held the door while Toni entered.

She led Toni up one flight of stairs and then across a hall to a room overlooking the playground. A cluster of women and one man were standing at the window looking across the courtyard.

Consuela turned when they came in the room.

"Sorry I'm late, Connie. I had a tenant problem."

Consuela looked back out the window. "Is that who he is? A new tenant?"

"Not him. Mrs. Fong."

"Oh, her—the firecracker lady. Is this Toni?"

"It is. Consuela Madrid. Toni Nelson. Consuela is the principal of Art of Learning."

"But I teach, too. So you want to be a teacher's aide?"

"She'd like to try it. She's one of my new employees on the salvage side, but she's out of a job while the INS still has *Terminal Lorraine*." *And after three days in* SubLorraine *she's not so sure she* wants *to be involved in salvage anymore.*

Consuela offered her hand to Toni. "Well, we definitely need some help in the afternoon and evening. We get a bunch of kids in the afternoons who go to the public school but come here for aftercare until their parents get home from work. Then we have some second-shift childcare until midnight—if you can stand the hit to your social life."

She beckoned to Toni. "Let's pop next door to admin, and I'll get you started on the paperwork. You can do that while we do our little meeting here."

"Okay," said Toni.

As the two women went into the next room, Patricia went over to the window and stood on tiptoe to see over one of the teacher's shoulders. Becket had opened his workstation on the patio table, but he was leaning back, fingers steepled, watching one of the afternoon classes as they swarmed over the play structure.

Christopher, their one male teacher, said, "Classic figure. Tragic face. Is he gay?"

Patricia frowned. "None of your bus—. I don't know. Don't *think* so."

Chris sighed. "Me neither. Not the way he watched you run across the courtyard."

Patricia blushed and turned away. "Aren't we supposed to be having a meeting?"

The others came away from the window grumbling.

Consuela returned from admin and looked at Patricia's face. "I missed something, didn't I?"

Christopher opened his mouth, and Patricia said, "Don't even start. After the meeting you guys can talk about me all you want. But. Not. Now."

Consuela blinked and struggled momentarily to find the proper expression. When her face stopped moving, the expression was carefully neutral. She picked up the paper in front of her. "The first order of business is the second-shift staffing schedule."

When Patricia came out of the meeting, she saw Becket crouched beside his chair, putting his eyes level with Marie.

"—well, I burned it," he was saying when Patricia got within hearing range.

Marie said, "That doesn't sound very smart."

Patricia winced but Becket laughed, a sudden surprised sound. Still chuckling, he said, "Well, no. Not as it turned out. Not very smart."

"Did it hurt too bad?"

Becket pursed his lips, considering. "No. I think it hurt just enough."

Marie looked confused. "Maybe you should have a grown-up kiss it and make it better."

Gravely he said, "I'll have to try that."

"Well, bye!" Marie turned and ran off, back toward her apartment.

"Buy you a drink, Commander?"

Becket looked up from watching Marie, his eyes unfocused, someplace else, but swiftly returning. "Oh. Ms. Beenan." He stared at his watch and then at the darkening sky.

"I'm very sorry," Patricia said. "The meeting went on longer than I thought it would." She kept herself from looking back at the school, certain she'd see faces watching from the next floor up.

Becket returned fully to himself and smiled. "It's quite all right. I got some work done and this is a very pleasant place to sit. And I had a visitor." He took a deep breath of air. "But I can't let you buy me a drink. You provided dinner and drinks last night. It's my turn."

"I didn't pay a cent for last night," Patricia protested.

"Not a cent," he agreed. "Just blood, sweat, and tears."

She looked away, discomfited. "All right. You can buy me a drink."

"Okay. Where?"

"I'll show you. Can you wait a few moments while I change?"

He gestured back at his workstation. "I'll be here."

She nodded, suddenly shy, then went through the patio door into her apartment. "Right back."

She picked clothing automatically, a silk tank top, a flowered skirt, and sandals, before ducking into the bathroom. She gave her hair a quick brush, washed her face, and brushed her teeth. *Why are you brushing your teeth?* She looked at herself in the mirror, at the dark smudges under her eyes from troubled sleep, and thought about the stash of cosmetics buried in the back of the bottom drawer. *No.*

She did reapply deodorant before dressing but froze before touching the knob.

Time to face the truth, girl.

She looked back at the mirror and almost didn't recognize herself. Aloud she said, "It's good to see you again."

He asked if he could leave his workstation and satphone in her apartment and she set the bag inside the door before locking up. They walked side by side, not touching, down the exterior stairs until they'd reached the public access. She turned away from the water and led him through an interior walkway, toward the center of the subdivision, past shops and shoppers pushing or pulling handcarts, through courtyards where taller units framed bits of dark blue sky far overhead, then past more residential buildings, the towers dropping in height again.

They emerged at the seawall, walking up a short flight of stairs, then walked along a cast seacrete path winding across a hex of growing soybeans and then a hex of wheat. At the far edge was a hardened concrete building facing the open gulf with a sign: Puesta del Sol.

The sun hung, suspended, just touching the far horizon, and Patricia imagined it was setting into the Texas coast, two hundred miles away, torching an already arid area of the Rio Grande Valley.

They followed the path to the far side of the building where a thin-but-long table-dotted veranda followed the outer edge of the seawall. Most of the tables were filled, their occupants watching the sunset or the slow waves breaking below on the submerged beach plates, foaming effervescently before subsiding back into the deeper water.

She stopped at a table by the railing. "Is this okay?"

"This is . . . truly excellent." He pulled a chair out for her.

"Good. I used to come here a lot. It's one of those places I've been avoiding."

He settled slowly across from her. "Oh? More painful memories?"

She shook her head. "Painful encounters—in the present. Geoffrey really likes this place, too. But I've decided that's his problem—not mine."

Becket smiled. "More extremes putting things in perspective?"

"Yeah." She turned her chair to face the sunset and sank down into it. "Be quiet for a bit, okay?"

"Sure."

She heard him lean back and settle into silence. If he moved or even breathed, the sound of the surf covered it. Her whole world shrank to the warmth on her face, the sound of the surf, the rhythm of her breath, and the liquid merging of the sun into the far horizon.

When the last drop of molten light dropped behind the earth she looked at Becket. He was leaning back in his chair, legs crossed, watching her. She struggled to take a breath. *Even so quickly may one catch the plague?*

"What does a girl have to do to get a drink around here?" she said. Around them, conversations increased slowly in volume.

Becket smiled. "I'll see if I can find a waiter. What do you want to drink?"

You. "A gin and tonic, tall, lots of tonic. I'm feeling very malarial." *Well, like I have a fever, anyway.*

"You don't have mosquitoes out here."

"No. All our bloodsuckers walk around on two feet."

Becket went away and after a moment came back followed by a barefoot waiter carrying two tall drinks.

"Which one is mine?" she asked.

"They're the same. I decided I'm feeling malarial, too."

She took a healthy gulp and held it in her mouth—three shocks—cold, bitter, sweet. Finally she swallowed. "Tell me about *Terminal Lorraine.*" At his blank look she added, "My boat."

"Ah. It's at BBINS. They've impounded it, but the charge of record is smuggling."

"Smuggling! Smuggling what?"

"Whatever you took off with you in your submersible . . . in other words, the charge has no substance, but it's also hard to disprove. How do you prove a negative after all?"

"Are they going to keep it?" *Are* you *going to keep it?*

"We're working on it. If worst comes to worst, I'll requisition it as evidence in my investigation and transfer it back to you, but it would be better if they released it directly. I don't suppose your mother might be willing to put some pressure on them?"

Patricia choked on her drink, coughing violently and nearly spilling the glass. Her mother had left another message on Patricia's phone, but Patricia hadn't acquired the nerve to call her back.

Becket was looking concerned.

Patricia used a napkin to wipe her lips. "My mother. Well, it's an idea. Or, perhaps I could just scrape my skin raw and roll in lemon juice."

Becket laughed. "Like that, is it?"

Patricia glared. "If you think it's so funny, *you* ask her."

Becket held up his hands. "I certainly didn't mean to offend, Ms. Beenan."

"Then stop calling me Ms. Beenan. It's Patricia."

He became very still. "Thomas."

She nodded. "I didn't think you were a Tom. What about Tommy?"

He made a face.

"Tomás?"

"Acceptable. Not Patty? Not Pat?"

"Not if you want me to answer."

He nodded, suddenly serious. "Patricia."

"Yes?"

"Just trying it. Sorry."

She grinned. "Don't be."

They had two more rounds and a basket of fried shrimp.

In the west a sliver of red marked the memory of the sun's passage. Above it the canopy darkened quickly to starspecked royal blue, then washed out again, behind them, as the city lights came on.

A waiter brought a glass-englobed candle and took away empty glasses and a neat pile of shrimp tails.

Thomas leaned back and sighed. "I still mean to buy dinner, too, but after the shrimp, it would be better to wait a bit."

Patricia, warming her hands on the candle, said, "We could walk. I know a nice restaurant in Playa del Mar. It would take us about thirty minutes down the seawall if we walked slowly."

"Are you cold?"

Yes. You better hold me. "Not really. There's just something about the flame-heat. When you lock out at twelve hundred feet and the water temperature is fifty-five Fahrenheit and you're breathing ninety-five percent helium . . . *then* you get cold. But you gain a real appreciation for heat—even when you're not cold."

"You work that deep?"

Patricia shrugged. "I've worked twenty-two hundred feet. Once. Not sure I'd do it again. The job took twenty minutes, but I was in decompression for four days. I prefer to work at that depth in *SubLorraine*—at surface pressure, dry. Inspection work, like I do for the Strand, is best."

He shook his head. "Walking is good, but both ways?"

She looked at her watch. "On the way back, a water taxi. Perhaps a gondola. Some of the gondoliers really came from Venice, you know, but I like the ones who are in the New Galveston Opera chorus. They have better voices."

He put some bills on the table weighed down by the candle globe and stood suddenly, moving to her chair before she knew he was ready to stand. She stood carefully as he pulled the chair back, steadying herself with a hand on the table. *Three drinks is too many.* "Bathroom break, first?"

"Good idea."

They met again outside the restroom doors. She pointed out the path, barely lit by low, solar-charged safety lights, following the outer edges of the hexes and zigzagging every time they met another hex. There was nobody else on the walk, and the low lighting and the persistent drumming of the surf increased the sense of isolation.

"I'm surprised there aren't people living out here," Thomas said. "It's nice."

"Oh, it's nice now," Patricia answered. "But when you get a cat five hurricane plowing through, the waves break well over our heads. All those tables and chairs back at Puesta del Sol have to be carted into the bunker and, though they hermetically seal the building, there's always some water damage."

"What about these crops?"

"Oh, you can write off the crops if we get one of those."

"I guess I meant, what about the soil? Doesn't it get too salty?"

She shook her head. "These are tailored crops—high salt tolerance. There's substantial salt uptake into the stalks and leaves and even a bit in the grain and beans, but the salt is continually removed from the soil just by the process of growing these crops." She pointed east, toward the inner edge of the seawall, 450 feet in. A lighted window gleamed on a raised structure. "There. Some people do live on the seawall. Just not on the outer edge."

The moon had risen in the east, nearly full, and so close to the horizon it appeared improbably huge, like a special effect from a movie.

Ahead of them the glow from Playa del Mar grew and began to resolve itself into individual lights. Patricia stopped for a moment and swung to face Thomas. "Feel like getting your feet wet?"

He shrugged. "Aren't there barnacles?"

"Not here. There's a stretch of beach matting." She stepped over the edge of the seawall and saw Thomas reach involuntarily for her. "It's okay. See?"

Thomas stepped forward and saw the narrow stair built into the outer wall of the hex, no railing, barely visible in the low light. She moved down it to give him room, watching to make sure he found the handrail built into the inner wall.

At the bottom she sat on a step and pulled off her sandals. "You better roll up your pants," she suggested.

"Why do I think I'm going to regret this?" Thomas sat and removed his shoes and socks, then rolled up his pants. He stuffed his socks in his shoes and, tying the laces together, slung his shoes over one shoulder.

The upper beach plate, where the stair ended, was a bare concrete surface mechanically pitted for traction. "We must be above the high tidemark."

Patricia laughed. "What's wrong with that statement?"

Thomas paused before saying, "Floating cities don't have high tidemarks. If the tide goes up, so do they."

"Right. He *can* be trained."

"And I work and play well with others, too."

She led him away from the wall, down the sloping plate. Before they got to the water, she reached the fibrous matting designed to keep the plate barnacle- and limpet-free.

Thomas grunted when his feet ran into it. "Ah. I've seen barnacles grow on everything up to and including floating feces—why don't they just attach to this stuff?"

"They do but their adhesive activates a reaction in the fiber, and it becomes brittle and breaks away before they can grow."

They reached the wet matting and Patricia began walking parallel to the wall. A wave broke and the foam lapped their feet. It was skin temperature, and Patricia wanted to rip her clothes off and plunge in. She contented herself with kicking flecks of foam before her.

Thomas said, "I guess you don't walk down a beach like this and look for seashells."

"Does anybody? Those kinds of beaches are mostly gone, aren't they? Drowned. I remember doing it in Galveston when I was a little girl, and on South Padre Island."

"I did it on Mustang Island, near Port Aransas." Another

wave sloshed over their feet. "They have some good sand beaches in North Africa, I understand. The Sahara was good for something."

Patricia nodded in the dark. "Beaches are geologic constructs made over geologic time. I guess that's what I hate most about the new Texas coast. It's all breakwaters or mudflats. It's not like we had a lot of rocky cliffs, like Maine or California. They've still got some great shorelines. We do have a sand beach here. It's another quarter mile that way." She pointed toward Playa del Mar.

"I've seen pictures, but I didn't realize it was real sand. Does it go on into the water?"

"Yeah. They put in a long stretch of submerged hexes and covered them with dredged sand. There's a submerged wall on the outer edge that keeps most of it in, but they lose tons every storm. They just keep bringing it in, barge after barge. There's even seashells."

Patricia's eyes were adjusting to the deep shadow cast by the rising moon, and phosphorescent phytoplankton gleamed faintly in the water. Occasionally the water would recede leaving tinafores caught in the matting, bright spots of glowing green jelly the size of her thumb.

"How far out do the beach plates extend? Here, that is. How far until you've got a mile of water under your feet?"

"It extends about sixty feet out from the outer corners." She pointed ahead where a hex corner extended toward the water.

They were even with the juncture between two hexes, and the meeting point was farther back from the water, a minicove almost. When they reached the corner, a few moments later, the water washed all the way up to the wall and Patricia held up her skirts to avoid getting them wet.

Behind her Thomas swore softly. "Well, I hope they'll let me in this restaurant of yours with wet cuffs."

Around the corner they moved back up the plate, where the waves were less threatening. Patricia bundled the loose edges of her skirt to one side and tied them in a knot, keeping her hem above her knees. Thomas took the higher ground and she wondered if it was to keep dry or to walk by her side.

"Do you swim much?" she asked him.

"Once upon a time." He looked down for a moment, at the foam around his feet. "I did water polo in college. I've got these long gorilla arms for blocking and I tread water well."

She took his right wrist and held his arm out horizontally. "My. Those are long. Do you brachiate?" *They'd wrap clean around me.*

He took his arm back. "Might as well check my knuckles for calluses while you're at it."

She thought his voice cooled a bit and she winced. "I just wondered if you'd be comfortable swimming without a lifeguard."

He stopped walking and looked at her. "The lifeguard isn't a problem. No swimsuit might be."

She shrugged. "It's dark." *Thank god.* She could feel her ears burning and knew she was probably blushing to her waist.

"Sharks?"

"We eat a lot of shark around here. Probability is low but even less if you don't do the wounded-fish routine. Don't flop around on the surface splashing."

He was still for a moment. "If you like," he said lightly.

She walked up the plate until she was above the beach matting, where another access stair clung to the wall. She dropped her sandals and untied the knot in her skirt, then shucked it and her underpants in one movement before pulling her tank top over her head and adding it to the pile.

Thomas was standing off to the side, turned slightly away, undressing just as quickly. It was dark, yes, but Patricia's eyes had adjusted quite a bit and the lines of his back and butt made her ache. She waited until he'd finished folding his pants and boxer shorts, then walked down to the water, ahead of him. It might have been her imagination, but she felt his eyes upon her.

She sliced into a low wave cleanly and stayed under, suspended in a warm liquid embrace. The receding water tugged at her, pulling her farther out before another wave came in. She felt the eddies stream over her body, between her legs, over her breasts.

What a week to choose to come back to life! She arched her back and raised her head out of the water, turning to locate Thomas, and found herself in the moonlight, far enough out from the wall that the rising moon shone full upon her.

Thomas followed, a shallow dive through a wave and up on the other side. Patricia released worries about him cracking his head on the plate and stayed where she was, her feet touching the matting when in the troughs and floating up on the crests of waves. He located her and swam near, but stopped when he was about two meters away.

"That does feel good," he said, his voice slightly hoarse.

A deeper than usual trough passed and she found herself standing, for an instant, waist deep in water, facing him. His eyes, half in moonlight, half in shadow, watched her and he licked his lips. He didn't stand when the trough passed but dropped with it, his shoulders barely above water.

Cheat.

"Whoa," Thomas said. "I'm feeling quite an undertow."

She smiled to herself. *The currents are strong tonight.* "Yeah. You have to be careful of it. If the currents are the right direction, you can get sucked under the seawall." When the crest of the wave followed, she slipped down into the water. "Of course, the opposite is as bad. You can get swept out to sea." She kicked off the bottom and swam parallel to the shore, sidestroke, gliding strongly between strokes into a slight crosscurrent.

Thomas followed, broadstroking strongly, gliding forward like a seal. His long arms swept phosphorescent eddies down the length of his body and Patricia had a hard time not watching him.

She felt sudden, terrifying doubt.

Is it just lust? Did I just open myself up for something really nasty? He is *INS, after all. Or am I just looking for something else to displace the memory of the bodies in the hold?*

She let herself sink, exhaling, to wait, one heel touching the matting of the beach plate. She used her skin to sense the pressure waves of his approach. She opened her eyes and in the burning salt water saw his blurred silhouette passing overhead. She reached one finger up and poked him in the stomach; then, kicking off the bottom, she shot back the way they'd come.

When she surfaced, she couldn't locate him at first, until she heard him laughing, behind her. In the dark, she smiled.

I didn't choose badly. This one is worth something.

She stood again, so he could locate her, and he approached again. She let herself settle back and arched, floating on her back, watching Thomas approach from the corners of her eyes.

Again, he stopped out of arm's reach.

For my protection . . . or yours?

Thomas turned over on his back, too, and Patricia peeked lower, but only Thomas's chest and face were above the water. *Heavy feet . . . or modesty.*

She reached out and found his hand, entwined her fingers, but didn't pull him closer. She saw him smile. They weren't able to talk while on their backs—the water filled their ears and the gentle surf was all she could hear. Overhead the stars in the west grew brighter, but the eastern sky was washed out by moon glow.

See my breath, a plume against the horizon, deeply blown, deeply drawn, before I return to the depths. She'd always identified with cetaceans, especially the deep divers like the sperm whale, which hunted a full mile down. There was something in that when she operated *SubLorraine*—even with the life support she couldn't stay down indefinitely. It was like a *really big* breath of air.

Floating in the warm surface water, her face above water, she felt the connection again, stirring, oddly connected to the sexual tension that was building within her. It felt appropriate that she was starting courtship behavior immersed in the sea.

She moved then, pulling on his arm and coming upright in the water. He raised his head, too, and she reached for him, closing the gap, sliding her free hand over his shoulder and behind his neck, letting her body come to rest against his, going directly to his mouth with hers.

His arms closed on her slowly, carefully, though he was responding to her kiss ardently and in other ways, too. Her lower body brushed his, and his degree of "interest" was substantially and delightfully apparent. His hands moved down her back and she arched, pressing her hips against him as he reached her buttocks.

He let the kiss end and moved his face back slightly. "Why?" he asked hoarsely.

"*So sweet a kiss the golden sun gives not.*"

"Shakespeare?"

"My vice, my liquor. *Love's Labour's Lost* in this particular case."

His voice was still hoarse. "Again, why?"

"Because." She kissed him lightly. "Because you're you. Because I'm me. Because it's time."

She started to kiss him again, but he turned his head, kissing her cheekbone, and said, "I can't do this lightly. It's getting too big, starting to mean too much to me."

She found her cheek up against the scarred side of his face and kissed it, feeling the texture with her lips, a crinkled, stiffer feeling than regular skin. "Yeah." She pulled herself even closer, pressing her body, wrapping her legs around his hips, cheek against his scarred cheek. She squeezed him, trying to maximize the contact, eliminating any spaces between them. "Ahhhhhh. I've been gone for a long time, too. And no, I'm not taking this lightly at all."

He kissed her, his tongue probing deeply, and she felt her breaths coming closer together.

"I just had a physical," he said. "A complete blood workup. You won't catch anything from me." He corrected himself. "Barring pregnancy."

She nodded. "Mine was last year, but I've been celibate for the last three years. I had my cycles turned off when I was still living with Geoffrey and I didn't see any reason to go back to tampons. So, pregnancy isn't an issue."

"Celibate. Yeah. Me, too." He nodded. "Trust is the issue. I don't know why, but I trust you."

She laughed. "You *don't* know why?"

He winced. "It's my job not to trust anyone. Not to believe anyone. To question everything. But I can't make myself question this. Well, I can't stop questioning, but I can't make myself *doubt* this."

"Doubting Thomas, you are well named. I've got the same problem—a thousand reasons this is a terrible idea. But my emotions are in control here." She giggled. "And my hormones, apparently."

He nodded then, firmly, as if something had been settled. "I've never done it in the ocean."

She smiled. "I have. But unless you've prepared with a water-insoluble lubricant, it can be uncomfortable. I didn't really plan this." *But I sure* wished *it.* "I suggest we save that for another time and move ashore."

His hands moved even farther down her back and she groaned. "Your arms *are* long. Let's move ashore *now*!"

He just walked out of the water without putting her down, hands cupping her buttocks, kissing her.

They passed back into the wall's shadow near the top of the matting, and she dropped her legs to stand and had started to pull him down on top of her when she felt him jerk.

"Dammit!" he swore quietly. "There's someone up there!"

She crouched suddenly, spinning on the balls of her feet.

"Where?" *Why now?* She saw them, two figures walking briskly up the path from Playa del Mar and, worse, two figures on the other hex walking from the north, from the direction of Matagorda and Puesta del Sol. They weren't looking in her direction, so perhaps the bright moonlight and the path safety lights had saved their modesty. She grabbed Thomas's hand and together they sprinted for the deep shadow at the foot of the wall, where their clothes were piled.

She stepped on her sandals before she saw them, then pulled Thomas all the way into the corner, at the very junction between the hexes. Here, where the gap wasn't tight, a shallow pocket had been eroded in the seacrete by past storms. She stepped into it and pulled Thomas's head down to hers, to kiss him. His hand traced her breast and moved down her stomach to tease the edge of her pubic hair, and she did a little reaching of her own.

I don't care who's *up there*. But she froze as she heard two sets of footsteps on the path, and then the other. She waited, willing them to move quickly, expecting the two couples to pass each other with a word of polite greeting.

She didn't expect them to stop. From the sound, they were about thirty feet away and just audible over the surf.

"Did you find them?" The man's voice was harsh, gravelly, grating.

A surprised tenor answered. "What? We haven't seen jack. You're kidding, right? They had to pass you."

"Christ on a stick!" the gravelly voice answered. "They must've doubled back on you while you were reporting in."

"No, they didn't! Thomas and the girl were moving south on that path, and I radioed while I kept them under direct observation. We waited for them to get well ahead before we followed. There isn't anyplace else for them to have gone."

Thomas twisted in the nook and held a hand to one ear. Patricia freed a hand and did the same. It helped a little, especially with the gravelly voice whose overtones blended easily with the surf.

"They could've met a boat on the lagoon. Or maybe gone into one of those inner-rim farmhouses."

"Isn't our boat over there? They would've seen something."

There was an electronic beep and the gravelly voice said, "Sea Eye, this is Top Dog—you see any boats stop on the seawall? Well, keep your eyes open. The target may have crossed over to the lagoon side. You see anything, let us know. Right. Out."

The tenor spoke again. "Damn, I wish we'd brought an IRIAD. They could've been hiding in the soybeans."

Gravel voice said, "We didn't know we'd be out here in the dark. When he left the hotel, he was dressed for the city. If we'd known he was coming out here, we could've put an entire squad in those fields and had a quick, clean kill."

Patricia felt Thomas tense beside her, his hand, which moments before had been doing wonderfully erotic things to her inner thigh, was now touching her mouth, cautioning silence.

Gravel voice continued after a moment. "All right, here's what we're going to do. Randy runs back to the bar, keeping his eyes open, then works slowly back. Pete runs back to the resort and does the same. We'll be working slowly out. If either of you acquires the target, give a squawk, but don't try for the kill unless you've got them clean, without witnesses. The idea is for them to vanish, not to cause more headlines. Understand?"

"Aye, aye, Chief."

"Sure thing."

"Then go."

Two sets of running footsteps faded into the distance.

Gravel voice said, "I picked them for their young eyes, dammit. How did Becket slip past us?"

The tenor answered. "Maybe he didn't. Maybe they're in one of those farmhouses. Maybe they went skinny-dipping."

"The old man said keep it small and tight, but *damn* I wish we had more men."

"Yeah. Well, we may have to abort and try again later."

"The old man is going to rip me a new one."

"We better get going. If we don't spot them, do you want us to go back to the drop-off?"

"No. Wait at the bar. If they're visiting someone, they'll probably be returning before long. They weren't carrying overnight bags, right?"

No, but that would've been nice. Patricia pictured a hotel bed with clean sheets and lots of pillows. An anonymous hotel room far away, just herself and Thomas. She tilted her forehead down against Thomas's chest and put her arms around his waist. Her desire was tapering off, replaced by a stomach-churning mix of anger and fear.

Above them, the tenor said, "Right." His footsteps moved back up the path to the north.

Patricia waited for the last man to move on. She wished she'd grabbed their clothes, but it hadn't seemed important. Now, even in the dark shadow, Thomas's black slacks lying atop his white shirt seemed painfully visible, a dark square on a white blotch.

She heard a scraping sound of shoe leather on concrete, then the jingle of coins in a pocket, then the sound of a clicking lighter. She shuddered. *A smoker. Yuck. No wonder his voice sounds like that.* She savored the taste of Thomas's mouth, still present on her tongue. Definitely *not* a smoker.

Thomas put his mouth to her ear. "His night vision will be shot for a moment. I'm getting our clothing before they spot it."

No! Don't move away from me. But she nodded while his lips still touched her and he could feel it. *Live first. Love later.*

Thomas walked out smoothly and picked up her garments, placed them on his clothes pile, then started back.

A coin dropped, perhaps from his pants pocket, perhaps from her skirt pocket, and rattled across the concrete, then danced around on its rim before coming to a stop. Thomas didn't hesitate, stepping quickly back into the nook.

Surely he wouldn't hear that over the surf?

A cigarette fell over the edge of the wall, trailing sparks when it bounced. They heard the electronic beep again and the sibilance of a whisper, but couldn't make out the words. Then a mechanical *snick-clunk* that Patricia associated with movie guns.

Thomas put his mouth to her ear again. "I'm going to run that way and draw him off. When he follows me, you run for the lagoon and try to find a residence."

She shook her head fiercely and pulled his head down so she could whisper in his ear. "Too risky. We'll both run for the point, instead, in the deep shadow."

He started to shake his head, but she said, "Listen! You're going to say it traps us, but we can go under the seawall. I've done it before. We need to do it now, though, before the rest of the goons get here!"

He stooped suddenly and grabbed his boxer shorts and fished his wallet out of his pants. She grabbed her underwear, tank top, and a handful of change from her skirt pocket.

"How do we get under the wall?" he whispered.

"Follow me." She took two steps out from the wall, turned, and threw the coins as hard as she could, over the wall, north, away from the man above. They both heard them hit the path with a clinking sound. Patricia turned and ran, as silently as she could, her panties and shirt wadded into one hand. She couldn't hear Thomas and turned her head, worried, but he was a few yards behind her, keeping pace, silently.

Go find my change, you asshole.

Chips of concrete flew off the wall over their head, stinging Patricia's shoulders and from behind came a sound like sustained coughing. They reached the water's edge where it met the hex's vertex and she ducked around the corner, into almost glaring moonlight.

"What now?" Thomas asked, looking back around the corner.

Patricia was pulling on her panties and tank top. "We swim out, hold our breath, and dive under the plate. The current's with us. It'll carry us under the wall."

Thomas frowned. "I don't think I can swim five hundred feet underwater while I hold my breath." He was pulling on his boxer shorts as he spoke and tucking the wallet into the waistband.

"I'd be very impressed if you could, but it's hollow under there, remember? It's the trapped air that supports the hexes. You don't even have to make it the sixty feet to the hex. There's pockets of air where the beach plates join the hexes."

The water around them exploded and Patricia could see a muzzle flash from the far hex, one of the other goons responding to gravel voice's radio call. She flinched back, dropping flat into the foam at the foot of the wall. Thomas copied her. The next burst struck the wall over their heads. "Shit! Hold your breath and let the undertow carry you out! We'll surface to take a breath over the plate's edge."

She kicked off the wall, knowing it was the surest way to get him moving. It hadn't escaped her attention that he'd placed himself between her and the gunfire.

Dammit, Thomas, if you get yourself killed right when I've found you— She hyperventilated briefly, then ducked under, kicking to stay on the bottom. One wave briefly kicked her back inshore and then the undertow took her, pulling her down the plate. She started kicking with it, a submerged broadstroke, concentrating on efficiency, making every molecule of oxygen in her lungs buy the best possible distance. She felt an eddy against her side, unnatural, and edged that way, then felt more.

It was Thomas, swimming hard. She brushed his hand, to make sure he knew she was with him, then kept going.

She felt him arch for the surface before she'd run out of air and followed him, turning carefully to push just her face above the water. Thomas broke water more forcibly and bullets splashed the water around them.

She flinched back under, her lungs half full, and felt for Thomas. *Did they hit him?* She met his hand questing for her. She waited, holding his hand, until he had to move up again. This time they surfaced in a trough, faces only. They floated like this, taking deep breaths, heads touching.

"Are we near the edge of the plate?" Thomas asked.

"Almost there. We can make it from here."

"If we wait much longer, they'll be at the point and can shoot down at us."

She said, "Deep breath. Don't kick your feet above the waterline."

A bullet hit the water beside her head and she lifted her arms from waist level, pushing herself under, letting herself sink a bit before she turned and dove down.

9

Becket: *Pasaje oscuro*

Another bullet hit the water short of them, but the angle was so shallow that it ricocheted, tumbling back up into the air with a buzzing sound, and passing close enough overhead that Thomas could feel the wind of it against his face. He took a last deep breath and pushed himself under with his arms, then tucked and dove.

He had to clear his ears twice on the way down, then intercepted the plate below with his hand, scraping it on an outcropping of mussels. *No beach matting here.*

He followed the current, keeping off the seacrete itself, and when the current suddenly shifted, pulling him down, he let it take him, under the edge and into pitch dark only occasionally broken by specks of phosphorescent green, as he wondered where Patricia was.

Trust her. She's better at this than you.

He let himself rise up, occasionally touching the beach plate overhead. He could feel it vibrate as the surf broke upon it above. His lungs were begging for air and, in the dark, he could see red spots swimming before his eyes.

I'm not going to make it, he thought, and then his hand broke into air and he kicked up, desperate to inhale, but the clearance was less than six inches and he slammed into the concrete above with his head, hard enough that he sensed unconsciousness threatening. He fought it off and rose again, more cautiously this time, sticking his face up above the water and taking whooping deep breaths. The water dropped momentarily, then rose all the way to the ceiling, and he kicked hard, finding the air interface farther in. He took another breath and waited to see if the water would obliterate the air space again, but though the water rose, it didn't rise all the way to the ceiling.

Now that he wasn't in danger of drowning, the bump on his head reclaimed his attention. "Ow, ow, ow, ow!" He touched his forehead and it stung, the skin clearly broken.

Out of the darkness came laughter and he felt overwhelming relief, strong enough to bring tears to his eyes. *God, I thought I'd lost you.* He swallowed before saying, "You have a very *different* way of showing sympathy, Patricia."

He turned toward her voice and saw her move toward him, a splotch of dark outlined in swirling phosphorescence. He reached out and met her hand.

"Must've hurt." She giggled again. "Come on, the overhead opens up the closer we get to the hex."

He thought about the slope of the beach plates. *Makes sense.* He stayed close enough to her to feel the eddies of her strokes and occasionally her legs brushed his arms, reassuring him. He wasn't sure of his direction, but when he checked overhead, the ceiling was steadily rising and soon was out of reach.

Ahead he heard Patricia say, "Ah," and he stopped swimming forward, treading water instead. Thomas cautiously approached and found her waiting beside a vertical wall.

"No handholds, I take it?"

"You said you could tread water."

He couldn't help laughing. "God, you sure know how to show a guy a good time!"

She started to laugh, then went into a fit of coughing. "Dammit, you made me blow water up my nose."

He caught a glimpse of light overhead, a thin crack of moonlit sky, and he said, "I thought this air was trapped under here, to float the plates."

"No. The plates hang off the seawall, but it's not airtight. That's why the water is rising and falling in here. If it had been day, you would've seen where the water sometimes shoots up between the cracks."

Thomas put an arm around her waist, treading water with his other arm and his feet. For a brief moment she let herself mold to him, her hips pressing his, but then they started to sink, and she pushed off slightly to keep treading water.

"Their timing was really awful," Patricia said.

Thomas groaned. "I was so mad, if I'd been armed I would've done something really stupid."

"*Todas las cosas tienen su tiempo,*" Patricia said.

Thomas half-laughed, half-growled. "As long as that time is soon!"

She touched him, tracing her finger down his stomach and across the front of his boxer shorts, then kicked away when he reached for her. "Soon. Right now we need our energy for something else."

"I'm listening." *I'm aching.*

"This wall goes down about thirty feet. Fortunately, you only have to come up about fifteen feet on the other side before you hit the air/water interface. It wouldn't be a big deal with fins on, but—"

"How thick is the wall?"

"About four feet at the bottom. It gets thicker as it rises, but it's mostly straight up."

"Why don't we just work our way south under the plates?"

"The current's wrong. When we hit the hexes that support the Playa del Mar sand beach, we'd still have to duck under. We can't swim back out to the edge of the beach plates. The current is too strong. Going under the seawall, the current works with us."

Thomas nodded in the darkness. "Got it."

"Be sure to keep a hand on the wall going down. It's very

easy to become disoriented in the dark. When you reach the bottom edge, you'll feel the current."

Thomas let his hand stray to her shoulder. "I feel every foot of that mile of water below us. It shouldn't feel any different than swimming in eight feet of water, but it does."

"We'll go together. You won't have to worry about cracking your head on the other side. The ceiling should be over twenty feet high."

"Very funny."

"Kiss for luck!" She found his face with her hands and kissed him long and hard, depending on his efforts to keep their heads above water. "Now," she said, breaking off. "Deep breaths—four should do it."

He listened, timing his breaths with hers, then ducked when she did, lifting his legs above the water to drive down, kicking and pulling with his arms. The first twelve feet were the hardest, but then the volume of air in his lungs compressed enough that his buoyancy went negative, and he worried less about making it down to thirty feet than stopping once he got there. He concentrated on keeping his ears clear, to avoid stopping.

He could feel the eddies from Patricia's strokes beside him, reassuring, a connection of pressure waves, no less real than reflected photons.

The current was even stronger than he remembered, perhaps because they were well below the beach plates and any conflicting eddies. He didn't so much turn to go under the wall as he was swept, pulled below the edge, scraping his leg on the concrete. He began kicking upward almost immediately, desperate for air.

He broke water before he expected it, relieved, then terrified. When he tried to take his first breath of air, it wouldn't go in, as if his lungs were paralyzed. Desperately, he tried again, and his throat, seemingly stuck closed, opened just enough and the air rushed in. After that, it was easy, deep breaths.

He heard Patricia break water, and he listened for her breaths. They came, like his, after an odd pause, a wheezing intake followed by more normal breaths that echoed oddly in the space above them. He spotted the glow from her watch face, distorted by water, moving with her hands as she tread water.

"Roll call," he gasped.

"Present and accounted for." She hardly sounded breathless at all.

They moved together through the phosphorescence. "This is a lot of work, you know," he said.

"Well, I think it beats playing catch-the-bullet with your head."

"Uhm. Can't argue with that. What's with that first breath? I nearly couldn't take it when I surfaced."

She put a hand on his shoulder. "I suppose I should've warned you. We've got half an atmosphere pressure differential going here. When you first surfaced, the volume in your lungs was substantially reduced from what it had been on the surface, almost pulling a vacuum, and your throat was squeezed shut by external pressure. Takes a bit of effort to get it open. Much deeper and we couldn't have."

"Oh." He shoved the resulting image firmly out of his head. "What now? I don't suppose there's a ledge under here where we can rest."

She sighed. "No. There isn't."

He groaned. "Of course there isn't. What do you suggest we do now? Beside treading water, that is."

"Well, I've been thinking about that. It won't be any big deal to swim across this hex, then duck under to the other. It's only fifteen feet down and fifteen feet up, and the air pressure will be about the same. Then we swim across that one, and we're at the lagoon. But our friends up above have a—"

"—boat out there. And they might have an IRIAD aboard, even if those guys didn't bring one ashore."

"And what's an IRIAD? I wondered about that."

"Infrared Image Acquisition Device. It's a set of fat binoculars that sees body heat. Live bodies in the water show up quite well on them. They're standard INS equipment."

Her voice came back smaller. "Oh. I was afraid of that, what with their 'aye, aye, Chief' and 'squad' and 'the old man is going to rip me a new one.' "

Thomas growled in the dark. "Yeah. That's my impression, too. It'll be interesting to find out if *Sycorax* is docked down at the Abattoir." He took another deep breath, trying to maintain some buoyancy. "Whatever we're going to do, we need to do it soon. I'm getting tired."

"Okay. I think we should work our way north, under the seawall, moving from hex to hex. This will get us away from their boat and we won't have to go too far to reach the populated edges of Matagorda Subdivision—about a half mile. If you can swim that far."

"I can try. What's the alternative? Cross over and let those bastards shoot us? Or perhaps stay where we are until we're so tired we just sink?"

"We have another limit on how long we can stay in here," Patricia said. "In five hours we'll pass the no-decompression limits for this depth and when we surface, we can get the bends."

Thomas laughed. "Five hours? I'm looking at drowning long before that."

"Okay. Let me find out where we are." She clapped her hands together once, sharply, surprising Thomas. Before Thomas could ask her what she was doing, Patricia touched Thomas's arm and pulled it. "Swim *that* way. It's parallel to the closest wall and that should be the one we just went under."

Thomas had heard the difference in the echoes, but interpreting the information gained was beyond him. He started sidestroking in the direction she'd pulled and whistled a light and bouncy phrase of music before the demands of swimming made him concentrate solely on breathing.

"What's that?" Patricia asked, keeping pace beside him.

"It's the overture to *Die Fledermaus.*"

"The flying mouse? Ah. Bats. Echolocation. You should see me with a sonar set and a good pair of headphones."

"I look forward to it." *I want to see* everything *you do.*

He stopped talking then and concentrated on long, gliding strokes. It was much easier than treading water and they came up against another wall in just a few minutes.

"Oops. Wrong wall," Patricia said.

"How do you know?"

"We hit it at too great an angle. We're probably just short of the corner. We just follow along." She started swimming along the wall and sure enough, they came to a corner almost immediately.

"There. This is the wall we want. There's another hex on the other side, like this one. All right, the easy part is that it's only fifteen feet down, okay?"

"Hmph. I have a feeling that I'm not going to like this next part." He had the feeling that she was smiling, but it was just a feeling. All he could make of her visually was an area of increased phosphorescence with a dark shadow in its midst.

"It's not so bad. It's just that when you put two hex walls next to each other, the thickness at the bottom is going to be eight feet, not four. Also, you're going to be swimming across the current, down there, instead of with it. It won't hinder, but it won't help either."

"How many times do we have to do this?"

"Uh, I'd say we were more than a quarter mile from Matagorda and less than half a mile. Call it seven to ten hexes. So, seven to ten times."

"Better sooner than later." The steady swim across the hex had actually helped him. Swimming was easier than treading water, and his muscles were loosening up.

She slipped closer to him and said, "Another kiss for luck."

He pulled her closer. "I don't need the luck, but I want the kiss." He did scissors kicks to keep afloat.

Patricia broke off after a moment. "I'm supposed to feel breathless after we dive under the wall. Not before."

"Suffer. And a one, and a two, and a—." He took two quick breaths and dove.

It wasn't nearly as bad as the earlier dive. He turned over on his back as he swam under the wall, touching the concrete above to find its end. It felt as if the entire structure above was sliding through the water rather than the current pulling him sideways, but it helped him orient himself, and he swam perpendicular to the motion.

He found the other side and ascended comfortably. He had no trouble breathing in after breaking the surface.

Patricia came up beside him, actually contacting his legs as she rose, and guiding herself clear with one extended hand, which he captured as she broke the surface.

"Roll call."

"Aye, aye. Six or so more to go."

They moved back to the wall and pushed off perpendicularly. His eyes were adjusting to the extreme dark and the phosphorescence seemed to be getting stronger and he thought he could actually make out the far walls, not by where they were, but by where the faint green glow ended.

He swam sidestroke, which let him keep one ear out of the water and talk, after a fashion. "What do you love?"

Patricia sputtered and broke her stroke.

He kept swimming and talking. "When I'm investigating somebody, if I can find out what they love—what they love to do, what they love about life—then I've taken a big step toward understanding who they are and what they're likely to do."

She was even with him again. "Are you investigating me?"

"Passionately."

She laughed softly in the dark. "What do I love? Hmmm. That's hard to say."

"You don't know?"

"That's not what I said."

Oh. It's hard to say. "Okay. What do you like?"

"Coffee."

"I guess I was thinking of things other than food."

"Coffee is more than a food to me—it's a, uh, sacrament. It's the prime ritual of my life. It's proof of the existence of God."

"I've gotten involved with an addict."

She splashed water into his face. He blinked it from his eyes and continued. "So, coffee. What else?"

"I like the way the sea looks when a storm is coming. The way the storm waves slam into the breakwater and you can feel it in your whole being."

"And thunderstorms? Lightning?"

"Of course."

He accelerated, crossed in front of her, and turned over, to sidestroke on his other side. "You seem to have a thing for great forces: storms, waves, thunder, lightning . . . coffee."

"And what do *you* like, Dr. Freud?"

I like you. "Ah. Well, I like getting it right."

"It?"

"Whatever. If it's an investigation, I like finding the truth. Not what's convenient or easy or popular. If it's a report, it's the right word or sentence. If it's sewing, it's making it strong and neat. So that people don't say, 'What a good repair!' Instead they should say, 'It was torn?' "

"You sew?" Her voice through the darkness was curious without being amused.

"I keep my uniforms in one piece."

"I like getting it right, too," she said, heavily emphasizing *right*. "What else do you like?"

Thomas frowned to himself. "I like helping people. I didn't join the INS, you know. Like my father, I joined the Coast Guard. I was going to rescue people. I got my chance, too, during the Deluge. Mostly people who didn't get out soon enough, or kept going back to their drowning homes one trip too many. We'd pull people off rooftops, telephone poles, water towers, you name it. Also dogs, cats, a lot of cattle, alive *and* dead.

"Then the refugees started moving—not just the American ones—and they passed the Emergency Immigration Act. We still got to pull lots of people from the water after we combined with INS . . . but it didn't necessarily help them. Well, at least they didn't *drown*."

She was quiet for a moment and Thomas wondered if she'd taken offense at something he said. Eventually, though, she said, "Helping people. That's what I was having trouble saying. I thought it sounded pretentious. But that's what I love. I don't pull them out of the water, though. I pull them out of the Abattoir."

"*Afuera de la Boca del Infierno*?"

"Now *that* sounds pretentious. I didn't start keeping count until Dad died. Dad did it, as well, in a haphazard sort of way. Señor Santos and his family, others along the way, but I've pulled over two hundred out of the Abattoir, sponsored them for city membership, found them jobs, places to stay. It's where I put my energy after Dad died. After I kicked Geoffrey out."

You couldn't rescue your father, so—"Any failures?"

"A few, especially at the beginning. It's not easy to take someone out of that environment and expect them to trust anything—themselves or others. Especially if they were born in there."

They reached the far wall and treaded water.

"I got better at picking people who'd make it outside with a little help. And I poured funds into an existing program to teach people the skills they needed to make it outside. Ready?"

He touched her shoulder in the dark. "No kiss?"

"All right. If you *insist*!" There was no reluctance in her performance of the physical act, though.

They dove.

Safely on the surface in the next hex, Patricia asked a question. "How did you end up in CID?"

It was Thomas's turn to pause. Finally he used her words. "That's hard to say."

"Oh, ho! And not because you don't know, right?"

He cleared his throat. "Ur, right."

"But you're going to tell me, anyway, right?"

She already knows me. How did that happen? "Yes."

"Then pretend we had this long, drawn-out exchange where you're terribly reluctant but I finally persuade you and get on with it."

"You have no respect for your seniors."

She laughed. "And just how senior are you? You probably knew my age before you met me."

"Thirty-four."

"Turnabout is fair play."

He switched sides again, letting her pass him, then catching up. "I didn't hear that. Water in my ear."

She splashed at him.

"Okay, if I were a dog, I'd be six."

She chewed on that for a moment. "Forty-two. So you're a dog-year older than me. That's not that senior. Stop changing the subject."

For the first time that night, Thomas felt cold, and it didn't have anything to do with the water.

"It was when I was a lieutenant j.g. I was XO on a patrol boat in the Northeast—New York to Maine. It was a small hydrofoil, sixty feet, and we were pulling interdiction duty. The short version is that my skipper and most of the crew had a smuggling scheme going. They'd 'inspect' various vessels and come away with 'contraband' and occasionally a 'prisoner,' but they never made it back to impound or detention. Mostly there were rich Dutch refugees and Turkish tobacco. It took me a couple of months to tumble to it, and then they assumed I'd go along, take a share, keep my mouth shut.

"When I refused a share, my skipper said fine, leave it. More for the rest of them. But I was implicated anyway. It had been going on as long as I'd been assigned there and the other officers would swear I was an active participant. I should consider the example of the three monkeys."

Her voice came out of the darkness, quieter than before. "See no, hear no, speak no."

"Yeah. Especially speak no."

"What did you do?"

He found it hard to speak for a moment. "I told him I'd changed my mind—that I'd take my share, that I wanted in. Then, next shore leave, I contacted CID. I stayed aboard for another two months undercover. I supervised a routine satlink overhaul that added an extra multiplexor linked to audiovid pickups I planted in several key locations, letting CID record from afar. The courts-martial took another two months and, when I was done, there wasn't a regular unit in the service that would have me."

"Can they do that?"

"Not officially. Unofficially . . . well, it happens. It was not a good time in my life. I was unhappy with what the INS did when they *were* performing their mission and unhappy with them when they *weren't*.

"I was about to resign my commission when CID offered me a post. It was the last thing I'd wanted to do with my career, but it's mostly worked out." He had his usual vivid flash of that awful moment with Eugene, the flames exploding out of the boat, but it didn't shake him like it used to. "Huh. That's the short version. And sometimes I still get to help people."

"Victims?"

"Mostly. Sometimes it's the perpetrator. Sometimes I can turn a petty offender around before he's ruined himself or others. A private word to him or his CO."

"Where do you draw the line?"

They reached the far wall. Thomas shrugged, then realized she couldn't see that. "Where does gray become black? I won't condone abuse of prisoners. I won't condone drug trafficking. Petty customs evasion? Maybe. Minor drug use? Depends. Dereliction of duty in the path of profit? No.

Suborning others from their duty—well, I've got a personal problem with that one."

She moved to him, touching his face. "I can see that. Ready to dive?"

He kissed her. "Yes."

It was getting easier, despite some fatigue. Diving down into the dark was hard because of the unknown. Knowing what to expect made it much easier. The lingering fear was that he'd surface on the other side and Patricia wouldn't.

But she did.

They stopped talking for a while, putting more of their energy into swimming, upping the pace a little to generate warmth. They kept the kiss before each dive, though.

After three more hexes, Patricia said, "Time to change, I think. Let's go downcurrent, now, across the seawall. There'll be another hex, then the lagoon."

"Aye, aye."

"Pay the toll."

They kissed and dove. The current pulled them easily under the walls, and they ascended holding hands, then swam across the hex. There was a glow visible from down in the water.

"City lights?" Thomas asked.

"Yeah."

"What can I expect on the other side?"

"It depends on how far we've come, but we clearly haven't come as far as the subdivision itself or we'd have another hex immediately on the other side of the wall and no light. On the other hand, the light means we're nearly there 'cause the stretch between Matagorda and Playa del Mar is pretty dark. So, we've probably got a bunch of floating docks and a bunch of boats. That's good,'cause if we come up under the docks, we're shielded from our friends with the IRI—?"

"IRIAD. Good. Anything else?"

"One very important thing. Breathe out all the way up if

you don't want a lung embolism. We're going back to surface pressure."

"Breathe out, or my lungs will pop like a balloon."

"You got it. Pay the toll."

Again, the current helped them under the wall, but the ascent on the other side was longer. Thomas let a steady stream of air bubble from his nose and, despite the burning, kept his eyes open, watching the light and dark blobs above slowly resolve into the fuzzy rectangular shapes of docks and the teardrops of boat hulls.

They came up between a dock and a boat hull, and Thomas tried to make his first great intake of air quiet, but only partially succeeded. Fortunately, there was plenty of noise to cover his gasp. Somewhere nearby the amplified *thump thump thump* of salsabilly music and the sound of many feet moving vibrated through the dock itself.

The light, though dim in their nook, was blinding after their journey beneath the hexes. He was treading water and suddenly realized there was a rope hanging down before his face. He grabbed it and tentatively pulled. It held. He snaked his other arm around Patricia and pulled her close, supporting her.

He whispered in her ear. "I've been treading water so long, I forgot I didn't have to." He pulled his head far enough back that he could see her. "I'd almost forgotten what you looked like."

"*Black as the pit from pole to pole.*" She smiled and he felt the muscular tension easing out of her. She slumped against him, resting her chin on his shoulder. "Whew. That was enough exercise for one night."

"We're not out of the woods—well, the water—yet. Sounds like a party."

She turned her head and kissed the side of his neck. "Yes. This is Marina del Paraíso—the tourist marina. They party every night."

"Animals."

She laughed softly. "Do I detect a streak of the puritan, Commander?"

He shook his head. "Envy, I think. I wonder what it's like not to have to worry about being shot." He transferred one of her hands to the rope, releasing her. "If we can find some clothes, the party will make good cover."

The top of the dock was just out of reach, but he pulled himself up on the rope, then caught the edge of a fiber-reinforced plastic plank with one hand, then the other. He pulled himself up until his eyes were over the edge and blinked in the light of strings of Chinese lanterns. The band was live, playing on a pavilion floating at the end of one of the piers parallel to this one. There were at least fifty people dancing and more scattered around the edges, but the immediate dock was quiet.

He turned his head and saw the seawall almost immediately behind him. He almost ducked down again, half-expecting one of *them* to appear at the parapet, gun at the ready. *Unlikely. We're well away from where we were and even if they realized we could go under the wall, they'd be checking directly across.* He looked around at the other boats, wondering if they could borrow one. *Ah.*

He dropped back down. "Follow me."

"What?"

"Clothing." He swam down to the end of the boat and then crossed to the next pier, away from the party. On the water side, away from the dock, a thirty-foot sailboat had laundry drying on its lifelines. The boat's portholes were dark and the piece of the hatchway visible from below was closed.

Patricia, swimming beside him, said, "Think anyone's aboard?"

"I'm hoping they're at the party or out to dinner. If they're asleep, they've got to be wearing earplugs."

Thomas unclipped a pair of drawstring pants, a brightly flowered men's shirt, and a white cotton skirt with an elastic waist, bundling them carefully and holding them on top of his head to keep them dry. "You want another shirt?" he whispered.

"No."

"Take my wallet," he said. "It's in my waistband. Clip a hundred on the line."

She nodded, and he felt her fingers move across his waist until she found the wallet. "That's a bit much, don't you think?"

"We've also robbed them of choice."

"Ah." She fumbled with the wallet and removed a bill; then, holding the wallet in her teeth, she pulled herself up and used a clothespin to hang the wet bill on the lifeline.

They swam to a dark corner where a larger motor cruiser cast a shadow against the seawall and, using its stern ladder, climbed out of the water.

Thomas staggered slightly, then caught himself. "I used to know how to walk." They sought shelter in an even darker corner, a nook formed by the seawall and some sort of storage locker. He offered her the skirt.

"Just a second," she said, and pulled off the tank top.

Thomas stared, his eyes wide. He'd seen her on the beach, he'd touched her, but the light was much better here.

She smiled at his expression but didn't stop moving, folding the tank top tightly, then wringing a double handful of water out of it onto the dock. She shook it out, then put it on again. She accepted the skirt and pulled it on, frowning as the waist proved large enough to fall past her hips. She gathered excess waistline together, folded and tucked it, then slid the lump around to the back.

Meanwhile, Thomas pulled on the shirt and the drawstring pants. The pants, too, proved of substantial girth, but the drawstring drew it tight and the shirttail, worn out, hid the resulting folds.

"Bend over," Patricia said. She toweled his head dry with the hem of the skirt, and then combed his short hair with her fingers. She did the same thing to her own head.

"There." She pulled him out into the light. "Interesting. How do you do that?"

He blinked. "Do what?"

"Make everything you wear look like a uniform. I guess it's not the clothes—it must be the way you stand. The way you move. You should slump a little, perhaps, tonight."

He pretended outrage. "Hey! I can be as casual as the next person." He let his shoulders drop and his head bend forward, until he was staring at the dock planks. "I'm glad we found these clothes—it's much better than my first plan." He took her hand and tucked it into the crook of his arm, then began walking toward the party.

Patricia leaned against him. "What was that?"

"I was going to approach an occupied boat and say we'd had to jump off ours because we were interrupted by your husband returning, and would they sell us some clothing."

She punched his arm with her free arm.

"Ow! I *said* this was better."

She muttered under her breath, "Interrupted, yes. Husband, no." She rubbed his arm at the point of impact. "What now?"

They reached an empty bench halfway up the pier toward the pavilion and they sat. Thomas groaned. "This may have been a mistake. I'm not sure I'll be able to get up again." He put his arm around her shoulders and she leaned into him. "I need to get a look at these guys, preferably without them knowing it."

"Well, I'm calling 911," Patricia said. "They tried to kill me." She started to stand, but Thomas pulled her back down.

"Wait a minute." He thought furiously, torn between his fear for her safety and his need to identify their attackers.

"You want to leave those assholes at large?"

"No. But I want to catch their bosses, too. But this might work. Yeah. Let's call the NGPD."

There was a bank of pay phones near the marina office. Thomas started to dial 911, but Patricia stopped him.

"Here, use this number instead." She punched in a different series and took the handset. "Major Paine? This is Patricia Beenan. Right. No, I'm not all right. About twenty-five minutes ago four men tried to kill me. Yes, I'm serious. Deadly serious. I'm putting Commander Becket of INS Criminal Investigation Division on the line now."

Thomas accepted the handset. "Hey, Barney," he said, and had to smile as Patricia's eyes widened.

Major Paine's voice was a pleasant tenor, carefully controlled. "What's going on, Thomas? Does this have to do with that mess Assemblywoman Beenan found near Houston?"

Thomas answered, "Almost certainly. I'll explain in detail later, but twenty-five minutes ago there were four men on the seawall between Matagorda Subdivision and Playa del Mar. They're armed with automatic weapons and I'm very much afraid they're rogue INS. We last saw them on the outer edge closer to the resort than Matagorda, but Assemblywoman Beenan took us under the seawall to get away from them when they fired upon us. We also heard them radio a boat, apparently on station inside the lagoon. They may have split, but there's also the chance they're still hunting us. Can you do something about that?"

"Descriptions?"

"Sorry. We heard voices only. One of them is named Randy, and another one is named Pete. One of them sounds like he gargles with gravel and he smokes, but you'll have to look for weapons."

"Okay. Don't hang up."

"Aye, aye."

He nodded to Patricia. "That was a good thought. I didn't know Barney's mobile line."

"How do *you* know Major Paine?"

"He was my instructor in interrogation at Quantico. When I joined CID, they sent me to the FBI academy for several special seminars. I've had dealings with him here, too, in the line of business." He touched his face, the scarred side. “We were working together on this, too, since the drugs were also being sold locally outside the Abattoir.”

“Oh.” She licked her lips. “I’ve been meaning to ask you why you haven’t done anything about the scar tissue. I could have sworn that medical technology was up to it.”

Thomas felt his chest get tight. “I did. You should’ve seen me before.”

She glared at him.

“All right. It’s not something I want to talk about right n—”

“Thomas?” It was Major Paine’s voice again, on the phone.

“Yes, Barney.”

“I’ve got a chopper and two boats headed that way, and we’ve alerted our beat officers in Playa del Mar and Matagorda. Where are you right now?”

“Uh, Marina del Paraíso?” He looked at Patricia who nodded.

“Ah, the perpetual party. That explains the music in the background. Why don’t you go hang out at the dance hall, where all those lovely deterring witnesses are, and I’ll have a patrol boat meet you at the taxi landing. It may be a while,” he warned, “since our first priority is your friends with the guns. Can I count on you to stay with the assemblywoman? I’d hate to lose her—she’s one of the few city officials I can stand.”

Thomas grinned to himself. “I think I can manage that.”

“Appreciate it. I’ll be down at central when they bring you in.”

10

Beenan: *Tumulto*

Patricia watched Thomas hang up the phone. She tried to push off the wall she was leaning against but had to try twice before she was upright again. "What's next?"

Thomas took her hand, naturally, and she felt an intense pleasure from the simple contact. He said, "Barney would like us to wait at the party. He'll send a boat to pick us up."

She looked over at the noisy bandstand. "Not very private."

He shrugged. "No. That's his point, though. He wants us public so our friends with the guns won't be tempted should they locate us."

She wanted to take him into one of the shadowy nooks by the storage lockers. *I haven't felt like this since I was a teenager, awash in hormones.* Not even with Geoffrey, she realized. Not even at the beginning.

"At least there'll be food," she conceded.

Thomas grinned at the thought. "Food is good."

They bought fish tacos from a stand at the edge of the pavilion, whitefish covered in onions, tomatoes, peppers, and lime, then sat on a bench while they ate. There was a bar, but they exchanged one look and both shook their heads. Patricia looked around and took off, pulling Thomas off balance.

"What!"

She halted three booths down.

"Oh."

If I can't have sex, I can at least have coffee. "Two lattes, triple shot, please."

Thomas looked at her and laughed. "Is one of those for me?"

She frowned. "Ummm . . . I guess."

He got out his wallet and began pressing wet bills between paper napkins. "Wasn't sure. Didn't want to come between you and your religion."

"You are wise." She found herself tapping her foot to the music, but her muscles rebelled. *Another time.* "Do you dance?"

He smiled. "Not without a lifeguard."

They took the coffees around to a table where they could watch the taxi landing. Thomas tapped her shoulder and pointed toward Playa del Mar. In the distance a helicopter, searchlight glaring, was moving up the seawall from the south. The beat of its rotors was barely audible over the band.

She saw his face change, a matter of intensity, and realized, *He wants to be out there. He's just here for me.* For a moment she considered telling him to go on, she'd be all right. *And let him get shot? I'm going to be more selfish than that.*

She eyed a taxi queued up at the pier. "Maybe we should just disappear. For all they know, they killed us in the surf and the only thing that will spoil that impression is if we show up again."

He tilted his head as he looked at her.

She went on, desperately. "They know your hotel and they know my building, but I know a nice hotel where guests don't necessarily show up on the registry. The rooms are small but the beds aren't, and room service brings food in from all the local restaurants." She let her hand drop onto his leg.

He groaned. "Get thee behind me, Satan." He dropped his hand to her thigh and squeezed gently. "As someone else once said, you want to leave these assholes at large?"

"You're not the only cop in the world, you know."

He blinked and his smile was touched with pain. "Is this how it's going to be?"

She winced. "What do you mean?" *You know* exactly *what he means.*

Thomas changed his voice, pitched it higher. "Do you have to go down in that dangerous submarine? You're not the only diver in the world."

She turned her face away from him, stung by the justice of his words. "When I dive, people aren't trying to kill me."

He cleared his throat and she remembered the helicopter firing at *SubLorraine*.

"Well, not usually."

He turned her face back toward him. "I'll give you that, but we're talking about risk here. Not just risk from human hostility. And we're talking about doing one's job."

She sighed. "And getting it right."

He breathed out and some of the pain left his face. "Yes. You change me, just by being who you are, but do you want to change me that much? You might not like the result."

She buried her face in his chest. *It's hard to give your heart without guarantees.* Her voice was muffled. "It's just a *little* chain. You'll hardly notice it. Except when you try to move. Or breathe."

He laughed and lifted her face, kissing salt water away from her eyes. "*Think'st thou there is no tyranny but that of blood and chains?*" He grimaced. "I, too, 'damn near married' her. She loved the man I was, but wanted to marry someone safer. When I wouldn't change into that safer one, she found someone who *was* safe. Divorced him, though, after two years."

Curiosity drove her question. "Did she come back to you?"

He frowned. "Well, she tried." He lifted his hand to the scarred side of his face. "I wasn't the same person she'd hoped to find." He shrugged. "It wasn't all her doing. I wasn't really back to life yet and living through a thick layer of cotton wadding—well, she moved on."

"She," Patricia said vehemently, "was an idiot."

"Ah." His eyes were warm coals, warming her more than her coffee. "That's our answer, you know. You offer me so much to live for that you make me want to be careful. I hope to do the same for you."

"Oh, shut up and kiss me."

He did, and she was content with that. When he broke off for air, he said, "Oops. Looks like our ride."

A thirty-foot NGPD patrol boat rounded the corner of Matagorda and flashed its blue strobes briefly. Thomas and Patricia were waiting on the dock when it pulled up to the landing.

Major Paine was waiting for them in dispatch, a slightly built man wearing a sport shirt, khaki slacks, and loafers. He was polishing his glasses with a handkerchief while he listened to dispatch traffic with a headset. Patricia knew that he'd come to the job from the FBI, but now that she knew he'd also taught at the academy, it fit, somehow. He'd always reminded her of her dad, an ex-academic himself.

Paine pulled the headset off when he saw them. "Let's go to my office." He led them through a door, past a large briefing room, through a reception area, and finally into an office with a view of the lighted city.

"Looks like they bugged out shortly after you started under the wall. A rim resident saw a boat pick up four men on the lagoon side about fifteen minutes before you called me. They were long gone by the time my guys got there."

"Did he get a look at them, or the boat ID?"

"He said it was an ElectraJet but didn't see what year. They had their running lights off. Between the rental agencies and privately owned boats, that narrows it down to one of about eight thousand."

Thomas groaned. "Very helpful."

"They did find some misfired ammo. Apparently they

were shooting caseless, but sometimes you get a misfire and the whole thing is kicked out. The ammo type fits several of the concealable fully automatics—Skorpion, Glock, Beretta, S&W. All of them are illegal out here but cheap enough to jettison." He shrugged. "That's the trouble with violent crimes out here. If you drop a gun in the water, it's *gone*." He waved a hand. "We'll look around in the morning for more evidence. Maybe we'll get some DNA where they climbed into the boat." He looked from Thomas to Patricia. "So, what else can you tell me about this?"

Thomas looked at Patricia and she nodded. "Take it away. You know a lot more about this than I do." She leaned back and rested her head against the wall. She'd finished her coffee on the boat and either wanted another one or to go to bed. Preferably, not alone.

Thomas said, "First of all, I need this to stay secure. As I said, we're probably looking at some form of rogue INS operation and I don't want to spook them before they're identified."

Major Paine spread his hands. "Anyone who has seen one of the newscasts knows that INS personnel are possible suspects. It's not exactly a secret."

"True, but I need to make sure the other evidence we've gathered does *not* make it on to the nightly news. Not unless we choose to release it to aid the investigation."

Paine nodded. "All right. It won't go past me unless it becomes pertinent to local investigations. Then it will be distributed strictly on a need-to-know basis."

"That's good enough for me, Barney. Here's what we have so far."

There were a few surprises for Patricia. The South American connection. The DNA evidence. As the two men talked, she was fascinated by their interactions, the way each knew what the other meant before sentences had been finished. Her interactions with Paine had been more formal than this, though she'd always gotten along with him. Paine was *concentrated*—in his person, in his speech, and especially in his attention. When he looked at you, the intensity of his gaze was palpable.

When Thomas paused, Paine asked, "Is this a Nat-Al matter?"

Patricia frowned. The name ticked a synapse, but she couldn't recall it. She looked at Thomas, who was also frowning.

"God, I hope not, but it's one of the things we'll be checking. It's not always easy to know—they don't carry membership cards and the raid on their known headquarters netted blatantly phony records."

Patricia blinked. "What's Nat-Al? Sounds Arabic."

Major Paine laughed. "Boy, that would piss them off. Nat-Al is a splinter group of the National Alliance, a white supremacist movement before the Deluge. Arabs are one of the many groups they're against. Nat-Al split off after the Deluge when the refugee situation started. National Alliance was always anti-immigration, legal or illegal, but Nat-Al takes matters into its own hands."

Thomas pinched his nose. "It's an ugly fact, but you find them everywhere. On mainland police forces, in government administration, and the armed forces."

Paine added, "Especially the INS."

Patricia remembered now. Her mother had mentioned them as part of her work on the Joint Immigration Oversight Committee in one of Patricia's brief visits to Austin.

"They've been a long-term project of mine," Thomas said. "It's the main reason Rylant sent me out on this job. And speaking of Rylant—I need a scrambled line, Barney. I need to bring my people up to date on this."

"Why don't you use my aide's line? He won't be in until morning."

"Got it." He stood and waved Patricia back into her seat. "Won't take a moment." He closed the door behind him.

Major Paine looked at her. "Well, Assemblywoman, is there anything else you'd like to add?" He took off his glasses again, and began polishing them with the same handkerchief.

Is that unconscious or do you do it to make me relax? The degree of correction in the lens didn't seem that great to her. *I bet you can see me just fine.* "I'll trade you Patricia for Barney," she said, smiling slightly.

He nodded. "Anything to add, Patricia?"

"Do you think they really want to kill me, too, or was I just with Thomas at the wrong time?" She was surprised at how cool she sounded.

Paine shrugged. "I don't see why they'd want to kill you. Any evidence you had you gave to the world. Your video did what you wanted it to. The INS evidence onsite now supersedes that, so killing you doesn't change things that way. If they *do* want you dead, it's because you know something else. Perhaps even something you don't realize you know." He narrowed his eyes. "Why were you with Thomas tonight?"

She blushed. *Christ, it's like being asked about your love life by your dad.* "We were going to dinner. We had drinks at Puerta del Sol, and I was going to take him to the sushi bar at the Playa del Mar Marriott."

"How long have you known him?"

And what business is that of yours? "Are you asking as a policeman, Barney?"

He tilted his head to one side. "I don't think so. I guess I'm asking as Thomas's friend."

Are my intentions honorable? "Two days." Patricia looked at her watch and blinked. "Make that twenty-seven hours." *Oh my god.*

"Ah. And you don't find him difficult to be with?"

She shook her head. "What on earth do you mean?"

Paine made an embarrassed motion toward the right side of his face. "There are many who find his scarring . . . troubling."

"Idiots."

Paine's eyes crinkled. "For what it's worth, I have a very high opinion of him."

"Well, duh! Why do you think I—?" *Was naked with him.* She stopped. "Do you know why he won't take the time to get his face fixed?"

Paine frowned. "I thought you didn't care about his scarring."

She flipped her hand. "Of course not. But I wonder about motivations. Is he punishing himself?"

Paine glanced at the door to the reception area. "Ummm. Thomas is a driven man and at least part of it is that he won't take the time. Last time I worked with him, he had over six months of personal leave accrued. A man who won't take vacations has little patience for lengthy and painful elective medical procedures. I know he blames himself for his ensign's death. I don't know what he could've done about it. Christ, he wouldn't even be burned if he hadn't gone into the boat after the explosion."

Patricia sat up, shocked. "He went *into* the boat? I thought he was caught in the initial blast."

Paine shook his head. "No. He was clear, but immediately after the blast, Thomas jumped into the flames, grabbed Eugene, and went over the side into the water. There was fuel burning on the water, too." He licked his lips. "Eugene was already dead, though. Inhaled flame."

Patricia was beyond words, eyes wide, mouth open.

Paine reacted to her expression. "Yeah. I don't think I could've done it. They gave him the Navy Cross for Gallantry, but you won't see the ribbon on his uniform. He skipped the presentation, so they tracked him down in his office, without warning."

"You sound like you were there."

Paine nodded. "I was—Admiral Rylant invited me because I was also there when the boat went up. But you didn't catch me jumping into that inferno."

"And Admiral Rylant is—?"

"Thomas's boss."

The door opened and Thomas came back in. His face was drawn, but he'd apparently heard the last sentence. Patricia immediately blushed and Thomas looked at her, smiling slightly.

"Should *my* ears be burning?"

She looked at Major Paine. Major Paine looked at the ceiling.

Thomas shook his head and snorted a smothered chuckle. "I see. Well, the man in question has just sent me to BBINS. I've got forty-five minutes to retrieve my satphone and workstation from Patricia's apartment and get over to the airport."

Patricia stared at him and saw mingled frustration and anger that matched her own. "They could be waiting there," she said. "They followed you from your hotel to there and then followed us from there."

Thomas nodded. "So they could."

Barney coughed. "I'll send a unit; no, make that two. One to stay with the assemblywo—with Patricia—and the other to take you on to the airport."

"What about your hotel room?" Patricia asked. *Are you keeping it? Will you be back that soon?*

Thomas exhaled. "Seaman Guterson is checking us out. He'll be meeting me at the airport."

Goddammit! She clenched her hands into fists and pounded the arms of her chair, once, before forcing her expression back to calm neutrality. "Why? Why now?"

"They finished towing *Open Lotus* to BBINS. They've found two more bodies aboard. One seems to have been engine-room crew, but the other one—"

"Yeah?" Patricia asked.

"He was INS."

Patricia felt awkward in the back of the boat under the watchful gaze of three NGPD officers, but it didn't stop her from leaning against Thomas on the ride to Matagorda. It added one more weight to the load of misery that was accumulating in her chest. *Don't you guys have something better to do?*

There was a little cabin forward, but she didn't quite have the nerve to drag Thomas in there and shut the door. But she wanted to.

Both units, eight police officers in all, came up from the landing. Perito stuck his head out of his loft window over the sub pen, and there was a bad moment as officers drew their weapons.

"Whoa—he works for me!" she shouted.

The sergeant in charge said, "Calm down, boys."

Patricia called up to Perito. "It's okay. *¿Has visto algún extraño?"*

"Uh, no. No strangers. I've been a bit *ocupado.*" A giggle came from the interior of the loft and Perito turned his head slightly, before looking back at them. "Is everything okay, Patreecia?"

Toni? She took a quick glance at Thomas. *At least someone is more successful at this than me.*

Patricia turned to the sergeant and said, "How about I just tell you if I see someone who doesn't belong here?"

The sergeant, a stern Sikh, nodded. "Of course. And perhaps the rest of us can avoid terrorizing the innocent inhabitants of the building." He added this last with a glare toward the three officers who'd overreacted to Perito's appearance. "Sanders. Jamal. Check with the concierge about suspicious characters."

The two officers peeled off toward the Elephant Arms water-level entrance.

"Things are all right," she called up to Perito. "*Mañana.*" Perito pulled his head back inside and Patricia felt another stab of envy.

The group went up the exterior stairs to the school and courtyard. Patricia walked close to Thomas, but her eyes were scanning the area, half because she was afraid the kill squad was here and half because she was afraid her "protectors" would shoot one of her tenants. They reached her front door without further incident.

"Good lock," the sergeant in charge said when she opened it. "Who has the combination?"

Patricia stood aside with Thomas as three of the officers moved inside. "My housekeeper and the concierge and myself. I had some trouble with an ex-boyfriend, so we changed it and limited it to us three."

The sergeant nodded. "Any chance they could be bribed to let someone in?"

"No. Threatened, perhaps. My housekeeper has a daughter. But that's a bit extreme."

"So is murder," said the sergeant. "And that's what they've already tried, I understand."

One of the NGPD officers stuck his head out. "Nobody inside. No windows or entrances forced."

"Very good."

Thomas reached inside and grabbed his workstation case. He looked at his watch and back at Patricia.

She shook her head, close to tears, then threw her arms around his neck and kissed him, hard. She tried to memorize the feel of his lips, his body, his arms, then, as abruptly, pushed him away from her. "Go. You'll miss the flight."

His face was a study in frustration. "*Yo te llamaré por teléfono.*"

The corners of her mouth turned down. She didn't know if the officers spoke Spanish, but she didn't care. "You better!" She crossed her arms across her chest to keep from grabbing him again.

He left, walking fast. By the time he was halfway across the courtyard, he was talking into his satphone. He turned once at the top of the stairwell to wave; then the group passed out of sight.

The NGPD sergeant said something and she turned to him, face blank. "I'm sorry, what was that?"

He repeated himself slowly. "I'm going to leave two men

here. One downstairs and one up here in the courtyard. If you need to go somewhere, please tell the man here, and he'll arrange an escort. If you see something that's suspicious, let him know or call in."

She nodded slightly. "Understood. Thank you for your help." *And for not shooting any of my tenants.*

He nodded, smiled slightly. "It's our job. I'll wait until you've locked the door, if you don't mind."

"Ah. Good night."

She went inside and locked the door, clicking the manual deadbolt extra hard so they would hear it from without. She heard a hand try the knob and then the faint sound of receding footsteps.

She turned and put her back to the door, her hands going to her face. The intensity and variety of her feelings threatened to overwhelm her: delight in Thomas, grief at the separation, anger and fear at the attempted murder. *What was it Thomas had said? Living through a thick layer of cotton wadding?* There was something to be said for that.

She didn't know whether to laugh or cry.

She showered off the dried salt water, drank two glasses of water, and tried to sleep, but her dreams were disturbed as the two recent influences in her life, desire and terror, manifested themselves in disturbing combinations. She finally dropped into a deep sleep near dawn, only to have her satphone wake her.

She scrambled across the bed to grab it, hoping it was Thomas. "Huwo?"

It was Major Paine. "I'm sorry to wake you, Patricia." He didn't sound sorry. She focused on the clock. It was after ten.

"S'all right. What's going on?"

"My men found some clothing that I presume belongs to you and Thomas. We also found lots of titanium fléchettes in the outer seawall where they shot at you and, thankfully, some undamaged projectiles that hit the water and got caught in the beach matting. We'll have good ballistics on these if we ever have a weapon to match them against.

"Anyway, I'm having the clothing brought around for you to identify. They'll be there in about fifteen minutes."

Goodbye, sleep.

She dressed for Thomas, an odd gesture, since he wouldn't see her—he was 250 miles away. She dressed in something she thought he'd like, an old green cotton dress that made the most of her modest bosom, clung at the waist, and flared out to midcalf. It had been her mother's. Her father had liked the way it brought out the red in Patricia's hair, but she hadn't worn it for a long time. She put on black flats and was combing her hair when the NGPD arrived.

The clothes *were* hers and Thomas's and, after she identified them, the policewoman left them with her. She sat on the couch, still sleepy, Thomas's shirt wrapped around her shoulders like a shawl, feeling foolish and smiling. *He's got to come back for his shoes, doesn't he?*

Another call came in on the satphone and she made herself wait for the second ring before she answered it. "Hello."

"Hi ther—" Thomas's voice broke off suddenly with a jaw-cracking yawn. "Sorry. Hi, there."

She couldn't help laughing. "Did you have trouble sleeping, too?"

"Who got to sleep? I couldn't, on the plane, because I was thinking of . . . the evening, and once I got here, there was too much to do. I'm about to go to bed now."

"I hope you sleep better than I did." She sighed. "When will you be back here?"

"I don't know yet."

Will you ever be back here? "How's your investigation coming?"

He hesitated. "What Alice said."

He doesn't want to talk about it. "Curiouser and curiouser?"

"That's the one. We'll have to talk about it later—wow! That's the biggest cockroach I've ever seen!"

The way he said it was odd, contrived, and she blinked, staring at the wall, concentrating. "Um, is there much of an *insect* problem there in Houston?"

He sighed relief. "Mosquitoes, cockroaches, *all* kinds."

"I'm glad I live out here. I can't stand cockroaches. I think it's those little antennae waving around."

"Exactly."

Bugs. He thinks the phone line is tapped. His? Or have they pulled the escrow keys for my satphone? This is worse than sitting in the boat with the police! "How will you get rid of them?" she asked. *Not even alone on the phone!*

He laughed. "I'd step on them, but they make a horrid scrunching sound."

"Some big strong male you are. How are you with mice?"

"They . . . well, they *squeak*."

"You are seriously in need of professional counseling. Or sleep."

"Yes. I wish you were here."

"Cockroaches? No way." She kept her tone light but felt on the edge of tears. "Better you should come here."

His groan was deep and heartfelt, cheering her immeasurably.

"You'll be hearing from me. We'll talk after I've gotten some sack time."

"Sweet dreams."

"Hace menos de cuarenta y ocho horas que te hallé."

Patricia shook her head. "I know. Less than forty-eight hours. Interesting choice, there. *Hallar*. So you *found* me. Were you looking?"

"I guess so." He sounded surprised. *"Hasta luego."*

"*Sí*. Be careful with my heart. I might need it back someday."

She hung up before he could respond.

11

Becket: *Arenque rojo*

Thomas, Jazz, and Ensign Terkel huddled in the dark cargo space of the chandler's truck as it bumped and rattled along pier 28 of the Buffalo Bayou INS Station. For his part, Thomas was silent, nursing a large coffee in a disposable cup. He'd only been awake for thirty minutes. Terkel and Jazz were talking softly, Jazz drawing Terkel out about some esoterica of baseball.

Good job, Jazz. Terkel had started the ride strung tight as a wire, but his voice was audibly relaxed now.

The truck slowed, then jerked to a stop, and Thomas held his coffee out at arm's length to keep it from slopping onto his uniform. He heard the front doors open and muffled voices.

Thomas stood and heard Terkel and Jazz follow his example.

A chief petty officer and five seamen were waiting at the back of the truck. Thomas had his ID out and extended. "Good evening, Chief. Commander Becket, INSCID." He pronounced it like the first half of *insidious*. "Would you please take me to your CO?"

The man's eyes were wide, staring at Thomas's face without once glancing at the ID, but he snapped to attention and saluted. The others in the crew also snapped to.

He knows who I am and he's very surprised to see me. Thomas jumped down to the pavement. *Is it because you didn't expect me in this truck or is it because you thought I was dead?*

Jazz jumped down behind him and took an equipment bag from Ensign Terkel, which he gave back to the ensign as soon as he'd dropped from the truck. The two formed up behind the chief petty officer and, as Thomas turned toward the sentry at the bottom of *Sycorax*'s gangplank, nudged him forward.

Two of the larger seamen from the work crew started to move forward and Thomas said, "As you were, gentlemen! You've got a truck to unload."

The sentry was armed with an M-21 automatic rifle and holstered sidearm. He stepped squarely in front of the gangplank and said, "Halt and identify yourself!" His voice held a note of panic.

All three officers held their ID's out in front of the sentry's face.

Thomas spoke, "Commander Thomas Becket, Lieutenant Hamilton Graham, Ensign Bartholomew Terkel, Criminal Investigation Division. I presume you know the chief, here. Stand aside."

The sentry shook his head. "This vessel is a gamma-level security installation."

Thomas shook his head. "Read the ID's, Seaman. We are all cleared to that level."

"Sir, you don't have *assigned* access!"

Thomas held his hand out toward Jazz, who slapped a piece of paper into Thomas's hand. Thomas unfolded the paper and read it aloud.

> *From: Adm. J. Peterson, CinCGulfOps*
> *To: Comdr. Randall Wall, CO Sycorax*
>
> The following personnel are to have complete and unrestricted access to *Sycorax* including secured gamma-level stations. Comdr. Thomas Becket, Lt. Hamilton Graham, and En. Bartholomew Terkel, as well as any personnel designated by Commander

> Becket as long as they have gamma-level security clearance or better. You will render them any assistance they require.

Thomas held the paper out to the sentry. "This order was *acknowledged* by your CO three days ago. I'll give you two minutes to clear this with the duty officer who should've let all sentries know. After that we'll just arrest you for obstruction."

"Uh, one moment, sir." The sentry picked up the station phone and talked into it.

Thomas looked pointedly at his watch. The *Sycorax* had pulled in an hour before, unscheduled, but their radio order for supplies to BBINS stores had been reported, thanks to some groundwork by Jazz. Thomas had no doubt that they'd have been out to sea again by dawn.

The sentry put down the phone. "Sir, Lieutenant Rodgers is on his way from the bridge."

Thomas took one step up to the soldier until he was right in his face. "Did the duty officer acknowledge our clearance?" His voice was loud and harsh.

The sentry flinched. "Uh, yes, sir."

Thomas lowered his voice to almost a whisper. "Then you've got two seconds to get out of my way before I take that gun away from you and ram it down your throat."

The sentry's lips turned white, compressed, and Thomas saw anger in his eyes, but the man stepped to one side and braced to attention.

Thomas walked past him without another word and heard Terkel's, Jazz's, and the CPO's footsteps on the gangplank behind him. They paused and saluted the ship's stern as they stepped aboard, then turned for the starboard stairway to the bridge level. The aforementioned Lieutenant Rodgers met them at the foot of the stairs. "What's this about, Commander?"

"Lieutenant Rodgers, I presume?"

"Yes . . . sir." The delay was deliberate.

Thomas rolled his eyes toward heaven. "Is your CO on the bridge, Lieutenant?"

"Commander Wall is dressing. He should be on the bridge shortly."

Thomas smiled mildly. "Fine. We can wait for him there. In the meanwhile, Chief, please show Lieutenant Graham and Ensign Terkel to your fifty-caliber machine gun storage." He looked at the CPO. "If you would be so kind."

"Aye, aye, sir." The chief petty officer's face was carefully neutral, though his eyes shifted briefly to Rodgers.

Thomas preceded Lieutenant Rodgers up the stairs. The bridge hatch was dogged open and he stepped into the interior. He'd served on a Witch Class boat many years before, but the *Sycorax* had been heavily modified, the compartments behind the room knocked out to triple the size of the usual bridge. It was still crowded, though, with several instrument and control stations beyond the standard.

A seaman stood watch near the helm cycling through some sort of menu on a touch screen, but he snapped to attention—with almost parade-ground rigidity—when Thomas and the lieutenant entered. Rodgers said, "As you were, sailor."

The degree of formality wasn't typical of the INS. *Commander Wall must run a tight ship.*

Thomas moved from station to station: remote piloting for the surveillance drone, two seats for sonar, a bank of five seats for electronic intelligence, and a raised command seat with repeater screens in the center.

He turned back to Lieutenant Rodgers, who was standing at parade rest, watching Thomas, expecting him to be impressed, perhaps. "Tell me about Machinist Mate Calvin McIntyre, Lieutenant."

Rodgers blinked. "McIntyre went AWOL eight days ago, when we put in at Abbott Refugee Processing Center. He had a two-hour pass to visit the Isabel Island Base Exchange and he didn't come back. One of our men saw him get on the ferry for New Galveston."

"What sort of sailor was he?"

Rodgers shrugged. "I wasn't surprised when he ran. He . . . well, he wasn't up to the standard we maintain on this vessel. His fitness reports have not been good in the three months he was with us."

Thomas nodded encouragingly. "Interesting. Who saw him get on the ferry?"

Lieutenant Rodgers frowned. "I'm not sure, sir. The XO, Commander Puffet, handled the inquiry and apparently talked with the shoreside authorities. He would know."

"Captain on the bridge!" bellowed the seaman near the helm.

The lieutenant and the seaman braced to attention as Commander Wall stepped into the room. He was handsome in a way Thomas had never been, even before the fire. Straight nose, clear blue eyes, high forehead, and blond wavy hair just short enough to avoid violating regs. He was half a head taller than Thomas, and his uniform was starched and perfect.

"Commander Becket," he said, nodding. He didn't offer his hand but stood in an aggressive parade rest. "I understand there was a mix-up at the gangway. We don't normally read the admiral's directives to seamen. If we'd received some notice of your intent to visit . . ."

Thomas turned over his hand, palm up. "Things *do* fall between the cracks, don't they? Like your notification to GulfOps about this provisioning stop. Your last reported position was over a hundred and fifty miles southwest of here screening traffic into Fort Bend County."

The skin around Wall's eyes tightened.

"Yes, well, we were shadowing a foreign freighter just outside the EEZ. They hadn't filed for clearance to an American port, but it looked like they might be trying for Louisiana. That brought us north. They filed, though, a couple of hours ago. Before returning to our station, I decided to reprovision."

Thomas smiled, "And a good thing, too. This saves me having to chase you down at sea."

From outside the bridge came a loud muffled *crack* and Lieutenant Rodgers jumped.

Commander Wall, his eyes on Thomas, said, "Stand easy, Anthony. That's just Commander Becket's men taking a ballistic sample from one of our M-2 machine guns. How is it done, Commander? A barrel of water?"

"It's a cylinder with multiple gel packs and rupture disks. Stops the bullet nicely without deforming it." Thomas nodded toward the door. "There'll be another in just a minute. Your vessel is the last one in the region we've checked. I see you've seen the news."

Wall pointed at the electronic intelligence consoles. "Oh, yes. Our reception is quite good. Everybody's talking about the *Open Lotus* and your investigation of fleet ordnance. It's amazing what people say over unsecured airwaves."

And secured.

"Could you tell me about your pursuit of the submersible that discovered the *Open Lotus,* Commander?"

"What's to tell? She ran when we did a routine hail, taking to her submersible. If we'd been any other INS vessel, we would have lost her in moments, but she was probably not expecting our sonar suite."

"You still lost her, though."

Wall's good looks twisted for one moment and Thomas thought, *Ah, there's the real man.*

"Yes, after six hours. She must've sat on the bottom and hibernated."

"So you chased because she ran. What prompted the hail in the first place?"

Wall blinked. "Just a routine check. The operator is known to employ aliens and has been caught working in the EEZ with them in the past. We want to keep her honest."

Thomas decided to leave that one alone. "You carry a

search-and-rescue helicopter on your fantail."

"Yes."

"Its crew seems to have opened fire on the submersible in violation of the rules of engagement."

Wall drew himself up. "According to *who*?"

Thomas winced. *Whom*. "Ms. Beenan."

"And you believe her?"

Another muffled shot came from outside, and all three men turned slightly before facing back to each other.

"Everything else she's testified about has independent corroboration. In this case, there's physical evidence." *I hope. She said there was.*

Wall blinked. "I'll look into it. Perhaps they fired warning shots. It wasn't in the encounter report."

"I'd be interested in your results. Why did you take three days to report Machinist Mate McIntyre AWOL?"

Wall turned to Lieutenant Rodgers and said, "Check on that provisioning detail for me, Anthony."

"Yes, sir." Rodgers left quickly.

Wall moved toward the electronic intelligence consoles at the back of the room, away from the seaman on duty. He gestured toward one seat and took another. When Thomas had sat, he said, in a lower voice, "I'll be honest, Becket. McIntyre was a bit of a puzzle. When he was assigned to this post, he had an excellent service record, commendations, and glowing fitness reports."

I know, Thomas thought.

"In the three months he was here, something happened. I don't know if it's the extra edge I demand of my personnel or if he had some sort of problem in his shore life that started affecting his behavior, but he started going downhill fast. There were several fights. One count of drunk and disorderly on duty. His execution of his duties became increasingly sloppy." Wall paused and spread his hands. "I'm a stickler for procedure but, frankly, I knew that if I reported him AWOL on top of the other violations he's racked up since he got here, he'd be dishonorably discharged. I was hoping he'd turn up immediately, and I could handle it with a captain's mast instead of turning it over to the JAG."

Thomas nodded. "Ah. And when he didn't show up, you went ahead and reported it."

"I did."

"I'll need to talk to the sailor who saw McIntyre get on the ferry at the Refugee Center."

Wall nodded and said smoothly. "Of course. I'll have to ask Lieutenant Rodgers for the name. He handled the inquiry."

The hair on the back of Thomas's head stood on end. *And Lieutenant Rodgers said the XO handled the inquiry.* Thomas realized his face was too still and coughed suddenly, covering his mouth. "Excuse me. Touch of bronchitis. I think I'll skip talking to the man for right now."

A loud stutter came from outside, much more distant, and Wall frowned and raised his eyebrows.

He'll know as soon as he has talked to his men, anyway. "That would be a ballistic sample from your helicopter machine gun. Sounds like my men are done. Thanks for your cooperation."

"The machine gun in the helicopter isn't fifty-caliber."

Thomas smiled. "Well, yes. I know. 7.62 millimeter and it has six barrels, so we needed ballistic samples from each one. Thanks for your time."

Wall stood with him and followed him to the bridge door but didn't follow him down the stairs. He met Jazz and Ensign Terkel at the gangplank. "All set, gentlemen?"

Jazz looked over his shoulder. The chief petty officer was right behind them, in earshot. "Ensign Terkel would like a word with you, Captain."

"What is it, Bart?" Thomas asked.

"If I could just show you something, sir," said Terkel, moving past Thomas and ostensibly closer to one of the deck lights.

As Thomas followed, he saw the *Sycorax*'s chief start to

move with them, but Jazz stepped in front of him, blocking him, and asking, "Perhaps you could tell me about Machinist Mate McIntyre, Chief?"

Thomas smiled and moved farther down the deck with Terkel. "Yes, Bart?"

"Sir, I checked the component-level inventory on their M-2 machine guns and the barrels match the inventory."

Thomas felt a stab of disappointment. "Oh."

"But the typeface is wrong." Terkel looked at Thomas as if this meant something.

Thomas shook thoughts of Wall out of his head and concentrated. "I'm not sure I know what you mean."

"Well, I've been crawling all over these M-2 machine guns for three days now and all the serial and part numbers stamped into these pieces use this one font. It's distinctive. The serial number on the *Sycorax*'s number-two machine gun is in a slightly different face, with a serif, and bigger. The color of the metal is slightly off, too."

"What are you saying, Bart?"

"I'm saying they probably took another barrel, welded over the existing serial number, machined it down, and stamped the old serial number there, but they didn't have the manufacturer's number dies."

I'm not terribly surprised. "Did you tell this to Jazz where any of their personnel could hear you?"

"No, sir. I wrote a note under the inventory sheet and showed it to him."

"Very good, Ensign. Let's get off this boat quick."

"Don't you want to pull that barrel for metallurgical testing?"

"Talk later. Quick, march."

Jazz, seeing them moving back to the gangplank, broke off his discussion with the chief. They followed Thomas off the ship in silence.

Seaman Guterson was waiting for them with a motorpool Humvee. He'd arrived five minutes after the chandler's truck, when the cat was out of the bag. Thomas didn't say anything until they were behind the piers on a rim road that ran around the base of the dike.

"I didn't pull the barrel because I don't want them to know we're on to them. Unfortunately, even if we prove the barrel has been changed, unless we have the barrel that *does* match our ballistics, it's extremely circumstantial. But most of all, I want them to think we're not really sure about them."

"*Them,* sir? Do you mean the entire crew—officers and men?"

"That's our initial assumption, gentlemen. With the possible exception of one Calvin McIntyre, may he rest in peace. Maybe I'm wrong. I hope so. It will make our job easier." He paused. "I asked Wall about McIntyre. He gave me a more-in-sorrow-than-in-anger story about McIntyre's fitness reports. He said he didn't report the AWOL because he hoped McIntyre would be back in time for them to handle it internally, so it wouldn't get him discharged. But there was one thing he didn't say."

Ensign Terkel was twisted around in the right front seat of the Humvee. "What's that, sir?"

"He didn't ask me why I was asking about McIntyre. We've kept a lid on this. Nobody but our unit and the old man knows our mystery corpse is McIntyre. So that means Wall knew McIntyre was aboard the *Open Lotus* when it went down. He knows we're asking because we've found his body."

"Pull the remote log, Bart."

Thomas, Jazz, Ensign Terkel, and Master Chief Bernstein were sitting in an office loaned by BBINS CID. Ensign Terkel was seated at his workstation, tied into the GulfOps administrative server.

"Yes, sir. There."

Every INS vessel over thirty feet burst-broadcast its GPS-determined coordinates along with its most recent log entries every five minutes. The coordinates were sent to determine dispatch priorities—which vessel was closest—for search-and-rescue or interdiction duties. Also, in the event of a disaster—an INS vessel sinking or under attack—response time was not limited by a request for position.

The file on Terkel's computer was ASCII, a series of paired longitude and latitude with a time/date stamp. Interspersed occasionally were log entries like, "Course change for radar bogie 325 deg. at 17.3 naut. miles." A bit later, "RPV launched for flyover of Bogie. ID US vessel Ready Wench, San Fran. CA. RPV recalled." Then, "RPV retrieved. Regular patrol resumed. 355 deg. 18 knts."

"Okay," said Thomas. "Give me a map plot of their position coordinates on the night of the twenty-seventh into the morning of the twenty-eighth."

Terkel held his hand before the screen, poised. "Animated or just the range with a course line?"

"No need to get fancy, Bart. Static with time marks."

"Aye, aye, sir." He went through a series of dialog boxes, bracketing the selected times and limiting the map to the western gulf.

The line appeared, starting from the south, about a hundred nautical miles southwest of BBINS, and moving northeast with four or five course changes to investigate radar-acquired subjects. At the assumed time of the attack on *Open Lotus*, the *Sycorax* was more than 150 nautical miles away from the wreck site.

Thomas stared at the data, frowning. His stomach rumbled. "Where's dinner?"

"Guterson should be back soon," said Jazz. "The data clears them."

Thomas shook his head. "I'm not so sure. Do the same plot for today, from fifteen hundred on. You can animate it this time."

"Aye, aye, sir."

The blip started 150 miles southwest, in good radar range of the EEZ border; the dot was vaguely hull-shaped, and it moved northeast, slowly, staying the same distance from the edge of the EEZ. At the top of the screen, the clock changed in five-minute increments every five seconds.

"Speed it up, Bart."

"Yes, sir."

Thomas watched Terkel do something to the keyboard, and the five-minute increments started coming every second. The blip stopped moving for a long time, holding station apparently, and then suddenly seemed to vanish. *No, there it is.* It was ten miles from the Houston dikes and moving through the navigation channel for BBINS. Thomas stared at the time. "Did you speed it up again? No, the time isn't different enough. Take it back slowly."

Terkel moved a pointer on a bar, and the blip moved slowly, backing out of the channel; then, between 2040 and 2035 hours it jumped three inches on the screen out to sea.

"I understand that the *Sycorax* is a technology test platform, but unless the lab boys have discovered a way to make a fifty-nine-ton vessel move one hundred and twenty-five nautical miles in less than five minutes, then someone is messing with the data."

Seaman Guterson came in with several paper bags. The sharp odors of Thai cooking permeated the room.

Jazz turned around and pulled a stack of printouts from the desk behind him. "As you said, they are an advanced technology platform. As a result, their personnel is a little advanced, too." He flipped through the pages. "Yeah. Master Chief Electronics Technician Benjamin Hughes. Bachelor's degree in electrical engineering. Double master's degree in computer science and communications technology."

Thomas nodded. "Someone like that would certainly know how to modify the data stream." He reached across the table and snagged a stick of chicken satay from where Seaman Guterson was unpacking the food. "Why isn't Hughes an officer?"

Jazz flipped pages. "Uh, he's applied for OCS three times, but it doesn't say why he didn't get it."

"Where's the peanut sauce?" Thomas asked. "He had a master's degree, yet officer candidate school turned him down three times? I'll bet he failed the psych review. We can't get that from the reviewing psychiatrist, but we might be able to find out from someone on the admissions board."

Jazz made a note.

"Okay," Thomas said. "We're sure about this room, right?"

Master Chief Bernstein nodded. "Yes, sir. Not only did we sweep for bugs, but it was a random assignment—nobody could've known it was going to be this room—they'd just cleared it for a file room, but the cabinets haven't come yet. We've had it occupied continuously since. It's clean."

Thomas nodded. "Good. I've felt nervous ever since we found out the nature of *Sycorax*'s ELINT suite."

Sycorax's electronic intelligence suite included a continuously updated set of FBI public encryption keys, the facilities for satellite-relayed taps and bugs, and enough computing power to defeat some of the lower-level encryption schemes used internationally. *Sycorax* was currently testing the suite, but its ultimate mission was gathering intelligence to support the interdiction of illegal drug and alien traffic into the country.

It had put a real damper on his phone call to Patricia.

"How many African Americans aboard *Sycorax*?"

Jazz shook his head. "None."

"How many Hispanics?"

"None."

"How many Asians?"

"None."

"And no women? The service is fifteen percent black, twenty percent Hispanic, and eight percent Asian. And nineteen percent female." Thomas shook his head. "There are probably other boats with monochrome crews, but it's suspicious. It couldn't possibly have been like that to start."

Jazz looked angry. "They probably treated them like Calvin McIntyre—made their lives a living hell, then gave them the chance to transfer out." He looked out the window. "It's been done in other units."

Personal experience, Jazz? "Well, they're not infallible. Tonight was a definite screwup. They were probably trying to avoid us—that's why they had the reported position out there, but the artifact is there, a clearly impossible blip."

Terkel was fumbling with his chopsticks, trying to break them apart, when they snapped at the wrong place. "Anybody got a fork?"

Seaman Guterson silently handed him a plastic fork.

"Thanks. If you look at the data, sir, you'll see they sent this one continuous position for as long as it took them to get inshore. Given currents and wind drift, it should've changed some, even if they were anchored. Maybe it was a malfunction. The GPS register stuck on the same position data."

Thomas frowned. "I don't think so, but you have an interesting point. It looks like it was set up so that, if the discrepancy was noted, they could cry computer glitch, either caught and fixed, or an intermittent that went away.

"I want a detailed review of the officers and crew, especially any Nat-Al associations or sympathies. Look for previous postings where they might have served together. Also, if we are, in fact, looking at an entire crew of rogue INS, I don't think it could've happened without someone in or above BuPers having put this particular crew together."

"Ugly," said Jazz. He was eating some pad Thai noodles but stopped with the chopsticks halfway to his mouth and put them back down. "Suddenly, I'm not hungry anymore. How widespread do you think this is?"

Thomas shrugged. "It would be nice if they'd concentrated all their bad eggs in one basket. Maybe somebody high up, then the rest of their active corrupt men on the ship." He sighed. "That would be nice."

Master Chief Bernstein snorted and kept eating.

Jazz poked at his noodles. "But you don't think so, do you?"

"I can hope. I think it must be pretty widespread and it may extend outside the service. We all know about Congressman Smithers."

Willie Smithers was a National Alliance candidate, elected on the Isolationist anti-immigration ticket. Thomas thought Smithers's speeches would sound familiar to audiences in 1935 Berlin. He was a very public figure, but there were many seemingly moderate Republicans whose campaigns benefited from National Alliance money.

Thomas sighed again. "But *Sycorax* was definitely near the Louisiana shore last night, when Patricia Beenan and I were attacked. So, the four rogue INS who tried to kill us were almost certainly not from the *Sycorax*."

Terkel raised a hand. "Are you sure about where they were? We've just shown we can't necessarily trust the data."

"Positive. They towed an oceangoing shrimper with engine trouble into Baton Rouge." Thomas switched to the kal pat, picking tiny shrimp from the rice.

"In three days, *Sycorax* supervises the detainee transfer at the Abattoir and stays the night. Wherever their crew drinks, whether it's the NCO club on Isabel Island or civilian joints in New Galveston, I want our men there, buying drinks and listening. Maybe even bemoaning the 'browning of America.' " He glanced at Jazz.

Jazz nodded back, his black face impassive. "Damn niggers and chinks and spics. What's going to happen to all my real estate investments if this goes on?"

Thomas smiled slightly and shook his head. "We also need to keep an eye on *Sycorax*. Do you think we dare plant a man aboard?"

Jazz made a face. "If you're right about the extent of this thing, I wouldn't give much for their life expectancy. I doubt he'd pull another AWOL, but man overboard is a real possibility."

Terkel, helping himself to some kal pat, said, "We can

monitor their radio traffic and take fixes. Maybe we should shadow them at sea."

Jazz shook his head. "*Sycorax* is the one with all the surveillance equipment. You can shadow them, but they're going to know you're there."

Seaman Guterson, straightening the containers, looked across the room and caught Thomas's eye.

Thomas shrugged. "I know, Mr. Guterson. But that's not really an option."

Jazz looked up. "What's not an option?"

Thomas looked around, gathering their attention. "It doesn't leave this room, okay?"

Bernstein swallowed a mouthful of noodles. "What doesn't leave this room?"

"Your word, gentlemen," Thomas said, glaring.

They assented.

Thomas wondered if he was betraying Patricia's confidence. He hoped not. "Patricia Beenan spent thirty-six hours with her submersible tied to the bottom of the *Sycorax* while *Sycorax* raced all over the gulf. And they never knew she was there. It's how she got back to the Strand."

Jazz's mouth dropped open. "Whoa. So if anybody could shadow the *Sycorax*, it's her."

Thomas shook his head. "Absolutely not. She's not even in the service, much less in our unit."

"Maybe she could lease us the submarine?" Terkel said.

"Why do we want to shadow them?" Jazz asked. "Don't you think they'll tread the straight and narrow for a while, after this?"

Thomas sat frozen for a moment. Finally he said, "It depends on why they did it."

Thomas got Guterson to drive him into town in the motorpool Humvee. BBINS was on the outer rim, reclaimed land built on the former Galena Park Subdivision. The Humvee left the base and drove through Clinton Park, more reclaimed land, new buildings built on the dredged debris of old structures. It always surprised him when they crossed the dike, for old Houston was down, sixty feet or so, as if in a shallow caldera, an ancient volcanic basin.

Loop 610 still existed, though it was raised well above its former altitude. Guterson got on it, heading southwest, and immediately hit bumper-to-bumper traffic, creeping around the rim road.

Ah, Houston. Even before the flood, Thomas could remember creeping around the loop. They edged past Interstate 45, which cut northwest through town but was reduced to an avenue on the outer side of the dike, a brief feeder into the reclaimed land jutting sporadically out into the brown water. Thomas saw the old Herman Barnett Stadium, its upper half sticking out of the new ground, its bottom half drowned—though now in rubble.

A mile past I-45 the traffic started moving again, and they passed the Astrodome before Guterson took the Stella Link exit. The access road dropped down into the shadow of the dike before steering them north to merge with the boulevard.

Here, if one didn't look behind, one could imagine the Deluge never happened. The cottonwood trees shaded frame houses and green lawns, recalling a different time.

But then one would pass a cross street and see new apartment towers rising hundreds of feet into the air.

They tried the mall first, the new one that straddled Highway 59 and rose eight levels into the air. There was a Houston police department volunteer auxiliary at each entrance, checking citizen ID, and the way they smiled at Thomas's INS uniform made him shudder.

"Good morning. Go right in."

Thomas didn't want to know, but he couldn't help himself. "What's with the ID check? Do you have a fugitive in the area?"

The auxiliary cop, a young man with an incipient potbelly, said, "Oh, no sir. We're paid by the mall. It keeps the riffraff out."

"Riffraff?"

"Wetbacks," said the officer. "Refugees—you know, the spics."

He looked at the man's badge: Warshofski. "And how long have your people been in America, Officer Warshofski?"

"Huh? Forever, of course."

Thomas raised his eyebrows. "Oh, I didn't realize that Warshofski was an Indian name."

"Hell, no. It's American—it's a Texan name."

Ignorance that powerful was hard to argue with. Becket left the mall without entering.

Instead, Guterson took him to a little shopping district in West University Place. The shoppers' ethnic backgrounds weren't as mixed as they'd be back on the Strand, but there were some Hispanics and blacks and Asians. A few stores lost Thomas's business by displaying signs stating Spanish Definitely Not Spoken Here. Ditto for the stores endorsing National Alliance Party candidates.

He felt more comfortable here than at the mall until he entered an antiquities store endorsing a New Tolerance Party candidate and three customers scurried out the door.

Dammit. I should've dressed in mufti.

The store owner glared at him and said, "*No hablo ingle'.*"

"*No hay problema.*" Becket said. "*Español es perfecto.*"

The man looked slightly less hostile, but only slightly. "*Quizá' una tienda diferente sería mejor pa' uste'.*"

But I like this *store.* Thomas tilted his head. The man's tendency to drop the endings of his words was very Cuban. "*¿De que parte de Cuba es usted?*"

The man's eyes widened. "*La Isla de lo' Pino'.*"

"Ahhhhh." Becket shook his head sadly. "*Inundada hace tiempo. Lo siento haber asustado a sus clientes.*" He dropped the Spanish. "I didn't mean to."

The man shrugged and smiled sheepishly. "Okay, I guess I do speak English."

Thomas smiled back. "That's a relief. I don't speak any Spanish. I'm looking for a gift *para mi amiga*."

The man cleared his throat. "For someone with no Spanish, you fake it very well."

They found the bomb, midmorning, in the engine room of the *Open Lotus*. Thomas and Jazz walked over as soon as the explosive ordnance disposal team had cleared out.

The interior of the *Open Lotus* still smelled of the sea, and a string of temporary power cable brought light to its lifeless interior.

"It was shoved here, beneath the mounting flange of the starboard diesel," Barbara Mendez explained. "The timer and detonator were in the spare-parts storage." She pointed at a locker far across the compartment.

Thomas scratched his head. "What? It wasn't attached to the plastique?"

"No. It's been smashed, too, the batteries removed. The EOD team leader said that it had been thoroughly disarmed even before the salt water got into it. We found some new cable ties cut by the main cooling pipe. If the bomb had been there, it would've opened the ship's interior to the sea and sunk it within thirty minutes."

Thomas nodded. "This is where you found McIntyre."

"Right. The door was dogged shut with pry bars from outside. There were fresh paint scrapes on the inside that seem to indicate that he'd dogged it shut from inside, but later, he must've tried to open the door again."

Thomas swallowed. "Like when the sea began pouring in."

"Right. He drowned, like those poor bastards in the hold. But first, it seems, he disabled the engines." She pointed out cracks in the engine heads and pointed at an eight-pound sledgehammer lying against the wall.

Jazz slapped his hands together. "You know, I'd wondered why they didn't sink her in deeper water. She was bound to be found here, but I suspect McIntyre threw a *sabot* in the works. I bet they intercepted her inshore and were moving her offshore to deeper water when McIntyre interfered."

Thomas looked around the room. "Hmm. But why not tow her on out? So he locked himself in here and disarmed their scuttling charge, but they locked him in from without, so what was their hurry?"

Thomas pulled himself up on the port diesel engine and looked up, examining the overhead vents. There were four large Belfor vents into the engine room, and standing on the engine, he could just reach the grillwork. He pulled the grill down, revealing a twelve-inch pipe, too small for a man to exit. But more than large enough to let the sea in when the boat sank.

He walked down the length of the diesel to the next grill.

"Ah." He eased the grill open carefully, holding his hand up to block the passage. There were two objects above, and he managed to get them out without dropping them.

"Look," he said. The first item was a standard INS hand-held VHF radio. Its power switch was on high and the selector had been pushed over to the automated SOS setting. The aerial had been extended up inside the vent. Beads of water fogged the inside of the LCD panel.

Investigator Mendez took the radio and Jazz steadied Thomas as he jumped down. Thomas landed lightly on the deck plates.

"What's that?" Jazz asked.

The second object was a bundle, about six inches across and eight long, wrapped in cloth, an engine-room rag by the looks of it. "Let's open it upstairs," Thomas said.

Jazz licked his lips and said, "Are you sure you shouldn't let EOD look at it?"

Thomas pursed his lips. "I don't think so. It's been soaking in seawater for four days and why would there be a second bomb? I think McIntyre hid it in there."

"And the radio?" Mendez said.

"Aye. That's why they had to sink her when they did.

They couldn't jam the signal all the way out into the deep gulf. The jamming would be as noticeable as the SOS. So they sank her immediately, to get the radio underwater. Even if it kept broadcasting, as little as fifteen feet of water would've blocked the signal."

They took the bundle up to the deck and over to the forensics worktable. The dry-dock walls rose high enough to block the deck from idle eyes ashore.

Thomas unwrapped it slowly. Inside, tied together by a piece of string were U.S. passports, Texas driver's licenses, and U.S. Social Security cards, more than could be conveniently counted. The driver's licenses, being laminated, were intact, but the ink on the Social Security cards had run.

"I knew we needed a document man," Thomas said. He began counting the driver's licenses, dividing them by gender into two piles. "Thirty in all." He counted the shorter pile, the women. "Twelve women. That makes eighteen men—the exact number of adults in the hold, right?"

Jazz nodded. "Right. Think they're genuine?"

Thomas peered closely at the holographic seals embedded in the plastic. "They look good, but I doubt it. I think those in the hold were illegals headed for the U.S., and they'd already bought good ID's." He carefully opened one of the passports. It was a joint passport, a young Hispanic woman with two small children. He shuddered.

"There's a chief warrant officer in the Houston field office named Patterson. He recently worked on a case involving really good faked ID."

"Let's get him over here."

12

Beenan: *Imagenes parlantes*

CONNECTED
ENTER USER ID CODE: XXXXXXX
PRESENT RIGHT EYE FOR RETINAL SCAN.
(IF YOU ARE WEARING GLASSES, PLEASE REMOVE THEM.)
WELCOME TO THE INSCID SECURE CONFERENCE SERVER MAJ. BARNEY PAINE. WOULD YOU LIKE TO INITIATE A CONFERENCE OR JOIN ONE IN PROGRESS?
CHECKING ATTENDEE LISTS FOR CURRENT SESSIONS. YOU ARE CONFIRMED FOR SESSION "FLEDERMAUS," ENCRYPTION LEVEL EPSILON. ATTENDING:
[BEEP] [VID WINDOW COMDR. THOMAS BECKET]
Hi, Barney. Thanks for setting this up.
[BEEP] [VID WINDOW MAJ. BARNEY PAINE]
No problem. No kinky stuff, though. I don't want to have to clean the console. I'll get her.
[VIDWIN BECKET]
Hi. Talk to you later, Barney.
[VIDWIN PAINE]
Hi. It's good—it's *very* good—to see you. Not as good as touching, but not bad. Is there still a problem with cockroaches?
[VIDWIN BECKET]
Not on this line, not with this level of encryption. My guys are certain. I wasn't very happy being, uh, constrained, on the phone yesterday.

[VIDWIN PAINE]
Who do you think is listening?
[VIDWIN BECKET]
Our friends on the *Sycorax*. Turns out it's a technology test bed for intercepting and decrypting communications. Its goal is to gather intelligence on drug and alien traffic, but that doesn't mean it isn't being used in other ways.
[VIDWIN PAINE]
Yuck. I have to come over here to talk to you without an audience?
[VIDWIN BECKET]
I'll try to come up with something simpler.
[VIDWIN PAINE]
So, since you aren't constrained now, what did you want to say?
[VIDWIN BECKET]
Well . . . I'm sorry I got you into that mess, with the guns.
[VIDWIN PAINE]
[VIDWIN BECKET]
Don't look at me like that!
[VIDWIN PAINE]
I guess I was hoping for something a little different.
[VIDWIN BECKET]
Well, besides being totally besotted with you, what is there to say? Surely you know how I feel. Doesn't it show?
[VIDWIN PAINE]
[VIDWIN BECKET]
Doesn't it?
[VIDWIN PAINE]
Let's just say I *suspected* it. I certainly hoped for it. I'm certainly feeling that drunken, reeling feeling, myself. And my life was really quite acceptable before. It was much easier walking across the floor when I didn't have to worry about hitting my head on the light fixtures. I had a meeting with the school staff this morning. I had to make them repeat everything.
[VIDWIN BECKET]

[VIDWIN PAINE]
Stop laughing.
[VIDWIN BECKET]
Sorry.
[VIDWIN PAINE]
When will you be back here?
[VIDWIN BECKET]
Wednesday for sure.
[VIDWIN PAINE]
Where will you stay?
[VIDWIN BECKET]
I'll be working. I'm still concerned about you. They might still try to get at me and if you're with me—
[VIDWIN PAINE]
And this is supposed to console me? My apartment building is an armed camp. There's police downstairs. There's police upstairs. It's the safest place on earth. And if that's not enough, I'll put you in *SubLorraine*, and we'll put a half a mile of water between ourselves and the rest of the world.
[VIDWIN BECKET]
We'll see. It's just that things—the investigation—has gotten a lot messier, a lot, uh, larger in scope, than previously thought. The number of bad guys is potentially greater.
[VIDWIN PAINE]
What's happened?
[VIDWIN BECKET]
I'll talk about it in person. For the time being, though, don't leave those policeman behind. I've already talked to Barney, and he's going to continue surveillance.
[VIDWIN PAINE]
How are you getting here? Can I meet your plane?
[VIDWIN BECKET]
I don't think that would be very safe for either of us. I won't leave without seeing you. Honest.
[VIDWIN PAINE]

You better not. Think of all those cute, young policeman who are following me around.
[VIDWIN BECKET]
Never happen.
[VIDWIN PAINE]
Says who?
[VIDWIN BECKET]
You prefer stronger vintages and older.
[VIDWIN PAINE]
[VIDWIN BECKET]
Right, then.
[VIDWIN PAINE]
Know-it-all.
[VIDWIN BECKET]
I have to go. We've gone from few leads to many.
[VIDWIN PAINE]
Safe hunting.
[VIDWIN BECKET]
I have to be—to come home to you.
SESSION "FLEDERMAUS" ENDS.
WOULD YOU LIKE TO INITIATE A CONFERENCE OR JOIN ONE IN PROGRESS?
DISCONNECTED

They found the bomb, midmorning.

"Hey, Pah-treeeeeees-ia."

Perito and Patricia were working on *SubLorraine,* getting it ready for the Engineering inspections. Patricia was standing on a ladder using Kevlar cloth and resin to patch the holes in the vertical stabilizer, while Perito was doing the maintenance check on all the through-hull fittings.

"What is it, Perito?" She was working the substrate up slowly, being careful to eliminate any air pockets that could collapse under pressure.

"What's this *nuevo* instrument package? Was it something you added for the Amoco job?"

The fumes from the resin were strong, and she should've had the doors open and a fan blowing. They were making her groggy. "What package?" The hydrocarbon detector had been there for years. She shook her head violently to clear it and backed down the ladder.

Perito was crouched under the submersible by the instrument bay, a recessed pocket that was at the rear of the hydrophone housing. Occasionally *SubLorraine* was hired for research tasks, and she had the bay and interface to handle specialized packages—everything from seawater chemistry sensors to a laser line scanner used to image the bottom in low-visibility conditions.

Perito had a screwdriver in his hand and was about to remove the restraining clamps to get at the strange box.

"Stop!" she said. She tried to say it as quietly as possible, but the intensity in her voice came through, and he jerked, banging his head on the hull.

"*Owwwwwww!* What did you do that for?"

She didn't answer him but crouched, frozen. *What to do, what to do?* One part of her wanted to pull Perito from the room and run, screaming. She looked closer. "Why did you think it was an instrument package—besides the fact that it's in the instrument bay?"

He started to reach up toward the bay and she intercepted his hand. "Best not to touch it, I think. It's a bit of a jury rig."

"Uh, there's a pressure transducer on the side. A Micron MP49."

She leaned over to view it and nodded. The transducer was just a small stainless-steel circular face on the exterior of the box, but Patricia recognized it. She had a box of them in a cabinet in the corner of the sub pen. They were used in every hex of New Galveston to monitor the water displacement in the float chambers. The higher the pressure, the greater the water displaced. They weren't terribly sensitive, but they could measure pressure to a quarter of a pound per square inch.

A thin-wire aerial ran down the side of the box beneath the transducer.

Unbidden, the memory of a gravelly voice came to her. *"The idea is for them to vanish, not to cause more headlines."* She shuddered. *Submarine goes down. It doesn't come up. Well, it's happened before.*

She held herself still, hoping Perito didn't smell the sudden tang of nervous sweat. "Right. I'll need to fiddle with it in a little bit, but I've got an errand for you right now."

"¿Sí?"

"Yeah. The lithium hydroxide cartridges are ready from the recyclers. I'd like you to take the boat over and get them, plus a kilo of activated charcoal."

"What about the through-hulls?" He held up the clipboard. The checkmarks only went halfway down the list.

"They close for lunch and I was hoping to start the engineering inspections this afternoon. You'll just make it, if you scramble. I'll finish the checklist."

"H'okay, *jefe*." He handed her the clipboard.

She followed him to the door. "Um, Perito, did you go out for dinner last night?"

He swallowed. "I did. I couldn't find anyone to watch the pen, but I locked it well. We were only gone for thirty minutes."

"We? Toni?"

"Claro que sí."

"Ah. Okay. See you shortly."

Perito left, nodding to the cop standing guard outside the door. She looked at the policeman for an instant, considering, but when she heard the motor on the company runabout fire up and pull away, she locked and bolted the door.

Giddy and a bit numb, she crouched before the submarine and said aloud, "How do I detonate thee? Let me count the ways. I detonate thee by the depth to which you descend, by lapse of time, by the distant caress of a digital radio signal, and by the passion of a tamper switch."

She longed to call Major Paine and the NGPD Bomb

Squad but thought, if they were watching, it would only take the arrival of more police to make them detonate it from afar, no matter how much they would prefer an ambiguous implosion beneath the waves. And she was not prepared to lose *SubLorraine*.

She licked her lips and moved, before fear froze her in place.

She used a pneumatic abrasive wheel to cut through the Kevlar composite, neatly separating the hydrophone housing from the instrument bay. Then, supporting the bay, she pulled the short bolts holding the tail of the bay to the titanium hull, and slid it backward, along the hull. She looked into the gap, at the instrument bus connector.

Thank god. They hadn't connected her instrument bus to the device. The cable pulled clear out of the now open end of the composite structure, and the entire thing lowered in her hands, the clamps still clasping the device tightly to the Kevlar enclosure. She kept it level, worried there might be a mercury tilt switch, and peered into the sawed-open end.

She swallowed. There was the gleam of a contact switch just visible between the case of the device and the top of the instrument bay. If she'd unbolted the box using the instrument restraining clamps, the switch would've popped out, closing a circuit or opening one—she didn't know which—but she was certain of the result.

When Thomas hears about this, he is going to kill me.

She set the assembly carefully down in the corner, cushioned on a pile of rags, then ran back and unbolted one of the floor panels, practically throwing it to the side, out of her way. Refracted sunlight painted flickering mosaics across the bottom of the sub and pen's ceiling.

If there was a timer, and she had to assume there was one, how much longer did she have? And how much pressure was the detonator set for? Surely greater than twenty feet—the submarine could still be in the harness; otherwise, when it went off. That could scarcely be interpreted as an unfortunate accident. Yet, if they knew about her upcoming schedule of hex inspections, they'd know she could easily do several days without ever getting below two hundred feet.

She grabbed a roll of duct tape and a two-kilo lead ballast weight used to trim the submarine when carrying extra equipment. *I would've set it at twenty-two psi, just over fifty feet.* She strapped the weight to the smooth bottom of the assembly, passing the tape several times around.

And if they set it to go off the minute it hits the water?

She envisioned a system of strings hung from the bottom of the sub and run to the door, allowing her to lower it from a distance. She looked at her watch. *And I could run out of time rigging something like that.*

She lowered the assembly slowly to the water's surface, through the gap in the floor. The lead weight touched the water first and she held her breath as liquid covered the device itself.

She let go and it dropped quickly, fluttering side to side and starting a slow spin, like an unusually stable autumn leaf dropping from a tree. She stared at it a moment, frozen, then shook her head. *Idiot!* She scrambled back until she was off the temporary floor panels, then stood and ran for the door.

I've got to open it before the pressure wave—

Her ears popped hard, and water geysered into the pen from the open floor panel, and then the floorboards were ripping up, bent and twisted, and the main sub-pen doors blew out, blasted open by air and water.

She found herself jammed into the corner near the smaller door, wet and twisted. She was having trouble seeing and realized that blood was running into her eye from a cut on her forehead. The small door flew open and a piece of the lock bounced off the floor in front of her; then the policeman who'd been guarding her door charged through, his gun drawn.

Oh, great. Shoot the bomb.
That'll learn it.

She didn't let them put her in the ambulance until they had four NGPD officers standing guard around the pen and she'd taken a quick look at *SubLorraine*. The submersible seemed fine. The pressure wave was generated far less than what it took routinely in a deep dive, and it had barely moved. She left a note for Perito to run a complete systems check.

Then, with a splitting headache, she let them put her in the ambulance—a hovercraft that did the run over to St. Joseph's in less than two minutes.

She didn't know if it was a slow day in the ER or the escort of four uniformed police officers, but she spent remarkably little time waiting. They took skull X rays and blood, peered in her eyes and ears, thumped her rudely all over her body, asked a million annoying questions, made her pee, stitched up her forehead, and finally transferred her to a private room.

She tried to nap, but just when she fell asleep, they woke her up to make sure she didn't have an epidural hematoma, or the bad dreams would return. It was almost a relief when Major Paine arrived to chew her out.

"It's all very well for you, but *you* wouldn't be the one having to tell Thomas the news. We have one instruction for police officers who find bombs. Can you guess what it is?"

Patricia was trying to look contrite. "Vacate the area and call the Bomb Squad?"

"Exactly. I don't care how expensive or irreplaceable your submarine is, *you* are not. What would they have done at the school, at your apartment building, in the assembly?"

The sob surprised her, half laugh, half cry. The tears and runny nose followed immediately.

Major Paine's face went from angry to distressed. "Hey, now. Uh, there's no need for tears—"

She held up her hand, tried to speak, but couldn't. She made a grasping gesture toward the box of tissues at the bedside table.

He plucked several from the box and handed them to her.

When she'd blown her nose and wiped her face, she said, "Sorry. It's not what you said. It's *how* you said it."

He frowned, puzzled. "Perhaps. I was a bit too—"

"No! It wasn't that. For a moment there, you were channeling my father. Word for word, almost, with the same facial expression. It took me by surprise, that's all." She blew her nose. "I'm sorry about the bomb, but *SubLorraine* is Dad's legacy. If they'd seen the Bomb Squad hovercraft pull up, I'm sure they would've blown it remotely."

"Dammit, you don't know that. If we'd been able to disarm it, we could've traced the components. Hell, even if it'd gone off, we'd have microtags to trace, but you sank those along with all the other components. What am I to do with you!"

She couldn't help smiling.

"It's not funny!"

She covered her mouth with her hands. "Sorry. You're doing it again. That was his expression. 'What am I to do with you!' Well, it's a bit like crying over spilt milk, isn't it? What about the things you *can* do, like seeing if somebody saw something? Perito was there continuously except for a thirty-minute window last night."

"We're on that." He sat down suddenly on the corner lounger and stuck his feet out. "Here." He took something from his breast pocket and flipped it through the air. It landed on the blanket between her legs.

She picked it up. It was a disposable pager—a three-by-two-inch piece of plastic barely an eighth of an inch thick.

Paine rubbed his face with both hands. "It was *my* daughter's. We just bought her a phone so she doesn't need this anymore, but the account is good for another three months. I gave Thomas the number over a secure line, so he can send you messages. It's not encrypted, but as long as he uses random phones to call you, it's secure enough."

She squeezed the dot in the corner. The surface opaqued, and an alphanumeric message appeared.

> YOUR HEART STILL SAFE IN MY KEEPING
> MINE IN GRAVE DANGER
> NO MORE BOMBS PLEASE
> T

She smiled foolishly at the words, then looked up at Major Paine. "These are waterproof, right?"

Paine nodded. "Yeah. Don't know about pressure-proof, but the battery and electronics are embedded. They're supposed to last a year, but Mildred always lost them before the battery could run down."

"When did you talk to him?"

"Right before I came here. He was not happy about the bomb. He suggested protective custody."

He must be upset. "But only suggested, right?"

Paine shrugged. "I came back with extended hospitalization, under guard. He liked that."

"How nice for *him*. When will the doctors let me out of here?"

Paine laughed, one short bark. "How long have you known Thomas?"

She glared at him. "I told you. Less than a day and a half before he went to Houston."

"He told me you wouldn't go for either of those options. So he told me to ask you to go the 'nice hotel where the guests don't necessarily show up on the registry.' "

"He wants me to disappear. On my own."

Paine nodded. "Apparently he likes that better than you being an open target."

He knows me. That was nice. *And maybe he could join me there.*

"It's a thought," she said. "It's definitely a thought."

There was a steady stream of visitors: teachers from Art of Learning, some assembly members, even Mrs. Fong with her grandson as interpreter. She thanked them for their flowers and cards and pleaded headache rather than go through the whole mess again and again. Finally she got the sympathetic staff to refuse visitors, saying she was sleeping, and to intercept the phone calls.

In late afternoon Major Paine sent her a woman police officer who arrived in the hospital room carrying a large suitcase and what looked like a tackle box.

"Dawlink, such things vee gonna do for you." She shut the door behind her and held out her hand. "I'm Officer Bowers y Romero. Call me Liz."

Liz, after hours, was one of the corps members of the New Galveston *Compañía de Noche,* a semipro theatre company. "Though it spills over into the day job. The detectives call me in all the time when someone has to go undercover and needs to change their image." She prodded Patricia from the bed and made her stand out in the middle of the room.

"Okay. The hospital gown is nice, I like the color, it shows off your legs, but the lines are *all* wrong." Liz untied the strings at the back, stepped in front of Patricia, and held out her hand.

Patricia pulled the gown off and handed it to her, standing there in panties. Her instinct was to cross her arms in front of her breasts, but she let her hands hang down by her side and raised her chin.

Liz walked slowly around her. "Mmmm. You're a tiny thing. Flat-chested, short. Yeah, we can do this, no problem."

She opened the suitcase on the bed and pulled out a large underwire bra. It wasn't empty. "Here. I use this mostly to dress small men as women, but you won't need the hip pads that go with it. You ever want bigger tits? They're overrated, but men like 'em for some reason."

She helped Patricia put it on, adjusting the straps and hooks. The falsies were some sort of gel pack, with a tendency to sag convincingly. "Here, slide your own tits up on top, and let the gel pack push up. There—cleavage. Works much better on you than guys. Hair and muscle. We can go with a low-cut dress."

She pushed Patricia in front of the mirror. "Any straight male looking at you isn't even gonna *look* at your face. Don't slump, dear."

"They're *heavy*!"

Liz turned sideways to the mirror and lifted her own largish breasts with both hands. "No heavier than the real thing, baby. You are so lucky. But you need to flaunt 'em. Back in a second." She went out the door.

Patricia turned around and around, bemused. The image in the mirror brought back memories of adolescent pain. In high school, the well-endowed Angela Bustamonte had called her "pirate's delight"—sunken chest. Well, she'd called Angela "mountain bust" in return.

Liz came back in, carrying a long Velcro strap. "Here we go. It's for broken collarbones, but you won't believe what it does for your posture."

The strap wound around Patricia's shoulders, forming a figure eight in back. Liz pulled it tight, drawing the shoulders back until Patricia thought her shoulder blades would grind together. The difference in the posture was amazing, changing her entire upper torso. She took a deep breath and watched the bra rise.

Liz inspected her, nodding. "I could've gotten you to pull your shoulders back, but unless you were aware of it every minute, you'd slump again. Better you shouldn't have any choice."

The next thing she pulled out of the suitcase was a pair of high heeled, midcalf boots. "These may be a little big. They've got lifts in them, though, and between the heels and the lifts, you'll gain three inches in height. You wear high heels much?"

Patricia rolled her eyes. "Oh, yeah. It's right up there with oral surgery—something I do as often as possible."

Liz laughed. "Well, think about your center of gravity being really low. Take your time as you step. Keep your weight on your toes and let your hips move. Nothing unnatural, just don't constrain their movement. You do that, they'll split their time between your breasts and pelvis with *maybe* a little attention paid to your legs."

The dress Liz produced from the suitcase, a simple red rayon dress with a moderate décolletage, was just a bit tight around Patricia's augmented chest.

"Perfect!" said Liz. "We'll double-date. I'll take your leavings." She opened the other case, revealing a mixture of theatrical and street makeup. "You want to make up your own face?"

"Uh. I guess. The color of this dress—it doesn't really work with my hair, does it?"

"Of course not!" Liz turned back to the suitcase and emerged with her fist upright, draped with a shoulder-length black wig. "But then, we're not going to let anybody see *your* hair."

Patricia left the hospital by the pediatric clinic entrance on the other side of the hospital from ER. Liz Bowers y Romero stayed behind, in her place, dressed in a hospital gown, a large gauze dressing on her forehead and her service automatic under the cover.

The small Band-Aid covering Patricia's own stitches was hidden under the wig's long bangs, and she carried a shopping bag with two other dresses, a stash of makeup, and her own dirty clothes. She caught glimpses of herself in the mirror, a stranger with lipstick the same shade as her dress and wearing large sunglasses.

The reflection reminded her of Toni more than herself.

She pulled cash from an ATM, wondering if they were able to trace those transactions. Then, passing a music boutique, she bought a replacement stereo for Toni, plus a replacement disc of the lost Grand Mal tape. The exact stereo was no longer available, so she went with a more expensive model. The clerk was extremely courteous and attentive. He arranged a messenger to deliver both and jumped around the end of the counter to hold the door for her when she left.

She was wondering what to do next when her bra started beeping, a faint musical chime. She pulled the pager from within, nestled deep between the gel bags.

MY NEW PAGER
32423 AT GTE DASH BEEPS DOT COM
PUBLIC TERMINALS BEST
REMEMBER OUR DEAL
KEEPING SAFE LETS US
COME BACK TO EACH OTHER
T

She spent an hour wandering around the downtown shopping district, buying another two dresses and some hosiery, an overnight bag, underwear, pajamas, and minimal toiletries. Men looked at her, but nobody seemed to be following her with the exception of one man who asked politely if he could buy her dinner and insisted on leaving his card with her.

Maybe I could give him the tits and he could take them *out to dinner.* He'd had the same kind of good looks as Geoffrey and she'd been more repelled than tempted. She dropped his card in the trash can as soon as she turned the corner.

The hotel, *Posada del Ángel,* was run by a cousin of Tío Rodolfo, and he accepted enough cash for a week and put Ms. Viola Sebastian in the computer. She made one trip out to a public phone and sent an e-mail to Thomas's pager.

GONE TO GROUND
THE ROOM IS SMALL
BUT THE BED ISNT

WHAT DO I KNOW THAT KEEPS THEM AFTER ME
P

She was back in the hotel room drying off from a shower when she got the next page.

THAT IS THE QUESTION
THINK ON IT
I AM
YOURS
T

She borrowed a line from Shakespeare and, wearing the wig, the breasts, and one of her newly bought dresses, sent a page from a public terminal before eating.

I HAVE UNCLASPD TO THEE
THE BOOK EVEN OF MY SECRET SOUL
AND CAN THINK OF NOUGHT
THE BED IS STILL NICE
(BUT TOO LARGE FOR ONE)
P

His answering page came back while she was drinking her after-meal coffee.

YOU MUST KNOW SOMETHING THAT SCARES THEM
YOUR TALK OF BEDS DISTRACTS ME
I'LL BE THERE TOMORROW
TO UNFOLD THE PASSION OF MY LOVE
T

Well, he worked it back around to Twelfth Night. She wondered if he knew the play or if he had Web-searched her phrase to get there. *And does he mean it or is it just wordplay for him?*

She went back to the room, locked the door, put on the

pajamas, and tried to sleep, but woke up bolt upright in bed, hands held out to push away the dripping dead.

She turned on the television and scanned the news channels. The bomb had made the local news.

The camera was apparently on a boat, well out from the dock, but the picture showed the blown-out doors on the sub pen and lots of yellow crime-scene tape. *SubLorraine* was visible through the door, she could see Perito talking to a uniformed policeman back in the hangar. "—Assembly Alternate Patricia Beenan is in guarded condition at St. Joseph's Hospital." The scene changed to a helicopter shot of a rusty coastal freighter held upright in a large dry dock, but Patricia didn't realize *which* freighter until the reporter's voice said, "Beenan discovered the sunken *Open Lotus* last week with over fifty dead aboard."

The dead. Well, I already remembered that part.

"Police have not commented about whether the two incidents are linked, but a source within the department indicates that this is the *second* attempt on Ms. Beenan's life in the three days."

Uh, oh. Bet that pisses Barney off.

The next bit of video put all thoughts of Major Paine and the bodies out of her head.

"U.S. Representative Katherine Beenan, mother of Assemblywoman Patricia Beenan, arrived in New Galveston this afternoon." The scene showed Patricia's mom walking through the terminal with a group of aides. She paused a moment to give a statement.

"I'm here for multiple reasons. Yes, I'm very concerned about my daughter, but I'm also here on behalf of the Joint Immigration Oversight Committee. We're very concerned with the horrible deaths aboard the *Open Lotus*. This sort of thing should not happen in U.S. waters."

A microphone jabbed forward, and a voice said, "Are you saying the INS should've taken the boat out of U.S. waters before sinking it?"

Patricia's mother rolled her eyes to the ceiling. "Why, no,

I'm not still beating my husband. If you have any proof linking the INS with this horrible crime, my committee will be glad to see it. We're not interested in a cover-up. We want to know what happened. My press secretary will notify you when we have more to say."

Although her mother was smiling politely on the screen, Patricia thought she could detect the inevitable onset of mal de mer. Still, Patricia didn't feel sorry for her.

Nobody was trying to kill *her,* after all.

She thought about all the unanswered phone messages. *Damn and damn. I'll have to go see her.*

13

Becket: *Brujas y madres*

On the way from the airport, Thomas's beeper went off.

ARE YOU HERE YET
P

At the Hyatt he used a public terminal.

I AM HERE
WITH ADORATIONS FERTILE TEARS
WITH GROANS THAT THUNDER LOVE WITH SIGHS OF FIRE
IVE MEETINGS ALL AFTERNOON BUT TONIGHT
T

They'd put Congresswoman Beenan on the concierge floor and one of her aides had to escort Thomas up. He left Terkel, Guterson, and the police escort that Major Paine had provided in the lobby. He wondered if he should've told Patricia that he was meeting with her mother. He was curious but also irritated.

Admiral Rylant had passed on the request and made it just short of an order. "If you *absolutely* don't have time to meet with her, then I'll send somebody from enforcement. But they don't know anything."

"That's not necessarily a bad thing. Congressional staffs leak like a colander."

"Well, I don't want you to tell her any details. It's more of a diplomatic mission. Let her know we're making progress."

I wish we were.

He almost refused, but curiosity finally pushed him over the edge. This was Patricia's mother, after all.

The concierge floor was richly appointed, thick carpet and gold-glazed fixtures mounted on mahogany panels. A city cop sat by the elevator and another stood outside the suite. The aide used a keycard to open the door.

Congresswoman Beenan was seated behind an imposing desk. She didn't stand. A single chair sat out in the middle of the room. It didn't match the furniture, so it must've been brought from the adjoining dining room. The drapes, but not the sheers, had been opened on the floor-to-ceiling window behind the desk, and the sunlight lit the sheers to painful intensity, silhouetting the congresswoman.

Thomas almost laughed out loud. *I wonder if this works on some people?*

The congresswoman gestured at the chair. "Please be seated, Commander."

Thomas walked over to the chair and dropped his hat on it. He was wearing his dress whites with all the ribbons. Guterson had even sneaked his Navy Cross onto the tunic, and Thomas left it. *What the hell.* He didn't sit down but continued walking, behind the desk, to the corner where the draw cords for the drape traverse were. He pulled them, closing the drapes and darkening the room.

"What do you think you're doing?" The woman sounded outraged.

He leaned over and turned on the desk light, then walked back around to the chair.

"If you want to run this briefing like an interrogation, you can always flip up the shade on that light and shine it in my eyes. That way you can intimidate me *without* exposing either of us to sniper fire." He picked up his hat and pulled the chair closer to the desk before sitting.

With the lamp on and the curtains closed, he could see her face now. The resemblance to Patricia was slight—a matter of the eyes and hair color. She didn't look as old as her fifty-eight years, but the anger on her face rendered her pleasant features ugly.

She leaned back suddenly, and her face went still, considering him.

Thomas crossed his legs and looked back, equally still. With the anger gone from her face, the resemblance was greater, and he found himself affected, wanting to relent, to be more polite, for Patricia's sake. He stilled the impulse.

"I wonder why Admiral Rylant would send someone so rude to brief me."

Thomas openly smiled. "I'm quite prepared to be polite. Or, if you prefer, I might be able to dredge up some nervous sweat and a stammer or two. What do you want? Information or subservience? I'm investigating the murder of fifty-four men, women, and children, and I was asked, not ordered, to make time for this *courtesy* briefing."

She straightened in her seat. "Fifty-four? I understood it was fifty-three. Did you find another body?"

I should've just said "mass murder." His felt his eyes narrow. "And who, pray tell, told you that figure, and when?"

She raised her chin. "Your boss. Three days ago. And who is briefing whom?"

Thomas smiled thinly. "Ah, that's the trouble with conversation. It goes in two directions. Perhaps you should've just asked for a written report. What else did he tell you . . . the better to shape my briefing?"

She sat back again and smiled slightly. "Why don't you just pretend I don't know anything and go from there."

I wish. "Very well. We have suspects but no proof. The investigation is proceeding. Progress is being maintained." He stood and placed his hat beneath one arm.

"Where are you going?"

"That concludes the briefing."

She pointed back at the chair. "Sit back down, Commander. We're not finished."

He did not sit, but turned to face her instead, in parade rest. "Do you remember the *San Luis* incident, Congresswoman?"

The woman's eyes narrowed. "Vaguely."

The *San Luis* was a small cabin cruiser with fifteen refugees aboard. It was sunk with all hands by an INS patrol boat. The three-man crew claimed they'd been fired upon, but the physical evidence did not agree.

"At the attorney general's order, INSCID briefed your committee on the ongoing investigation, complete with a detailed summary of the evidence and suspects."

She didn't say anything.

"The details were in the *Washington Post* the next day. The two suspects skipped the country after killing our most important witness."

She waved her hand as if brushing at gnats. "That was the committee, seven members and their aides. They traced the leak to Senator Nole's aide."

Thomas didn't say anything.

"Commander, I've got a right to know. I have a *need* to know. It's my job to safeguard the people's interests, to make sure the Constitution is not subverted. You can have my assurance that it won't leave this room."

Thomas shook his head. "You voted for the Emergency Immigration Act. You approved the Displaced Americans Disenfranchisement. You voted for the impeachment of Justice Libby. I'm not so sure the Constitution is safe in your hands."

She looked aside at that. "That was very early in my career." She raised her eyes back up. "But since you're so interested in my voting record, you'll also find I've voted on every attempt to end the Emergency Immigration Act and, in fact, when this election is done, I think you'll find we actually have the votes to finally do it. You'll see that my presence on this committee has kept the National Alliance from destroying what vestiges of immigration we still have."

Thomas paused. "I admit, madam, that I'll take you over Congressman Smithers, any day."

"Thanks, I think. Why don't we begin again?" She touched a button on the phone. "Meredith, could we get some coffee in here?" She looked back at Thomas. "And how do you take your coffee?"

It wasn't a big step, but it was in the right direction. He turned his hand over. "With milk," he said mildly. "If you would be so kind."

One of the aides came into the room and put a piece of paper down in front of the congresswoman while she was still talking into the intercom. She picked the paper up, then looked at Thomas. "Do you really want to find out who sunk the *Open Lotus,* Commander?"

"That's my intent, Congresswoman. That's my mission."

"No matter the cost?" She was oddly serious.

Thomas straightened to attention. "I won't kill or torture to find out, and I would prefer not to die. I won't subvert the Constitution. Anything else goes. My word on it."

She turned to the aide. "Have them send her up."

The aide left the room.

"There's a young lady downstairs who claims to have information on the involvement of the INS in the sinking of the *Open Lotus.*"

One of the congresswoman's aides had a jacket that wasn't quite too small for Thomas's shoulders. He put his uniform jacket and hat in the closet and sat in the congresswoman's seat behind the desk to hide his uniform pants and shoes.

If this mystery woman knew that the INS was involved in a mass murder, she might hesitate to discuss it before an INS officer.

Congresswoman Beenan stood in front of the desk and leaned on it.

The woman came in with an aide on one side and a New Galveston police officer behind. She was wearing a red dress, sexy with lots of cleavage, with shoulder-length shiny black hair, bright lipstick, and sunglasses. She was looking at the congresswoman, but when her head swiveled to take in Thomas, her mouth dropped open.

Thomas took one look at her face and froze, his hand going to his mouth.

Congresswoman Beenan pushed off the desk and offered the woman her hand. "I'm Katherine Beenan. I understand you have something to tell us?"

"What are you doing here?" the woman hissed, stepping past the congresswoman's offered hand as if it wasn't there.

Thomas looked her up and down and whistled. *How on earth? "Good madam, let me see your face."*

The congresswoman, annoyed, looked from Thomas to the stranger.

The woman in the red dress said, *"Have you any commission from your lord to negotiate with my face? You are now out of your text: but we will draw the curtain and show you the picture."* She took off her sunglasses. *"Look you, sir, such a one I was this present: is't not well done?"*

The congresswoman was twisting her head, staring at the brunette.

The voice reminds her, but she still doesn't get it. Aloud, Thomas said, *"Excellently done, if God did all."*

Here Patricia sighed and departed from the play. "No, in truth, God and nature had a shitload of help." She pulled the wig off and dropped it on the desk, then turned to the congresswoman.

"Hi, Mom."

Thomas hadn't expected tears—first the mother's, shocked from her, apparently; then Patricia's, in response.

Thomas waved the aide and the cop out, then sat back and drank his coffee, carefully looking away from the two women. When they pushed apart from each other, he slid the box of tissues across the desk toward them.

"Did you get your breasts done, Pea?" the congresswoman asked a few moments later.

Pea?

Patricia blew her nose. "No. They're as false as the hair. I've had more doors held for me in the last twenty-four hours than in my entire adult life, and I don't think it's the hair."

The congresswoman looked back at Thomas, and some of her rigidity returned. "Did you two set this up?"

Thomas shook his head. "Surprised the hell out of me. I had no idea she was going to be here."

Patricia was looking at Thomas, smiling. "I was surprised, too. Mom, can I borrow a T-shirt and some shorts? This rig," she gestured at her chest, "chafes me sorely."

The two women left the room. While they were gone, he put his uniform coat back on. In a few moments, Patricia's mother returned.

"She's scrubbing her face. You must've seen her in that disguise before," said the congresswoman.

Thomas shook his head. "No. Never."

Patricia came back in, barefoot, dressed in shorts and a cotton shirt. She was drying off her face with a hand towel.

Thomas stepped forward when she lowered the towel. "Ow, that had to hurt." He leaned forward, looking at the stitches.

She laughed. "It sure hurt when they put them in, that's for certain." She searched Thomas's face, her mouth parted. "I didn't really feel it when the bomb went off."

The congresswoman shook her head, unable to let it go. "Then how did you recognize her when I didn't?"

Thomas felt the small package in his jacket pocket. "Ah, well, I have an idea about that, but it's kind of personal."

"Personal?" Patricia's mother was clearly baffled. "What on earth does *personal* have to do with you recognizing her?"

He looked back at Patricia. She had a question in her eyes, her head tilted.

Thomas took the plunge. "Well, you didn't recognize her

because you only lived with her for the first part of her life, whereas I—" he took the box from his pocket "—intend to live with her for the rest of it."

He held his breath and offered the box on his fingertips, his palm flat, like one might offer sugar to a horse.

Patricia dropped the towel on the floor and he thought for a second that she was about to bolt, but she cautiously reached out and took the box, then opened it.

Christ, this has got to be the scariest thing I've ever done.

She looked up at him and there were more tears in her eyes. "Oh, Thomas, are you sure?"

"I am sure of everything but the timing and the audience. *Give me thy hand; and let me see thee in thy woman's weeds."*

Her response was physical, passionate, and deeply gratifying.

It took a moment for them to realize the congresswoman was talking to them, or at least *at* them.

"Either you carry an engagement ring around on the off chance you meet a likely bride, or I can assume you two have been introduced."

Thomas backed off from a heroic kiss and traced the line of Patricia's jaw. "We were to meet later this evening. I was going to ask her then." He touched Patricia's lips with his fingertip. "I didn't mean it, by the way, about *thy woman's weeds*. I mean, you looked great in that dress, but I like you just fine in shorts. Or jeans. Or coveralls."

"Or nothing?" she suggested, then blushed, her eyes darting sideways at her mother. "Well, I think your uniform is very nice, too."

Her mother snorted. "I think I better order up some champagne." She picked up the phone and talked briefly, then walked back to the entwined couple. "Let me see the ring."

"The ring?" said Patricia. She was still staring at Thomas, and he laughed.

"Did you even look at it?" he asked.

"Of course," she said.

"What color was the stone?"

She buried her face in his neck. "Okay, I'm a fraud. What color is the ring?"

Her mother found it the box, dropped on the floor by the towel. "Green. It's an emerald bracketed by two smaller diamonds. Looks like an antique. Very nice. A family piece?"

Thomas shook his head. "No. I found it in an antique shop in Houston. It dates to the eighteen eighties. I did go into one of those malls—" He shuddered. "Your hand, Patricia." He took the ring from its box. "I had to guess at the size." He slipped it on her left ring finger. It stuck slightly at the knuckle, then went over.

"Perfect," Patricia said. "I wouldn't want it to slip off. Oh. It *is* nice." She kissed him again.

"I think I'll go see if there are any champagne flutes," the congresswoman said. She closed the door behind her.

Oddly, this privacy seemed to constrain Patricia more than the presence of her mother. She backed off, staring at Thomas as if he were suddenly strange.

"I didn't even consider this. I've been concentrating on getting you into my bed the *first* time." She looked down. "Not for all time. This is so strange. Nobody gets married without sleeping together first—not unless they're hyper-religious."

Thomas's voiced husked. "I'm more than willing to sleep with you before we get married. You know I want you—we've just been . . . interrupted." He smiled. "My one worry is that we'll get shot at every time we try."

She shrugged off the joke, her face still serious. "You don't have to marry me to sleep with me. I want you, too."

Thomas dropped to both knees and held his arms out. "I love you. I am overthrown. I hadn't read *Twelfth Night* in years, but I've read it three times in the last twenty-four hours. I've even been reading *sonnets*, so bad do I have this plague. Christ, I've been giving my men orders in iambic pentameter!"

She sobbed, a short laugh, with tears.

He pushed on. "*Love alters not with his brief hours and weeks, but bears it out even to the edge of doom.* I'm in this for the long haul." He pointed at the scarred side of his face. "The question is, can you put up with this?"

She crouched and cupped his face with her hands. "*Make me a willow cabin at your gate, And call upon my soul within the house; write loyal cantons of contemned love and sing them loud even in the dead of night.* Oh, Thomas, I do love you."

He stood again, taking her in his arms, but she pushed back, another look of panic on her face. "Where will we live? I don't even *know* where *you* live."

"I've a room at the Washington Island INS Depot BOQ and some things in my parents' attic in Victoria. I don't plan to uproot you, girl. If I use up all my accrued vacation, it will carry me into my twenty-year retirement option."

She grabbed his upper arms and searched his face. "Are you sure? Don't you want to make admiral or something?"

He shook his head. "No. I might have limped on, after this case, for want of something better. But I *have* something better. *Todas las cosas tienen su tiempo.*"

She blinked. "*After* this case."

"Well, yes. After all, even if it wasn't worth solving in and of itself, they've tried to kill us. How can we have a life together until that's stopped?"

She sighed. "You made me forget, for a moment."

The dead.

"Well, yes. You do that for me, too."

The door opened, and the congresswoman came back in, followed by a hotel room-service waiter with the champagne and glasses.

"I know I'm not exactly in the mainstream of your life, Pea, but after Geoffrey I never heard about you seeing anybody else." She waved the waiter out after he'd managed the cork. "How long have you and Commander Beck—I guess Thomas is more appropriate—known each other?"

"Four days now," Patricia said absently, eyes locked with Thomas's.

The congresswoman, pouring from the bottle, knocked one of the flutes over. "What?"

Thomas looked over at the suddenly distraught face and felt sympathy. Looking at it from the outside, it *was* insane.

"They've been a very *intense* four days," he allowed.

He picked up Terkel and Guterson and their police escort in the lobby. Terkel, after a nervous glance at Thomas's expression, said, "Are you all right, sir? Is the congresswoman making waves?"

He stared at Terkel. "No, she took it rather well. I was surprised."

In fact, she'd followed him to the door after his reluctant farewell to Patricia and whispered, "Thank you for letting me be part of this. We've been apart so long—" She'd been unable to continue, settling for squeezing his hand before letting the door close.

"Took *what* rather well? The briefing?"

"No, the engage—" He stopped himself. Terkel had no way of knowing about the engagement. Until Thomas had given Patricia the ring, even he'd been unsure whether he'd have the nerve. "There was some trouble at first, but the congresswoman and I have reached an understanding. She won't be looking over our shoulder, and she won't be interfering.

"What did my face look like, just now, that made you ask?"

Terkel shrugged. "Uh, serious. Perhaps a little, well, *sad*." He looked embarrassed to say it.

He hadn't wanted to leave Patricia; that was certain. And the depth of this commitment, this new course in his life—well, that was a bit scary. *I'm surprised he didn't say I looked* terrified. "Don't worry about it, Bart." He remembered the press of Patricia's body against his—the promise of it. "I'm better than all right."

They made the run out to the Abattoir in ten minutes, both police patrol boats planing at over forty-five knots, hooting slower craft out of their way with a burst of their sirens and flashes of light.

When they delivered Thomas to the Abbott Detention Center landing, the police escort stayed with their boats. Terkel and Guterson followed him through the layers of security into the prison.

At every checkpoint he studied the guards, the men behind the armored glass throwing switches, the distant figures standing watch atop walls. He wondered if any of them spoke with a gravelly voice. *Jazz didn't want me to come. I hope he wasn't right.* Thomas had argued, "What good would it do to take me out? Surely they must know it wouldn't stop the investigation."

Chief Dallas, Thomas's escort to Admiral Pachefski the last time he'd come, met them inside. "Your man is in hex fifteen, medium security for felonious but nonviolent offenders. We've arranged for an exercise court, as you requested, though it's not the safest way. We'll have guards up on the walls, but out of earshot. I reviewed the record—I don't see why he'll talk to you when he wouldn't talk to reduce his sentence."

Thomas shrugged. "No harm in trying."

"What does he have to do with the *Open Lotus*?"

"Perhaps nothing. But if he does, then it's not something I'm free to discuss, Chief."

"Right, sir. Just making conversation."

Still probing for the admiral?

At the entrance to the exercise court, Thomas waited while the guards coordinated the remote unlock with central control.

"Go ahead, sir," Chief Dallas said. "They'll send him in from the cellblock side."

Thomas turned to Terkel and Guterson. "You guys hang by the gate. I want to try him alone."

"Aye, aye, sir," said Guterson.

Terkel nodded.

The court was bare, gray seacrete walls and netless basketball hoops beneath a sky made brilliant blue by the drabness below. High on the walls two guards with rifles were silhouetted against the blue at opposite corners of the court. A rack with basketballs and soccer balls stood against the wall. Rectangles painted on opposite walls represented soccer goals.

A door of bars clanked open on the other side, and a single figure walked into the court dressed in bright orange prison shorts, shirts, and sandals.

Thomas pulled out the copies he'd made of the passports and driver's licenses and left the briefcase with Terkel. Patterson of the Houston Field Office had confirmed the driver's licenses were like those Armando had been convicted of selling. They would pass a cursory computer check and the embedded anticounterfeiting measures were all in place indicating stolen legitimate stock.

He walked slowly across the court, trying to look as nonthreatening as possible. He'd deliberately left his dress uniform on, the better to differentiate himself from the detention center personnel.

"Hola, Armando. ¿Cómo estas?"

The figure froze and said, "I'm okay."

Thomas kept his face still. They'd done a good job. The man looked like Armando, but the Armando from the records—his booking photograph, not the Armando he'd seen delivered here just four days before.

He wondered if it was a mistake or deliberate. Perhaps even the prisoners had switched places on their own, or the guards pulled the wrong prisoner because of the resemblance. There were sixty thousand prisoners in the detention center, over seventy percent male.

"What happened to Armando?" he asked quietly.

"What do you mean?" The man asked. He was sweating.

"Surely they told you Armando doesn't speak English."

The man's eyes widened. "I learn."

"Or that I was personally acquainted with him?"

The man's hand was wiping his right palm on his shirt as if to dry it. "Ah. *No me dijeron eso.*" Even the accent was wrong—Mexican Spanish, not South American like Armando Ortega's.

The man was trying to be casual, but his entire body seemed tense. He turned the wiping motion into scratching, moving over to his ribs. He leaned closer, "It's like this, señor." His scratching hand moved around his side, to his back.

Thomas didn't see it coming, but he *sensed* it. The man's entire body was tense to an unbearable degree, a man desperately determined and/or afraid. It was a powerful thrust, upward, toward Thomas's heart, and he was turning his hips as it came in, blocking with the back of his hand, keeping the arteries, tendons, and nerves of his arm away from the blade. He felt it rip through his uniform tunic and score his skin, but by that time his body was out of the way and the knife was tangled in the uniform. He brought his arm down on top of the knife arm and rotated his entire body, twisting the arm and wrist up in front of his face, locking the elbow and forcing his attacker's torso down.

The man started to resist, and Thomas twisted his hip back into him. The man screamed, and Thomas felt something "pop" in the vicinity of the man's elbow. The knife dropped to the court with a metallic clatter. He shoved the man away from him, intending to pick up the knife, when a bullet scattered concrete chips where his attacker had just been.

"Hold your fire!" he yelled. He scooped up the knife. One of the guards on the wall had his rifle leveled at the prisoner. Thomas stepped into the line of fire.

Terkel and Guterson were running across the court toward him.

Thomas swiveled his head at the other guard. *"Stand*

down! If either of you fires another shot, I'll arrest you!" To Terkel and Guterson, he said, "Shield the prisoner. I don't want him *conveniently* silenced."

Chief Dallas came through the door, two armed guards with him. "Are you all right, Commander?"

"Stay back, Chief! All of you!" Thomas pointed at the guards. "Stop right there."

"You're bleeding, Commander!" said Chief Dallas.

Thomas looked down. His dress whites had a spectacular red stain spreading across them. "I'm obliged to you. You can have one of the prison doctors join us inside, but first of all I want to talk to Admiral Pachefski. Immediately!"

Thomas made them clear the corridor before he and Terkel helped the prisoner out of the court. They took over the hex guardroom, evicting the two guards on break and posting Guterson outside.

The knife was a prison special, some unidentified scrap of carbon steel shaped and sharpened on concrete with a handle of wrapped cloth and tape. Thomas tried it on a piece of paper and shuddered as the edge sliced through the paper as easily as an X-Acto knife.

"So, since we know who your aren't—who *are* you?"

"El muerto andando," the man said. He cradled his arm, hunched over it, and rocked back and forth. His skin was white around his lips. "*Ay, mi pobre hija.*"

"Why are you the walking dead? And what about your daughter?"

The man shook his head.

"What did they say they'd do to her?"

"I've failed so they *will* do it."

Thomas crouched before the man, trying to catch his eyes. "If they're going to do it anyway, why not tell me? Perhaps I can stop it."

For a moment he saw hope struggle with despair and pain. "No. These men are unstoppable. They are untouchable."

"Is she a prisoner here?"

"She should not be, but she is."

Thomas winced. He was pressing a handkerchief to the slice over his stomach and the position was awkward. "Why shouldn't she be here?"

"They took her from the camp last night and showed her to me through a *espejo,* a two-way mirror. She didn't commit any crime. The *pendejos* brought her to make me do this."

Thomas felt sick. He'd requested the prisoner interview yesterday at noon. Whoever it was moved quickly.

"What did they say they would do?"

"*Violación. En cada orificio. Despues, muerte.*"

Terkel raised his eyebrows—his Spanish was rudimentary. Thomas stood and stepped over to him. Quietly he translated, "Rape, in every orifice; then death." He felt slightly dizzy. The wound, though superficial, had bled a great deal. He sat on a tabletop against the wall. "They wanted him to kill me; then the guards were to kill him, as a reaction. When he failed, they still tried to kill him, though it's defensible. They can say they thought he was still a danger to me, but mostly they wanted to cover their tracks."

Terkel had been present when Jazz had argued against this visit. "But why? That would bring CID down on the Abattoir like the Inquisition."

"Wouldn't it though," Thomas said thoughtfully. He crouched before the prisoner. "*¿Su nombre verdadero? ¿Y su crimen?*"

"Maximilian Vigil." He pronounced it "vee-heel." "*Mi crimen es violación de la frontera.*"

"Illegal entry into the U.S.," Thomas said for Terkel's benefit. "They picked him because he looked like the real Armando, and he had a convenient daughter they could threaten. *¿El nombre de su hija?*"

"Zaneta Vigil. She is only fifteen." He began crying silently.

The doctor and Admiral Pachefski arrived together.

The doctor looked at Thomas's bloody front and started forward. "It's a scratch, doctor. Señor Vigil here has a severely dislocated elbow."

"He won't bleed to death with a dislocated elbow. Let me see."

"Why are my personnel being kept out of this room, Commander?" asked the admiral.

"Because I believe your personnel tried to kill this prisoner before he could talk to me. By the way, do you vouch for this doctor? He *is* a doctor, isn't he?"

Pachefski narrowed his eyes. "Yes. Lieutenant Lotts is known to me. I believe he's a trauma specialist."

"That's right, Admiral," the doctor said. "Please open your tunic, Commander."

Thomas let the surgeon help him remove his tunic and shirt.

The surgeon pulled the handkerchief away from the wound. "Your definition of a scratch is a little different from mine, Commander, but you're right. This won't kill you anytime soon. Keep the pressure on. We'll have you over to the hospital in a bit, to stitch you up." He turned his attention to Vigil's elbow.

Admiral Pachefski spoke. "It's better than the last injury you received out here, but I'm beginning to think people don't like you, Commander. So, are you going to tell me what this is about, this time?"

Thomas froze. *Is he or isn't he involved?* Well, there was one way to find out.

"Yes, sir. Here's what happened and *here's* what I think is behind it."

Pachefski was being very obliging. He allowed Thomas's New Galveston Police escort access to the prison, and he let them guard Thomas and Maximilian Vigil as they crossed the detention center to the hospital.

Aliens have replaced Admiral Pachefski with a pod person.

Doctor Lotts detailed a chief health service technician to suture Thomas's cut, a seven-inch slash that went from his left lower ribs to midstomach. The technician did a subdermal row at the deepest point, a full centimeter deep where a bit of abdominal muscle had been sliced.

"No sit-ups for a while, Commander."

"Umm." He was lying on his back sipping lemon electrolyte prescribed for blood loss.

The technician was just finishing when Thomas heard Vigil's voice in the next treatment room weeping, huge heartbreaking sobs. *Oh God, they've found the daughter . . . and she's dead.* Thomas waved the medtech aside and rolled to his feet. "One moment!" He stuck his head next around the corner.

Admiral Pachefski had returned. Vigil's good arm was clinging to a slight, dark-haired teenage girl and shaking with previously suppressed grief.

Pachefski was watching them, his face drawn, but he turned when he saw Thomas, and stepped out into the corridor.

"His daughter," he said, gesturing. "Whoever it was didn't touch her. She was actually in the camp, in her assigned compound, but says she *was* called over to the prison last night, ostensibly to see her father who was gravely ill. They left her in an interview room for twenty minutes, then sent her back, saying a mistake had been made—a different Vigil was sick, not her father."

The admiral took a handkerchief from his pocket and blew his nose. "You'd have to be stone to be unmoved by his face when I brought her in."

Thomas nodded. "Do you believe his story?"

Pachefski nodded. "Yes, until I have strong evidence to the contrary. The guards who were on the wall didn't belong in that unit. They relieved the regular guards, saying the unit CO had authorized it. The unit CO denies it, but he was at his desk, two hexes away, and the regular guards didn't check with him." He glared at Thomas as if this was somehow all Thomas's fault. "I hate to say this—" He shook his head again, his face contorted like a man sucking on lemons. "I *really* hate to say this, but you were right to avoid briefing me on your investigation. I have no idea how far this thing spreads."

Thomas looked away, embarrassed. He cleared his throat and asked neutrally, "Where are the false guards, now?" He let the medtech steer him back into the treatment room.

Admiral Pachefski followed. "We don't know. They faded almost immediately."

"And their names?"

Pachefski shook his head. "The regular guards *think* the names were Jones and Smith." He exchanged a cynical look with Thomas. "I've got over three thousand INS personnel in the prison alone. We're running the file pictures past the guards who should have been on duty, but I don't have much hope. This is ugly, Commander. Even uglier than that last mess you investigated."

The medtech stuck a medicated dressing over the stitches and then wrapped an elastic self-clinging bandage all the way around his torso to keep it in place.

"Did you find the real Armando Ortega?" Thomas asked the admiral.

"Yes. They simply switched them. Ortega was in Vigil's cellblock over on the minimum-security side. He's on his way right now." He was watching Thomas's face and quickly added, "I sent my aide and my orderly, both of whom have been with me for years. They know not to trust anybody else. And we checked his retina pattern."

Thomas subsided. The medtech went to a closet and pulled out a set of surgical scrubs. "Looks like you bled on your uniform pants, too, Commander. Would you like to borrow these until you can get another uniform?"

"Excellent, Chief. I appreciate it."

The medtech smiled and handed him the clothes, a piece of paper on top. "Here's a handout on taking care of those sutures. The inner ones will dissolve, but you need to have the surface set pulled in ten days. The lidocaine is going to wear off in about an hour, so you might want something for pain. You get any of the symptoms on the list, you high-tail it to a medical facility." He pulled a plastic bag out of a cabinet. "You can put your uniform in here."

"Aye, Chief. Thanks again."

Pachefski waited until the medtech left before speaking. "I imagine you'll be camped out here for quite some time, checking this out."

Thomas shook his head. "No, sir. Not a bit."

"What?"

"I believe this was an attempt to get me to divert my investigation, to turn it away from where it really belongs. Between your intelligence unit and facility CID, I'm sure *your* people can get to the bottom of what happened here last night and today."

He paused and drank some of the electrolyte. "I am concerned, though, about the Vigils. Would you consider an administrative discharge? I mean, the man was in for border crossing, right? What is that—three months? How much of it has he served?"

"The man tried to murder you!"

"The man is more of a victim than I am. Don't *you* have a daughter, Admiral?"

Pachefski looked away.

Thomas pressed the point. "I won't bring charges against him, but I'm afraid he's at risk. He's another one who could identify those involved. And they might snatch his daughter, to keep him from testifying."

Pachefski looked back. "The man did ten weeks of thirteen. Yeah, I have administrative leeway over misdemeanor offenders, but if these villains are INS, they could still get at him in the camp."

Thomas nodded. "You let him go, and I'll get them sponsored into New Galveston and hidden. I'll take them now, when I go, after I've met with Ortega."

"I can't discharge Ortega. Felonious offenders require

judicial review, and they're mad at him anyway, since he wouldn't cooperate."

Thomas nodded. "I understand." He offered his hand to the admiral. "I'm extremely grateful."

Pachefski stared at the hand for a moment and then shook it. "You're welcome."

Thomas walked through the hospital to a public comm terminal.

FATHER AND DAUGHTER
NEED HIDDEN SANCTUARY
FROM THE MOUTH OF HELL
YOUR UNCLE PERHAPS
T

They moved the Vigils down to an empty observation room guarded by the civilian police. Thomas met with Armando Ortega in an empty lounge down the hall.

"*Buenos dias,* Armando. *Es bueno verlo.*"

Armando looked surprised. "*Señor Cicatrizado. Mucho gusto.*" He pointed at the surgical scrubs Thomas was wearing. "*¿Es un doctor ahora?*"

Thomas lifted up the shirt to show the bandage. "*Se cortada. Mi uniforme está ensangrentado.*"

"*¡Que lástima!*"

Thomas shrugged and showed Armando the copies of the forged ID's. "*¿Conoces a estas personas?*"

Armando glanced at the pages and his eyes widened slightly. He handed them back without looking any closer. "*No puedo decir.*" He licked his lips and looked around the room.

Cannot say? "¿Por qué?"

Armando shrugged.

Thomas tried shock. He tapped the pages and said, "*Todos están muertos. Todos ellos.*" *All dead. Every one of them.*

Armando turned white and sank down onto the lounge's couch. "*¡Esto rompe el acuerdo!*"

What agreement is broken? "*¿Cuál acuerdo?*"

Armando seemed no longer in the room, his gaze far away and distressed. "*Entre las Encinas y el Cartel de Gomez.*"

"*¿El cartel de la droga? ¿En Colombia?*"

Armando came back to himself and stared up at Thomas. "*¿Qué? Nada. No tiene sentido.*"

Thomas tried for several more minutes, but while Armando was polite, he wouldn't expound further on what he had said. He would only repeat, "*No tiene sentido.*" Only a thing without sense: nonsense.

Reluctantly, he turned Armando back over to the admiral's aide. "Try to keep him alive, please."

"The admiral has taken special measures. Solitary and guards who'll watch each other as well as him."

Thomas's pager went off before he went into the Vigils.

IVE A SOFTNESS FOR FATHERS AND DAUGHTERS
THRICE WELCOME
MY UNCLE AWAITS THY PLEASURE
IF YOU ARENT WITH THEM
THE WORD IS
DROWNED VIOLA
P

I love you, Patricia.

14

Beenan: *Los colores*

After Thomas left, Patricia's mother told her, "Your father and I knew each other for four years before we became engaged. Didn't guarantee a successful marriage." She leaned over and kissed Patricia. "Just a wonderful child." The congresswoman blew her nose. "You do what's right for *you*."

Patricia stared back, openmouthed. *Aliens have replaced my mother with a pod person.*

They ate a room-service lunch together and for the first time in a long time, Patricia felt she'd found her mother again. *Maybe we're both done blaming each other for Dad's death.*

She left after lunch, reluctantly, to let her mother pursue her official agenda.

When she got Thomas's page, she went to a public phone, voice only, to ask Tío Rodolfo if he would take in Thomas's "father and daughter." Rodolfo had agreed with remarkably few questions, which made Patricia very uneasy. What if these two were a disaster, throwing the restaurant into disorder? Or thieves?

Oh, Thomas, I must trust you a great deal.

She sent the page and returned to the Posada del Ángel, alternating between staring at her engagement ring and worrying about Rodolfo and the refugees.

Finally, unable to avoid it, she did a full makeup job: foundation, powder, eyeliner, eyebrow pencil, mascara, and lipstick; then she put on the "rig"—the false boobs, the shoulder strap, and the boots with lifts, plus a newly purchased dress, a white linen sundress that she had to admit she'd bought to maximize her false cleavage. *Take that, Angela Bustamonte!*

The Posada del Ángel was in the same subdivision as Cosas Muertas del Mar, but she took a water taxi anyway, from the far side. The driver kept turning his head until Patricia said, "No tip if we run into something."

He grinned and kept more of his attention on the water.

Standing on the wharf at the restaurant, she rewarded him by bending forward when she paid him. His eyes never met her face.

She shook her head, amused and disturbed. O, *peace! now he's deeply in: look how imagination blows him. Disguise, I see, thou art a wickedness, wherein the pregnant enemy does much.*

Tío Rodolfo was standing at the reception station. He'd watched Patricia arrive but moved his eyes back out to the bay to watch traffic. He handed a menu to Ferdinand, one of his nephews, and nodded toward Patricia, but his attention was still out there on the traffic.

Ferdinand approached. "One for dinner, señorita?" He was very dignified, very serious, which Patricia thought funny since his usual manner was comic, snapping dish towels at the busboys and imitating the more pompous customers back in the kitchen.

She said, in an artificially husky voice, "Go on, Ferdi, I want to talk to Rodolfo."

Ferdinand looked puzzled. "As you wish, señorita." He clearly didn't recognize her. He conducted her over to Tío Rodolfo. "*La dama quiere hablar con usted.*"

"Madam?" Rodolfo turned and bowed slightly. "How may I be of service?"

She took the menu from Ferdinand and put it back with the others in the reception station. With the husky voice she said, "Run along, Ferdi. *Privado*."

Ferdi bowed and backed away, searching his uncle's face for a clue, but Rodolfo was also puzzled.

"I see you know my nephew."

She used her own voice. "*Claro que sí, Tío. Como mi hermanito.*"

Rodolfo's jaw dropped. "Patricia?"

"Shhh. It's a disguise—*un disfraz*."

He shut his mouth and looked her up and down. "*Muy atractivo*," he finally said.

She shook her head. "Have they come yet?"

"Your refugees? No. Señor Becket called. He's sending them over in a taxi. A special taxi driven by a police officer. Who are they?"

"*No sé*."

Rodolfo raised his eyebrows.

She shrugged. "If they become a problem here, I'll find another place for them."

"Señor Becket asks this? And you are willing to do this for him?"

"This and more."

"Who is he?"

She hesitated. The INS were not Tío Rodolfo's favorite organization and frankly, a lot of their reputation was earned, but he would have to know sooner or later. "Thomas is a commander in the INS. He is investigating the *Open Lotus*, the drowned ones I found."

Rodolfo's face closed down. "*Lobos de la frontera*."

She nodded and held up the ring. "*Éste lobo es mi compañero por todo la vida.*"

"*¿Se casaron?*"

We haven't had the time to get married—or anything else.

"*¿Sin su bendición? Claro que no.*"

"My blessing, eh." He looked at her. "Does he love you?"

Even to the edge of doom. "He does."

"And you love him?"

"Oh, Tío, so very much."

"You will have to invite me to the wedding."

Patricia breathed a sigh of relief. "Who else would give away the bride?"

They stood together in contented silence for a few moments; then Rodolfo gestured. A taxi was approaching from the bay side, ordinary enough, but farther out, a police patrol boat paralleled it.

"Your refugees?"

"*Quizás.*"

A Hispanic man wearing his right arm in a sling got out of the taxi, helped by a teenage girl. There was no exchange of money, and the taxi pulled away as soon as the two of them were on the dock. Tío Rodolfo took two menus from the station. "Here, you be the *recepcionista.* Take them to the *patio de la familia.* I'll meet you there." He turned to the back of the restaurant.

She walked forward to meet the pair. The man was staring at her, his eyes large. The girl was swiveling her head back and forth, trying to take in everything.

"*Buenos días,*" she said. "*Bienvenidos. ¿Dos para cenar?*"

The man blinked. "I would like to speak with Señor Santos."

"Of course. Your names?"

"*Vigil. Maximilian y Zaneta.*" He indicated his daughter.

"*Mucho gusto. Me llamo* Viola."

The girl stopped looking around. "Viola, but that's—. I heard you drowned." Her English was good, with a slight Texas drawl.

"Commander Becket always exaggerates," she said, letting them know they'd definitely come to the right place. "Follow me, please." She led them back through the kitchen, then down the hallway to the patio where she'd told Thomas about her adventures with the *Open Lotus* and the *Sycorax.* Tío Rodolfo was waiting.

"Señor Maximilian Vigil *y* Señorita Zaneta Vigil. Señor Rodolfo Santos."

Tío Rodolfo was standing with his arms behind his back, formal and severe. "*Bienvenidos. ¿Vigil? ¿Conoces a Eduardo Vigil de Tampico?*"

For the first time since he'd stepped from the taxi, Maximilian smiled. "*¡Mi abuelo!*"

Rodolfo's face went from polite to delighted. He slapped his chest. "*¡Fue tío de mi madre!*" He spread his arms wide. "*¡Primo!*"

Patricia, bemused, shook her head. *What is that? Second cousins? First cousins once removed?* Whatever. It wasn't that surprising—the Deluge had scattered families like chaff from wheat, and lost and unknown relatives reconnected at the oddest times.

It looked like Thomas's refugees were going to work out.

MOST RADIANT EXQUISITE
AND UNMATCHABLE BEAUTY
CAN YOU MEET ME
AT BARNEY'S OFFICE
1800 HOURS
T

IS THERE A BED
P

AFTER
T

ON YOUR ATTENDANCE, MY LORD
P

Patricia went by the hotel for casual clothing, but kept the disguise on. She took the Intercity ferry over to Palacios and walked through the shopping district, spending time in shops, pretending to look at the back side of window displays, but, in fact, looking for anyone interested in her.

As she went in the public door of the Central Precinct, she wondered if any of these police might be Nat-A1 sympathizers or outright members.

She doubted it—the ethnic mix of the New Galveston police reflected the Strand's diverse culture. A lot of care was taken to recruit multilingual men and woman with psych reviews for bigotry and xenophobia.

Still, she didn't give her own name at the desk. "Viola Sebastian to see Major Paine by arrangement."

The desk sergeant put the call through and, before Patricia could sit down, a policewoman came from the back to escort her out of the public area.

"A bathroom first, please?"

"Certainly, ma'am." The officer showed her a restroom outside of dispatch. "I'll be right here."

"Okay. It'll be a minute."

She used the handicapped stall, packing away the dress and falsies, wig, and the elevator boots. When she came out of the bathroom, she was wearing comfortable sandals and Thomas's dress shirt over shorts, and all the makeup had been washed down the sink.

The policewoman looked at her, then past her, then back again, to take in the shoulder bag, the same bag Viola Sebastian had been carrying.

"I'm ready," Patricia smiled.

"Wow," said the officer. "Assemblywoman Beenan. This way, please."

A door on the far side of dispatch opened onto a room labeled Special Operations. A set of communications consoles ran around the room and a conference table was in the middle. She saw Thomas, in jeans and a sport shirt, leaning against the near side of the conference table and talking to Major Paine and to two INS officers in uniform.

Three uniformed police manned comm stations, headsets on.

The officer who'd escorted her from the front closed the door behind them both and took a seat at one of the other stations. Thomas stopped talking in midsentence when he saw her and breathed out, a deep sigh ending in a smile. The other three men turned around, but she didn't really see them.

"What's wrong? Why are you so pale?" She'd dropped the bag and moved forward.

Thomas looked surprised.

Major Paine bent over suddenly, laughing. "I'll break it to her gently, he said! It's only a scratch, he said!"

Thomas glared at Major Paine. Then he stepped up to her, taking her hands in his. "I'm glad to see you. I expected you to show up in your Raquel Welch outfit."

She shrugged. "I just changed out of it. What's 'just a scratch'?"

He shrugged as if it were nothing. "They tried to get at me today, in the Abattoir." He touched the left side of his stomach. "They had to put in some stitches."

One of the INS officers, a black man, said, "Fifty-three, right? Thirteen internal and forty out—"

"*Thank you, Jazz.* You are, uh, precise, even if not exactly helpful."

"Shouldn't you be in a hospital?" she asked.

"No, I shouldn't," he said firmly. He turned back to the INS officers. "Patricia, I would like you to meet Lieutenant Jazz Graham, my executive officer, and Ensign Bartholomew Terkel, our newest investigator. Gentleman, Patricia Beenan."

She shook their hands. *Fifty-three stitches?* "Was it a knife? Did you lose a lot of blood?"

"A nasty little prison knife. A bit of blood, yes. But in the end, it bought much. We know who the victims were on the *Open Lotus*."

She blinked, confused. "I see, you walked up to someone

and said, 'If you tell me who the victims are, I'll let you cut me open'?"

He shook his head. "It's not that straightforward."

"Why am I not surprised?"

He drew her over to the conference table and held a chair for her. "Here, let me tell you a story."

She pulled him around the front of the chair. "*You* sit." She pulled out another chair for herself and watched as he lowered himself and then winced as he leaned back. She intoned, "*Ay, ay, a scratch, a scratch; marry, 'tis enough. Where is my page? Go, villain, fetch a surgeon.*"

Thomas groaned. "Do you know *every* line of Shakespeare? Or was that somebody else?"

"It's no good if you don't get the reference. It was Mercutio shortly before he croaks, in *Romeo and Juliet*. We have a deal, remember?"

"Okay, I get it. I get it. No bombs, No knives."

She flushed, remembering her bomb. "Go on, tell me this story. Is it in iambic pentameter?"

"It could be. What is that line from the beginning of *Romeo and Juliet*? *Two households, alike in . . .*"

She closed her eyes for a moment. "*Two households, both alike in dignity, in fair Verona, where we lay our scene, from ancient grudge break to new mutiny, where civil blood makes civil hands unclean.*"

"Yeah, that's it. Well, trade Bogotá for Verona, and the Gomez family can be the Capulets and the Encinas family can be the Montagues. Change *both alike in dignity* to *both alike in land ownership*."

"Oh. And from which family do we draw our victims?"

"The Monta—that is, the Encinas family. The ancient grudge is there. The Gomez cocaine cartel has been after the Encinas mountain coffee plantations since before the Deluge, as often as not with open warfare. There have been periods of truce and periods of bloodshed, but it really heated up about five years ago."

"How did you identify them?"

"Well, when we found the bomb—"

"My bomb?"

"Oh, no. There was a bomb on the *Open Lotus,* on it before it was sunk. Remember I told you we found two extra bodies on board when we brought the *Open Lotus* up and that one of them was INS?"

She nodded. "That's right. It was the reason you went dashing off to BBINS."

"Yes. Well, we found a bomb in the engine room that McIntyre apparently defused." He saw the confusion on her face. "McIntyre was a machinist mate on the *Sycorax*. His was the INS body. We think he interfered with their plan to scuttle the *Open Lotus* in deeper water and that was why they sank her where you found her."

"I don't think it's very fair of you to criticize my handling of bombs if you've been doing the same thing."

Thomas glared at her. "*We* let the bomb squad handle it."

She looked away. "So you think it was the *Sycorax*?"

"We're pretty sure, but we don't have clear evidence." He told her about the discrepancies in the *Sycorax*'s reported and actual positions, as well as the suspected alteration of the fifty-caliber machine-gun barrel.

"Can't you arrest them?"

"It's very tenuous."

She shook her head. "I still don't see how this ties into the Encinas cartel."

Thomas gestured to the far side of the table, and Ensign Terkel stepped around and slid a file folder across. "We found some fake ID's in the engine room of the *Open Lotus* after we took a better look." He opened it and set it on the table, showing her color copies of driver's licenses and passports. "I knew of a recently convicted documents provider in Detention out here, so I went to see him."

Lieutenant Graham added, "And got yourself sliced."

"Give it a rest, Jazz. I promise, next time *you* can go."

Jazz subsided with a grin.

"What happened out at the prison? Did this documents man attack you?"

"No. Somebody had switched Ortega, the documents guy, with Vigil. Vigil attacked me."

She stood up so quickly that her chair fell over backward. "*What!* You let me place a murderer in Tío Rodolfo's home?"

Thomas held up his hands. "They used his daughter, Patricia. They said they'd—well, some pretty awful things ending in death if he didn't kill me. They'd also set up some guards to kill *him* immediately after. He's not the villain in this act."

She licked her lips and turned to pick up the chair, but Ensign Terkel had already recovered it. She settled back down to perch on the edge. "Okay. Is that why you got them out of there?"

"Yes. Besides the chance they might carry out their threat against the daughter, both of them have seen these men. They might be silenced to keep them from ID-ing the bastards. Have you heard whether they are getting along with Don Rodolfo?"

She nodded. "I attended their arrival. It worked out very well—turns out they're family, distant cousins, previously lost."

"Really? That's weird." He shook his head. "The prison did find Ortega, eventually, in Vigil's cell. He took one look at these," he tapped the pages on the table, "and clammed up, but when I told them they were all dead, he let slip something about an agreement broken, a truce if you will, between the Encinas family and the Gomez cartel. But he wouldn't say anything else."

Patricia waited.

"Enter the DEA. We sent copies of the ID's to the DEA unit in Colombia, and they identified the entire group, then filled in the background." He licked his lips. "Uh, where's that Barf-Aid?"

Ensign Terkel fetched a bottle of flavored electrolyte replacer from the back of one of the comm consoles.

"Thanks, Bart. Doctor's orders," he said to Patricia, and

took several deep swallows, then made a face. "The background: apparently, in the last three months, the Gomez cartel effectively won the long-term war, destroying the Encinas family's coffee crops, burning their warehouses, and killing many of their employees with the help of bought government troops. The Encinases gave up—sued for peace, and the agreement, *el acuerdo,* stopped the fighting and allowed the Encinas family to withdraw, to leave with the remnants of their fortune, much of which was in bearer bonds and precious metals."

Patricia blinked. "Which wasn't aboard the *Open Lotus.*"

"Certainly not when *we* searched it," agreed Thomas.

Patricia's face twisted, "Was it piracy, then? A mass mugging? Did they kill all those children for the *money*?"

"That's what we need to find out."

In fair New Galveston *where we lay our scene.*

She had an odd frisson as she thought about that play. *The refugee community is mine, the Capulets, ranged against the INS, the Montagues. Thomas is my Romeo, and I his Juliet.* She sighed. *We're going to have to rewrite the ending.*

Patricia sat on the conference table, her feet dangling at Thomas's right shoulder; he was seated in a chair. Like everyone else in the room, she wore a wireless headset with a channel switch and listened.

All the comm stations were occupied, and Major Paine paced behind the operators, his hands folded neatly behind him. Ensign Terkel and Lieutenant Graham were arranging a series of personnel file folders across the table for ready access. The room still smelled of Chinese food; the containers had been cleared away moments before.

Patricia rested her hand on Thomas's shoulder and he covered her hand with his.

A voice, on a canvas of turbines and wind, reported, "Hover ferry away. We count nine of them aboard. Nobody got off at Isabel Island, so Red team is aboard. Blue team is still watching the ship."

Major Paine's voice came across. "Copy that, Red One. Green, Orange, and Yellow teams, heads up. ETA fifteen minutes."

There was a series of beeps from the comm consoles, and the c^4 status screen, a large display currently showing an overall map of the Strand, flashed acknowledge symbols against the grouped team members' names as they responded. There were three member's in each team. "Green two," said Major Paine. "Did you copy that?"

The last missing symbol appeared.

"Might as well start ID, Major," said Thomas.

"Certainly, Commander. Take over."

Thomas released Patricia's hand and touched his headset. "Red One, we'll have the video now, if you're ready."

A dark image appeared on a screen on the Red team console.

"Switch to image intensification mode, Red One."

A man's silhouette flared into view: blond crew cut, with a thin, nearly invisible mustache. He was wearing a loud tropical shirt.

Terkel had the file and answered on the channel. "Mowett, Richard. Damage Controlman, First Class."

The image shifted to a heavier man with a thick walrus mustache, balding, in a collarless shirt. Patricia leaned forward and whispered, "Where's the camera?"

Thomas said, "Hmmm. Red team has theirs in a satphone. Takes some practice to aim it."

Graham meanwhile was identifying the man on screen. "Hughes, Benjamin. Master Chief Electronics Technician."

"Ah," said Thomas, leaning forward. "The guru. The master of time and space."

Patricia was confused, but they were moving on through the group, identifying faces, then coming back again, once the names had been found, to catalog the clothing.

Master Chief Hughes was the ranking member of the *Sycorax*'s crew on the ferry. There were no commissioned officers with them and only one seaman. The rest were specialist petty officers of one stripe or another. There was a senior chief radarman, a chief gunner's mate, a senior chief telecommunications specialist, and an aviation survivalman, first class.

When the aviation survivalman was identified, Thomas turned to Patricia and said, "You've met him before, sort of."

"I don't recognize him."

"He would be the diver they put in the water, from the helicopter. That's his duty."

"He was just wet-suited limbs and a face mask, bobbing like a cork. I did not tarry there."

Thomas touched his headset. "The ferry stops first at the Palacios terminal, then across to the airport, then back. If anybody stays aboard, Green team will board at Palacios. Red team exits at Palacios so the profile changes. Red and Green, acknowledge."

The c^4 console operator reported, "Red and Green teams acknowledged."

But all of the *Sycoraxers* left the ferry at Palacios, so Green team stayed on the pier.

Thomas looked at Major Paine. "Would you take over, Major? You know the city better."

Major Paine nodded and lifted his hand to the handset. "Red team head for the taxi stands. Yellow team to the Intercity ferry queue. Orange team to the Palacios walkways, now. Green team, stay back. Green One, give us some video."

Earlier, Thomas had told her that, except for Blue team, back at the Abattoir, there were one New Galveston police officer and two members of Thomas's CID unit with each team. Blue team, expected to operate strictly in INS territory, was all CID.

An image on the Green console appeared, a wide-angle shot of the crowded ferry pier. Patricia had trouble discerning which group of figures was the crew of the *Sycorax*, but by watching the video's motion, she identified the block of men, two walking in front, then four, then three following.

They were walking down the center of the pier, neither turning toward the taxis or the Intercity ferries.

Major Paine began talking quickly, splitting Orange team and sending them ahead, down three different possible avenues. He did the same thing with Yellow team, covering three others. He had Red team move in parallel with the quarry, up the pier through the crowd, and he had Green team stay put, less some of them turn back.

The group stopped at the foot of the pier, and they turned inward, talking.

"Red Two, see if you can capture any of that."

There was a beep from the console; then, on the Green Team console, she saw a figure walk close to the group and bend down, to tie a shoe.

There was the murmur of crowd noise and "—the girls are cuter at Elephant and Castle."

"The beer is better at Yardo's."

"Why not split up?"

"Belay that! No splitting up. Those were the conditions for this liberty, remember? We're not leaving anyone behind."

"Aye, Chief. Shall we vote? Or flip a coin?"

"Vote," said the first voice, the one who wanted the pretty girls.

Good beer won out.

"Out of there, Red Two, before they make you. Red and Green teams meet transport at the far end of the taxi stand. It'll take them fifteen minutes to walk around to Yardo's." He switched to another channel and Patricia heard him ordering an unmarked boat to the pier. Then he switched back to their operations channel. "Yellow and Orange teams, spread out on Shore Walk, Yellow first, Orange second. Leapfrog them when they pass, using the Mall Walk. Report any deviation of path and if anybody splits off. As they pass, silent report with two beeps."

Major Paine released the transmit stud on his headset and said, "Emma, let's switch the status map to the four grids comprising the southeast quadrant of Palacios."

The map at the c^4 station changed and the team symbols—formerly overlapping colored numbers—resolved to individual team members. The orange and yellow numbers were moving rapidly, a few up Shore Walk and the majority cutting behind, a full hex inward, then using local paths to reconnect to Shore Walk. The clustered red and blue numbers were out in the water, now aboard their boat, heading southwest.

"How are they tracking them?" Patricia wondered aloud.

Major Paine said, "Calibrated GPS." He pointed at a console. "We receive the same GPS signals here, a known, fixed point, and calibrate from that. Accurate to five centimeters." He touched his headset. "Red and Blue team, we'll want to force a table at Yardo's, if possible. If necessary, I'll call the manager, but see if you can do it without."

"Force a table?" Patricia asked quietly.

Thomas leaned against her knee. "Like a magician forcing a card. Preselecting a card for them but making them think they've picked it themselves."

"What good does that do?"

Thomas grinned, a flash of white teeth, predatory. "Well, we're going to bug the table."

Major Paine turned his head, "Or tables. That might be best, even. Divide the juniors and the seniors, and either group might talk more freely." He touched the headset. "Red One, it's your call on the tables. Get plenty of *chicle* ready."

Red One replied, "Copy that. We're chewing so hard our jaws hurt."

"What's the gum for?"

Thomas laughed. "To hold the bugs to the bottom of the tables. They're small enough that the gum covers them completely. Even if they look under—" He shrugged.

"Won't the gum muffle them?"

"The table itself becomes a diaphragm."

Yellow team was reporting the passage of the quarry, and

the c^4 console operator, Emma, was manually moving a blinking dot up Shore Walk to reflect the information. The red and blue numerals moving in the bay curved back into Palacios, then touched and moved inward, the dots moving quickly.

The quarry moved past the last Yellow team member and into Orange team's purview. Emma zoomed in on the c^4 display again, as the boundaries of action shrunk. The outlines of individual structures were clearly delineated now.

"Control, this is Red One. We've got four open tables, all six-seaters. We're going to bug them all with trilobed spacing." There was loud music in the background.

"Copy that, Red One. We'll need a reference source on that music."

"Yes, sir. How much time do we have?"

"The quarry is still five minutes away."

"Back in a moment."

Thomas turned to Patricia. "The reference source is so they—"

She interrupted him. "—can subtract the music out of the bugs signal. We do the same thing in sonar—engine noise or waves."

Red One came back on the air. "I've assigned the four tables channels seven through ten. We've got a mike five feet in front of a PA speaker on channel twelve. Repeat, reference is on channel twelve. Tables are seven through ten."

"Copy that. Let us know which tables, when they're seated."

A horrid thought occurred to Patricia. "If the *Sycorax* has all that fancy radio monitoring equipment, couldn't they be intercepting this traffic?"

Major Paine nodded. "They could be, if they could find it. We're actually working inside the Channel Seven television analog broadcast signal, a hidden digital stream. Once they found it, they'd have to decrypt it, too, figuring out which bit is part of which channel, and that's constantly changing, too. So, while we're not certain, we're *comfortable*." He touched the transmit stud. "Red Three, are you positioned for some entrapment?"

A woman's voice answered, "Such things vee gonna do to them."

Patricia burst out laughing. "Liz?"

Major Paine nodded. "Where are you set up?"

Liz's voice continued. "At the bar. I'm draped over a bar stool, and I'm sitting quite demurely for the moment, but when they get here, the amount of leg I show will be *shocking*."

Major Paine chuckled. "Carry on, Red Three."

Thomas looked at Patricia and raised his eyebrows.

"Liz is the police officer who set me up with the tits." She mimed lifting large breasts with her hands. "Hers are real."

Thomas's lips made a silent "Oh."

"Okay," Major Paine said. "Heads up everybody. They'll be inside momentarily. As soon as they enter, Yellow team sets up on Shore Walk east, west, and right out front. Orange team sets up on Mall Walk east and west plus the utility path on Yardo's back door. Yellow One give me some video. Red and Orange, I'll want video when they're settled."

The remote video display on Yellow team's console lit up with a view of the nine *Sycorax* crew members coming up Shore Walk, then turning and climbing the low steps into Yardo's.

Patricia found herself holding her breath, waiting, waiting.

Red One's voice said, "The hostess has put table eight and nine together. Repeat, channel eight and nine."

Patricia exhaled.

Curtain up.

15

Becket: *La evidencia de la cantina*

The initial audio coming out of the main speakers was gibberish, a hint of voices, sliding chairs, and the louder sounds of elbows on the table, all overwhelmed by the music.

Major Paine said, "Porter, subtract the reference signal."

Immediately, the voices leapt into comprehension.

"Our beer special today is Barro Añejo in bottles and Conejo Aplastado on tap. We also just cracked the barrel on our winter lager from Yardo's own microbrewery, Yard o' Ale. The rest of the beers are on the list. Your waiter will be here immediately."

"Thanks, dawlin."

Video appeared, a view on the Red team console. The combined table, seen from across the room, zoomed to fill the frame. On the Green team console, a different angle, higher, shot down the length of the table, providing a better view of faces.

Thomas took a sip of the lemon electrolyte and wished he could have beer instead. He'd had the Barro Añejo, a lovely dark brew, almost a stout, from Cuba. *Certainly better than this lemon piss.* He leaned back, acutely conscious of Patricia's bare knee against his shoulder.

The local on his stitches had worn off an hour before, and he'd avoided the pain meds they'd issued, wanting to keep his head clear. It wasn't too bad if he held still.

The men at the table ordered stuffed potato skins, onion

rings, buffalo wings and three pitchers of the house ale. "To start," said a voice identified as Hughes, the electronics master chief.

The men made small talk while they waited for the beer, certainly nothing that Thomas could construe as being about the sinking of the *Open Lotus*—but it was all being recorded anyway.

When the beer came, two of the men tried to chat up the waitress who'd helped their waiter bring the mugs, but she politely ignored them and went back to working her own tables.

They poured the mugs full, but nobody drank until they all had a full stein. They turned their heads expectantly to Hughes at the head of the table.

Hughes lifted his mug and intoned, "Saint Crispin's day."

The figures on the screen responded, "Saint Crispin's day."

"What? Is Hughes a Catholic?" Thomas looked behind him and swore silently as his stitches pulled.

Jazz looked at the file. "No, he's listed as Church of Christ."

"Crispin. Rather esoteric choice for a saint, too," Paine said.

Emma, the c^4 console operator, said, "Unless you're from Soissons, France, where they died. Crispin *and* Crispinian. They were brothers. Martyred in Gaul by Emperor Maximian. Patron saints of shoemakers." The others in the room stared at her. She shrugged. "Before I was a cop, I was a nun."

"When is Saint Crispin's feast day?" asked Thomas.

Emma furrowed her forehead. "Uh, same as Saint Tabitha—October twenty-fifth."

"Next Tuesday," said Major Paine.

Patricia cleared her throat. "There's a famous speech in *Henry the Fifth*—they call it the Saint Crispin's day speech."

Thomas smiled. "Shakespeare again. Does it have any bearing?"

Patricia considered. "Perhaps. It's the speech Henry makes before they fight the French at Agincourt, six thousand Englishman against twenty-five thousand." She cleared her throat, "*That he which hath no stomach to this fight, let him depart; his passport shall be made and crowns for convoy put into his purse: We would not die in that man's company that fears his fellowship to die with us*. And so on."

On screen the beers were being refilled.

Paine added, "The French became mired in the mud and the archers killed over five thousand. The English lost about two hundred men." Dryly he added, "It was a famous victory." He tilted his head at the screen. "They do have that look, a sort of precombat jitters."

Thomas watched the faces. They were pale, serious, not the faces of men bent on partying. "If I'd been involved in a mass murder, I might look like this. Say a battle, though. What battle?"

"What *desperate* battle," amended Patricia. "That might happen next Tuesday."

At Yardo's the food arrived, and the conversation was limited to "Pass the blue cheese" and "Don't be such a pig; you already had two potato skins."

Paine spoke, "That guy with the red shirt is only picking at his food. Nervous? Second thoughts?"

Terkel said, "That's the air survivalman, Peter Fraser."

Thomas studied the face. Fraser was clean-shaven, with narrow eyes and a long nose. His body language was closed, slightly hunched, elbows held close. He didn't look happy, but none of them did. The rest of them didn't look particularly scared, though, and there was an element of that to Fraser. "I agree. We might be able get to him."

Paine nodded. "Let's cut him out from the herd, then." He touched his headset. "Red Three, we think the subject in the red sport shirt is a possible." He released the stud and turned to Terkel. "Where is he from? College? Interests?"

Terkel flipped through the file. "Boise, Idaho. Two years

at Boise State University, then he joined up. He likes to dive. He's got a commendation for some in-water repair work for the *Sycorax*'s sonar array. Two reprimands for prejudicial conduct toward a fellow serviceman."

"That fits," said Jazz.

"What's it mean?" asked Patricia.

"Hate crime. Words or actions related to racial differences." He looked at Thomas with a question in his eyes.

"Go ahead," Thomas said.

Jazz continued. "We've found an unusually high number of this offense in the crew's records. Nearly all of them with the exception of Commander Wall, the CO. There were a few incidents at the academy for Lieutenant Rodgers, before he graduated. The XO, Puffet, is actually related, by marriage, to Congressman Smithers, of National Alliance fame."

Paine touched his mike again. "Red Two. He's from Idaho but if you can't fake that convincingly, don't try. Bit of a bigot. Likes to dive. Looks worried about something. See what you can do."

As the food disappeared, the conversation became more animated. It seemed like they were shouting, and Thomas had to remind himself that the loud background music wasn't being processed out for *them*. "The conversations are splitting up, Major. Do you think we could split the two channels three ways—two solo and one combined?"

"We can. Porter, make that happen. On the combined, do that thing where you filter out the difference, leaving only the stuff *both* channels have."

"Yes, sir, the AND algorithm. Shall I leave any of them on the speakers?"

Major Paine looked at Thomas.

"Ah, perhaps, the signal at Hughes's end of the table."

Porter nodded and did something with the console. The number of voices dropped markedly. "I've put the filtered combined on channel Charlie and the other end of the table on channel David."

Thomas turned around and said, "Jazz, you take Charlie,

and Bart, you take David. I'd appreciate it, Patricia, if you would concentrate on Hughes. If he has a Shakespearean bent, he might say something that we'd miss."

She smiled at him. "If you like."

He settled back and concentrated on the screen. It really helped to watch who was talking, to make sense out of the different voices.

Hughes was talking with the senior chief telecommunications specialist and the senior chief radarman. Their voices were lowered and their body language excluded the rest of the group.

"—discipline is definitely a problem, especially among the ratings. We need to keep on top of them in a careful sort of way. Nothing vicious, or we might get another McIntyre."

The other two grunted agreement and the radar chief said, "At least it's not that long. Next week, then it's over."

The telecommunications chief sighed. "Aye. And a whole different set of problems. When it comes to setting them, I hope that bastard Collins comes through. We'll need even more hands than he can provide."

Hughes raised his beer. "*No, my fair cousin: If we are mark'd to die, we are enow to do our country loss; and if to live, the fewer men, the greater share of honour.*"

The radarman got a sour look on his face on hearing this, but didn't say anything. The telecommunications chief raised his beer in response.

Thomas looked at Patricia and she nodded.

"Same speech. Henry Five. What did they mean about 'setting them'?"

Thomas was very still. He hadn't been happy to hear that, either.

Patricia went on. "You set anchors, you set sails . . . and you set charges. And there's already been two bombs in this play."

Thomas nodded. "We'll have to see." He held a finger to his lips and gestured to the screen.

The radar chief was saying, "—not sure that waiting isn't a better option."

Hughes said, "We've been over this. CID is too close. If those idiots in detention hadn't blown it, we might have distracted them, but—" He shrugged. "They're holding eight-fifty-three for the new year, and Puffet was told it stands a good chance of passing."

The radar chief raised his mug. "God damn McIntyre to hell."

"Amen," responded Hughes. The three drank.

Thomas looked around the Ops Room. "Eight-fifty-three. Any clues, anybody?"

When nobody spoke, Patricia said, "Perhaps it's a bill. A piece of legislature."

On the screen, Hughes went on talking. "Well, watch 'em like hawks. We don't want another McIntyre." He looked at his watch. "And make sure they don't talk to anybody."

The waiter showed back up and took the dinner order and, though they listened carefully, there was no treason to be learned. Thomas was glad he'd already eaten, though. The entrees ordered evoked memories of texture, taste, and smell.

"I could phone my mother," said Patricia.

He looked at her blankly.

"About eight-fifty-three."

"Oh! Good idea. Major Paine, is there a phone Ms. Beenan may use?"

Major Paine pointed at the Blue team's console. "Tell Martha the number and she can assign it a channel for your headset."

The console operator said, "Switch to channel F—Foxtrot."

Patricia tapped her headset and Thomas saw her lips moving. He switched channels on his headset in time to hear the console operator say, "It's ringing, ma'am."

He started to tell her that he was on the line when a

male voice said, "Congresswoman Beenan's phone. How may I help you?"

Patricia said, "Mark, it's Patricia. Is my mother available?"

"Only to you, ma'am. That's what she said. Hang on."

"Thanks."

Again, in the pause, Thomas drew a breath to tell her he was listening, when Congresswoman Beenan's voice came on. "Pea?"

"Hi."

"What's that noise. TV?"

"Sorry, it's a restaurant. Can I ask you a quick question?"

"Does it have to do with scheduling your wedding?"

"No, actually. Have you heard of a bill eight-fifty-three?"

There was a sharp intake of breath on the other side. "How did you hear about *that*?"

"Well, it seems to have something to do with the *Open Lotus* thing."

"How could *that* be related?"

Patricia said, "We don't know, but then, we don't know what the bill *is*."

"Oh. It's a combined measure calling for the repeal of the Emergency Immigration Act and the stepped naturalization of all INS refugee-center populations. It's not even officially on the docket. It was deliberately delayed in committee because it doesn't have a chance under the current Congress, but after the new year, when the new members are sworn in, we stand a chance." The congresswoman cleared her throat. "I wrote the first draft."

"Does Smithers know about this?"

"God, I hope not, but it's hard to keep anything completely secret in the Capitol. How can this have something to do with that mass murder?"

Patricia said, "Don't know yet. What would that do to the Abattoir?"

"The what?"

"Sorry, that's a nickname for the Abbott Refugee Center."

"Ah. Well, over a period of five years, those who wanted it would be phased into the naturalization process starting with green cards and progressing through to citizenship. The center itself would revert to New Galveston, per the long-term lease agreement, though the INS might maintain Isabel Island as a base."

"Oh. Thank you, Mother. I don't know if it is significant or not, but at least we know."

"I have to get back to Washington tomorrow afternoon. How about breakfast? You could bring Thomas."

Thomas heard Patricia's intake of breath. "Perhaps lunch? I'm going to be up quite late and was hoping to linger in bed."

Thomas grinned to himself, keeping his face forward.

"No good. I've a working lunch with Admiral Pachefski."

"I'll go with you to the airport, then. Can't speak for Thomas."

"Well, try. We have a three-thirty-five flight, so two-thirty, at the hotel?"

"All right. Gotta go, Mom."

Thomas switched back to the command channel. Red Three was saying, "—switching to channel eleven and making my move now."

The camera's view on the Red team console widened, taking in more of the restaurant. Thomas saw a gorgeous, large-busted blonde undulate across the room, moving toward the hallway at the back, where the pay phones and restrooms were. She was glancing at the end of the table where Fraser was sitting.

Thomas looked at the other screen, the one still on the table, and he watched Fraser's posture change dramatically and his eyes widen. When the blonde—Liz?—Thomas was having a problem thinking of her as Red Three—reached the hallway, Fraser stood abruptly. Thomas wasn't listening on the channel at that end of the table, but he heard distantly, "athroom break."

Thomas cycled through the channels until he had eleven.

The camera operated by Red One zoomed on Fraser's back as he entered the hallway, and Fraser suddenly bent down, retrieving something off the floor.

"Clumsy me," said Liz's voice. "Thanks."

Fraser's voice, formerly confined to monosyllabic responses, said, "You're very welcome. I, um, look, I'm really not this forward, but I'm about to go out to sea, and well, I'd really like to buy you a drink."

On the other screen, Hughes, at the main table, jerked as if stung. He reached down to his belt and pulled forth a satphone. *It must've been on silent ring.* The expression on his face, as he answered, was annoyed, but his eyes widened immediately thereafter. He spoke briefly, then shut the phone, and took a look around him, his eyes narrowed.

"Did we get any of that conversation?" Thomas asked.

"He said, 'Hello,' " reported the Green team console operator. "Then, 'a few minutes ago' and 'in a noisy restaurant, just to Pinkerton and Maisey.' " Pinkerton was the radar chief, and Maisey was the telecommunications man.

Meanwhile, Liz was answering Fraser's question. "A drink? I think that would be just the thing. Out to sea, eh? Tomorrow?"

"Tonight. We've got this thing to do."

Back on Red screen, Hughes clapped his hands together sharply, twice. "Liberty's over, gentlemen." He pulled his wallet and dropped a great wad of cash on the table.

Thomas felt his stomach sink. *They know.*

Hughes looked across the room, to where Fraser was escorting Liz toward the bar. His eyes narrowed, and he cupped his hand to his mouth. "Fraser! Recall!"

Fraser, on Green camera, was looking back and forth between Liz and Hughes. "Oh, fuck!" he said. It sounded louder than it probably was in the restaurant since channel eleven had the reference signal subtracted, eliminating the overriding music.

Liz made one more attempt. "Eventually. What about my drink?"

Fraser dropped his head. "I'm sorry." He started to turn away.

"Well, take my card, sweet cheeks. Give me a call."

Fraser paused, took it, and managed a pained smile. "I will."

Thomas had an unwilling flashback to three nights earlier, when his evening with Patricia had been interrupted and he'd had to rush for the airport. He felt an unwilling pang of sympathy. Aloud he said, "How did they find out? Do you think they found your frequency?"

Major Paine frowned. "I doubt it seriously." He went back to directing the exterior teams, distributing them back toward the ferry. "Red and Green, stand by in case they head elsewhere." He turned back to Thomas. "Let's keep the faces fresh."

But the *Sycorax* crewmen crowded into two water taxis, at the landing across Shore Walk.

At Thomas's worried look, Major Paine said, "Don't worry; both of them are ours. Give us channel three on speakers, Porter."

The speakers, silenced when the crew had left the restaurant, came back on. "—acios Ferry Terminal," Hughes's voice snapped. "If we make the eight-fifty ferry, the tip will be substantial."

Fraser's voice, barely audible over the accelerating motor, said, "What's the deal, Chief? I thought we had until midnight."

There was a pause, and Fraser's voice came back, "Ohhhhh."

Paine talked into his headset. "Taxi One, did you see any of that?" He listened and turned to Thomas. "Hand signs. Hughes touched his ear and his lips. They do know. They may not know about the taxi, but they're not taking any more chances." He took off his headset. "Emma, take over—record everything, and page me if they do anything but head back to the *Sycorax*. Commander, Assemblywoman, would you join me?"

Well, it's not a joint bathroom break.

Patricia and Thomas followed the police commander out into the main dispatch room, then down a hall, away from his office. He stopped at a nook crowded with file cabinets and empty of personnel.

"How did they find out?" asked Patricia.

Major Paine tilted his head to Thomas. "What do you think, Thomas?" It was an echo from his days as an FBI instructor.

Thomas stared past them at the featureless wall. His side was aching, but it receded into the background. "One, they found the frequency and deciphered it. Unlikely, but possible. Two, you have a security problem in special ops, either in the field or in that room. Again, unlikely. Three, my unit does. Unlikely. Four, there's some sort of leak at the congresswoman's. Either an assistant, or her phone or her room are being tapped."

Patricia nodded. "I asked her about eight-fifty-three and told her it seemed to be linked on the *Open Lotus*. Almost immediately after, Hughes gets a phone call. What did he say?"

Thomas said, "He said, 'a few minutes ago' and 'in a noisy restaurant, just to Pinkerton and Maisey.' "

Patricia nodded. "And if the other side of that conversation was 'Did anybody just mention eight-fifty-three?' and 'Where?' it fits." She slapped her forehead. "If they were bugging her phone, they may have even recognized some of the voices in the background. The speakers in the room were going full blast."

Thomas added, "Given *Sycorax*'s decrypting technology and ELINT suite, it fits."

Paine's face lightened. "Ah. I'm relieved, almost. Stupid of us, but at least I don't have to conduct a witch-hunt in my department. What is eight-fifty-three? Did your mother know?"

Patricia repeated what her mother had told her.

While Major Paine thought about that, Patricia asked,

"Did you hear what that kid said to Liz? 'Tonight. We've got this thing to do.' "

Thomas nodded. "Yes. They have to go back on patrol."

Patricia shook her head. "That isn't a 'thing,' really. He said 'this thing' like it was a specific thing."

Thomas leaned against the wall. "Hmmm. I better see about getting some sort of vehicle to shadow the *Sycorax*. We know they diddle their position data, after all."

"Why can't you use satellite imaging?" Patricia asked.

Thomas spread his hands. "Their heat signature is large enough that we could probably track them through the forecast cloud cover, but I'd get no detail. If they met a ship, I might be able to tell that, but not *what* ship."

"Will you be going?" Patricia asked.

Thomas thought about being at sea with his stitches, constantly shifting his center as the vessel pitched, and the pain flared anew. He thought of Patricia, naked in the moonlight. "I'll be sending Jazz and Bart."

Patricia grinned. "Good."

Thomas found the patrol hydrofoil he'd requisitioned for the machine-gun inspections was a mere fifty miles north of the Strand and was available. He was dissatisfied with the arrangement—he had no idea if she carried Nat-Al members aboard. He was able to get her without giving her intended mission to GulfOps and he hoped that would do. He would've preferred to take a vessel from Major Paine, but the NGPD didn't have anything seaworthy that the *Sycorax* couldn't run rings around.

"Keep stealthy, Jazz. Minimum radio traffic. No radar. You know the drill."

"Aye, aye, sir."

They were in the police motor pool, hidden from spying eyes. Major Paine had a boat standing by to run Jazz and Ensign Terkel out to the hydrofoil, a rendezvous set for the mouth of the North Civic Channel on the New Galveston side, miles away from the *Boca del Infierno* with the entire bulk of the Strand between them and the *Sycorax.*

Patricia was back in her disguise, an illusion so strong that Thomas found himself looking elsewhere for *his* Patricia. She was almost exactly his height with the lifts on, and he contented himself with her eyes, framed with mascara and eyeliner but still hers.

Thomas wore a floppy panama, its brim tilted to cast a shadow across the scarred side of his face.

Holding hands, they watched the patrol boat pull away, until it turned the bend in the tunnel and headed for the municipal lagoon.

"Ready?" she said.

"Oh, aye."

One of the NGPD faux cabs awaited their pleasure, bobbing gently in the wake of the patrol boat. Even in heels, Patricia was aboard quickly, settling herself neatly. Thomas groaned and oozed aboard, holding his side. Patricia muttered, "*Ay, ay, a scratch.*" She stood to help him sit, then pushed the button that closed the canopy.

The driver pulled away, and as the engine noise rose, Thomas let himself groan.

"Are you sure about that hospital?" she asked.

"I need a bed," he said. "But not in a hospital."

"I'm afraid to touch you."

"Oh, please don't be. I could use some *gentle* touch."

She laughed. "We've had enough of the other." She leaned over and kissed him, keeping her weight off. As she started to pull back, he stopped her, prolonging the kiss. She broke off to take a deep breath. "Ah. I've been wanting that. And more." She cupped the falsies and pushed up. "You like my boobies?"

He laughed. "I'm grateful for your boobies, but I can't pretend to like them. If they keep you safe, hidden from harm, great. But what you were born with is more than enough for me."

She dropped her hands to her lap and sighed. Thomas wasn't sure whether she was sad or happy.

"What's wrong?"

She laughed. "Absolutely nothing. Every man I've interacted with in this outfit has had trouble meeting my eyes—except you."

Thomas smiled. "I did something right?"

She took his hand in both of hers and leaned against him.

The hotel was not on the water's edge and they had to go four hexes inward to reach it. Thomas tried to walk without limping, to present a tourist's facade, carefree. The room was on the third floor, but she knew where the freight elevator was, saving him from the stairs.

The room *was* small and the bed *was* large. She started to push him down on it, but he said, "Let me use the bathroom first. Once horizontal, I don't want to get up again."

She nodded. He closed the door and urinated, then washed his face and hands. When he came out, he carried a glass of water and two tablets.

"What have you there?"

"Pain meds. I haven't had any yet, and I'm told with two I'll sleep like the dead. I figure we'll have half an hour after I down them. I'm sorry, but it's getting a bit much for me."

"Well, take them! Don't be a martyr for my sake."

He shook his head. "It's purely selfish. I'll take them when you come to bed."

She said, "Well, then, I'll be right there. Will you need help undressing?"

He smiled. "I don't think so, as long as I can drop these pants on the floor without bending over."

She turned off the overhead light and threw a room-service towel over the bedside lamp, muting its glow; then she went into the bathroom, closing the door.

Thomas undid the shirt, kicked off his shoes, dropped his pants and underwear, as promised, and was sitting on the edge of the bed trying to remove his socks with his toes when Patricia came back in, naked, her face scrubbed clean of makeup.

"I'll get those," she said, stooping. "You take those pills."

He stared at her, his mouth suddenly dry. "You know, the pain just went completely away." He swallowed the pills as she pulled his socks off; then, with her support, he lay back on the pillow. He was unable to take his eyes off her.

Patricia laughed. "*Now* you're having trouble meeting my eyes." She traced her fingers over the elastic dressing wrapped around his middle.

He reached up and lifted her short bangs, where they drooped over the stitches on her forehead, then traced his hand down the side of her face, then her neck, and down to the curve of her breast.

She inhaled sharply and pinned his hand there with hers, bending over and kissing him slowly.

They progressed carefully, gently, Patricia on top, and as they moved and kissed and touched, he felt the drugs take hold, modifying the sensations, making things less urgent. There was a bad moment when her knee brushed his bandaged side, but she moved it away immediately when she felt him flinch.

She came first but it triggered his climax, moving together like slow thunder, a velvet earthquake that lasted into ecstatic aftershocks.

With a sort of breathless laugh, spoken with lips against the skin of his neck, she said, "You see? We *can* do it without being shot at."

He felt her slide down beside him, nestled under his armpit on his uninjured side, head on his shoulder, and with this happy contact, fell asleep.

16

Beenan: *Muertes diminutas*

Patricia drowsed initially, savoring the warm contact of Thomas's body down the length of hers. *This is good. This is very good.* She resented the few square inches of bandage that kept her from contacting him skin to skin *everywhere* their bodies pressed together and laughed quietly to herself about it.

Wake up, slugabed.

She wanted to talk to him, to kiss, to touch, to make love again. She wanted to try things with Thomas that, with Geoffrey, she'd only done reluctantly. She felt hungrily wanton and eager.

Still, his face asleep was now relaxed, different, released from the pain. *He did his best to hide it but you could see it around his brow, his eyes.* It was probably better that he slept and recovered. *—the death of each day's life, sore labor's bath, balm of hurt minds, great nature's second course, chief nourisher in life's feast.*

Yes, sleep, for now, she grinned. *I won't be so gentle in the future.*

He wasn't a mouth breather, she noted, nor a snorer. She wouldn't know for sure, she supposed, until she saw him asleep without drugs. She hoped he didn't mind that *she* snored.

Geoffrey had told her often enough that she did.

She remembered Thomas's face against her neck, her

cheek, her breast, and she realized he'd had his facial hair suppressed. It made sense, she guessed, while he was in the military. She'd done the same herself with her leg and armpit hair when she was younger and though she felt differently about such things now, she'd never taken the time to have it reversed.

He had other scars besides the burns. There were three puckered spots high on his left pectoral and matching holes over his shoulder blade showing where the fléchettes must've exited. *Or entered—he could've been shot in the back.* She smoothed her hand over the three on his chest, as if by rubbing gently she could erase them. Thomas slept on, oblivious.

She tried to sleep but her fatigue was not enough to overcome her joy, and her brain, untethered, flew from the past to the future, from the fantastic to the practical.

What does he like for breakfast? Is he pleasant when he wakes, or does he need time? Is he religious? Does he want children? Is he good with children? Does he like broccoli?

The things that had been worrying her all day, ever since he'd proposed, came back to her transformed. Whereas before they'd seemed like insurmountable obstacles, rocky mountains on the horizon, now they seemed like wrapped packages in some labyrinthine postal system, surprises to be opened and dealt with when they finally arrived on the doorstep. Dread had transformed into pleasant anticipation—even delight.

She wondered what their days would be like. Would he get a job? Would he like to work with her, learning to pilot *SubLorraine* or skippering *Terminal Lorraine*? Maybe he really wanted to retire, though she found it hard to picture him working in a garden or watching television all day long.

She had an image of herself returning from a city inspection, surfacing in the pen, to see him waiting for her, a toddler on his shoulders.

Damn, the city inspections. I've got to get going on them. They were how she earned her hex's utilities, municipal school fees, and city membership dues. She was able to keep nearly a hundred sponsored refugees in job training because of that arrangement.

She inhaled, her nose right against Thomas's skin. There was some sweat, some musk, a hint of deodorant. She darted her tongue out to taste him—slightly salty—and found herself intensely aroused.

What relish is in this? How runs the stream? Or I am mad, or else this is a dream: let fancy still my sense in Lethe steep; if it be thus to dream, still let me sleep!

She crept from the bed, sliding out from under his arm and covering him with the blankets. The muted light was still on, and she watched his face for a moment, the motion of his eyes behind the lids, in REM. *Dream of me.*

She turned off the lamp and went into the bathroom, showering with water colder than was comfortable. When she climbed back into bed, she warmed herself against him until sleep finally came.

And if she dreamt, the dreams did not trouble her.

Thomas's satphone woke them both to bright morning light shining around the edges of the room's drapes.

Patricia sat up, instantly awake, and heard Thomas grunt in pain as he tried to sit up directly, using his stomach muscles. She pushed him back. "I'll fetch it."

His phone was hooked to his pants belt and she retrieved it from the floor, flipped it open, and handed it to Thomas.

"H'lo?" he managed.

She looked at him. He was still fogged with sleep or the aftereffects of the pain meds, and he was blinking hard.

"Righ'," he said. "I need a shower to wake me up. I'll call back in five minutes." He stabbed at the phone with his forefinger, trying to turn it off, managing it after two more tries. He stared at the phone for a moment and she took it from him. He focused on her and suddenly took a deep breath.

"You."

She grinned at him. "*Tu. ¿Recuerdas mi nombre?*"

"Don't lay traps, *mi dulzura*. Drugs or no, I remember *mi novia*."

She kissed him.

"Help me up," he said, after. "I've got to get this fog out of my head."

She lifted his shoulders and he swung his feet to the floor, cradling his side.

"Does it hurt much this morning?"

He shook his head. "It's throbbing a bit, but not like last night. I'd like to take a cold shower, but I'm not supposed to get the dressing wet."

While he urinated, she found a plastic laundry bag in the closet. Splitting it, she was able to fasten it tightly around his chest, draping the bandage.

She hovered as he climbed into the tub, worried about his balance, but he managed and turned the cold water on, with no ameliorating warmth. She jumped back from the cold spray and, at arm's length, tugged the curtain shut. In her mind's eye lingered the vision of Thomas, teeth clenched, thrusting his face into the stream of cold water.

She hovered, listening for some cry or gasp, but he was silent. She laughed quietly. *In voices well divulged, free, learn'd and valiant*. Especially valiant. When he emerged, she handed him a towel and untied the plastic, then took another towel and dried his back. "*Quiet untroubled soul, awake, awake! Arm, fight, and conquer, for fair England's sake!*"

He mimed snapping his towel at her, then limped back into the room to his satphone. "Can we get coffee up?"

"Yes. And breakfast?"

"I don't know." His face fell as he added reluctantly. "I may have to leave."

She winced but turned back to the room phone as he turned to the satphone. Rather than go through the hotel, she called to a coffee shop the next hex over and arranged the delivery of two large lattes and muffins. *He can always take his with him.*

By the time she was done, he was just finishing up.

"—at NGPD? Right." He looked at his wrist and, finding it bare, looked around the room until he spotted the television clock's readout. "It'll take you a bit, so oh-nine-thirty? Great." He looked at her and licked his lips. "We've an hour."

She threw herself down on the bed and said, "Then let's not waste it."

They took a water taxi to Palacios, hidden below the canopy, necking slowly. She didn't wear her disguise. He got out at the NGPD public landing and she took the cab on, looking back from the window, not just because she wanted to watch him, but to make sure he moved inside quickly.

She had the taxi pull right up to her sub pen, alarming the police officers stationed there, but they relaxed when she emerged. Perito had rehung the pen doors, though they were sadly bent and folded and didn't quite meet in the middle, and through the gap she heard salsa played loudly from within.

The dockside door was locked, and when she punched the combination the lock clicked, but the manual bolt was engaged and the door wouldn't open. She pounded on the door, hard, seeking to be heard over the music. Inside, the volume was turned down and Perito's voice said, "Who is it?"

"*Su jefe.*"

He threw the bolt and opened the door wide. She walked in quickly, driven by an itching feeling between her shoulder blades that didn't subside until the door was shut behind.

"*¿Qué pasa?*" She looked first at *SubLorraine,* noting that the floor panels were back in place, though many had new holes drilled for the bolts into the dock. Looking over at the workbench, she recognized the stereo that was playing the music. "Isn't that Toni's new stereo?"

"*Sí*. She, uh, she moved in with me." He looked up at the ceiling, toward the apartment. "But she's up at the school right now."

"Really? And how did her parents take that?"

"*Bien y mal.*"

"Mixed feelings? How so?"

"They have more room with her gone."

Patricia laughed. "And on the other hand there is the *hombre desacreditado* their daughter is living with."

He drew himself up. "*¡Claro que no!* Am I not the trusted employee of the eminent assemblywoman?" He slumped back down again and tapped the back of his forearm. "But I think they're not so sure about *el color de mi piel*."

"And *la rubia*? Does she care what color your skin is?"

Perito grinned. "She likes it."

"Then don't worry about *los padres*. They'll get over it." She put down her bag and gestured at *SubLorraine*. "How is she?"

Perito pointed at the floor panels under the middle of the sub where a pneumatic sander lay, the hose snaking across the floor to the compressor outlet in the corner. "I was smoothing down the mess you made of the instrument housing. Everything else is set—the absorbent, the activated charcoal, the oxygen, the reserve air bank, and the natural gas. I tested the turbogenerator for a few minutes, then spun up the flywheels using city power, uh—." He looked at his watch. "Two hours ago."

Patricia smiled. "The most *trusted* and *dependable* employee of the eminent assemblywoman."

She moved over to the phone and dialed the Engineering Office.

Assistant Director Martinez was glad to hear from her. "The way you've been all over the news, I could've sworn we wouldn't be talking to you for a long time. Are you all right?"

She looked down at the ring and thought of the way Thomas had felt against her. She grinned. "Actually, quite all right. I'm going to start where we left off, hex three-sixty-two, isn't it? Framing the Number Three algae farm? Unless you have some indication of a problem somewhere else."

"No, that's good. We've got that stretch; then we're overdue for the inspections of the seawall and beach plates around the refugee center."

"Well, barring problems, I don't see why I can't finish the algae farm today and move on to the seawall stuff tomorrow."

"Great. Pachefski's engineering staff has been bugging me, wanting to know when you'll get to their end, but with all your adventures, I haven't been able to tell them. You'll e-mail the inspection video at the end of the day?"

"And drop off the water samples at the lab. Right. See you."

She let two of the NGPD officers escort her up to her apartment to pick up some comfortable working clothes, but the trip, which should've taken five minutes, took over an hour.

She felt like a ship accumulating barnacles.

The first person to stop her, to make sure she was all right "after that horrible explosion," was Celeste, and then Marie ran up shouting, "Tante, I lost a tooth, I lost a tooth!" This slowed her enough for the next person, Toni, to reach her, wanting to talk about moving in with Perito, and then Consuela saw her from her office window and grabbed her to authorize some expenditures and an emergency hire. By the time Patricia made it into her apartment, there was a small crowd surrounding her that didn't quite dare to follow her inside.

She shut the door and stared at the bust of Shakespeare. *Will, I should've worn the disguise.*

The phone rang and she glared at it, but the number of unheard messages on the display was up to over a hundred and she didn't want to add to it. "Hello."

"Assemblywoman Alternate Beenan?"

She froze. She knew that voice. It was a hoarse and gravelly voice, the voice of a heavy smoker. The voice she'd heard on the seawall when they'd tried to kill her and Thomas.

She reached out and hit the message button, causing the phone to start recording. "No. The asseeemlywom-an, she no here. You weesh to leave a *mensaje*—a message?"

"Yes. There's a bomb in the school. Do you understand?"

She felt adrenaline shiver through her like ice water in her blood. "A bome?"

He snarled. "*¡Una bomba en la escuela, estúpida! ¿Comprendes?*"

"*Sí. Una bomba. ¿Por qué?*"

"You should be asking 'cuándo'!" He hung up, hard.

She ran out the door, nearly knocking over her police escort. "I've just received a bomb threat on the school! Get the bomb squad!"

The officer reached for his radio but grabbed her arm as she started for the school. "Wait, ma'am!"

"There are sixty-three kids and seven adults in there!" She twisted her arm, breaking out between the thumb and forefinger. "Call the bomb squad, dammit!"

She could hear him talking on the radio as she ran, the other cop right behind her. She paused at the door and said, "Keep everyone out!" She threw open the door, punched the combination on the inner door, then stepped across the inner hall and pulled the fire alarm.

The bell began ringing immediately.

Down the hall, Consuela stuck her head into the hall, her eyes wide. She called to Patricia, "*¿Es real?*"

Patricia beckoned her closer and said quietly, "Bomb threat."

Consuela's mouth opened, then her jaw firmed. "Right. We'll need to get them out of the courtyard, too." She grabbed a teacher just coming out of her class, twelve kids behind her like ducks, and whispered in her ear. "Tell the others." She turned back to Patricia. "Straggler sweep?"

"I'll take the third floor."

"I've got two."

Patricia turned to the policeman who'd followed her inside. "Will you check this floor for stragglers?" All four classrooms were now emptying, and orderly lines of kids who started out bored, but became excited when they saw the policeman. "It's just these four classrooms, but there's the bathrooms, kitchen, and lunchroom."

"Yes, ma'am."

Patricia ran for the stairs, heart pounding. *Please be a hoax, please be a hoax!* The entire hex was being watched by the police—she didn't see how a stranger could've got in, but they couldn't take that chance.

She passed a distraught teacher on the upper landing, leading her class of fourth-graders down. "I'm missing one! Antonio went to the bathroom right before the bell, but he's not in there!"

"Right," Patricia said. "Get these kids out—I'll see to Antonio."

She didn't bother to check the bathroom, but started a methodical sweep of every room, dropping to the floor to peer under the tables, then moving on. Antonio was in the janitor's closet and jumped when she threw the door open.

She didn't bother talking to him, just took his hand and yanked.

"Hey!" he shouted, surprised.

She went out through the walkway to the play structure and shoved him in the long tube slide, then leaned over the railing to make sure he came out below. His own teacher, trooping by with the rest of the class, took him in tow.

She went back in, checked the last two rooms, then went down the stairway to one. Consuela was there before her, dithering at the door. They left together, leaving the inner door unlocked for the bomb squad.

All of the policemen were standing there.

"Is everyone out?" the corporal in charge asked.

"Yes," Consuela answered. "We did a sweep. We'll double-check with a head count. You're not going in, are you?"

The corporal shook his head. "Do I look stupid?"

Patricia, remembering her own recent bomb experience, blushed. "Hey, who's guarding the sub?"

The corporal licked his lips. "Well, I thought this was a priority. The kids and all."

"And this might be a diversion. The kids are all right, now."

He ducked his head. "Right. Carter, Matiz, and Wing, get back downstairs. The rest of us will keep anyone from entering the courtyard. You two take the inner stairway; I'll take the outer. Ladies, if you'd please join the others—if a bomb does go off in the school, this whole area will be filled with flying glass."

The adrenaline stopped flowing, and Patricia felt suddenly limp as she and Consuela were walking down the outer stairs to the waiting children. They were crowded in front of the apartment building, sitting by class. By now, some of the kids' parents, locals living in the Elephant Arms, were mingling, talking to each other and the teachers.

Everyone's eyes got particularly big when the bomb squad hovercraft pulled up to the landing and the team moved quickly up the stairs in their padded armor carrying bomb sniffers and cases of other equipment.

Patricia turned to Consuela. "I think it's time for a trip to Enrico's, on me." She took her bankcard out of her wallet and pressed it into Consuela's hands.

Consuela opened her eyes wide. "The entire school?"

"And whatever parents want to go along. Definitely," she held up her watch. "There's plenty of time until the end of school. Maybe they'll even have the school cleared by then."

Enrico's was an upscale ice cream and sorbet parlor two hexes away.

"You're the boss," Consuela said. She spread the word, teacher to parent to teacher, and got the students formed up and moving, two by two.

Patricia checked in with Perito and the police officers back on guard downstairs.

"No, nobody tried to get at the sub."

She sighed. What did they want? Were they attacking the school for revenge? What good did that do them? Were they even attacking the school at all? Maybe this was just another form of attack aimed at her. It certainly kept her from getting any work done.

She called Martinez at the Engineering Office and postponed, yet again, telling him briefly about the bomb threat.

"*Cobardes,*" he said. "*Sin caras.*"

"*¡Esto es verdaderamente demasiado!*"

She went as far up the stairs as the police would permit and waited to hear from the bomb squad.

"The call was from a pay phone outside the base exchange on Isabel Island. Of course, nobody knows specifically who was using it at that time," said Major Paine.

The bomb squad had been over the school building multiple times without results. When they'd been apprised of the normal security in the building, as well as the temporary presence of NGPD officers in the area, they declared the building clear.

Thomas listened to the recording again. "It sure sounds like the voice from that night."

They were in Major Paine's office.

Patricia had gotten over her initial fear for the children and teachers, had gone through relief when the building was declared safe, and was now working on a towering rage. "God damn them and their games. Martinez had it right—they're *cobardes sin caras*—cowards without faces. What do they want?"

Thomas shook his head. "I wonder if they just did it because you showed up again. That someone saw you arrive back at your hex."

She shook her head, disgusted. "I'd like to give them a ride on *SubLorraine*, on the *outside*, without life support." She exhaled through pursed lips, trying to expel some of the rage, and picked up Thomas's hand. In an artificially squeaky voice she said, "And how was *your* day, honey?" More normally she added, "What's with *Sycorax*?"

Thomas's mouth became a straight line.

"Oh, did something happen?"

"Something *didn't* happen." He clenched his free hand into a fist. "*Sycorax* seemed to be heading toward three freighters well beyond the EEZ when Jazz surprised the radio operator making an unauthorized transmission. The operator says he was just testing his equipment, that nothing went out, but the transmit light was on and Jazz is no fool." He released the fist and rubbed his forehead. "Anyway, *Sycorax* radically changed course almost immediately. It might have been some sort of rendezvous with one of the freighters or even something over the horizon. But we don't know—possibly won't ever know—not if we can't observe their activities without being blown."

Major Paine nodded. "Where's *Sycorax* now?"

Thomas looked at his watch. "As of twenty minutes ago, it was inland, between here and McAllen, in the Bay of Matamoras."

"I've got a V-36 we use for long-range air-sea rescue," said Major Paine. "But it's not exactly inconspicuous on a radar screen—it does have twelve-hour endurance in fixed-wing mode." He shrugged and said, "I'd have to charge you for the fuel."

Thomas shook his head. "I could probably come up with the funding, but if they can see it, it's not very useful."

"At the moment of the rendezvous, it would be good," Patricia said. "If you knew when and where, you could close pretty fast, flying low. They wouldn't know you were there until the last thirty miles or so and what's that? Maybe six minutes' warning, tops?"

"But you still have to know when the rendezvous is. And to do that—"

"You need my submersible."

Becket looked down at the floor. *He's thought of it already. He doesn't like it though.*

"How hard would it be to train me to pilot it?"

She shook her head. "Not really an option—and I'm not just being stubborn. I could train you in basic piloting, enabling you to handle some basic operations and the bare minimum emergency procedures, in about three days. To do this remora thing, under the *Sycorax,* I wouldn't be comfortable with less than a month and that includes lots of trail runs using friendly boats."

Thomas looked down at his hands. "I can't ask this of you. It's not your affair."

"Well, they've, by god, made it my affair! They've shot at me, more than once, they've threatened my property and my employees and the children from my school, and they've tried to blow me up. This has to end. If this will do it, then I'm all for it."

Major Paine frowned. "I don't like it. It'll be dangerous."

She sat up and squared her shoulders. "*Women and children of so high a courage, and warriors faint!*" She slumped down, abandoning the posture. "I go to spy on them, not fight. And I'll do so *with an invisible and subtle stealth.*"

Thomas stood up suddenly. "Oh, stop it, please." He looked at her and she watched him carefully, but his look wasn't anger or irritation. It was fear, and it silenced her far more effectively than his words.

We had a deal: no more bombs, no more knives.

She stood up, her head bowed, and leaned into him. "I'm sorry," she said, mumbling into his chest. "I know it's dangerous."

He put his arms around her. "Maybe I should just arrest them all? Surely one of them would testify, for consideration."

"And if they don't," Major Paine said, "you've blown the entire investigation."

Thomas growled deep in his chest and it vibrated against her face.

In a very small voice she said, "Let's get it over with."

The design had really been in her head ever since Thomas had mentioned the suction collars they use on the deep submergence rescue vehicles. She had a circular plate of one-inch steel, two feet in diameter, grooved for a half-inch-thick O-ring around the rim. Within this circle she had the machine shop mill away three-eighths of an inch, forming a shallow dish. Next they drilled and tapped a half-inch through-hole, a foot off-center. The last stage was to weld a D-shaped tab for mounting, directly in the middle.

"Are you sure it can be done in time?" Thomas had asked.

She'd nodded. "Your job is to get them close enough to the Strand that I can latch on. I'll be ready by midnight."

Mounting the flange to the sub was accomplished by replacing the forward lifting eye with a vertical post, braced to the stern by another steel member, against the edge of the pilot's hatch. A ball-bearing joint connected the brace to the suction plate, letting it rotate and tilt in relation to the sub. This held it like some odd hat, three feet above the top of the front portion of *SubLorraine* and a foot above the vertical stabilizer at the stern.

An armored vacuum hose was run from the forward trim tank and screwed into the tapped hole in the plate.

This is going to take knots off her speed, thought Patricia. She greased the mounting point at the bottom of the plate so that it could rotate slightly, forward and back. *Well,* SubLorraine's *thirteen knots was never going to match* Sycorax's *forty-five, anyway.*

When they put a sheet of aluminum across the plate and turned on the pumps, the plate stuck tight, then deformed, dimpling in the middle. They turned the pump off and watched the gauge but there was no leakage, and all efforts to dislodge the plate failed until the vacuum was deliberately breached.

She changed into clean shorts and a long-sleeved sweatshirt and took the rig underwater, ten-thirty at night. The wind was picking up outside, generating a heavy chop in the lagoon, but it was calm and still underwater. The plate interfered with *SubLorraine*'s pitch control, slowing her normally snappy response, but not dangerously. Patricia cruised over to the Intercity pier and clamped on to the bottom of the four-fifteen ferry while it was loading. The ferry towed *SubLorraine* neatly over to Palacios without missing a beat, oblivious to her presence.

There's something to be said for this.

She detached and dove under the dark mass of Palacios and, eventually, found the police motor pen, nicely lit among the dark shadows of Palacios's support hexes.

Thomas was waiting when she surfaced, as promised, with the food, water, and a special secure radio. Seaman Guterson put a rope around the suction-plate bracket and another over the snorkel.

"Well?" she said as she opened the hatch.

Thomas was staring at *SubLorraine* with wide eyes, and she realized, *He's never seen it before.*

"It's so *tiny*!" he said.

"Look, dear, haven't you heard that size isn't important?" She remembered Toni. "You're not claustrophobic, are you?"

He shook his head. "I used to spelunk, in high school."

"What about the *Sycorax*? Did you manage it?"

Thomas sat on the edge of the dock and held *SubLorraine* off with his feet. "*Sycorax* will be in the *Boca del Infierno* in three hours to refuel, as a favor to the depot supervisor who has a bad leak in his tank and needs to lower the level so he can work on it."

"And we're sure about the depot supervisor?"

"Doesn't matter. When he leaves, the hydrofoil will be following them again; then it will receive an emergency response order that will make them break off, leaving *Sycorax* 'in the clear.' " He pointed his finger overhead. "And with Tropical Storm Hermia moving into the area, they may feel safe from aerial surveillance, too."

17

Becket: *La sanguijuela*

Patricia used the external floodlights as they traversed the Strand, and Thomas's eyes followed the inverted topography of hexes and the plunging tubes of OTEC intake pipes. The flickering patterns of schooling fish swimming in and out of the beams mesmerized him, lulling his mind.

It wasn't silent, either. Besides the sound of *SubLorraine*'s motor, there was a continuous *thud-swish* that faded and increased based on their proximity to various OTEC plants.

He was propped against the hatch that separated the pilot compartment from the lockout chamber, his lower back and butt padded by a sleeping bag. He looked forward occasionally but spent most of his time looking up through the transparent acrylic hatch over his head. He yawned suddenly, and it echoed in the humming interior of the submarine.

There was a chuckle from the pilot's seat. *"I'll give thee fairies to attend on thee, and they shall fetch thee jewels from the deep, and sing while thou on pressed flowers dost sleep."*

He vaguely remembered the source. "Oh, don't be an ass."

She laughed again, and he closed his eyes for a moment, listening to it echo. *I could listen to her voice forever . . . well, for a very long time.*

The submarine seemed to jerk sideways, and he opened

his eyes, his hands flying out to brace himself. "What was that?"

"I entered an OTEC discharge stream to hitch a ride on the current." Patricia seemed unconcerned. "It saves us energy."

She did it several more times as they passed different plants, before she turned off the lights. "Softly, now," she said. She throttled back the motor to the faintest whine. "That's the depot ahead."

There was a barge tied up near the depot, and she raised *SubLorraine* carefully to its flat bottom and started the trim pumps. There was a slight *thud* as the Sucker grabbed hold, and Patricia's shoulders dropped. She rotated the seat to face him, putting her feet down between his, a set of headphones on her head, one ear on and one ear off.

There was a glow coming down through the water, filtered dock lights, but by the time it lit the interior of *SubLorraine,* it was dim, flickering. It silhouetted Patricia's head and, though he could see a slight gleam from her eyes and teeth, Thomas couldn't read her expression.

"I'm tired," she said. "Getting the Sucker ready was a lot of work." He saw her shoulders move. "Make that tired and hungry. We didn't stop for supper."

Thomas sat up and reached behind him, unlatching the hatch to the lockout chamber. He felt around and came back with an insulated bag and a thermos. "Here's your sacrament. And here's something Tío Rodolfo prepared with his own hands." He unzipped the insulated bag and the scent of garlic, shrimp, and onions wafted into the room "I ordered it by phone sent Mr. Guterson to pick it up. The Vigils are doing fine, by the way."

"If I didn't already love you, Thomas, this would do it." She took the thermos and poured herself coffee while he unpacked the tortillas, cardboard containers, and napkins.

They hadn't finished when she held a hand to the headphones and said, "Ah, she comes."

"Are you sure it's her?"

"Jet-turbine water jet drive boats that large are very uncommon. Besides, I spent thirty-six hours attached to her bottom. I *know* what she sounds like."

"Should we be getting ready?"

She shook her silhouetted head. "They're probably fifteen miles away still, coming full bore. We've got time to finish eating. It'll take them another twenty minutes to get to the breakwater and another ten minutes to negotiate the shipping channel. I don't know how much fuel she'll take on, but that can't take less than a half hour. We've got lots of time—I may even nap." She rotated the chair back to the front and hit a switch.

"What are you doing, if you don't mind me asking?"

"I'm pumping out my middle trim tank, to take *Sub-Lorraine* negative. That way, when I release the Sucker, we'll drop immediately." She rotated the seat back to face Thomas. "I had the weirdest feeling running up here with you behind me. You're much bigger than Toni—the crew member I had with me when I was running from *Sycorax*—but I spent that entire time resenting her presence. I'm much more comfortable with you."

Thomas smiled to himself. "Maybe this Tony fellow wasn't your type."

Patricia chuckled. "No, she wasn't. But it's more than just the relationship. Toni couldn't hold still. She was constantly shifting, throwing off the trim, and when she did move, she jerked, always banging herself against something."

"Well, my shoulders are almost touching on both sides. I don't really *dare* move." But he knew what she meant. He'd realized immediately upon entering the sub that he'd have to take a Zen meditative attitude. *You must sit like a* rock! That's what his sensei used to say. "I'm glad you're comfortable with me. I wouldn't have asked you to be *mi novia* if I didn't feel the same way."

She shoved the cardboard containers to one side and put her knee down, shifting carefully to him, then kissed him. He pulled her closer, causing her weight to rest against his good side, and let his hands wander down her back.

"Oh damn," she said after a few minutes. "I've put my knee in the *frijoles*." She was breathing heavier than the exertion warranted. So was Thomas.

"Let me see. I'll clean it off."

She shifted back and he pulled the container off, then leaned forward, careful to avoid bumping his head on the ventilator fan housing.

Patricia jerked, then breathed in sharply. "Well, that's *one* way to clean it off." She leaned back in the seat and added somewhat breathlessly, "And the beans don't go to waste."

Thomas finished with her knee and moved a few inches up her inner thigh. Patricia gently pushed his head away. "*That* is entirely too distracting . . . at this time."

He returned to his position with a sigh. "Name the time, lady." He forced himself to lighten the tone before he drove himself mad. "Did I tell you *when* I decided to marry you?"

She shook her head.

"I think it was when I bumped my head under the seawall and you laughed at me. I figured it was the only punishment suitable."

Her laughter was an echo of that earlier time.

"See!"

She put the earphones back on. "Ah, they're slowing at the seawall. Time for one more cup of coffee."

Thomas bagged up the trash and stored it in the lockout chamber. "I never asked, but what do we do about a toilet?"

"You can't hold it for three days?"

He didn't bother responding to that.

"There's a 'comfort bottle' with a catch spout for urinating.. We brought extra bottles this time, though last time Toni and I ended up cycling the lockout chamber to empty the bottle more than once. I feel bad about that. During all of my inspections I take water samples, which are checked for urea and *E. coli* contamination. It's the boat people who are the worst."

"What about the *maquiladoras*?"

"There've been some accidents, but the industrial compacts are strict. Violation of the environmental or work safety regulations is grounds for termination of license and confiscation of hex. They can sell or remove their factory equipment, but they can't do business anymore."

"And they still build out here?"

"It's only been exercised three times. Look at the positive side: we have cheap power, an excess of workforce, and no taxes, just the city membership dues, which, while not cheap for a factory hex, are a flat rate not tied to income.

"And real estate. We have to make it, but compared to the cost of land and facilities on the mainland since the Deluge, it's very attractive." She paused. "Uh, that inquiry, about the toilet . . . was that theoretical or was there a more pressing need to know?"

He laughed. "Theoretical. The coffee will make it a practical matter in the due passage of, uh, time."

She took the headphones off. "We want to be pretty quiet, now. Their sonar operator was pretty good."

Thomas dropped his voice to a whisper. "Yes, that would be Chief Marine Science Technician Hallett. He was a naval sonar operator in nukes. He was not *allowed* to reup at the end of his term, but they didn't dishonorably discharge him so he passed screening for INS."

"Did you find out why?"

"Same story. You can't be a bigot on a nuclear submarine. The navy is well mixed and quarters are too tight. He got top marks, though, on job performance."

The *Sycorax* pulled up to the dock. Thomas couldn't see it, but the noise of her engine plant and water jets could be heard and felt through the hull.

"Okay. Let's get on while she's still noisy." Patricia did something to the controls and *SubLorraine* dropped, then tilted slightly forward, banking to the left, under the adjoining hex.

By tilting his head, Thomas could see the flat screen monitor. Engine thrust was zero. "How are we moving?"

"We're gliding—flying if you will. We're negative, so we're sinking, but we have wings, just like a plane."

Thomas looked up through the top hatch and could see the glow of the dock lights defining the barge they'd just left, the edge of the hex, and now the pointed prow of the *Sycorax*.

"You can see the sonar dome," Patricia said. "That rounded tip on the bottom of the bow." The sub was receding, moving deeper and to the west. When they were parallel to *Sycorax,* Patricia threw another switch, and there was a soft pumping sound.

"And now?" he whispered.

"Pumping out the trim tank, taking us positive. Now we're going to glide *up*."

SubLorraine continued parallel to *Sycorax,* but now she was rising slowly. He had to crane his neck, now, looking back to see her; then Patricia was banking the sub to the left, a medium turn that brought them back out from under the hex and right at the stern of *Sycorax*.

"There's the jets," Patricia said. "There's the intake grate ahead. I want to grab on between them." She was still ten feet below the hull. She pitched the nose forward and the sub slowed markedly, momentum trying to drive it forward and buoyancy driving it back. After a moment it stopped and began moving slowly backward. "Let me know where we are in relation to the jets, please."

"They're still aft, about six meters? Five. Four. Three." As he spoke, the hull of the *Sycorax* was also getting closer. "Two."

Patricia raised the nose again. *SubLorraine* drifted back a bit more, then slid forward again. Patricia was leaning forward, twisting her head between the hull overhead and her compass, while muttering to herself, "Come on, baby, just a little more." She threw a switch and Thomas heard water rush into a tank. *SubLorraine* hung suspended, level, seemingly motionless, neither dropping or rising.

"I *think* we're still positive," she whispered. "Ever so

slightly, but I can't tell if we're rising or not. The fathometer isn't that sensitive and I can't see well enough in this murk." She reached out and touched a spot on the monitor that said, "12 FSW." Suddenly it changed to eleven and Patricia exhaled.

She was right. There was no way I'd be able to try piloting this without her years of experience. He felt confused. At least he hadn't risked her life for *no* reason, but was it good enough? Was this safe enough? *Safer with her at the helm.*

The Sucker bumped the hull and Patricia stabbed at the switch. The pump went on and there was a slight *thud* as it clamped on. Patricia let the pump go until it was laboring, then shut it down.

"Mr. Shark has a remora, now."

The weather started getting rough, the tiny ship was tossed.

Tropical Storm Hermia was moving the waves with diligence and, once *Sycorax* cleared the INS ship channel, she was moving across waves ten feet high.

"You better give me one of those bags, Thomas. When it gets like this, I'm liable to lose it."

Thomas, wondering the same thing, said, "I'd like to hear a play."

It was dark, though not as dark as their passage under the seawall. Phosphorescence, generated by the wake of the *Sycorax,* streamed by the acrylic nose of *SubLorraine,* outlining Patricia's head. "A play? What play?"

Thomas swallowed convulsively as a higher than average swell caused them to drop suddenly. "Well, a comedy would be good. I've seen enough death lately to not want one of the tragedies. But I'll settle for any one you've *con'd* complete."

"Complete? Hmmm. I don't know if I've ever tried that."

He swallowed again. "Here, I'll prompt you. Setting, Duke Orsino's palace. Enter Duke Orsino, Curio, and other lords; Musicians attending. Duke Orsino says—"

"If music be the food of love, play on . . . "

He didn't know whether she missed any of it—he'd only just reread it, but he certainly didn't know it by heart. The parts he could remember, she certainly knew.

She was into act two, where the drunken carousing of Sir Toby and Sir Andrew awaken the person and ire of Malvolio, when the engines of *Sycorax* revved up and, at this higher rate of speed, her stability increased greatly.

Thomas felt his stomach settle.

Patricia's recitation, overwhelmed by *Sycorax*'s engines, stopped. She leaned forward. "Thanks for the distraction."

He kissed her. "You weren't the only one who needed it. I was enjoying the play, though."

"It's too noisy to continue."

He moved his hand up the front of her shirt and stroked the underside of her breast. "Well, what else can we do?"

In the tight darkness, moving carefully to avoid banging knees, elbows, and wounds, they found *something* to do.

Later, Thomas said, "I feel guilty."

"Aren't you supposed to save that for the morning after?"

He held up the luminescent dial of his watch. "It *is* morning. I feel I'm neglecting my duty."

She laughed and he could feel her moving, her hand searching the floor. "Where did my underwear go? Ah. Duty is a two-edged sword. What about your duty to your *novia*? You did that duty right well—I may have trouble walking." She reached out and patted his knee. "The woman distracted you. Don't worry, I'm all business, now."

Three hours after they'd left the Strand, they received a coded signal on Thomas's secure radio—two beeps—that indicated the hydrofoil was breaking off. As arranged, they did not respond.

"In this weather, it might not be pretense," Thomas said.

Ten minutes later, *Sycorax* changed course and increased speed, heading southeast, for the EEZ.

"Oh, shit!" said Patricia, listening on the passive sonar.

"What is it?"

"My prop blades are cavitating. It's noisy and they might pick it up."

"Ah. How fast are we going?"

"Forty knots."

He whistled. "They'll spring a leak in these seas if they're not careful. What can we do about the cavitation?"

"I don't know. If I'd thought about it, I might have removed the prop and stored it in the lockout chamber. I *think* it would fit through the hatch. Of course, then we'd be severely hampered if we had to maneuver at short notice."

"If they pick it up, maybe they'll think it's some hull noise of their own."

"Maybe. I hope so."

They followed the position using their GPS data. Thomas wondered what position the *Sycorax* was reporting in its log data and made careful note of times and locations to compare, later.

The waters brightened, a gray diffuse light that lit up the surface waves. After a while, Thomas could make out rain, hard driven, chewing up the troughs. The peaks were wind-torn and foamy.

Just after they'd crossed the EEZ, Patricia said, "I have another vessel, just off our course line. Diesel, two conventional props and hull pounding. It's taking a beating in these waves."

"How far?"

"I don't have a baseline, but with all this surface wash noise it can't be that far."

Almost as if they'd heard her, *Sycorax* make a five-degree course change. "Now it's dead ahead. *Sycorax* must have her on radar. What range would that be?"

Thomas crouched forward, carefully, so he could see her readouts. "Um. With the mast on *Sycorax*, she probably made contact at seventy nautical miles or so, but you think it's closer than that?"

"Much."

"Well, maybe they were both cruising for a particular point, but now it's clear the diesel ship isn't going to make it there and *Sycorax* just changed course to make directly for her. We're well out of U.S. waters so, unless this is a distress response, which we haven't heard on your VHF, it seems like a prearranged rendezvous. Of course, if it's a U.S. vessel, INS can board them anywhere in the world." Thomas let his hands rest on Patricia's shoulders and kneaded gently. She leaned into the pressure. "I know, though, that *Sycorax*'s operational orders are specifically for interdiction patrol up to but not crossing the EEZ."

Sycorax dropped speed markedly fifteen minutes later, and her velocity-driven stability disappeared.

"Oh, god," Patricia said. "Here we go again." *Sycorax*'s bow plunged into a trough and the stern, with *SubLorraine* attached, rose and then dropped.

Thomas, still leaning forward, bumped his head against the ventilator fan housing. He eased back to the hatch and braced himself with his heels against the base of the pilot chair.

"There it is," Patricia said, gesturing to her right.

Thomas craned his neck, but he couldn't see what she was talking about through the overhead hatch. "Describe it, please."

"Well, I can only see the hull, but it's pretty clean, no weed, a bit longer than *Sycorax*. I'd say it was a freighter. It's not built for speed. They've both turned into the teeth of the storm and are slowing down. I'd say they were about to transfer something."

Thomas felt his gut freeze. "I hope so. Let's hope it's not another *Open Lotus*."

Patricia had set her radio to frequency hop, scanning up and down through all the frequencies. "Still nothing on the VHF. No hail, no directions. Surely they wouldn't do that *again*?"

"How deep is the water here?"

He saw her shoulders tense up. "Thirteen hundred fathoms. About a mile and a half."

"Hopefully what they're doing is receiving what they bought with the money from the *Open Lotus*. How fast are we moving? Can we unclamp and get back on?"

"What do you want to do?"

"I want to get a look at that freighter."

"It depends. If they're just querying them, *Sycorax* could be gone the minute we unclamp, and we'd never catch them, not with their legs."

He fell silent, considering.

"They're moving closer together," Patricia said. "Risky, in these seas. I think you're right. They're trying some sort of transfer. We're down to four knots. I can do this, fairly stealthily, too, but if they bug out on us, we'll have to wait out the storm below, then take eighteen hours to cruise back to the Strand."

Waiting would just increase the chance that they'd complete the transfer.

"Do it."

She punched the trim-tank valve control and shoved the stick forward. *SubLorraine* dove sharply forward running on momentum alone; then they were in the jet wash and being shaken. She kicked in her thrusters and tilted the sub up. The noise of *Sycorax*'s engines faded dramatically, a numbing relief. "It's going to be rough on the surface," Patricia said. "And there's the chance they may spot us."

They broke the surface in a trough, then rose sharply as a swell broke over them, twisting them forty-five degrees on their axis.

The wind was ripping the tops off the waves and throwing them horizontally, and heavy rain pounded off the hull, sounding like hail. The two ships were dark blotches dimmed by the airborne water, but Thomas peered anxiously at the rounded stern of the freighter. The letters were barely legible: *Kim Jong,* Democratic People's Republic of Korea.

The freighter had a crane boom extended over the water between the two ships, and there was a cable running to a dark object that dangled over the water. From that, another cable ran to a utility crane forward of the helicopter fantail on the deck of the *Sycorax*.

Another wave slammed into them, twisting the entire sub violently. "Enough," Thomas said.

Patricia didn't bother replying, just put the nose down and dove, trying to get out of the turbulence on the surface. She eased down to fifty feet, then eased forward, just slightly faster than *Sycorax*'s four knots.

"At least the visibility was so bad they probably didn't see us. I hope their sonar operator is helping with that cargo transfer," she muttered. "At least they're not actively pinging." She brought the submarine up slowly, trying to match speed, but the entire hull of the *Sycorax* was moving up and down with the swells.

"Democratic People's Republic of Korea. Is that north or south?"

"North. Arms dealers to the world. They've been doing a booming business with Honduras lately."

They were closer to the starboard side of *Sycorax* this time and Thomas was watching through the pilot hatch, trying not to visualize what would happen if the hull came down more suddenly than Patricia allowed for. *We're a long way from anywhere.* He grinned to himself. *Well, only a mile and a half from the bottom.*

Something splashed into the water forward of them, dropped off the side of the *Sycorax,* and began sinking slowly.

"What was that?" Thomas said, his view distorted by the extreme angle through the upper hatch.

"A man!" Patricia said. She shoved the stick over and they banked sharply to the right.

It was a man, a good thirty feet below the water, kicking and flailing desperately, his feet and hands oddly together.

Patricia moved closer, and Thomas saw a glint of reflected light at the wrists and ankles.

"Christ! He's shackled at the feet and hands!"

He was sinking rapidly, slowed only by his efforts. Thomas, already shocked, swore as he saw a length of heavy chain threaded through the handcuffs on the man's ankles.

Patricia said, "I'm only going to get one shot at this! Get in the lockout chamber and prepare to equalize it. It's the red handle." She was rapidly closing on the wiggling, sinking figure, but the depth gauge now read fifty feet.

Thomas moved, throwing as many of the provisions as he could from the lockout chamber forward. He glanced up just as *SubLorraine* seemed about to dive under the sinking man; then Patricia rolled the submarine ninety degrees and Thomas fell heavily against the bulkhead. There was a sudden clanking sound on the hull; then Patricia righted the sub and shouted, "Did I get him? Did I get him?"

Thomas looked up through the pilot hatch and saw a silhouetted figure folded over the Sucker support.

"Yes!"

"Use my mask and fins and the pony bottle. Shut this hatch, unlatch the exterior hatch, and equalize the chamber. It's the red valve. The hatch will open when you've equalized." The sub tilted back as she headed back for the surface.

Thomas slammed the door and latched it, then unlatched the exterior hatch. He threw the red valve and pulled on the face mask. Air shrieked in and his ears popped hard; then he was awash in water as the hatch dropped open while the sub still rose. He grabbed the pony bottle and twisted the valve, then put the regulator in his mouth. He threw his shoes off and ducked out, not bothering with the fins.

Patricia had stopped the prop, but there was still some forward momentum. *Dammit, I should've worn the fins.* He clung to the hatch, then climbed, pulling himself from the hatch hinges to the vertical skeg before it. Then, as *SubLorraine* slowed even more, he was able to kick his way up to, the man.

It was Fraser, the air survivalman.

He'd stopped struggling and his eyes were closed. He was folded around the support at his waist and, considering the speed *SubLorraine* had been going when they hit, the support probably had driven the rest of his air out of his lungs.

Thomas tried to get him to take a breath, putting the regulator in his mouth and hitting the manual exhaust button, but he was unresponsive. The air blew past slack lips. Thomas took him by the chain between his handcuffs and pulled him around, working his way down the length of the sub. Then, with the heavy chain at the man's ankles pulling his body down the port side of the sub, Thomas went down the starboard side, pulling Fraser's wrists. He reached the hatch as the chain pulled across the top of *SubLorraine* and dropped, but Thomas was halfway in the hatch by the time the chain started dragging Fraser down.

The chamber was half flooded, and Thomas twisted the red valve again as he pulled Fraser up to the air pocket. The shrieking noise of the air was brutal, but he ignored it, tilting Fraser's head back, verifying that the tongue was clear, then starting mouth-to-mouth as soon as both their heads were above water. He tasted blood and hoped Fraser didn't have internal injuries. *Or any bloodborne disease. I'd much rather be doing this with Patricia.*

He was vaguely aware that Fraser's body was dropping as the water was forced back out the hatch by the air pressure. He guided him down to the floor, still breathing.

He felt for a pulse at the neck without stopping and couldn't tell if there was one. *I could use some help in here!* But he knew Patricia couldn't leave the pilot's section until the pressure between the two chambers was equalized and, when Thomas looked through the acrylic hatch between the two compartments, she seemed to have her hands full.

Fraser convulsed, and water and bile spewed from his

mouth. Thomas barely turned his head in time, and the liquid splashed onto Thomas's cheek. He pushed Fraser over to one side while the man first vomited and then went into a paroxysm of coughing.

Thomas looked at the vomited fluid. It was mostly clear—no blood. Good. He looked around. The chain and Fraser's feet still hung in the water, out the hatch. Thomas pulled both inside, then snaked the hatch up and latched it. The chamber wasn't big enough for Fraser to stretch out, so Thomas bent Fraser's knees and rested the man's shackled feet on the large tank labeled Salvage Foam clipped to the aft end of the chamber. *Better for him. Elevated feet for shock.*

He looked through the acrylic hatch. Patricia was twisted in her seat looking back at him. *She didn't tell me how to pump the air back to surface pressure.*

An intercom box mounted over the hatch squawked. "Thomas? The hatch telltale shows closed. Correct?"

He pushed the transmit button. His voice sounded strange to himself—too calm, given the circumstances. "Affirmative. Closed and latched."

"Is that him coughing?"

"It is. Well done, woman. How do I equalize the lockout chamber?"

"The switch labeled 'Exhaust Pump.' It has an auto-cutoff, but watch the gauge. It's the zero line—actually one atmosphere but zero gauge."

"Aye, aye."

He pushed the rubber-coated switch and heard a compressor start. The gauge currently read 15½ psi, opposite an inner ring that read 35 fsw. It began to drop, headed for the zero, but slowly.

Fraser's gasping coughs had subsided to a labored wheezing. Thomas shifted him slightly, lifted his head, and slid one of his shoes under it—a poor pillow, but better than the titanium hull. He looked around for the other shoe and realized it must've washed out with all the water.

Fraser's lip was split and the flesh on his upper left cheek was so swollen that the eye was closed. *So that's the blood I tasted. I don't think he got that running into the submarine.*

The gauge dropped to 12 psi.

He heard *SubLorraine*'s engine noise increase and the pitching worsened. The intercom came back on and Patricia's voice said, "Dammit, they seem to have finished their transfer. *Sycorax* is revving up."

"Can you catch her?"

"I'm trying, but I'm afraid they may hear me."

Thomas bent over Fraser. "How you doing there, Fraser? You sure are one lucky son of a bitch."

Fraser moaned, and Thomas couldn't tell if he was conscious or not.

The intercom came on again and Patricia's voice sounded severely strained. "Thomas, we may have a problem."

"What?"

"I'm getting active pinging from a source separate from the *Sycorax* and I hear very high-speed screws in the water. I've never heard this before, but it's been described to me."

Thomas stood very still. *That sounds like a—*

Patricia continued. "I think it's a torpedo."

Fraser's voice, hoarse and weak, said, "It is."

18

Beenan: *Pillapilla*

Thomas's voice came back over the intercom. "Patricia, Fraser here says it is!"

"Oh, god!" Patricia said aloud, but without hitting the intercom's talk button. Every instinct she had told her to run, dive deep, turn away from the active pinging.

She turned toward it, instead, and pushed the throttle all the way to the stops. *SubLorraine* accelerated to twelve and a half knots, only a bit off her maximum speed. She turned her own active sonar on, cranking the power, and stabbed the talk button. "Is that a U.S. Navy torpedo?"

After a pause, Thomas's voice came back. "It's a mothballed Mark forty-six, Mod five."

She tried to remember what she knew about that model. Over the years, as the active operator of a submersible, she'd met many current and ex-navy submariners, all with stories to tell. The Mark 46 could move almost three times as fast as *SubLorraine* and it carried a hundred pounds of high explosive. It could home using both passive and active sonar, and had enough mono fuel to travel over four nautical miles.

The only bright side was that it was designed to target *much* larger craft than *SubLorraine* and, while *SubLorraine* might be relatively slow, point to point, she *was* nimble.

So, Patricia turned toward the path of the torpedo to present the smallest possible target.

She had no illusions as to their survivability if that warhead exploded anywhere within a hundred yards of them. Incompressible water would transmit the pressure wave like a hammer. But she doubted it would detonate without a direct hit. It was designed for targets *much* tougher than *SubLorraine*.

She had it now on her sonar screen, less than four hundred yards away, closing at a combined speed of forty-four knots—almost twenty-five yards a second. She cursed the Sucker attachment, which was limiting her vertical maneuverability.

Behind her she heard the hatch open and she said loudly, "Don't move. I've got her trimmed." The torpedo closed to two hundred yards. Visibility was poor. The water was clear, but the storm had severely reduced the amount of sunlight. She flicked on the floodlights, the highest setting, and hoped the torpedo didn't also home on infrared. She estimated she had about a hundred feet of visibility.

She was suddenly intensely glad they'd taken the time to make love in the sub. "I love you, Thomas," she said.

"You must."

What the hell did he mean by that?

One hundred yards. They could hear the pinging through the hull now. Seventy-five. Fifty. Thirty. *There.* She saw it and skewed the rudder over hard, kicking the nose to starboard, then rolled the entire sub. Behind her she heard bodies thudding around the lockout chamber like sneakers in a dryer.

Oh, god, I didn't— But large as it loomed, the torpedo *did* miss, flashing by, passing close enough that she could make out letters on the side, just clearing the Sucker plate. Patricia continued the roll and shut off her active sonar, dropping the throttle back to a bare five percent, enough headway to maintain stability, but quiet.

Behind her, Fraser had started coughing again and, when he wasn't, he was swearing.

She looked back. Thomas was shifting Fraser, helping the

man lie down on his back again. Fraser was cradling one elbow. Thomas had a cut on his forehead that was trickling blood down across his right eye.

"It missed?" Thomas said.

"We're not out of the water yet. That thing will try to reacquire us and it can go for another three and a half minutes before it runs out of fuel." She had a horrible thought. "Fraser! Do they have more than one torpedo?" *Why wouldn't they?*

Fraser stopped swearing long enough to say, "They could only get one."

Patricia muttered. "One might be enough."

She brought the nose up. "I'm going up. It's going to be rough, but we have a much better chance of eluding it if we're hidden against the surface-scatter zone." She looked back, guiltily. "Uh, try not to bang around too much. That thing tracks on passive as well as active sonar."

Thomas, holding one hand to his cut forehead, raised his other eyebrow. "We'll *try*."

She looked back at the controls, pulling the sonar headset back over both her burning ears.

Sycorax was powering away to the northwest, over a mile away, and well out of their range. *And if the torpedo did lock on to them, they could simply outrun it.* The Korean freighter was moving toward the southwest, but the storm was still in its teeth and its headway was slow.

Thomas was talking, barely audible over the headphones. "So, Fraser, what did you do that caused your friends to drop you in the water? And before Saint Crispin's day, too."

The torpedo was circling now, still actively pinging. Patricia thought about her tail section, the right-angled planes of the vertical and horizontal stabilizers joined together by the circular prop shroud. *Lots of nasty reflective corners.* Dad had never intended *SubLorraine* to be sonar stealthy.

The bearing stopped changing abruptly and she shuddered. Did she dare try the chicken maneuver again? She pinged the freighter and got a return at five hundred yards.

The torpedo had run away from them for a good minute before reacquiring them and, while she didn't have an exact range, it had to be over a thousand yards. How much over would determine whether they'd live or die.

She shoved the throttle all the way forward and ran for the freighter.

Fraser was in midsentence, answering Thomas's question, but he stopped talking when the sub accelerated. "What's happening?"

Patricia asked, "What sorts are they, on the Korean freighter?"

Fraser said, "They're arms dealers. This is just a stop on their regular run to Honduras, supplying the junta."

"Did they have lifeboats?"

They were still over four hundred yards from the freighter.

"Uh, I think so. It's hard to take in every detail while you're being beaten, chained, and thrown overboard."

"Thomas, do you remember?"

"Yeah. They had a bright orange capsule mounted on davits. Why?"

"We've been reacquired. I *think* I can reach the freighter before the torpedo reaches us."

"Oh. No other options?"

"What did you mean when you said, 'You must,' when I told you I loved you?"

He sucked his lips into his mouth and released them with a slight popping sound. "You must love me to let me put you in such danger. I love you, too, by the way. Are you saying we're about to die—*again*?"

The freighter was three hundred yards away.

"Not immediately." She shrugged. "We'll know for sure in about forty seconds."

Behind them the pings from the torpedo were coming at closer intervals, indicating a lessening of the distance, but she couldn't take an active ping without turning *Sub-*

Lorraine around. "I'd rather be leading this thing into *Sycorax*, but she's keeping her distance."

She turned around to look at him. "Hey, Thomas, do you want children?"

Thomas laughed out loud and Fraser was looking at both of them like they were insane. "I would like to have *your* children," Thomas said.

She breathed out and turned back to the controls. "Well, that's nice to know. Another thing that would be nice to know is, What did the *Sycorax* transship from the Korean boat?"

Fraser cleared his throat but didn't say anything.

Thomas said, "Why not tell us? If we're about to die, what does it matter?"

Two hundred yards. The screws were louder, behind them. Ping interval dropping.

Fraser said, "One-oh-five-millimeter armor-piercing rounds and some special acoustically controlled detonators."

Thomas said, "Why on earth? Does the *Sycorax* have a one-oh-five cannon?"

"They're recoilless rifle, but no, they don't. It's the second shipment we've taken. The detonators are put on the recoilless rounds, and the entire thing is waterproofed, then fitted with an inflatable collar that keeps it pointed up."

"Why? In case a plane flies over?"

"No. To penetrate three feet of seacrete."

Patricia felt soundless thunder shake her world.

"Oh, god, Thomas! They weren't after *me*, they were after *SubLorraine*. They were trying to stop my scheduled inspections under the Abattoir!"

One hundred yards.

"That's right," Fraser said. "Even back when you found the *Open Lotus*, they wanted to make sure you didn't get your submarine back to the Strand. They didn't want you to find the devices before . . . well, before they sank the Refugee Center."

Patricia felt numb. Some part of her kept refining her course, listening to the torpedo, its pinging again audible through the hull, and watching the instruments. Another part of her gaped in horror. *Almost half a million people.* She remembered her mother talking about Bill 853. *They'd rather kill them than see them brought into the U.S.*

The hull of the freighter loomed out of the murk, and she drove straight for it. *Gotta remember she won't dive as fast with the Sucker.* Still she almost waited too long, pushing the nose down as it loomed before her. The Sucker just missed the hull, but she heard the top of the vertical stabilizer slam into and scrape along the hull. Then they were under the keel, and she pulled up again, on the far side of the ship.

The torpedo's pinging dimmed in volume, and the acrylic nose of *SubLorraine* shot out of the water halfway up a large swell just as the torpedo exploded on the freighter's hull.

The water whitened around them and the entire sub, already half out of the water, went airborne. "Hang o—."

SubLorraine slammed into the trough, jarring even Patricia, strapped into the padded seat. They slewed around broadside to the wave and it folded over them, pushing them back under. The monitor bracket snapped in two and the flat panel display dropped across her lap. She killed the throttle and turned her head around, anxious about Thomas, but he had turned sideways across the lockout chamber and braced himself, legs across Fraser to the port hull, back braced against the starboard hull, and arms extended up to the ceiling.

His head was swiveling back and forth to take in the submarine, Fraser, and Patricia. "Hello," he said.

"Hello, yourself, *novio*." She gave him one quick heartfelt grin, then turned back to the controls.

Though the display bracket was broken, the cable was not, so the readouts were still working, though something seemed to have happened to the GPS. She tried the throttle, and *SubLorraine* responded relatively quickly. None of the leak indicators had turned red. *Being partially out of the water saved our asses.*

They were still rising and falling with the swells, so she dove, letting *SubLorraine* drop down until she could no longer feel the surface turbulence, then headed away from the *Kim Jong. It's an arms ship. One explosion might lead to another.*

She tried the passive sonar but all she could pick up were rumbles, the echo of the explosion reflecting off the bottom a mile and a half below, then off the surface, and back again. She tried to locate *Sycorax,* but couldn't. *Is the sonar broken?*

The water outside was murky, even with the floodlights, and she realized what had happened. The underwater explosion had liberated—shocked—dissolved gases out of the water to form billions of tiny bubbles. This formed what submariners called an ensonified zone—a section that messed up sonar, reflecting sound waves. But how long would it last?

Thomas was asking Fraser something. "How many of those devices have been deployed?"

"About five hundred. We—they needed another one hundred to be sure the whole thing would go down at once."

Patricia was doing some quick thinking. "There are over thirteen hundred hexes, not counting the seawall, but, yeah. If you holed enough of them, they'd tip the others, spilling the air."

Thomas asked, "And these detonators—how do they work?"

"They were the expensive part. *Sycorax* had to play a digitally pulsed sonar sequence to set them all off at once."

"There's no other equipment that can do it? I mean, those Nat-Al members who work in the Abattoir can't set them off?"

"Don't think so. It takes a sonar set specially linked to a digital signal generator. It was Master Chief Hughes's special project."

"How far away can they be and still set them off?"

Fraser shook his head. "No idea. That wasn't my end."

Thomas looked annoyed. "And what was your end?"

"I'm a diver. I trained others. We placed the charges. We've been working like dogs for the last two weeks."

"And you got fed up with it?"

Fraser turned his head away.

"What happened? Why the change?"

"*Open Lotus* surprised most of the crew—Wall gave the orders for the scuttling charge to the gunner's mate, but he sent McIntyre along to position it. McIntyre waited until the gunner's mate was on his way out, barricaded himself in the engine room, and started broadcasting an SOS. Wall himself took the fifty-cal and the XO commanded the cannon. By the time the rest of the crew realized what was happening, the freighter was completely underwater."

He shuddered. "Even though most of us had signed on for the full mission, *Open Lotus* opened our eyes to the reality. Anyway, last night I tried to talk Mowett into blowing the whistle with me, but the asshole turned me in to Wall." He laughed, a short bitter bark. "Wall made Mowett push me over the side. I hope he has nightmares."

Patricia had been thinking. "Thomas, you can't let *Sycorax* get anywhere near the Strand."

"How near?"

"It has a powerful sonar. I wouldn't risk anything less than twenty miles. In this storm, they might not *need* the extra mines. If they blow what they have, the storm may do the rest."

Thomas chewed his lip. "This storm is the problem. I don't know what sort of intercept we can arrange. Certainly not anything airborne. Well, we won't know until we try. We'll need to surface so I can radio."

"No. I've got a deployable buoy. I don't want to get up there anytime soon."

She pushed the deploy button and heard the electric motor unwind the buoy, but when the panel showed sufficient cable out to reach the surface, she couldn't hear anything on the VHF and the GPS was still dead. "Damn." She used reverse thrust and backed the submarine enough to bring the line in view through the top hatch, stretching up to the surface.

Patricia swore. "It deployed. We must've scraped off the antennae when I dove under the *Kim Jong*. That's the same antenna we were hooked into before. Is there an aerial on your radio?"

Thomas shook his head. "Did you bring your satphone?"

She shook her head. "No. Didn't want the distraction."

"Neither did I." He looked aside. "I can't believe I was so stupid! Isn't there another radio aboard?"

"There's the GPIRB, but that'll just send our position and distress notice through the COSPAS-SARSAT-GEOSAR satellite networks. You can't use it to send particular messages, and *Sycorax* would be the first to receive that information. Given their intentions, I'm not sure we want them to have it." She paused. "We've got the Gertrude, the underwater telephone, but that's no good for this. The only one who could hear it would be *Sycorax*."

"Is there any way we could disable *Sycorax*? Make it unable to send the signal?"

Patricia had been thinking of nothing but. "The only thing I can think of is to ram her sonar dome and that's iffy. Can't be sure it would take out the transducers. I'd have to put you guys topside with the Koreans, put on my full diving equipment, and rig an extension for the stick, so I wasn't in the part that got scrunched. Then I'd have to go out through the pilot hatch or the shattered nose, depending. If *SubLorraine* got stuck, I'd have to go out the lockout hatch."

She looked back at Thomas. He was shaking his head grimly. "And if the collision didn't kill you, you could save that until you were sucked into the intake jets."

"Well, maybe then I'd foul a water jet." She licked her lips. "Wish we had that torpedo. *Sycorax* is a worthy target.

Make a note: stock Valium *and* limpet mines."

Thomas winced. "She's millions of dollars of taxpayers' property."

"And if we let her get to the Abattoir, what's the cost in lives? Almost half a million people, including INS personnel. Did they target Isabel Island?"

Fraser shook his head.

Patricia went on. "Or, for that matter, in property. I know my own hex cost three quarters of a million to cast, before we put a single building on it. Multiply that times thirteen hundred—"

Thomas shook his head. "You've made your point. I'd drop a missile on it if I could. I don't suppose we could block her intake with the sub?"

Patricia licked her lips. "Not with the sub, no."

Patricia did a large circle, coming out of the ensonified zone, and detected hull groaning, the sound of a ship under stress. The *Kim Jong* was sinking but, as of yet, had not generated further explosions.

She circled the ship, forty feet under, and was relieved to find the bright orange hull of the lifeboat in the water, circling the ship. It was a modern pod, completely covered, unsinkable even if it rolled. She didn't envy the crew their ride in the storm-tossed waters, but they'd survive.

She could hear *Sycorax* now, moving fast enough to be stable, but not anywhere near her top speed. The bearing was changing rapidly, indicating she was moving near right angles to *SubLorraine*, but she was still a ways away. If Patricia pursued at her top speed, *Sycorax* would hear her. If she pursued her stealthily, she'd never reach her.

"Okay, boys, you're on." She handed the mike to the Gertrude back to Thomas. *"Today on* Towntalk, *'Men and Their Toys and the People They Kill with Them.' Let's go to Tomás, from D.C."*

Thomas held the mike. He cleared his throat and said, "Mayday, mayday. Any U.S. submarine. This is INS Commander Thomas Becket. Mayday, mayday. Request immediate interception of INS vessel *Sycorax* before she can detonate explosive devices intended to sink the Abbott Refugee Center. Repeat, immediate interception and interdiction are necessary to prevent the total destruction of the Refugee Center and great loss of life. Current position is North twenty-three, fifteen, twenty-seven; West ninety-one, forty-five, thirty-two." He began repeating it.

Now, do they hear it? And if they do, do they believe it? Do they believe there's any chance of the message being heard? That there could actually be navy subs in the area? She pursed her lips. *Stranger things have happened.* The explosion of the torpedo had to be picked up by the SOSUS net, but explosions were used in seismic sounding for oil. *In the middle of a tropical storm?*

Sycorax's bearing stopped changing, became fixed, and her engine and wake noise increased. "She's moving," Patricia said. "Don't know if it's toward us or away."

The Gertrude receiver suddenly started screeching, a harsh warbling sound that moved up and down the spectrum. Patricia turned down the volume and smiled.

"Well, they heard us, at least, and they're taking it seriously enough that they're sonically jamming the underwater telephone. I think it's time to go hide behind the *Kim Jong*, at least while she's still on the surface."

They stayed down below fifty feet. The *Kim Jong* was heeled over on her starboard side, and her stern was still awash, but the bow, where the torpedo had hit, was hanging down, well under. Patricia could see great bubbling columns of air pouring out of the hatchways and didn't think it would be long before the entire vessel sank. She could hear the lifeboat's small diesel engine northwest, where the wind and waves had swept it.

She stayed close to the edge of the hull, where she could track *Sycorax*'s jamming signal, a tone more discernible than the ship's turbines and water jets. Here, even under active sonar, *SubLorraine's* profile would merge with that of the *Kim Jong*.

Maybe we should go try the lifeboat's *radio? Uh, hi, we just sank you, but would you mind terribly if we used your radio?*

"I don't suppose we can get any weapons off the *Kim Jong*?" Thomas asked, looking over her shoulder.

"It's going to go down, really soon. Do *you* want to be in one of their holds when it does?"

She looked over at the *Kim Jong*'s bridge, even with them. "Thomas! They have a VHF antenna, and we can get to it without going inside. Hell, I'll bet I could get close enough that you can reach down through the lockout hatch!"

They put Fraser up in the pilot section, behind Patricia, while Thomas pressurized the lockout chamber again. She would've rather done it herself, but there was always the chance the *Kim Jong* would sink and she'd need to move quickly to keep *SubLorraine* from being pulled into the downwash. Also, she had no intention of leaving Fraser where he could reach the controls, regardless of handcuffs and change of heart.

"Got it," Thomas's voice said over the intercom. "Looks like a standard fitting. It's a bit corroded and I had to use a crescent to get it off, but it should work. Should I go on out and try and install it on your buoy?"

"No. That antenna isn't standard. We'll have to hardwire it into your radio, but *Sycorax* is closing. We need to get ready for our other trick. Button up."

"Aye. Hatch is shut. Starting exhaust compressor."

Sycorax was actively pinging now and slowing, to maximize her ability to listen. *They're going to get seasick.* She was close enough that they were hearing *Sycorax*'s turbines through the hull again.

"Fraser?" she asked. "You're sure the Sycorax doesn't have any more torpedoes?"

"Yes, ma'am. The Nat-Al guy at the navy depot could only get one, like I said. That, and a few depth charges."

"*Depth charges!*" She moved *SubLorraine* completely behind the *Kim Jong*. It chose that moment to tip the final balance between trapped air and weight, and dropped completely below the waves, sinking.

Several semitrailer cargo containers, clamped on deck, tore free and bobbed to the surface, or floated, near neutral at depth. *Thank god for small favors*. She moved in to one of these near-neutral ones, a container that was moving up, very slowly.

Sycorax had turned again, toward them, sonar apparently telling them they didn't have to worry about running into the *Kim Jong* anymore. Patricia held her breath. *Hey, maybe they'll smash the sonar dome on one of those containers.*

Sycorax disappointed her by nimbly avoiding them, but it was still coming toward them. She let the container rise faster than *SubLorraine* and, as *Sycorax* moved slowly overhead, she moved under it, then up.

Below, the dropping *Kim Jong* began creaking again, as sealed compartments contorted and ruptured. Patricia used the noise to cover the sound of her blowing her trim tank. They were rising rapidly now, toward the stern of *Sycorax*.

Pressure equalized between the compartments and Thomas opened the hatch.

"Shhhh," Patricia hissed.

A barrel-shaped object splashed into the water ahead of them and began sinking rapidly.

"I love you, Thomas."

"Not *again*!" he said.

She kicked the thrusters in and pulled up, headed for the *Sycorax*'s hull. *Hopefully they set it to explode deep enough that it wouldn't rupture their own hull.* Another part of her said, *Well, their hull is a lot tougher than yours, isn't it?*

Sycorax was moving slowly enough that *SubLorraine* passed the intake jets easily. This time Patricia wanted to clamp forward of them—even if it meant being closer to the sonar dome. She turned on the Sucker's trim pump and left it on. *Sycorax* was rising and dropping with the swells, and Patricia had doubts about her ability to touch gently.

She was watching it descend toward her when the depth charge went off two hundred feet below and several hundred feet behind.

The explosion ran *SubLorraine*'s hull like a bell, loosened a thru-hull fitting for the depth meter, spraying water across Patricia and, incidentally, pushed the sub the last few inches toward *Sycorax*. The sucker clamped on with a bump, and *SubLorraine* immediately began dropping and rising with *Sycorax*.

Patricia killed the throttle and threw her hand over the leak, trying to keep the spray off the electronics. "I need a crescent wrench here!"

She heard Thomas scrambling through the tools and then coming back. He passed it to Fraser who; two-handed, passed it to her.

"They must've mistaken some of those sounds from the sinking freighter for us," she said, cranking on the fitting. The spray stopped immediately, but there was a slow seep she didn't like. She verified the sump pump was working. As long as they had electricity for the pump and the leak didn't worsen, they'd be all right. *Panic later.*

The flywheels were down to less than twenty percent. The charge could've lasted days, with them clamped on in leech mode, but she hadn't counted on them having to dodge torpedoes or perform man-overboard rescues and multiple evacuations of the lockout chamber.

She didn't think much of their running the turbogenerator in this weather. The seas would wash over the snorkel. And there were no submerged drilling platforms around here with convenient bubbles of air.

One thing at a time.

She rotated the hydrophone until it was pointed sternward, and then she pulled out the headphone jack. Immediately, the sound of the turbines, already audible without aid, became richer, transmitting frequencies not heard through the hull.

She cranked the seat around and carefully squeezed over

Fraser, and into the lockout chamber, kissing Thomas quickly as she moved back to the toolbox. "Okay, as I remember, the intake grid on the water jets had six-inch-square openings." She was pulling tools out and laying them on the floor. She took heavy wrenches, a two-pound sledge, and screwdrivers. "How tough are those impeller blades?"

Thomas pursed his lips, then licked them. "Well, on the Witch Class boat I served on, we had to replace them occasionally, especially if we were working inland waterways. Sand in the water chews them up. The stuff that could really crack them—rocks or metal debris—doesn't float."

"Not usually."

She pressurized the entire sub. Not only would it lessen the leak in the pilot compartment, she didn't want to leave Fraser in there alone. Thomas braced his shoulders against the ceiling and pushed down on the hatch with his feet to get it open against the current streaming by. Patricia blocked it open with a ten-inch box-end wrench. Water bubbled and swirled around the opening, reminding her, oddly, of a flushing toilet.

"Monkey wrench number one," she said. She took an adjustable pipe wrench, perhaps fourteen inches long and weighing about two pounds, and used the salvage-foam tank nozzle to encase it in sticky, buoyant foam. They had to squeeze it through the gap in the hatch, and then it was gone in the current.

She heard it bump, once, against the shroud around *SubLorraine*'s prop; then there was another bump as it was sucked up to the intake grid. "It might stick crosswise," she warned.

Thomas held up another wrench. "It might, at that."

This one, released, went through the grate. They heard a series of clanking noises followed almost immediately by a dreadful screeching.

"Sounds like they lost an impeller blade," Thomas said. "Ah, gee. They better shut it down before they lose a turb—"

The screeching noise stopped and the overall noise level dropped markedly. There was still one turbine running and one water jet. Thomas held up the two-pound sledge.

Patricia eyed its geometry doubtfully. "I don't know. Can't hurt to try."

As she suspected, foamed enough to float, it stuck in the grid.

Thomas held up the bolt cutters and Patricia said, "No way—too big, but—." She took the cutters and used them on the chain running between the handcuffs on Fraser's ankles. "Hold still." The steel was extremely tough and wouldn't cut for her, but Thomas was able to do it, bracing one handle against the floor and using his weight.

She snaked up the released heavy chain, the deadweight used to sink Fraser. It was two feet long and weighed over five pounds. "Now *that's* what I'm talking about," she said. "Poetic justice. *Go, sir, rub your chain with crumbs.*" She foamed it and dropped it out the hatch.

The remaining water jet died a spectacular death. The chain broke two of its impellers and it went into asymmetrical convulsions before *Sycorax*'s crew could disengage it.

"Oh, my," Patricia said, listening to the speaker. "Sounds like it tore the casing open. They've got a leak." With both turbines shut down, they could actually hear shouting transmitted through the hull. *Sycorax,* battered by wind and wave, stopped quickly. "Time for the next step."

She put on her fins and mask and the pony bottle; then, dragging the tank of salvage foam with her, she dropped through the hatch and swam back to the intake grid. She thrust the nozzle within and held it down. It took five minutes to empty the tank and, just before it quit, foam was extruding through the grating, having filled the interior of the water intakes.

Even after *they replace the impeller blades, I seriously doubt they're going to get any thrust out of this engine.*

The pony bottle was empty by the time she climbed back

into the sub. "You got that antenna wired to your radio yet?"

"Aye, aye, ma'am. I do."

"And have you tested it?"

"Not yet. I was a little concerned about you. When we start broadcasting, I'm worried they may start dropping more depth charges."

"Then, let's away from here!"

She pumped negative and released, gliding away from *Sycorax* and banking hard for her stern, to keep away from her sonar dome, still gliding. Then, low flywheels or no, she powered away from them until they were over a half mile away.

The radio worked, with the sub surfaced and the antenna extended into the acrylic nose section. Thomas told Jazz enough details to start things moving. "Call Admiral Rylant on the secure link. Tell him *everything*. Get Major Paine's bomb squad working on the devices under the Abattoir."

The seas were lessening and, with great discomfort, Patricia kept the sub on the surface until the INS *Witch of Endor*, backed up by the U.S. Navy missile frigate *Samuel Eliot Morison*, arrived three hours later.

19

Becket: *Diapositivas de tiempo*

For Becket the rest of the day dissolved into a series of crystalline moments framed with timeless stretches of fatigue fog. There had been too little sleep, too much coffee, and too much adrenaline.

SubLorraine being plucked from the sea by a utility crane on the navy missile frigate as if it were the slightest bit of flotsam and deposited gently on her aft deck. A warm meal in an incredibly spacious wardroom. The taste of spaghetti with Italian sausages.

Commander Wall being transferred to the other INS Fastship on a stretcher, in a body bag. When his surrender was demanded by Captain Heins of the *Witch of Endor,* he'd gone back to his cabin and used his service automatic.

Watching Major Paine's VTOL V-32 come out of the fog and rain, then land on the fantail of the *Sycorax* to disgorge Jazz, Ensign Terkel, and the rest of Thomas's CID team, there to start documenting evidence.

The *Witch of Endor* also left a damage-control team and skeleton operation crew on *Sycorax* to repair the impellers and clean the salvage foam out of the intake jets, then bring her in. They'd be taking it directly to BBINS when they were done.

Standing with Patricia and Fraser in New Galveston, where the two ships docked at a pier normally used for cruise liners as the handcuffed crew of the *Sycorax* was brought off the *Witch of Endor* by NGPD officers.

Rylant had authorized the use of the non-INS officers. "The witch-hunt on this is going to be ugly," he'd said on the phone. "I don't want any more suicides or any escapes. Keep them clear of INS until we know who else is involved."

The faces of the crew—stoic, depressed, closed—changed markedly when they saw Fraser, back from the dead. Eyes widened; jaws dropped. Mowett, the damage controlman who'd pushed Fraser over, recoiled into his escort and nearly went over the gangplank railing.

"What a good idea!" Fraser was hopping up and down, shouting. "*You* try to swim with handcuffs!" When all of the crew had passed, Thomas sent Fraser off with an NGPD protective-custody team.

Patricia was not amused. "He's far more outraged that they tried to kill him—not that they drowned those children in the *Open Lotus*."

Thomas nodded. "Give him a little credit. He drew the line late, but he did draw it."

She shook her head. "Tell it to los Encinas."

Becket saw her point, but Fraser had already identified six Nat-Al participants on staff in the Abattoir and had seen others that he would be able to identify from file photos. *And hopefully, the fact that he's alive and talking will encourage others to cooperate.*

Major Paine's office, examining one of the floating recoilless rifle shells, the detonator removed. "There are too many of them for my boys alone, so we've got INS EOD, my bomb squad, and every recreational diver on the force under there. I hope you don't mind, but except for a percentage, for evidence, we're puncturing the floats and letting them sink. It's the quickest way to deal with them."

"As long as you're keeping track of the number."

"Right."

"Would it have worked?" Thomas said, leaning over and looking at the tip of the shell.

"Too well. Not only would it have compromised the hex flotation, my bomb squad supervisor says it would have sent seacrete flying like shrapnel topside, killing and wounding enormous numbers even before they started drowning. You know how crowded it is over there."

Patricia sighed. "About as crowded as the hold of the *Open Lotus*."

Thomas drooped. "Yes. About that crowded."

A videophone conversation with a shaken Admiral Pachefski, furious at the attempted destruction of his facility and his charges. "I can't even begin to fathom how people like that *think!* They have no empathy, no human feeling."

Thomas answered him. "That's why, I suppose, most of them had to be people not from your facility, who've actively avoided seeing the refugees as people. The crew of the *Sycorax* was insulated from them, thinking of them not as human, but only as *other*. Others with different skins who wanted to move into their neighborhoods, take their jobs—all that fear-of-change stuff."

Thomas felt numb, emotionally depleted. "Even the six we know about, who did work for you, are from the detention facility and that's a bit different. No children, mostly felons. I imagine they found it easy to keep from identifying with them."

"Yes, well, we got five of those, but we're missing one. Master Chief Gunner Stuben. He was on the sick list, but he wasn't in his quarters. We've forwarded his picture and details to Major Paine—they're watching the airport and the ferries and the commercial shipping. I imagine, when the news breaks, they'll be putting his face on television. It won't take long."

"When the story breaks? Do you think it will?"

Pachefski sighed. "It has to. This has got to end. Congresswoman Beenan is right." He shook his head and looked off to the right. "I was wrong, you know. When I suggested you look outside the INS for the perpetrators. I thought maintaining the status quo was the way to take care of this, but I see now it isn't."

And finally, the long, seemingly endless climb up the stairs at Patricia's hex.

Major Paine had kicked both of them out of police central, saying, "Jeez, go get some rest. You guys look like death warmed over."

Thomas climbed slowly. "Did they add a couple more flights of stairs while we were gone?" His stitches were inflamed from either his exertions or their immersion underwater—or both.

"Men are *such* babies! I suppose you'll complain about the stairs up to my loft as well." She was walking with his good arm across her shoulders and her arm around his waist. The farther up they went, the more of Thomas's weight she was supporting.

"I don't mean to complain," he said mildly. "In truth, I've little to complain about. I'm alive. You're alive. We're together. The other end of the Strand still floats, and half a million people still scurry, sleep, love, eat, and get in each other's way."

"And you've probably infected your cut. We should probably go to the hospital instead."

He shook his head. "No. In the morning, perhaps, if it's not better. *Thank god!*" They'd reached the top of the stairs, the courtyard with the play structure and Art of Learning School. "That is by far the most impressive play structure I've ever seen. It must've cost a fortune."

Patricia cleared her throat and said nothing.

Thomas raised his unscarred eyebrow. "Just pretend I repeated the question. I'm too tired to actually do it."

"All right. I'm a criminal. In violation of the Flood Salvage Act, I lifted those pieces from sunken Burger Kings and McDonald's all up and down the Texas coast."

Thomas said, "Hold out your wrist." He slapped the back of her hand lightly, then shook his finger before her face. "Bad Patricia, no bone."

Thomas was glad to see there was a police officer still stationed outside Patricia's door. He was an older officer, heavy, who didn't exercise enough. His uniform gapped slightly at the shirt buttons. *Looks like he'll have to go up to another size soon.*

Patricia greeted the policeman, smiling. "All quiet?" she said.

The policeman ducked his head.

Patricia punched the combination on the lock and opened the door. Thomas followed, curious. He'd never been inside this apartment, yet it was going to be their home.

He got one step inside the apartment and tried to turn, sensing movement. Something hard struck him on the back of his head and he went to all fours on the floor. Through the pain, he heard the door slam and someone lock it. He shook his head and staggered back to his feet.

"Stop right there!"

The voice was the same. Their old friend from the seawall, the man who'd phoned in the bomb threat to keep Patricia from inspecting the Abattoir.

When Thomas could focus, he saw the policeman standing behind Patricia, one arm across her throat, the nine-millimeter police automatic pressed against her temple.

"Chief Stuben, I presume. I should've realized it wasn't your uniform. Is he still alive?" Thomas's head was pounding.

Stuben hesitated. "Probably, but you're asking all the

wrong questions, Commander." The man's face was twisted, all civility dropped from sight. He ground the gun into Patricia's head and she winced. "Hold still, or I'll blow your head off!"

"What do you want, Stuben?" Thomas kept his voice quiet. "You weren't on the *Sycorax* when she sank the *Open Lotus* and you failed to kill us on the seawall so you can't be charged with murder. Wouldn't it be better not to compound your crimes?"

"Give it a rest, Commander. I'd have gladly operated the cannon on the *Sycorax*. I'd have gladly pushed the detonator to set off our charges under the Abattoir. And I put the bomb on the submarine that *this,*"—he twisted the gun again, bringing a cry of pain from Patricia—"bitch found. None of those were crimes. They were the highest form of patriotism. It's you and your fucking brown-skinned sympathizers who are betraying your country."

"What do you want, Stuben?" Thomas asked again.

"I want a long-range helicopter, INS or NGPD, I don't care, set down on the roof of the school. It will be fully fueled. You and the assemblywoman here will join me in a short trip shoreward, but if I don't get what I want, you two won't live to see it."

Patricia narrowed her eyes and closed her mouth into a straight line.

Don't do it, Patricia.

She mouthed, *I love you.*

Oh, no! He looked around, moving just his eyes, looking for anything to use as a weapon. "I'll have to make a call," he said.

"What are you doing?" The voice was young, female, and came from overhead, from the loft.

Thomas looked up to see Marie, the small black girl he'd met in the courtyard, looking over the railing.

Stuben jerked the gun up, twisting Patricia around, and fired. Wood splinters exploded from the edge of the loft, and the small girl screamed and ducked back.

Patricia twisted inside Stuben's grip, bringing up her right elbow, the same maneuver she'd used on Geoffrey the first time Thomas saw her. The elbow caught Stuben in the face, knocking him back, but he still had his gun. Thomas scooped up the heavy brass bust of Shakespeare by the door and threw it, underhanded. It was heavier than he'd expected and well below Thomas's chosen target, Stuben's head, but it smashed into the man's upper shin with painful force, and he bent over, a gasp of pain forced from his lips.

Patricia scooped the bust and lifted it hard, bringing it up into Stuben's elbow, and the gun flew up, from nerveless fingers. Stuben tried to reach for it with his other hand, ignoring Patricia, and she swung the bust into his stomach. Then, when he bent over from this, she brought her knee into his face. She was screaming, "Don't you ever mess with my kids!"

Stuben fell over backward and Thomas hobbled to the gun, where it landed on the couch. Patricia raised the bust and took a step toward Stuben, lying on his back, breathless, his nose bleeding.

Thomas said, "Whoa, girl. You whupped him."

She looked around at Thomas, the wild look on her face still there, but it faded when she saw the gun in his hand. She turned away and yelled up, "Marie? Are you all right?"

There was silence and then a quavering voice said, "I'm sorry, Tante. I promise not to sleep in your bed anymore, only please, *please*, don't shoot me!"

And after the fatigue fog had been dealt with.

They were sitting on the couch with the curtains drawn aside, watching children swarm the play structure on the other side of the courtyard. Their shrieks and shouts carried dimly through the glass.

"Try it again," Thomas said.

Patricia put her arms on his chest and said, "Thomas, I love you."

He sat bolt upright and looked wildly around.

She slugged him on the arm. "Very funny. Ho, ho, ho. It is to laugh."

He kissed her. "Face it, an alarmingly high percentage of the times you've told me that you love me, it's meant, 'Look out, we're about to die.' "

"We've given that up, though," she said.

He shook her slightly. "*We* never took it up in the first place. *We* think it's much better to find a path through life where people don't try to kill you. It was all those other crazy people who took it up."

She leaned against him. "And they're all behind bars."

"Most of them. We'll have to see who else is named."

He closed his eyes and breathed in, his nostrils against her hair. This was more like it. They'd slept. They'd eaten. They'd made love. And, just when he'd been about to go to work, he'd been called by Admiral Rylant and informed that the FBI was taking over the investigation, to eliminate any perception of conflicts of interest arising from an INS unit prosecuting INS personnel.

They still needed him, but as a witness, not as an investigator. He'd immediately put in his leave request.

"We could pick up *Terminal Lorraine* from BBINS for a honeymoon trip," he suggested to Patricia.

"They'll release it?"

He grinned darkly. "They'd better. Haven't you been watching the news?"

She blushed. "The public will forget soon enough. I hope to God."

The official press release went out from INS Washington. Thankfully, they'd realized a cover-up was impossible. Credit for stopping the destruction of the Abattoir had been given equally to Patricia Beenan, daughter of the eminent congresswoman, and Commander Thomas Becket of the INS.

There was movement in Congress to vote on Bill 853 even before the new members were sworn in and thanks to the *Sycorax* incident, it looked like it would pass.

Meanwhile, a police guard kept the press out of Patricia's hex, and the phone calls were being filtered by Toni.

"One more time," he said.

"Thomas, I love you."

He shook his head and sighed.

"What?"

"Just a tiny adrenaline rush. Really, it's nothing. I can take it. I'm tough."

She bit him.

"Ow!"

"You certainly are. I think it's your bachelor genes kicking in. You're trying to get out of marrying me."

He shook his head, crossed his heart with his right index finger, then pulled his thumb across his throat.

She laughed. "Cross you heart and hope to die? I do love you."

He slowly looked around, rising up slightly. "Okay. That wasn't bad at all. No torpedoes, no bombs, no guns, no knives, no little girls in the bed. Just don't stop saying it and perhaps, eventually, I'll get used to it. Okay?"

"Okay." She pulled the book onto her lap and indicated the place with her finger. *"Plight me the full assurance of your faith; that my most jealous and too doubtful soul may live at peace."*

And he skipped the part about following the priest, going straight to, "*—and go with you and, having sworn truth, ever . . . will . . . be . . . true.*"

Acknowledgments

There are large amounts of Shakespeare sprinkled through the text, including quotes from *The Tempest, Love's Labour's Lost, A Midsummer Night's Dream, The Life of King Henry the Fifth,* and *Romeo & Juliet,* but mostly it's *Twelfth Night.* William Ernest Henley's "Invictus" has a brief appearance as does Lord Byron's "Sardanapalus." Certain minor events in the text were lifted from Dorothy L. Sayers's *Busman's Honeymoon.* Her fans will recognize them. More generally, the wonderful relationship between Lord and Lady Peter Wimsey was in my mind as I created Patricia Beenan and Thomas Becket.

If you're going to steal, steal from the best.

I'm indebted to Rodolfo Gonzalez, jazz flautist, who helped me with the *español* in the text. Melinda Snodgrass, Sage Walker, Pati Nagle, and Sally Gwylan read the book in draft and had many helpful—"Women do not act like this, Steve!"—suggestions.

And I couldn't have written this without my constant reader, Laura J. Mixon.